Bohemia

Published under licence by The Self-Publishing Partnership Ltd, 10b
Greenway Farm, Bath Rd, Wick, nr. Bath BS30 5RL, UK in partnership
with Silver Crow Books, Frome
www.silvercrowbooks.co.uk

www.selfpublishingpartnership.co.uk

ISBN printed book: 978-1-83952-922-1
ISBN e-book: 978-1-83952-923-8

Cover design by Christine Molan
Internal design by Andrew Easton

Printed and bound in the UK

This book is printed on FSC® certified paper

Bohemia

Somewhere between Rome and Shepton Mallet

Sian M Williams

Silver Crow Books

AUGUST 2012

At the fraying edge of old Somerset, just beyond the ever-expanding conurbations of Bristol and Bath, there's a forgotten valley, a deep fault lying between the villages of Crubscombe and Earwick. Motorists who explore its strangely convoluted lanes in the hope of dodging urban traffic jams find themselves winding through green tunnels made by unkempt and exuberant vegetation. They may have a sense of plunging deep into an untouched wilderness, but behind the impenetrable hedgerows is a landscape which has been used and discarded. The land, here, though green, is poor, fit only for pasture or the pursuit of game, but beneath the thin soils lie riches.

Deep coal mines were sunk along the ridge overlooking the north side of the valley, and scattered rows of stone cottages built to house the colliers and their families. Seeking to impose order, the Ordnance Survey named the area Upper Crubscombe. The old dwellings, and the spoil tips known locally as batches, are all the passing motorist can now see of past lives, lived in a harsh world of industrial toil.

To the south, much of the hill below the village of Earwick has been quarried for roadstone aggregates. Once they had extracted as much limestone as was economically worthwhile, the quarry company moved on down the valley to more accessible deposits. The lanes and footpaths were re-routed around the new workings, and the old ones were left to be re-colonised by nature.

The abandoned Earwick quarry is now a series of flat-bottomed basins, backed by pink and grey cliffs and occupied by skeletal concrete buildings, rusty plant, half-buried railway tracks and overgrown spoil dumps.

More lucrative than the limestone were the outcrops of Silurian volcanic rock on the steep scarp of Crubscombe Hill. Hard and seemingly indestructible, these rocks, known to geologists as andesitic lavas and to the locals as basalt, were ideal for the manufacture of extra-strong concrete and for surfacing airport runways. The oldest workings, where ancient ash flows had been followed and hacked out of the hillside, became mysterious canyons, deep and dark, damp and slippery underfoot. More recently, a massive basalt deposit, upended by tectonic mayhem into a series of vertical piles, was identified close to the old village, on Crubscombe Manor Farm. To reach this rich source of revenue the company duly blew the pastures away, along with most of the playing field that it had previously provided for its workers, until there was nothing left but a very deep hole, bounded on the village side by a steeply terraced rock wall. Above the wall, all that was left standing was the Manor farmhouse, its outbuildings and orchard, along with the quarrymen's social club and the cricketers' scoreboard.

A few hundred yards south of the farmhouse the Boundary Stone Rock – a sheer black crag surmounted by a roughly-shaped pillar, reputedly of Saxon origin – stood out from the edge of the quarry like the last remaining tooth in a diseased gum. Despite its raffish appearance, the Boundary Stone is a scheduled ancient monument In the mid-1980s there was a successful campaign to preserve it from the advancing excavations, which resulted in the closure of the quarry.

The workings were instantly abandoned, as if the company had been forced to flee some overnight invasion. Ever-rampant plant life swiftly encroached on the rock wall terraces. The basalt pit filled with water which was bitterly cold, even in summer. Nevertheless, this became an informal bathing place for wild swimmers and local teenagers and the villagers renamed it the Lower Pool. Looming high above it, the Boundary Stone continued to defy all who came near it. Below the stone, a sheer cliff plunged down to the dark water of the pool, while, behind it, narrow paths offered unauthorized access to would-be swimmers willing to thread their way through tangles of vegetation.

On a hot afternoon in the middle of August, a week after the triumphant conclusion of the London Olympics and six months or so before this story begins, a group of teenagers clutching towels and forbidden caches of cider came skittering and tripping down one of the many stony, bramble-strewn paths from Crubscombe to the pool. They picked their way over jagged shards of rock, cursing and laughing as they stubbed their toes and barked their shins, until they reached the thin strip of gravel at the water's edge. The boys, struggling out of their jeans, hopped and stumbled. The girls, stripping more decorously to their bikinis, smeared themselves and each other with sunblock.

All cast discreet glances at Jason Chawner, who unzipped his denims with a flourish and stepped out of them gracefully. With his cropped, blond hair and muscular body, he looked like a Greek god, or the latest reincarnation of James Bond. He loved sport of any kind and was good at it, particularly swimming. His parents had even managed to get tickets for the Olympic diving competition and his towel, a souvenir, was printed with the Union Jack. He picked it up and wrapped it around his shoulders. Screwing up his eyes against the sun, he looked up at the Boundary Stone as if answering its challenge, then sprang in easy strides up the treacherous path which led to the top of the rock. The others stopped what they were doing and watched.

The boys cheered and jeered.

'G'won, Jace!'

'Plonker!'

Jason knew little of the Boundary Stone's historical significance, only what his dad had told him about the hippies from the old Manor farmhouse getting the quarry closed down because it was a monument or something. He wasn't bothered. There were still plenty of working quarries. As soon as he was eighteen, he'd get his HGV licence and work for his dad, hauling aggregates from the Mendips to roadworks and building sites across the nation.

Reaching the top of the rock, he stood tall and took an end of the towel in each hand. Swaying from side to side, he waved it for the benefit of his admirers below. Still holding the towel, he stepped between the stone and the edge of the rock, confronting the Lower Pool. Then he jumped.

As the Union Jack floated and bobbed on the waves caused by the impact of Jason's body, the bitter grey water closed over the boy's head. The watchers waited, wondering what game their leader was playing this time, until realisation dawned and understanding took root, followed by panic.

Some called out to Jason, begging him to stop being a pillock. One boy tried to run into the water. A group of girls dragged him back. Others stumbled up the path towards the village, swiping wildly at their mobile phones. But there was nothing to be done.

CHAPTER 1

I

'Down In yonder green field
Down a down, hey down a down
There lies a knight slain 'neath his shield'

The singer was a small woman, her shape obliterated by a floor-length greatcoat and an endless woollen scarf. Heavy boots protruded under the hem of the coat.

Jimmy Sullivan stopped mulling over his list of performers to give her his full attention. Not all the wannabe performers merited this, but Mary had a beautiful voice. It seemed to float above the smoky fug of cigarettes and candles, and the occasional discreet spliff. Idly, he wondered how anybody could sing with such power and feeling and support so much clothing at the same time. It was the beginning of January and the heating comprised two portable gas heaters.

The folk club met in what had once been Crubscombe Quarrymen's Sports and Social Club and was now a decaying shack close to the edge of the abandoned basalt quarry. Officially the club had closed at the same time as the quarry but Jimmy Sullivan and his folk club had never got round to moving out. Not even the drowning of Jason Chawner in the water-filled pit, six months ago now, had prompted it to move on. It continued to trespass on the quarry land with little concern for safety or the law.

Twenty-five years, Jimmy mused as the song neared its tragic end. He returned to his list, a serious responsibility. Anybody, the good, the bad and the hopeless, in his secret estimation, could have a go and would be allowed a maximum of two songs. He nodded to Terry the barman, who was already lifting his guitar from its usual place propped against a rickety cabinet underneath the optics.

Best get it over with.

Terry was a staunch and loyal friend, a co-founder of the club. He was not the most gifted man musically or intellectually, but he kept, and supplied at cost, the best beer in Somerset.

Mary's song ended, followed by a communal sigh of appreciation. There was a shifting of bodies and feet and a jockeying for space on overloaded tables as earnest balladeers, feminist song writers, environmentalists, fox hunters and guitar-toting troubadours put down their drinks and applauded as one.

'Thank you, Mary,' Jimmy said, 'that was delightful.' This time he meant it. 'And now...' he proclaimed with more energy than conviction, 'we have our own, inimitable Terry Mivart.'

Terry moved into the space which the club used as a stage, a tiny clearing at one end of the room, lit by a single spotlight. Behind this area were the kitchen door and a serving hatch. The bar was immediately to the performers' left, while to their right a jumble of musical instrument cases and bits of broken furniture encroached from a neglected dumping ground, requiring each act to manoeuvre itself into position with great care.

Jimmy took Terry's place behind the bar and topped up his own glass, while Mary, receiving her accolade with due modesty, backed away into the kitchen.

Moments later the massive bulk of Frankie Dando could be seen working its way behind the performers' space to the kitchen door. Here, he stood leaning against a jamb, filling most of the open doorway and scanning the audience with beady eyes while Terry gave them Bert Jansch's 'Needle of Death'.

Rebellion against Terry's assault on music was unlikely. One of the folk club's few rules was that everyone, however abysmal their performance, would be listened to in polite silence. But tonight, club members had been asked to make a controversial administrative decision. Small squares of paper had been given to all tonight's participants on entry and the motion put.

The issue was smoking. The European Union had long since enacted a ban on smoking indoors, which the club ignored. It was not interested in the law, or safety regulations. Its risk assessment amounted to: *If you fall into the old quarry on the way home, you're a twat.* But the singers had begun to notice that their voices were sweeter, drinks tasted better and there were fewer sore throats in venues where the smoking ban applied. There was no constitution, or any kind of legal status, but the club was democratic; so, Jimmy had organised a secret ballot.

All those in favour of a ban wrote 'Yes', and those against, 'No'. The papers had then been collected by Frankie in a hard hat he had loaned the club for the purpose. Now, in the kitchen Mary was counting the votes while Frankie watched her protectively so he could later guarantee to those unhappy with the result that there had been no tampering.

Terry's performance staggered on. 'Needle of Death' was followed by a barely recognisable version of 'Streets of London'. Leaving the maintenance of order in the large and stern hands of Frankie, Jimmy got stuck into his beer and let his mind wander.

After mulling over the pros and cons, he had voted 'Yes'. The opposing faction had declared themselves to be libertarians or bohemians, and had insisted that no law should impede their god-given right to choke themselves and their friends and companions to death. Jimmy was a singer and a caller for a ceilidh band. He needed to look after his voice and hadn't smoked for twenty years. He remembered the terrible winter when he and his wife, Gaynor, had given up, each supporting and cajoling the other. They'd made it, largely thanks to Gaynor's persistence, and Jimmy had been forced to admit that he felt better for it. His wife's increasing preoccupation with health issues was, he supposed, well founded. Perhaps she'd even come back to the club and sing with him again if a smoking ban were enforced.

He looked over the heads of the audience and artistes towards the feeble glow of the exit sign above the door to the Gents; at least fifty people in tonight. In spite of all their musical differences they were a community, happy and safe, as long as everyone was careful. Jimmy knew all the right people, councillors, senior police officers and magistrates, in fact all the venal pillars of the local establishment. He was confident that he could deal with any legal or logistical problems that might arise.

During one of their increasingly frequent rows, Gaynor had compared him to the Road Runner, legging it over the edge of the canyon.

'Which is all very well,' she'd observed acidly, 'as long as you don't look down.'

Jimmy resolved not to look down. Too many folk clubs were fading away, squeezed out of previously friendly venues by the rising cost of health and safety.

'Streets of London' in all its tuneless agony concluded. Terry bowed and the audience cheered. Effort was appreciated, as was cheap beer. Mary and Frankie, hovering in the kitchen doorway, caught Jimmy's eye. He made his way over to them for a brief consultation before edging his way back to the spotlight.

'Ladies and gentlemen! We have a result!'

All conversation stopped.

'The Ayes to the right...'

The laughter was punctuated with cries of 'Get on with it!'

'Yes votes: thirty-five. No votes: seventeen.'

'Fix!'

'It's a substantial majority,' Jimmy pointed out. 'From next Thursday onwards, I must ask you all to step outside if you fancy a drag.'

It was a far bigger margin than he'd anticipated. The silent majority, it seemed, had prevailed.

'Health and safety gone mad,' grumbled one of the 'nos' pointing the stem of his tar-encrusted pipe at Jimmy in a gesture of defiance.

The noisy minority concurred.

'Why don't you come over here and give us one of your brilliant hunting songs, Brian?' Jimmy suggested. The man had already sung twice that evening, but he calculated that the feminists, hunt sabs and vegetarians – likely members of the 'Yes' faction – would be too flushed with victory to object to this blatant act of favouritism.

'Well, would you believe it? Who'd have thought this place would be obeying the law?' Jimmy turned to find Luke standing next to him. They'd known each other for years, bonded by Irish ancestry and music. Their friendship went back to the Cardiff days. Luke and his wife, Jen, had rented a room at the Sullivans' farmhouse, back in the days of the hippy commune. They hadn't been sorry to leave, Jimmy remembered, but they'd bought themselves a pretty stone cottage on Crubscombe Hill and stayed in the village.

'What you having, Luke?'

'You can get me a shandy.'

'You driving?'

'I've got the van here.'

'It's only half a mile to your house!'

'It's got all the band's instruments inside,' Luke said. 'You volunteering to carry the harp home for us?' Luke played the box in the ceilidh band. These days, Jimmy thought, he was becoming distressingly middle-aged.

Jimmy ordered the shandy, and another pint of beer for himself. 'Time for the third half, I think. Give us some tunes would you, Luke, as soon as Brian's slaughtered his fox.'

It was after eleven and time for respectable working people and their babysitters to be in their beds. The company began to thin out while the survivors – dedicated musicians and drinkers – unclasped instrument cases or sat around chatting. First there'd be Irish jigs and reels, then maybe a bit of klezmer and, when inebriation finally took hold, French café waltzes.

Leaning on the bar, pint in hand, chatting to friends, acquaintances and newcomers, Jimmy, amiable and emollient, was the perfect host. He noticed that Terry, ever loyal, was attempting to pacify the losers by offering them free beer and wondered if this was altogether wise. Fortunately, most of tonight's survivors were musicians. Always eager to join a session and paying no attention to political disputes, they tuned their instruments and followed Luke's lead into the reels and jigs. Music always wins, Jimmy thought fondly.

Midnight passed unnoticed. The music flowed with rising levels of virtuosity, inspired, and occasionally hampered, by rising levels of drink. Jimmy sang a funny song.

In a corner near the entrance to the Gents, a little knot of nerds discussed the engineering problems encountered during the building of the Rio-Antirrio Bridge.

There was no rent, no insurance company to placate, no neighbours to complain, no grumpy landlord putting chairs on top of tables and observing that it was 'past his bedtime'.

Come this Easter they'd have clocked up twenty-five years, from

1988 to 2013 – a remarkable achievement, Jimmy thought. The club had kept going through economic boom and bust, the advent of social media, in which it had little interest, and all the bitter personal disputes that had dispersed the original founders. Old friends had left, but new people kept coming, alerted by the folk world's bush telegraph. The gifted and the hopeless still dropped by and gave it their all. Famous members of the 'folk aristocracy' looked in now and again, many of them contacts Jimmy had made during his time as social secretary of Cardiff Students' Union. Over the years, the club had acquired a reputation as a good place to try out a new set.

Jimmy squinted through the thickening twilight of the smokers' last hurrah, wondering if he should have another pint. He pushed his mug over the bar.

'Give me a half would you, Terry?' As he fished in his pockets for change, he noticed, not for the first time, that his jeans were getting tighter.

Terry said, 'Cheers.' They clashed glasses and Jimmy watched in awe as his friend swallowed at least a quarter of his in one go. Terry had been boozing from the cradle and hadn't an ounce of flesh on him. With his unruly tangle of thinning grey hair, he looked like a mangy floor mop with a beaky nose and wire-rimmed glasses. Jimmy's own brown curls, though still abundant, were sprinkled with silver threads. Furthermore, he was finding it harder to read the running order in the dim light of the old clubhouse.

He had to admit, if only to himself, that age and the concerns of the modern world were closing in. Now that the old workings had claimed a young life, health and safety were on the march. *Stupid little sod*, Jimmy thought, but he pitied the Chawner family and those poor kids who'd witnessed the whole grisly business. He wondered what his own daughter and her friends had done after bounding out of the back door to play. They'd been warned about the quarries, but, if they'd been anything like him, the warning would have passed them by, like a fairy tale from a distant country.

The tragic event had been a media sensation, all over the local news bulletins for a day or so, before the flood tide of new stories had washed it away.

The boy's family, and their supporters in the village, had started a campaign to make the area safe. Gaynor, a lifelong political activist, and now a parish councillor, had been persuaded to chair the committee. Jimmy resented this. She was overworked already. She had a full-time job as well as all the work she did for the community. More concerning were the aims and objectives of the campaign. They wanted the quarry company to level the old spoil dumps, landscape what was left of them, return the valley to some semblance of the green and pleasant land they all supposed it to have been at some time in the past. The old quarrymen's social club would be swept away in a frenzy of clean living and order.

Gaynor was already trying to involve him, insisting that the campaign needed his local knowledge and his contacts. He conceded that some means should be found to deter idiot kids from jumping off the Boundary Stone Rock Rock into the Lower Pool, but he would rather not get involved in a campaign that could mean the end of the folk club. With any luck the villagers would soon lose interest, their anger dissipated by the preoccupations of day-to-day life.

Give it time, he thought as he landed back on earth. He leaned over the bar and called to Terry to top up his glass.

As the musicians moved on to the French café waltzes, a tall, grey-haired figure stumbled out of the murk, from the direction of the toilets, and stood before him, swaying but dignified. The apparition fixed him with a watery eye:

'It spans the Gulf of Corinth.'

'Pardon?'

'The Rio – Annnt....irrio Bridge.' Having deposited this nugget, the speaker lurched out of the clubhouse into the freezing darkness beyond.

'Night, Cyril,' Jimmy called after him. 'Take care.'

II

Gaynor Sullivan stared at the screen of her laptop. It was late, but Jimmy wouldn't be back for hours. Before going out he'd made another of his periodic attempts to coax her back to the folk club.

'We'll be voting to introduce a smoking ban,' he'd insisted.

'Good for you,' she'd sighed, both eyes focused on a lengthy piece of A-level prose translation, half an ear listening to her husband. She corrected a word here and there and added a judicious scattering of red ticks. The next time she looked up, Jimmy had gone. A smoking ban was all very well, but she wasn't a folk singer any more, hadn't been for years. Motherhood, her job and her work for the community consumed all her energy.

Her marking done, pupils' exercise books and folders neatly packed into supermarket carrier bags and placed by the back door ready for the early morning exodus, she checked her inbox one last time before going to bed. At the top of the latest entries was another one from Bron.

Bron, now happily married, her demons laid low, apparently, had, after years of near silence, emailed her for the third time in a week to say she intended to return to Crubscombe and drop in for a catch-up. She would be expecting an answer, which could be difficult.

Years ago, Bron and Gaynor had been close friends. She and her ex-partner, Miles, had lived in the Manor farmhouse with

Gaynor and Jimmy and shifting tides of assorted bohemians for nearly ten years. She'd been the most visible and vociferous leader of the protests against the basalt quarry. Bron had always been a formidable campaigner.

Gaynor's eyelids drooped. She should open the email and deal with this now, but her mind wandered into the distant past, before Crubscombe, before Jimmy and Miles. Once again she saw the advancing headlights and heard the tense chatter of wound-up people speaking Breton and French, with a smattering of English and Spanish.

Shadows behind the headlights had resolved themselves into a slow procession of trucks towing the mobile-mairies.

'Portakabins we call them in England,' she'd remarked to a middle-aged woman standing next to her in the crush. She remembered being able to feel the lumpy contents of the woman's overcoat pocket – a bag of small, round stones as it turned out – and how she'd watched the movement of the woman's arm as she raised her hand to a powerful catapult that hung round her neck; a twentieth century Frondeuse. Demonstrating in France was different. She'd been warned. Here the police were known to be armed with long, heavy truncheons – the dreaded matraque Un *coup de matraque* could dash your brains out and then what chance would she have had of a place at Girton? Their opponents had been ready, with catapults and Molotov cocktails. Bron, standing on the other side of her, had done her Dolores Ibarruri impression.

'No pasarán!'

'No pasarán!' Gaynor had echoed. She was terrified.

She'd been on holiday, an exchange visit, with her Breton penfriend, Isolde. But the French government, in its insolence, had decided to build a nuclear power station on the Pointe De Raz, the unspoiled western tip of Brittany, where families like Isolde's spent their summer holidays walking, swimming and picnicking in the sunshine. It was a place where occasional British tourists clambered over the terrifying rocks of the 'Inferno of Plogoff' to experience the 'Land's End of France', and where locals kept modest hotels, tended flocks of sheep, fished the treacherous inshore waters and minded their own business. The *centrale nucléaire* was not to be tolerated.

The whole of Western Brittany had risen in rebellion against this madness from Paris. Gaynor, seventeen years old and in the middle of her A-level year, had been swept along. In the bars and folk gatherings of Quimper, she and Isolde had consorted with environmentalists, Breton nationalists and other assorted rebels. It was at one such 'Fest Noz' that she'd met Bron, a Welsh nationalist and long-time campaigner for the Welsh Language Society, who'd also come to Plogoff for the fight.

Every night the authorities had tried to move their 'mobile-mairies' along the only feasible road, carried by a narrow bridge, onto the Pointe de Raz. Every night, the Plogoffistes had held that bridge with their catapults, Molotov cocktails and desperate human bodies.

'They shall not pass!'

Gaynor roused herself, trying to concentrate on the present, but her mind insisted on roving through the past. How had she got away with it? Parents were more lax in those days. All hers knew was that she was a gifted linguist, something to do with her growing up speaking both Welsh and English, according to the educational psychologists. Holidays with the daughter of a respectable Breton family had seemed appropriate.

Steeling themselves by singing Breton nationalist songs, Gaynor and Isolde had stood firm. Then the middle-aged woman set a stone into the cradle of her catapult, took aim and fired. It had whizzed past a helmeted policeman's right ear and smashed into one of the headlamps on the leading truck.

The Plogoffistes cheered.

Immediately, a phalanx of police charged towards the bridge, keeping the middle-aged woman in their sights. An old man, wearing the sash of the Legion d'Honneur over his scarf and woollen coat, stood at the entrance to the bridge and harangued them.

A policeman had shouted back: 'Go home you old fool! Why are you fighting against your government with these Breton traitors and communists?'

'Tell your government to piss off! I fought with de Gaulle against the Nazis.'

They dragged the old man away. Gaynor recalled hoping that the police, though notoriously stupid, had anticipated the image problem they would inflict upon their political masters by beating up an elderly hero of the Resistance.

The images in her head moved on to the shadowy, masked figures hanging around the back of the crowd flicking cigarette lighters. Molotov cocktails started to fly over the heads of the protesters, crashing in bursts of flame around the feet of the police. Finally, the police turned and ran.

She returned once more to the present just in time to stop her head from crash landing on the computer's keyboard and chuckled at the memory. In the end the 'Plogoffistes' had won, and Gaynor had learned that a community united could achieve anything.

She had also decided that there was no way Catrin, her eighteen-year-old daughter, would ever be allowed to take such risks.

Bron's legacy was rather different. Her daughter, Eirlys, had been born nine months after the battle in Plogoff, the baby's paternity the subject of much speculation, but never disclosed.

Gaynor had not seen Bron since she, Miles and Eirlys, a

teenager by then, had left the Manor farmhouse. Over the seventeen years since their departure, she and Jimmy had gradually become accepted, then won the respect of all factions in the village. They had put on events in the village hall and helped to prevent the closure of the post office. Those who paid enough attention to public affairs appreciated Gaynor's long service on the parish council.

Bron, on the other hand, had been a divisive figure. The old villagers, many of whom depended on the quarries for employment, disapproved of the hippy encampment she'd established next to the Boundary Stone and the 'die-in' outside the offices of the quarry company in Bath. And, once the quarry closed, they muttered about how Bron was away too much 'dying in' and living in trees along the proposed routes of new roads, making trouble for other innocent, hard-working people. They also complained about 'that boyfriend of hers'... *Miles*.

Jimmy had been at school with Miles. How delighted he and Gaynor had been when their two friends got together. Gaynor shuddered. Miles was affable, fun, amusing and so plausible. It had taken years to find him out. In the intervening time he had pursued, and frequently seduced, every pretty young woman in the village, and *God knows where else*. Bron, preoccupied with saving the planet, had failed to notice her partner's treachery, but she'd got more than her share of the blame.

Women always do, Gaynor thought angrily. She opened the email and skimmed through it, fearing the worst.

The tone was unexpectedly apologetic. 'Really sorry,' it said, 'change of plan. Darren and I have just completed the purchase of a little farm in Brittany, near Quimper.'

Just like that? thought Gaynor, *Typical Bron.*

The email went on to describe in detail the delights of Bron and Darren's 'forever' home: traditional décor, enough land to grow all the food they could ever eat and only two kilometres from the nearest beach.

'And no quarries?' Gaynor said softly to the screen. She'd grown up surrounded by the slate quarries of Snowdonia. Her feelings about mineral extraction could be best described as conflicted: the drama and the danger; love and hate. Perhaps she'd agreed to live in Crubscombe because she missed them? But there was no time to think about that right now.

Bron's missive concluded with an invitation to Gaynor, Jimmy, and Catrin, to stay with her and Darren over Easter and join their Breton reunion party. Isolde would apparently be there, and Eli and Jean and Marianne.

'Perfect', Gaynor whispered, 'problem solved.'

She typed a reply assuring Bron that nobody in Crubscombe would be offended that she hadn't honoured her promise to visit Somerset, and happily accepted her invitation, on behalf of the whole family. She supposed she should have discussed it with Jimmy first, but reasoned he'd be likely to go along with it. He'd always enjoyed their holidays in Brittany.

If he has any objections, he should have been around to air them, damnit!

She shut down the computer. Making her way out of the kitchen and switching off lights, she pondered the next move of the Crubscombe Environment Committee. There'd have to be another meeting, soon. Although she and her friends had started the campaign against the basalt quarry, they had not finished the job. And a young man had lost his life because of their negligence.

CHAPTER 2

The following Sunday Jimmy decided that it was time to have another go at raising the matter of the club with his wife. Every Sunday morning, religiously, he and Gaynor took it in turns to chop a few vegetables and hurl them into the Rayburn with whatever joint of meat happened to be hanging around in the fridge or the freezer before escaping to the pub. It was their day of rest: time to catch up with their friends and neighbours and, theoretically, with each other.

Once in the Jolly Collier they liaised with the Crubscombe community. Jimmy, engulfing pints of real ale, exchanging banter with the men, while Gaynor, sipping viscous Australian red and longing for a nice light pinot noir from Burgundy, chatted to the women. This time, Jimmy noticed as they strolled home, she was still sober. Perhaps it was the menopause. Congratulating himself for his empathy and tact, he decided not to enquire.

He waited until lunch was over and their eighteen-year-old daughter, Catrin, had scurried away to her bedroom to do whatever it was teenagers did all day, which they invariably described as 'homework' or 'studying'.

Gaynor was talking to him about something and, though a notoriously cunning strategist, Jimmy could think of no way of diverting the conversation.

He stared across the kitchen table, looking for inspiration

but finding none in the remains of the Sunday roast, which sat on a greasy plate congealing between piles of books and papers. His gaze passed on to the door to the back stairs and then to the window, alighting briefly on the dust-encrusted casement before passing through and coming to rest in the orchard, home to the disorderly skeletons of assorted fruit trees, which probably hadn't been pruned for at least fifty years. Between the bare boughs he could see the high stone wall, bits of it falling into ruin, separating the orchard from the disused quarry. On the other side of it there was a strip of scrub-covered hillside, threaded with steep, narrow paths which led to the remains of the playing field and Crubscombe Quarrymen's Sports and Social Club.

It was a perfect set-up, a short step away from the farmhouse. They had an electricity supply; not entirely legal perhaps, but safe. He and Jerry the Spark had laid a cable from the house after the quarry company left. There was the on-going issue of the electricity bill, but he was sure that was mostly down to Catrin. Teenage girls were always using electrical kit, like – hair dryers, for example. The club used hardly anything.

And now they even had a smoking ban. *What was not to like?*

The afternoon light was fading; Jimmy watched as the sun sinking behind the Boundary Stone managed a faint pinkish glow. For some reason his thoughts drifted into the past. He and Gaynor had fallen in love with Crubscombe. The landscape had a kind of ruined glamour. The sheer cliff faces and dark pits in the abandoned and working quarries gave what would have been a green and pleasant land an edge.

The farmhouse, a six-bedroomed, seventeenth-century residence for a gentleman farmer, his family and his servants, a charming jumble of old stone and steep gables, had been on the market for some time at a very reasonable price. Miles had found out about it from George Archbold, a fellow inmate of his and

Jimmy's public school, eldest son of the quarry company's owner. Eager to escape from urban life, Jimmy, Gaynor, Miles and Bron had viewed the property on a bank holiday weekend, when the quarry was silent, and closed the deal with the Archbolds the following week.

'Jimmy!'

Jimmy shook himself out of his hazy recollections and focused on his wife. She was talking about Bron, which was probably the reason that she and Miles had floated into his wandering thoughts.

'You're not listening!'

'Yes, I am…Bron? Right?'

'She and Darren have got married.'

They looked at each other for a moment.

'He's a bit…' Gaynor ventured.

'Boring?' suggested Jimmy.

'He's always carried a torch for her.'

'Really?' Jimmy couldn't imagine anybody carrying such a thing for Bron – her bags perhaps?

Gaynor nodded. 'They've bought a farm in Brittany.'

'They're living in Brittany?' Jimmy approved. 'Sounds good. She's always …er…loved Brittany, hasn't she?'

'They've invited us for Easter.'

Jimmy made no comment. Shortly after leaving the farmhouse, Bron and Miles had gone their separate ways in a storm of mutual recrimination. Miles had left the country, rumour had it to try his luck in Hollywood, and nothing more was heard of him. His penchant for drunkenness and adultery was cited by Gaynor as the cause of the break-up, but Jimmy had his doubts. Bron could be difficult. He reached for the open bottle of red wine still standing in the middle of the table, lifted it and inspected its contents in a theatrical manner.

'Shall we kill this?'

Gaynor watched him as he poured equal measures of the remaining wine into their glasses. He met her censorious eye.

'You drink too much, Jimmy.'

'We,' he corrected her.

'I only drink at weekends.'

'I only drink at weekends, and on Thursdays.'

Gaynor sighed. 'That bloody club.'

'You used to love it.'

'I grew up, Jimmy.'

'You don't grow out of something like the club. It's a cultural institution.'

'It's a shebeen.'

'Twenty-five years old, this Easter.'

'Time to move on then.' She gave him a disparaging look, picked up the empty wine bottle and strode across the room, through the back door and into the utility room. There was an ear-splitting crash as the bottle landed on top of its late companions in the recycling bin.

Jimmy watched as she returned to the table. She'd kept her slender figure but her long black hair hung dejectedly at either side of her oval face and there were crow's feet gathering under her blue eyes. Years of teaching modern languages to ungrateful Somerset youth at Hales Mead Comprehensive had instructed her in the art of dealing with teenage miscreants and staffroom tyrants. It had also made her suspicious and, Jimmy reflected sadly, eroded her sense of humour. She looked tired but the indomitable, tenacious and sometimes alarming woman he'd always loved and admired was still there. She needed to chill; start singing again. It had been established by published and peer-reviewed medical research that singing was good for you.

'Jimmy!' Gaynor's wedding ring wafted to and fro an inch or so from the end of his nose. 'While we're on the subject of the club –' she appeared to have been reading his mind, again – 'and its environs –' she dragged her chair round the table, sat beside him and pulled him round in his seat to face her – 'apart from the illegal sale of alcohol –'

'We have a club premises certificate,' he reminded her.

'For that place? It's a death trap.'

'We don't allow smoking anymore.'

'I can't imagine why they haven't blocked the entrance...'

'To the car park?'

'It's not a car park any more, Jimmy. It's a patch of land at the edge of a very deep hole.'

'Nobody's complained.'

'Well, we're complaining now. The club car park,' she elaborated with a shudder, 'is right on the edge of the basalt pit.'

'We got it closed down didn't we? There's no more pollution.'

'It's only a matter of time before one of your drunken mates rolls through the fence and crashes down into the Lower Pool.'

'It's taken twenty-five years so far.'

'Don't be facetious! You might think that one young life in twenty-five years is OK...'

Jimmy felt obliged to concede. He nodded mechanically while Gaynor marshalled her thoughts, preparing the main thrust of her attack.

'The thing is,' she continued gently, 'we fought a good campaign. We got Archbold's to close the quarry, but they never finished the job; they just downed tools and buggered off.'

He was sure he'd heard all this before. He looked intently into her eyes and switched his mind into autopilot, making a note to himself to wake it up if anything new was introduced.

The sermon continued. If the disused quarries were cleaned up, the pools drained, the spoil dumps levelled, the holes backfilled, the crumbling and rusting plant dismantled and taken away, then the whole area could be landscaped tastefully. It would become a happy playground for the whole community, especially the children. If she and her committee, with Jimmy's help, raised the necessary funds, it could be done. Jimmy was good at that sort of thing. He knew all the right people. They could build a new community centre and Jimmy's folk club could meet there in comfort and safety.

His whole being recoiled from this. There'd be bills and fees, food hygiene regulations, no more cheap beer or cider and all this restrained jollification would have to come to an end by midnight. There would be no more third half. He could feel the walls of the old people's home closing in around him.

'Poor Eve Chawner. She's lost her son, for God's sake! Somebody's got to take responsibility.' Gaynor's insistent tone tripped the wake-up switch. It was possible she could tell he wasn't really listening. For a moment he considered the washing-up as a possible means of escape, but decided, instead, to offer some thoughts.

'There's nobody to take responsibility. The old company, Archbold's, no longer exists.'

'Yes it does. It's just been swallowed up by some multi-national; Aggrementos, I believe it's called these days. They're blowing tons of rock out of the working quarries as we speak.'

'It's been through a number of …' Jimmy concentrated for a moment … 'iterations.'

'Why don't you talk to your old school chum?'

'George Archbold? He's not my chum.'

A barrage of sound, like a ghostly blast from the basalt pit, exploded above their heads. Catrin was listening to something she considered to be music. Deep rumblings from the bass made the windows rattle.

'What the hell is that?' groaned Jimmy

Gaynor looked up at the ceiling listening intently. '"Yes", I think. One of your old bits of vinyl.'

To her parents' astonishment Catrin had retrieved most of her father's vinyl collection from the boxes in the dining room, where it had been dumped and forgotten, along with the turntable and amplifier, which she and one of her boyfriends had restored to working order.

'I thought all those old boys were dead,' Jimmy said.

'Prog Rock lives on, especially if it's on vinyl.'

Jimmy sensed a welcome return of humour. 'Is this a Hales Mead thing?' he asked.

'The sixth-form intelligentsia. Retro. Catrin says it energises her, helps her to write her essays.' Gaynor laughed, then, returning to her hobby horse, raised her voice above the racket. 'George Archbold? His family still owns most of the land around here, and he's still involved with the quarries, isn't he?'

'CEO of Aggrementos. I didn't actually like him.'

'Oh, come on, Jimmy! You've no objection to using the old school tie when it suits you.'

The door opened. Catrin's head, dark brown eyes fringed by brown curls, so like her father's, appeared round it.

'Phone!'

'Well, answer it,' Gaynor said.

'It'll be for one of you. I don't do landlines.'

Jimmy got to his feet. A blast of cold air greeted him as he went out into the hall. The plaintive bleating of the telephone was barely audible above the wall of sound descending from on high. He picked up the handset.

'Jimmy Sullivan speaking.'

'Jimmy!'

The voice at the other end was clear and recognisable, a startling reminder of the past. 'Miles? What the...?' Jimmy lowered his voice and carried the phone into the dining room, closing the door carefully behind him. 'What's brought you out of the woodwork?' he whispered.

'Hello Jimmy!' The voice had lost none of its uninhibited bonhomie. 'Have you got a cold?'

'No! No, I'm fine.'

Jimmy glanced at the back of the solid wooden door. There was a gap underneath it. A draught wafted in from the hall stirring ancient cobwebs that flourished undisturbed in the corners between the walls and the ceiling. Since Miles, Bron and Bron's teenage daughter, Eirlys, had moved out, the room had been abandoned and was known in family circles as the 'oubliette'. In the middle of it, under jettisoned relics of the family's past life, there was a dining table, surrounded by dusty chairs. Musical instruments in various states of disrepair stood against the walls between bookshelves and piles of cardboard boxes stuffed with papers. Old coats were dumped on the chairs, along with other items of clothing. Amplifiers and speakers and yards of electrical wire were stashed under the table and forgotten about. A faint whiff of damp books and something that might be drains hung in the air.

Wrinkling his nose, Jimmy spoke into the phone. 'Where the hell are you?'

'Bath.'

'Not still hanging out in L.A. then?' Jimmy asked cautiously.

'Noo! I've come home.'

Jimmy considered asking why, but decided against it.

'The old country is calling to me. Time to make a comeback.'

The conversation paused momentarily.

'How's it going?'

'Brilliantly! Lap of luxury, mate. I'm staying with George and Alex.'

'George?'

'George Archbold. You must remember him.'

'Yes! Yes, of course,' Jimmy said, taking care not to sound judgemental.

'George is all right, in spite of being...'

'An unscrupulous, capitalist bread-head?'

Miles laughed. 'Same old Jimmy! Dear old George has been Mr Generosity, and Alex is a sweetie.'

'That would be the third Lady Archbold?'

'Yes, possibly. One has trouble keeping up. They've given me carte blanche, Jimmy. I can stay as long as I like. Have to admit they've been wonderfully kind and hospitable to the old school chum.'

'Jolly good,' Jimmy said, with genuine enthusiasm. Pleased as he was to hear from the 'old school chum', he was relieved to know that he had his feet firmly established under someone else's table. 'Oddly enough, Gaynor and I were just talking about dear old George.'

Miles sighed. 'How is the lovely Gaynor?'

'On a health and safety trip,' Jimmy said carefully.

'Are we in danger?'

'I shouldn't think so,' Jimmy reassured him.

They both laughed.

'The past is another country, as they say,' said Miles. 'I am relaunching my career.'

Miles' career had once been meteoric, starting one Sunday afternoon at a session in the Pendragon Hotel in Cardiff when they'd all watched, with kindly amusement, the then five-year-old Eirlys, skipping and twirling to the music. Inspired, Miles scribbled the lyrics of 'The Little Dancer' on the back of a copy of the pub's lunch menu. Later he added a cute little tune and recorded it on his latest CD. He released it as a single in 1987, in the summer, when the record-buying public is at its least judgemental. It rose to number five in the charts and paid a substantial chunk of the deposit on the old Manor farmhouse. Multiple gigs and tours had followed.

'I still get fan mail, you know,' Miles continued. 'The fans are hungry. Miles Hollowtree is back!'

Jimmy didn't doubt this. There were corners of the folk world where Miles' name continued to be spoken with awe. He'd been up there with Bert Jansch and Ralph McTell for a while. He was, Jimmy recollected fondly, a brilliant comet, flashing across the night sky and then fading, remembered by some but lost in the vastness of space.

'He'll have to come and do a set at the club,' said Jimmy, pleased to be able to offer some help.

'Good God!' Miles guffawed. 'Is that still going?'

'Same time, same place, every Thursday night without fail,' Jimmy said proudly.

'I'd be delighted.' Miles stopped to think for a moment. 'Is Frankie Dando still minding the door?'

'Yes, still the same old Frankie.'

'I shall be on my best behaviour, scout's honour!'

Jimmy laughed. 'Looking forward to it, mate.'

Back in the outside world, the kitchen door creaked open. Gaynor's footsteps approached along the hall. Jimmy froze, then relaxed as they diverted to the staircase.

'Catrin!' The footsteps ascended the stairs.

It occurred to Jimmy that he'd been on the phone for much too long. He suggested a date and then, bidding his old friend a cheery farewell, hit the red key and carried the phone back into the hall. It would be good to catch up with Miles, he reflected, longing to resurrect the jollity of the old days.

He hoped Frankie would see it in the same light. The club's

enforcer had never rated Miles as a musician and, a perfect gentleman himself, had disapproved of his womanising. Perhaps it was his upbringing. Frankie's family were upright, god-fearing Methodists, but the only time he'd been near the Wesleyan chapel in recent years had been to attend his mother's funeral. Nobody knew what was going on under Frankie's rough-hewn carapace. He never confided in Jimmy, or in anybody else, as far as one could tell. But a chap knew when another chap needed support. *Better keep an eye on them both,* Jimmy thought as he replaced the phone in its cradle.

Gaynor appeared at the top of the stairs. 'Who was that on the phone?'

'Work,' Jimmy said firmly. He strode into the kitchen, walked resolutely to the sink and got stuck into the washing-up.

CHAPTER 3

I

On the day of Miles' comeback gig at the folk club Frankie Dando finished work at lunchtime, which he did as often as possible on a Thursday. He was not in the best of tempers. Noticing a couple of young men sitting in an unmarked van outside his neighbours' front gate he scowled at them before turning into his own front path. As he entered the house, he found yet another airmail letter lying on the mat. Displeasure turned to rage and ignited into a blaze of fury. He decided to relieve his feelings by de-cluttering.

He stumped up the stairs to his bedroom and, using a largeish proportion of his considerable strength, picked up a sofa, which had been sitting there for many years quietly annoying him, and hurled it out of the window, without taking the trouble to open it first. The sofa burst out into the air carrying with it shards of broken glass and twisted segments of 1960s steel frame. It bounced into the middle of what had once been a lawn and, sagging, but intact, came to rest upside down under the washing line. Dust, scraps of fabric, squashed beer cans and other bits of rubbish, released from its interior, came to earth over a wide area, landing in unexpected places.

In the garden in Cherry Close, which backed on to Frankie's residence, a neighbour, darting out to her washing line in the bitter cold to feel for any suggestion that the things hanging on it might eventually dry, looked up for a moment.

'Frankie's on one again,' she muttered, then shrugged and retreated indoors.

The van took off, exiting Apple Close in a spreading plume of oily smoke.

A chilly wind poured in through the window, rattling the remaining bits of glass and broken metal. Frankie went back down the stairs, threw the letter into the living-room fire place and put a match to it again and again until there was nothing left and the vicious through-draught carried its ashes up the chimney, scattering them over Upper Crubscombe. Satisfied, he picked up his guitar and his cranky old amplifier and went into the bathroom to sing the blues.

Crubscombe settled down to listen again, whether it wanted to or not. The neighbours gossiped and grumbled but they endured.

I went down St James' Infirm'ry
Saw my baby there...

'Talented man.'

'Oh yeah? I'll give him...'

But no one argued with Frankie.

'He's on one again.'

'Hangs round with that Jimmy Sullivan.'

'Hippies.'

'Down that folk club.'

'Maybe he's practising.'

'Maybe he's just got his electric bill!'

'Council will kick him out this time. Perhaps he'll lose his job.'

'He's all right really.'

'He's got an explosives licence, did you know that? Does the bang for all the quarries. Shouldn't be allowed.'

'It's that little girl I feel sorry for, Rosie...'

Let her go let her go God bless her...

II

Over in what had once been the Quarrymen's Sports and Social Club Jimmy and Terry Mivart, still the 'Hon Sec' and licensee, were making essential preparations for the evening's entertainment. They were testing the beer. More domestic arrangements, such as seating and heating, could wait until later.

It was early March, less than a month till Easter, but the weather was still freezing. A miserable grey twilight hung over the clubhouse, the car park and the rickety post-and-wire fence which stood between it and the edge of the basalt pit. Just inside the fence, afforded a small degree of shelter by the remains of the cricket club scoreboard, half-rotten chairs, too damp and smelly even for use by the folk club, had been arranged in a semi-circle – the last redoubt of the smokers.

Looking out of a grimy window, Jimmy noted this development with genial tolerance. He zipped up his puffer jacket and held his faceted beer mug up to the struggling light. The ale was chestnut brown and clear. Even in this feeble luminescence it glowed like a brown diamond.

'He've settled nicely,' Terry observed.

'You do a good job, Tel.'

'Ah yeah. Considering I haven't got a proper cellar.'

'We manage though, don't we?'

'Suppose I do. Had to ditch the end of the last barrel, mind. We was getting complaints.'

They sipped and swallowed. The beer from the newly-tapped barrel was heavenly.

Terry, setting his glass down on the bar with an exaggerated sigh of contentment, winked at Jimmy. 'What you doing this afternoon then, mate?'

'Site meeting with the owner of a potential venue for an art installation, underground, no wi-fi or mobile coverage.'

Terry chuckled. 'He must be wondering where you are.'

'He would be if he actually existed.'

Terry thought this over for a moment, then guffawed. 'You'm a crafty bugger!' He was impressed, but he could see a possible flaw. 'What about your boss? Don't he ever ask you about all they site visits you do on Thursdays?'

'Who? Bill Ryan? Used to be a Morris Man back in the day. Quite a livewire in his youth as I recall.' Jimmy looked into the chestnut depths of his beer, remembering. 'I do my job, not necessarily in office hours, of course. He leaves me alone.'

For Terry no such manoeuvres were necessary. Since the quarry had closed, he'd worked for Chedgy's, his cousin's brewery, purveyors of the finest real ale in the county. Terry saw to it that they supplied the folk club with large amounts of 'Original' at very little cost in recognition of his unusual and surprising gifts as a brewer, and his friend Jimmy's long-standing acquaintance with the MD.

Jimmy pulled out a chair and lounged, placing his precious mug on a nearby table. The chair protested. He wondered if he should heed his wife's advice and cut down on the beer. *Not yet, please.* Mondays and Wednesdays were now alcohol-free. Gaynor had insisted, conveying with a look the message that she did not want a husband who was dead or fat, so he complied. Thursdays, on the other hand, were for song and ale. Jimmy leaned back in his chair watching with an envious eye as his friend waded into his beer. *He must have hollow legs.*

'Keeps it in the space between his ears,' Gaynor had once remarked.

Terry fussed over his taps and pipes, sparkling islands of cleanliness in the generally filthy premises. He rubbed them down with a brand-new J-cloth, chattering excitedly.

'Gotta have it all nice, see, for our guest.'

'Miles?' Jimmy laughed.

'Miles Hollowtree.' Terry's voice sank to a reverential whisper. 'He's a legend. How'd you get him to come back?'

Jimmy looked around. Seen in the light of day the décor was beyond hideous, featuring orange relieved with splashes of ochre and damson – classic 1970s – the whole liberally sprinkled with black mould. He chuckled, 'Must be the pull of the bright lights.'

Terry frowned. 'Think we should clean the Gents?'

Situated at the opposite end of the clubhouse from the bar and the kitchen, accessed through a door marked 'Fire escape', the Gents was a rugged, stenchful cavern, including changing rooms and showers (some still leaking) for long dead or retired sports teams.

'Difficult to tell,' Gaynor had once sniffily observed, 'which are the showers and which are the urinals.'

Nobody ever cleaned it and nobody, when sober, lingered.

'Shouldn't bother,' said Jimmy, 'Miles won't care. He's an old folkie.'

Terry looked at his watch. 'Where's he to? He should be here by now.'

'Plenty of time,' said Jimmy. He never panicked, at least not outwardly.

He changed the subject. 'I wonder what's happened to Frankie?'

'Dunno, haven't seen him today.'

This, Jimmy thought, might be cause for concern. Frankie had seemed a bit miserable lately, but nobody could say why. Jimmy felt he deserved more respect than he was given by fearful villagers and suspicious guardians of the law. He was a gifted musician; his interpretation of the blues, learned during youthful misadventures in the Mississippi Delta and other obscure corners of the southern USA, was unsurpassed in Somerset and, possibly, the whole of the United Kingdom. Perhaps he was avoiding Miles.

Having given his friend's state of mind a cursory inspection, Jimmy let it go. All would be revealed in due course – nothing too dangerous probably. It could be dealt with when, and if, anything untoward actually occurred. He hoped whatever it was would have blown over by the evening. With numerous extra punters expected to witness the comeback gig of Miles Hollowtree and the best real ale flowing at £1.50 a pint, he could do with some help with security.

III

At the T-junction in Fry's Bottom, Miles Hollowtree stood on the roof of his serviceable Peugeot estate desperately shouting into a mobile phone, which he held as high as possible above his upturned face. The back of the car was packed with guitars and other musical instruments, and something electronic in a silver flight case. An ageing troubadour, he was, in the parallel universe of folk, still a famous man, deferentially discussed on Mudcats, the website for discerning folkies. He was lean and tanned, his face still handsome but lined, slow roasted under an alien sun.

'Haven't got the faintest idea where I am, Jimmy!' he shouted into the mobile. 'I've been driving round in circles for three hours.'

'Can you see any landmarks?' Jimmy's voice sounded as if it was a thousand miles away.

Turning round gingerly on the slippery steel roof, Miles looked again at the mutilated road sign which pointed, more or less, up and down the larger of the two roads.

ROME 3   SHEPTON MALLET 14

'It says Rome, Jimmy. I'm three miles from bloody Rome, apparently.'

Static, or possibly heartless laughter, crackled out of the phone.

Miles looked around impatiently. All he could see over the top of a rambling hedge were ranges of untidy farm buildings.

'Sounds like Fry's Bottom,' Jimmy informed him through the static.

'What? What the hell am I doing there?'

'Main route into Crubscombe now.'

'What happened to Blackdown Lane?'

'It got blown up.'

'Terrorists? Huh! Can't say I blame them.'

'Stanedown Quarry. It expanded.'

'Is Frome still there?'

'Last time I looked. Which way are you facing?'

'Shepton Mallet.'

'OK! Turn right...'

Miles tried to concentrate on the hissing flood of turnings and landmarks, knowing that he would probably forget it all the minute he got off the phone. The thing went dead anyway, so he scrambled and slithered back on to the road and, wrenching himself away from the grasping tendrils of a hedge plant, staggered round to the driver's door.

The air smelled richly of distressed pigs.

IV

Rosie Dando, newly released from the school bus, dressed in mufti – a sixth-form privilege – turned off Upper Crubscombe High Street into the Orchard Estate. She was tall, like her dad but, unlike him, remained slender and graceful. Her hair, a mass of rich dark- brown curls, had been tied back severely to facilitate a day's study and was beginning to pull on her scalp. As soon as she got home, she'd have a shower and then release it. After a few years of experiment, she'd gone for the natural look, her look. Her boyfriend said he loved it, which, though this was not the point at all, mattered. She had inherited her mum's dark-brown skin. Her wide-set eyes were black flecked with green and sometimes changed colour, depending on the light, like shot silk. In spite of her colouring, she looked a lot like her dad. Her parents had been a handsome couple, or so she'd been told.

She smiled as she strode past the low concrete walls, iron gates and improvised parking spaces. She was going out tonight, meeting up with her mates, and with *Him*.

As she approached the corner of Apple Close she heard the keening guitar.

Now what?

She let herself into the house and made her way to the kitchen window slowly appraising the devastation in the back garden.

'Dad!'

The house filled with exquisitely executed melancholy, achieved by inserting a finger into the neck of a broken glass bottle and sliding it up and down the fretboard of the guitar. But Rosie was not impressed.

She ran up the stairs, threw her rucksack in through the door of her bedroom, advanced on the bathroom door and thumped it with a peremptory fist.

'What's it about this time, then?'

The slide guitar stopped, but Frankie continued with a rambling succession of miserable picks and chords.

'Never you mind. I'm out of sorts.'

'I'd noticed.'

The guitar continued, gently weeping.

'Dad! I need the bathroom!'

'Use the one at the back.'

'I need a shower.'

'Why? You going somewhere?'

'I'm going out with Catrin, right? I don't stop you from going down the club, do I?'

Frankie shifted his position on the bog seat and, retreating further behind the guitar, noodled around a few minor chords.

'Got a big guest on tonight, 'Frankie remarked with bitter irony. He moved his fingers up and down the fretboard, looking for minor chords, then, remembering his parental duties, asked suspiciously, 'You off to Bristol?' He understood that kids liked to go to Bristol, or worse, Cardiff, with the intention of getting into bad company. He suspected an unsuitable boyfriend.

'I'm not going anywhere if I can't have a fucking shower!'

'You ought to mind your language.'

The doorbell rang.

Rosie glared at the bathroom door. 'That'll be the neighbours.'

She trailed down the stairs and opened the door to her next-door neighbour.

'Lisa! I'm really sorry.'

'It's all right, my love,' said Lisa, shoving a large, warm plate, wrapped in a cloth, into her hand. 'I have come to say thank you.'

'What for?' As far as Rosie was aware Lisa, though she tolerated the blues, was not a fan.

'We've had the bailiffs round, or we would of if they hadn't seen your dad first. He did tell them where to go.'

'But not in so many words, right?'

'Didn't say nothing. Doesn't need to, does he? They run away. Skinny little gits they was, in a van. When they heard that sofa come out your window they buggered off.'

Upstairs the guitar continued its wailing hymn of grief.

'He's a good man, your dad, but he's troubled.'

'He will be when I get in his face.'

'No kidding?'

'He's a gentleman. Never hit a woman in his life. I take advantage.'

'Well, I have baked you both a nice rabbit pie for your tea.'

'Right. Thanks, Lisa.'

Rosie left the pie on the kitchen table and went upstairs again to look into her dad's bedroom and assess the extent of the damage. She supposed Lisa had a point.

Troubled as he was, her father had gone to war with furniture. Furniture had made him a lonely divorcee, furniture made him drink, in the past it had got him into trouble with the police. Furniture was conspiring to make her, his beloved daughter, grow up and leave him for some distant university, and it had to be punished.

Pushing against the draught, she put her head round Frankie's bedroom door. After a swift assessment of the damage, she retreated to the landing, allowing the door to slam behind her.

'You're going to end up in jail,' Rosie informed the frustrated artist in the bathroom.

She went into her bedroom, emptied her school stuff out of her rucksack and replaced it with towels and toiletries. Then, flicking speculatively though her wardrobe with one hand, she eased her phone out of the pocket of her jeans with the other. She tapped and swiped its surface with a flying thumb.

'Catrin? Hi, it's Rosie. He's on one again... I can't get in the fucking bathroom.'

V

Grey dusk was closing in on the old Manor farmhouse and its grounds. Between the orchard and a patch of grass known as the lawn, a small vegetable plot, untended so far this year, lay dormant in the unseasonable weather. The farmyard, surrounded on three sides by stone outbuildings, roofed with corrugated iron, used now only as storage space for garden paraphernalia, was looking drab. The house itself, with its ill-fitting casements and open fireplaces, was an ice palace. In spite of its rustic charm, it only had one feature of outstanding architectural interest, a staircase, which, hidden in a stone turret attached to the back wall, gave access from the kitchen to the servants' bedroom. On account of this, the whole building, and everything in its curtilage, had been awarded the status of Grade II Listed.

Just important enough to attract the attention of council bureaucrats, thought Gaynor, sitting at the long wooden table in her picturesque kitchen, shivering under a blanket as she worked her way, red biro poised over them, through a seemingly bottomless pile of blue exercise books. *Not enough, though, to attract a grant from English Heritage.* The place soaked up money and there was seldom anything to show for it. All their reserves had gone when they remortgaged to buy out Bron and Miles, and then they'd had to replace the roof. Thoughts of a nice, modern semi ran through her mind...*gas central heating...* She sighed and blew on her freezing fingers, coaxing them back into action.

She'd got home from school by four o'clock, earlier than usual, because she had to chair a meeting of Crubscombe Environment Group's steering committee at eight. If she set aside an hour for tidying up and managed to find the tin of baked beans and half-loaf she was sure she'd seen in the cupboard that morning, there should just be time to clear the most urgent pile of marking.

8H. They were the lowest band, twelve- and thirteen-year-olds maintained, more or less, in statutory captivity, restless and resentful. H, according to staffroom wits, was for hopeless. She reached for another little blue book. Jordan Fishlock...a few grudging words of laboriously formed but scarcely intelligible letters... 'je suis...Jorden...'

For God's sake! The boy can't even spell his own name. At least he'd handed it in.

He wouldn't dare not. Years of quelling the mob at Hales Mead Comprehensive had given Gaynor, now Head of Department, an aura of institutional terror. The girls were easier. They subconsciously admired her elegance, her height and the thick black hair, sometimes streaked with grey, these days, when she hasn't got round to dyeing it. But all feared her sharp tongue, a gift from her north-Welsh granny, honed and refined on the field of battle. She struck fear into the hearts of the rebellious, like a Disney witch.

The witch shivered and pulled the blanket tight around her shoulders... *It's March! Surely this horrible cold winter will end soon.* She wondered if Jimmy had remembered to order some more coal for the Rayburn. Probably not...she'd have to remind him.

The door opened...

'Jimmy?'

Catrin bounced in, impetuous, like her father.

'Rosie's coming over for a shower, all right?'

'Yes, fine,' Gaynor murmured distractedly.

Catrin went over to the Rayburn. 'It's gone out.'

Gaynor nodded.

'Sorry, Mum. Maen ddrwg genni.' Speaking Welsh was a bond with her mother which her father did not share.

'Not your fault. Your father forgot to order the coal.'

'Can I put the immersion on?'

'Go on then.'

'I'll put the fan heater on for you, you're freezing to death.'

'Oh, all right.'

'We're not that broke, are we?'

'No. Of course we aren't.'

Catrin bounced out with the parting shot. 'You'll get hypothermia.'

'Catrin!' Gaynor called after her.

'What?'

'Cae drws!'

'Sorreeee!'

Catrin returned, closed the door and could then be heard galloping up the stairs to her room.

She'd been very good lately, bit edgy perhaps, maybe not sleeping properly…stress probably. The exams were only a matter of weeks away and she, along with Rosie Dando, had been offered a place at Cambridge to read modern languages. Two in the same year, a huge academic coup for a bog-standard comprehensive.

Gaynor viewed her daughter's achievements with satisfaction. She lacked Rosie's focus and work ethic but she had a facility for languages, probably the result of her bilingual upbringing. The Easter break in Brittany would do her good. She wouldn't remember Bron, having been little more than a year old when the ructions started. In spite of them, the family holidays in France with Isolde and Marianne and their children had remained an annual fixture and Catrin always enjoyed them. No wonder her French was so fluent.

The red pen hovered over Jordan Fishlock's feeble offering. What on earth was she going to say? *Never mind, dear, they'll let you give it up next year?* Hardly.

Her mind wandered again, this time to Rosie. Girton College, no less, had offered her a scholarship. 'Ticks all the boxes,' according to Al Messenger, Deputy Head, responsible for Ridiculous Initiatives and Careful Conservative Values.

'Nothing to do with her being clever and hard-working, then?' Gaynor had said mildly, fixing him with a cool, hard stare.

She thought of Rosie's mum, Estelle, remembered afternoons

in the school holidays drinking coffee or red wine. They'd talk about anything and everything, reviewing the latest literary sensation or laughing at the assortment of drunks and fools, most of whom claimed to be friends of Miles or Bron, who hung round the farmhouse.

There was nothing to keep Estelle in Crubscombe: no work for an African-American college dropout, no intellectual stimulus at home. Frankie was kind, she had always insisted on that, but, Gaynor felt guilty at the thought, no match for her intellectually. Supported by Gaynor, Estelle had decided to return to the United States and resume her studies; and Frankie had pulled down the shutters. He clung on to his daughter by any means the law could provide and there was nothing Estelle could do about it. Gaynor vowed that she would watch over Rosie. She had kept her word, sending Estelle regular bulletins about her daughter's progress by letter and email. But nothing could break down the adamantine wall that Frankie had built between himself and his ex-wife. Gaynor shook her head, looked down at the red biro in her right hand and addressed it. 'No getting through to him...' At least Jimmy seemed to be able to keep him out of trouble, sorting out his quarrels and interceding in his confrontations with the law. As a result, Frankie had stayed out of jail and retained his explosives licence; quite an achievement, really.

Jimmy used his contacts, pulled strings, conducted negotiations in pubs and bars, the way men do. In the past he and Gaynor had worked well together, their skills complementary. They still agreed about most political issues, but lately he was becoming difficult.

With a sigh Gaynor ticked the two more or less correct words in the Fishlock oeuvre and threw his book on to the 'done' pile.

The school was digitising, persecuting its staff with spreadsheets, apps and a never-ending stream of emails. More distinguished and trustworthy pupils were issued with tablets and could submit their homework online. The Fishlocks of this world used exercise books.

How many more...? Ten? Fifteen? They had to be finished by tomorrow morning, when she would be handing the class over to the trainee, who would have to learn to deal with year eight refuseniks *sometime...*

She flicked open the next exercise book. Teresa Bryant, a tryer, poor kid.

Pondering the symptoms of hypothermia, she moved her feet as close to the fan heater as she dared and peppered the meticulously rounded letters with big red encouraging ticks, and some corrections.

She heard the door of the utility room open and slam shut. Then the back door opened, admitting a whiff of mouldy damp, and Jimmy.

'Hiya! Bad day at the office?'

With unquenchable jollity he charged into her presence, swept her hair back from her face and kissed her on the forehead. She could smell beer.

He rushed round the kitchen, like a ball in a bagatelle, opening cupboards and inspecting their contents.

'What are you looking for?'

'My turn to make supper, isn't it? What do you fancy?'

'There might be some beans somewhere. You'll have to use the electric cooker because somebody forgot to order the coal.' She pulled the blanket tight around her shoulders and glared at him.

'Ah!' Jimmy said. 'Sorry! I'll do it now.' He patted the pockets of his jacket, located his phone and fished it out. He stared intently at its shiny face for a moment, then started swiping and poking it with a fat finger.

Gaynor looked on amused but infuriated. 'No point trying them now, is there? The office is closed.'

'Not a problem, my sweet. I will sort it.' He paced round the room, holding the phone aloft, looking for a signal, collided with the piles of exercise books on the edge of the table and sent them cascading to the floor. The marked and unmarked came together in a single heap.

'Jimmy!'

The call connected.

'Hello! 'zat you Jimmy?' The voice was faint and indistinct.

'Speak up, Terry!' Jimmy bawled at the phone. 'Stand on a chair. You'll get a better signal!' He prodded an icon that seemed to represent a loudspeaker and Terry's voice filled the room.

'You at home, Jimmy?'

'Yeah, yeah. Can you get your Michael to drop some coal off asap? My wife's freezing to death up here.'

'Sure, mate. I'll give him a call.'

'Thanks! I owe you a big drink.' Jimmy turned triumphantly to face his sceptical wife.

'Do you think that's a good idea?' she said.

'It'll be fine. Michael won't mind. He's Terry's cousin.'

'Buying Terry Mivart a big drink.'

'That you, Gaynor love?' enquired the voice on the end of the phone. 'You coming down the club tonight?'

'No, thank you.'

'You should do. We got a special guest tonight. He's a' old friend of yours'

Jimmy found the red telephone symbol and stabbed it with a desperate forefinger, but it failed to respond.

'It's Miles…Miles Hollowtree?'

The red telephone finally connected and cut off Terry's flow.

A brief silence followed.

Gaynor put down her pen and watched while Jimmy, resuming his search of the cupboards, extracted a tin and turned to face her.

She caught his eye and held it. 'Miles?'

He held up the tin. 'Baked beans?'

'Miles is playing at the folk club tonight?'

Jimmy cleared his throat. 'Is there any reason he shouldn't?'

Gaynor said nothing. In all honesty, she couldn't think of one.

'He's an artist,' Jimmy persisted, 'a performer. He's relaunching his career. That's what the club does. We support artists, and the community,' he added hastily. 'We provide entertainment. Miles is still popular. A lot of people will be very glad of the opportunity to come and hear him. They remember "The Little Dancer"...'

Gaynor winced. 'His pop song?'

'People love it.' Jimmy paused for a moment, his pleading brown eyes gazing into hers. 'Why don't you come along? Come and have some fun. Remember fun?'

Gaynor remembered: the shouting and door slamming, the cries of anxious children, the procession of angry husbands and fathers who shunned them in the pub and the Co-op and, occasionally, turned up at the farmhouse threatening violence; the money, waylaid by drink, which never found its way into the household budget. In the end, Jimmy had agreed to conduct the painful negotiations that led to Bron and Miles' departure. How could his memory be that short?

'I've got a meeting tonight,' she said stiffly, 'Crubscombe Environment Group.'

Jimmy opened a table drawer and rattled through the oddments inside. He was looking shifty. 'Where's the tin opener?'

Gaynor lost interest in her blanket and sat up straight. The memories were in full flood.

'There is no force upon this earth, no wind, no wave, no army, no base cajolement that could induce me to go anywhere near that over-rated, lying, hypocritical old tart. He destroyed my oldest friend – broke her heart, and her daughter's. He was the only father figure that poor girl ever knew. He dumped them both. They never heard from him again.'

Jimmy, backing away physically from her arctic blast, tried to introduce a sense of balance. 'I thought she'd thrown him out.'

'What else could she do? He was screwing every available female in the district, and lying about it.'

'She wasn't around much herself, was she? How can you be sure she wasn't doing the same?'

'No! Bron never did anything like that.'

Jimmy raised an eyebrow.

'I can't stop you,' Gaynor said grimly, 'from "supporting" him at the club, but he's not coming here, Jimmy. Don't even think about, don't even contemplate inviting him to this house.' She paused, studying his face intently.

'Why would I? He's staying in Bath, with the Archbolds, living the life of luxury, I gather...' Jimmy's voice tailed off as a tangential thought appeared to cross his mind. 'I could ask him to arrange an audience with his Lordship, if you like, to talk about the quarries? The man dislikes me for...well...all sorts of reasons, but he might listen to Miles.'

Gaynor snorted. 'Let's see if he's telling you the truth first, shall we?' She paused, taking a long, deep breath before pronouncing, 'If you find that he has, in fact, got nowhere to go, you will cast him into a ditch and leave him there to die, slowly and miserably.'

'Yes, miss,' said Jimmy.

With a perfunctory tap at the back door, Rosie strolled into the kitchen. She was carrying her backpack and a heavy dish wrapped in a tea towel.

Gaynor and Jimmy jumped like guilty lovers and greeted her in bright innocent unison.

'Hello Rosie!'

'Sorry, Gaynor,' said Rosie. 'Dad's on one again. Catrin said I could use your shower.'

'Yes, of course you can,' Gaynor said.

Rosie laid the dish carefully on the table and lifted off the cloth revealing a crusty meat pie with a single wedge cut out of it. 'It's one of Lisa's.'

The scent of rich gravy and herbs wafted round the kitchen.

Gaynor stood up. 'I'll find some plates. Better get rid of the evidence before any of the vegetarians arrive for the meeting. Jimmy! Go and call Catrin!'

'I left a piece for Dad,' Rosie explained. 'Not that he deserves it.'

'Oh dear,' said Gaynor, 'What's up?'

'How should I know? He won't come out of the bathroom.'

This had always puzzled Gaynor. 'Why the bathroom, for heaven's sake?'

'He likes the acoustic.'

CHAPTER 4

After his unexpectedly sustaining and wholesome supper, Jimmy returned to the clubhouse.

Miles was sitting on a high stool at the bar attacking a bag of fish and chips, slowly recovering from his extended journey. He was drinking lime and soda and seemed a little jumpy. 'It hasn't changed much, Jimmy.' His gaze swept over the clubhouse, which, in its pre-set state, was lit by a single fluorescent tube that concealed nothing. 'Something's been eating the upholstery. Have you got rats?'

Jimmy studied the benches that stood along the back and side walls, conceding that lumps did appear to have been bitten out of their plastic and foam-rubber coverings. 'Possibly,' he said.

The two men looked at each other for a moment. Like Terry, Miles had retained his slim build, but there were hard lines etched into his face, especially round the eyes and mouth. His skin was tanned and cracked like vellum and Jimmy noted with satisfaction that his hair was definitely receding. There were fifteen or more years of their lives to recover, which might require a modicum of tact.

'I gather Bron has left the country,' Jimmy observed cautiously.

Miles grinned. His eyes twinkled. 'Gone to Brittany with Darren.'

'So I've heard.'

'Well, bloody good luck to him.' Miles raised his bright green glass and drank, making an effort to gain emotional sustenance from lime and lemonade. 'She threw me out, you know? Cast me into the street, then sold the house in Bath and buggered off to live with the Teepee people in Wales.'

Jimmy nodded, conveying understanding and sympathy.

Terry, standing on the other side of the bar lingering over taps and other liquor- dispensing paraphernalia, made an attempt to offer his hero a beer.

'It's our "Original". You used to drink it, didn't you?'

'Sorry, mate, I'm on the wagon. I'm getting back into touring. Got to look after my health.'

''Tis all natural ingredients. It'll make the place look better an' all.'

Miles stared at the beer barrel like an ancient cat sighting a sparrow in some inaccessible tree. He shook his head. 'Grim reality for me from now on.' He eyed Jimmy's brimming glass with avuncular concern.

Jimmy took a guilty sip and changed the subject. 'We've lived in worse places than this haven't we?'

'Ah! The old alma mater?'

'Y' what?' said Terry.

'Our old school,' Jimmy explained. 'We went to a public school.'

'More like a public lavatory,' said Miles.

Terry looked puzzled. 'I thought you went to one of them posh schools.'

'In the best British – well, Welsh in our case – tradition,' Jimmy assured him. 'Cold, damp…'

'When the north wind whistled up the stone steps into the cloister,' Miles elaborated, 'you'd have to move pretty swiftly or you arse would fall on to the flagstones and shatter.'

'You didn't like it, then?'

'Best days of our lives,' Miles reflected sourly.

Jimmy smiled. 'There was one happy resident – an enormous fat rat that lived under the bread bins in the pantry.'

'We called it Clarence,' said Miles, 'after the housemaster. I wrote a song about him.'

'Ooh,' sighed Terry, 'yes... I know that one. "Clarence The Rat".' He started singing with tuneless abandon. 'Clarence the rat, tappety tap, he prowls around with his spring-loaded cane, looking for boys to beat...'

'The very same.' Miles twinkled at Terry, acknowledging a true fan.

'Is that true, like?'

'Oh yes,' said Jimmy. 'We were beaten most days when we were in the junior school, and sometimes after that.'

'Not that we ever did anything wrong, did we, Jimmy?'

'What us? Nooo!'

Terry stared at them, eyeballs almost touching the lenses of his steel-rimmed glasses. 'It must have been a terrible place.'

Miles looked thoughtful. 'Oh I don't know, quite liberal really compared with the old days. It was the 1970s after all. Buggery, at least, was optional.'

Terry backed away.

'Not that we took up the offer.' Miles winked at Jimmy. 'We used to ride our bikes into the nearest town to pick up the local scrubbers.'

'Speak for yourself,' said Jimmy, 'I had to make do with beer and a song or two at the Bryn Bugail folk club.'

'You were a good boy, Jimmy,' Miles said pityingly.

'We were a double act,' Jimmy said. 'I mean singing and playing the guitar. We called ourselves "Miles Away".' He and Miles looked at each other over the tops of their drinks and laughed.

'God we were dreadful!' said Miles. 'I reckon they must have felt sorry for us.'

'Everybody's welcome at a folk club,' Terry said solemnly, 'even if they're a bit, you know,' he lowered his voice, 'they're beginners like.'

Miles made no comment. He nodded and lifted the giant glass of green stuff to his lips.

Jimmy was still tripping down memory lane. 'It used to get a bit hairy sometimes. I had to pull him out of the hedge at the bottom of Llanfedw Hill on at least one occasion.'

'Blasted bike threw me.'

'Upside down with your little legs thrashing the air, singing "I'll fathom the bowl".'

Jimmy enjoyed his friends' laughter, then, duty calling, he turned to see how the preparations were going. Nearly time to open the doors.

He found himself catching a forbidding glare from Frankie who, drawn from his bathroom by habit and loyalty, was leaning against the wall next to the entrance observing the frivolities at the bar with evident displeasure.

Circulating quietly among the tables, Mary was setting out wax encrusted bottles, removing the burnt-out stump from the neck of each one and replacing it with a fresh candle. Jimmy was surprised to see her. She was a member of Crubscombe Environment Group, a formidable campaigner. In more generous and less corporate times she would have been the postmistress, in charge of her own shop. Now she was relegated to a glass-fronted cell at one end of the counter in the Co-Op. This she defended with a mixture of good humour, guile and the occasional outburst of leafleting and demonstration. Her campaigns had been aided and supported by Jimmy and Gaynor and had resulted in Crubscombe's being the last post office left standing in an area of about twenty square miles. Though she was on Gaynor's committee, she had decided to come to the club. Jimmy was touched by her loyalty.

Frankie detached himself from the wall and went to give her a hand.

Jimmy's phone spluttered, managing to ring – just. Another stranded customer. He dragged a chair to the edge of the bar and, using it as a stepladder, climbed on to the cracked Formica, balancing unsteadily with his head wedged against the strip light.

'Yes...yes... First left, then right...what does it say? RUBS BUM...? OK... drive along the top road...main drag, yes... Go to the chippy and ask. They'll know where we are.'

He leapt down from the bar with a bit too much bounce and vigour and was obliged to spend a few moments attending to a knee.

'Big crowd,' he said jauntily. 'You're packing them in, Miles. Only one song each tonight for the punters.'

Miles looked him austerely in the knee. 'We're not getting any younger, Jimmy.' He sipped his drink.

'Chin up, Miles! Best foot forward. It's not over till the fat lady sings.'

'You'll see a few of them tonight.' Terry could see a man deprived of good beer and judged him to be in dire need of cheering up. 'That Jessica and her lesbo mates...'

'They're not lesbians, Terry,' said Jimmy, 'they're feminists. Well, they might be, I suppose...none of our business.'

'Oh, I don't hold with none of that political correctness.'

Miles winked at him.

II

Back at the farmhouse Gaynor dragged the last of the dining-room chairs into the kitchen, found a gap near the top of the table and placed it there. Then she ran a damp cloth, the nearest available J-cloth that wasn't actually slimy, over the ill-assorted furniture, removing thick accretions of dust. She counted chairs. Would there be enough? There'd have to be. Hosting meetings of Crubscombe Environment Group was expected of Gaynor. She was a parish councillor (returned unopposed) and she had the biggest house. The biggest, but not the cleanest.

With coal delivered, as promised by Terry Mivart's cousin, the Rayburn was roaring away so Gaynor had decided on the kitchen. It was the only room with a big enough table anyway; and there was marginally less dust.

The tabletop was now an empty pine plank desert, sprayed with disinfectant, lithified food deposits scraped away with a metal pan-scourer. The piles of books and the assorted domestic flotsam had been swept into cardboard boxes and polythene bags and dumped in the dining room.

She trailed the damp cloth one more time over all the visible surfaces, ran it under the tap and threw it into the cupboard under the sink. Then she poked around with the hoover until the place looked more or less passable. How did other people keep their houses so clean, even most of the artists and musicians, the bohemians, who lived in the old stone cottages which clung to the side of Crubscombe Hill? Their houses were furnished eccentrically and cheaply, but tastefully, and they were never dirty. Gaynor was impressed by their homemaking skills. She even felt a stab of envy for the more conventional incomers who had moved into the modern boxes on the new estates, warm and dry with wall-to-wall carpets in pastel shades, and not a speck of dust anywhere, but she had always preferred books to housework.

Catrin and Rosie racketed down the stairs and charged into the kitchen shouting something about going to Di's, or was it Si's? They were wearing jeans and boots *not going dancing then.* The back door slammed behind them causing all the jars and bottles on the shelves to jump and rattle as if in a minor earthquake, and new deposits of dust to float down on to the surfaces. Gaynor retrieved the damp cloth and went over them again.

There was no prospect of ever persuading Jimmy to sell the place, but, as soon as Catrin finished university, Gaynor vowed she would raid every savings deposit bank account and pension scheme for any remaining cash and there would be gas central heating. She glanced over the unusually naked tabletop at the Rayburn, silently informing it that it was on death row.

CHAPTER 5

I

For the sake of professional courtesy, Miles endured as much of the first half as was humanly possible.

The place was heaving. According to Jimmy a whole Bristol folk club had come by hired coach, at least thirty people.

The floor singers came and went. 'One song only tonight, I'm afraid,' Jimmy said. He squeezed between tables, collecting names in his little notebook as he went, and summoning the next performer to the space in front of the bar with a nod or a whisper.

He nodded to Terry, waiting eagerly behind the bar, guitar strapped to his chest, nervously fingering the frets. With doom and foreboding in his heart, Jimmy announced brightly: 'And now, all the way from Upper Crubscombe, our own Terry Mivart.'

There was a scintilla of rebellion, a repressed under-breath mutter by some of the regulars. This was instantly quashed by a hard stare from Frankie, who had now assumed his usual position near the entrance, beer mug in hand.

Terry hugged his guitar and gazed solemnly at the audience. 'I am going to sing a sad old song about the evils of drug abuse, "Needle of Death".'

Something stirred in the front row. Frankie put his pint pot down on the nearest table, looming over the ill-disciplined mass, as one of the Bristolians whispered to his neighbour: 'Oh no! I was going to do that.'

Another stage whisper joined it from the depths of the crowd, 'So was I!'

Miles had always loved Bert Jansch, an early role model. Gagging for a fag, the one addiction he could not break, he endured the terrible onslaught.

They're a pretty job lot, he thought. Always were, of course, but now they're getting older, all of them tired and lined, with even the good voices cracking and fading away. So far there'd been a succession of greying and balding men on stage, some gifted, some most assuredly not, and most preceded to the spot by enormous beer bellies. The women were a particular disappointment: fat and defiantly decked out in garish robes and hair dyes, or thin and sour – flat of voice and chest. What had become of all the youngsters?

The high spot had been Mary, who'd sung Joan Baez's 'Diamonds and Rust', accompanied by Frankie, of all people. As far as Miles could remember, Frankie, though a technician who could cope with any genre, did not lower himself to playing folk for anyone. *Whatever.* He made a mental note to delete that particular number from his own playlist.

He returned, suddenly, to the sweaty, orange-hued present. Silence had fallen. A pretty, trembling girl – sixteen, or thereabouts – was standing in front of the bar. She started singing an old ballad, sweetly and with feeling. Then, catching the rapt fascination with which she was being received, she panicked and forgot her words. Some of the audience tried to reassure her by taking up the song and singing it softly back to her. But she burst into tears and fled, crashing through the porch into the night.

Jimmy rushed out after her, and then Frankie, who had paused to gather up her shoulder bag and coat.

Typical, thought Miles, *the only one who's really got it and she doesn't know*. He slid out of the hut, hoping to be able to offer some words of encouragement and comfort. But she'd gone. There was just Jimmy walking back down the track towards him.

'Terrible stage fright,' he said. 'Such a shame.'

'Talented kid,' said Miles.

Further up the track, Frankie handed the sobbing girl her coat and bag and insisted on escorting her as far as the road.

'Come back next week,' he said, in a concerned but detached manner, 'when there's less...' He glared over his shoulder towards smokers' corner, where Miles was now heading, rolling up as he went, '...people about.'

There was now standing room only at smokers' corner, but a chair was willingly given up and offered to Miles. He accepted it graciously and lounged there, fielding questions and requests for autographs and listening idly to the conversation.

Cyril, folded into a very small chair, chin almost touching his knees, held the floor.

'"*Pussy Pegs*",' he observed, staring morosely into the darkness on the other side of the fence.

Luke, sitting three seats away, paused in the act of making himself a roll-up and scrutinised him from under the brim of a stylish felt hat. 'You all right there, Cyril?'

'Dental hygiene for cats.'

'Right?'

'It was an advertisement. They're telling us we've got to clean the cat's teeth now. The world's gone mad.'

One of the standees sympathised. 'It's the internet, innit. Load of cobblers.'

'It was in the free paper.'

There was a general muttering on the subject of health and safety.

Luke pinched a few stray filaments of tobacco from the end of his roll-up and searched through his pockets until he found a lighter. 'Does this *Pussy Pegs* kit include chainmail gauntlets?' he enquired.

Terry emerged from the clubhouse carrying a folding chair and squeezed in next to Miles at the end of the semi-circle, one chair leg projecting under the fence and dangling over the void.

''T was a' old volcano once,' he informed Miles.

'Really?' Miles, looking out over the dark, slimy waters of the abandoned quarry, inclined his head politely.

'Basalt, see? Very valuable rock.'

'It's andesite, Terry,' Cyril corrected him. 'Pyroclastic flows. Like what killed all those people in Pompeii.'

'I hope nobody suffered.'

Luke finished his cigarette and cast his dog-end over the fence. 'No, they didn't. Mostly because they were graptolites – primordial worms – no brains or central nervous systems, y'know?' He regarded Terry with quiet amusement from under the brim of his hat.

It all looks much greener these days,' Miles said, peering towards the trees and scrub which had colonised the steep terraced walls of the basalt pit. He could just see glimpses of their foliage in the shadowy area beyond the glow from the clubhouse's outside light.

'If anyone was to fall over the edge,' Cyril informed the gathering, 'they'd probably be saved by one of those bushes. They'd be found hanging there like the ram in the thicket.'

Joyous singing, in powerful close harmony, erupted from the hut, until it appeared to tremble on its uncertain foundations:

'*Oh good ale you are my darling*
You are my joy
Both night and morning!'

'You know what,' Terry said to Miles, 'you could do with a beer.'

Miles sighed and shook his head. He didn't want kidney disease; he didn't want cirrhosis of the liver; he didn't want to get old and fat.

A shadow fell between him and Terry. He looked up and saw that Jimmy was standing next to him.

'It's the interval in a minute, Tel,' Jimmy said. 'I think Mary could do with a bit of help behind the bar.'

II

'Marmalade!' declaimed Vicky Anstruther, wildlife painter, founder member of Crubscombe Environment group and dedicated bringer of bad tidings.

Marmalade? Gaynor thought of the thick, chunky sweet amber delight that was the only bright spot in her morning routine – a fleeting moment of pleasure between the alarm clock and staggering out to the car with her heavy bags. Grinding her teeth, she flicked through a pile of newly printed A5 leaflets, trying to focus on their contents.

Vicky frowned at the amber jar sitting harmlessly on Gaynor's kitchen dresser, through her thick, heavy-framed glasses. 'Marmalade is a hidden killer.'

'Why? What's the matter with it?' Gaynor murmured distractedly. She looked round the table from one earnest face to the next. Ten of them. All women who for various reasons cared about the environment. Not a bad turn-out, she supposed.

'It contains citrus fruits,' trumpeted Vicky, 'which are sprayed with chemicals, fungicides and insecticides – all of which are neuro-toxins.'

'I always make my own,' said Stella Palmer, 'and I wash all the fruit first.'

'Yes, but it's still over fifty per cent sugar.'

'Oh dear. Should I be using honey?'

'Honey's just sugar with bee grubs in it.'

There were bottles of wine on the table, red and white, alongside cartons of fruit juice, fizzy water, and crisps. Remembering her duties as a hostess, Gaynor handed them round.

Vicky declined. 'Eighty per cent fat and salt,' she remarked, turning her nose up at a passing bowl of crisps.

'Would you prefer some plain bread?'

'No thank you, Gaynor. I've just had my supper.'

Some heads nodded in sympathy with Vicky's strictures, but nine hands dipped, more-or-less eagerly, into the bowl. These were high-end nibbles – Penney's 'West Country potato crisps', made from potatoes grown by rosy-cheeked Somerset peasants, hand fried in South Somerset rapeseed oil and dipped in an assortment of sweet, cheesy and fiery flavourings.

Gaynor gave out some of the leaflets. 'Now, if we could return to the matter of the old quarries? Stella?' She looked across the table at Stella Palmer, a newcomer to the village, about the same age as herself, though she looked older with her tidy haircut and fawn jumper above the sort of trousers that used to be called slacks. She lived in one of the new houses in the estate opposite the pub, which had suddenly become a place of environmental interest when a four-hundred-foot mine shaft opened up in one of the back gardens. She had no experience of campaigning, but at least she was prepared to take on the job of secretary. Her carefully manicured hands hovered over the keys of her laptop.

'We've got less than two weeks till the public meeting,' Gaynor said. 'We've already discussed the safety implications of the old quarries in their present state. Does anybody have anything to add before we move on?' She refused to look in Vicky's direction. Instead, her eye came to rest on Lisa, the Dandos' next-door neighbour, who seemed to have something on her mind. 'Lisa?'

'Crubscombe's a tip. Nobody've ever done anything for us. Int nothing here for us or our kids. The bosses and the councillors, they takes what they can get and then they bugger off.'

Vicky sat up straight. Her shoulders tensed. She often found Lisa's views to be questionable, but this time she favoured her with a grudging inclination of the head.

Encouraged, Lisa drove home her point. 'Nothing here for us, is there? They don't give a...'

'Thank you, Lisa,' said Gaynor. 'What we need to know is who, if anybody is actually responsible. We've done some research.' She nodded at Stella, who activated her screen and started scrolling furiously, 'And,' she added, 'what they are legally required to do.'

'Bugger all,' Lisa said. ''Tis Archbold land innit?'

'Used to be,' said Gaynor.

'He's a lord. They do make the laws.'

The meeting fell silent, drinking and chewing crisps. It appeared to be thinking. After a while Vicky piled in. 'The House Of Commons make the laws, Lisa.'

Claire Stybie, the vicar, who had been sitting quietly next to Gaynor at the head of the table, passed round another bowl of crisps. Gaynor shot her a grateful look. She knew that Claire would much rather be at the folk club, holding forth about the crayfish and the piss-pot and similar gems of English folklore, but the cares of her flock always prevailed.

Lisa dived into the crisps and munched without inhibition. She was lean and rangy. Her spiky hair was hennaed and her bare arms tattooed with flowers and vines. She looked as if she would eat anything she could catch.

'They must have had planning permission,' Claire said. 'Were there any conditions attached?'

Gaynor remembered that Jimmy had promised to find out. She assumed he'd forgotten. 'Does anybody remember?' she asked, looking at Mrs Edwards, a relative of the Chawners and the oldest villager present.

'Sorry, my love. I dunno. The men did work there. That's all I know.'

Trying not to lose patience, Gaynor asked Stella to read out the various iterations of the quarry companies from Archbold and sons, via AA Aggregates, Con-Co, Bristol Aggregates and Fuels, and Inter-Road Aggregates PLC to the present company, Aggrementos. A mass of tedious detail revealing next to nothing.

She was woken from a reverie involving vague curses aimed at her husband by an urgent rasping croak from the front door bell. Startled, she rose to her feet, and went out into the hall. Nobody ever used the front door, apart from the postman. Built of some sort of hard wood which had weathered over the centuries into a dense, impregnable mass, it had probably been designed to repel the New Model Army. The massive iron bolts, which had last been used twenty years ago when a visit from the Drugs Squad was a realistic possibility, were now rusting in their moorings. Kicking aside the decaying duvet which served as a draft excluder, Gaynor pulled the door open to find herself standing face to face with Eve Chawner and her husband Ray.

'Eve! Ray! How good of you to join us!'

Ray stepped over the threshold in front of his wife. 'Something's got to be done, Gaynor.'

'Come in,' Gaynor said, trying not to stare at the advancing trucker's gut and bum by looking past him to his wife. She'd never had much to do with Eve Chawner – just another body in the pub on a Sunday lunchtime, at the other end of the bar, with a different group of women. She had once been a brilliant blonde, chatty and full of raucous laughter. The figure hesitating on the doorstep looked defeated and drained; the roots of her hair matched the bags under her eyes.

Gaynor forced a smile. 'Come in and sit down, Eve, this way.' Pushing the door to the oubliette closed as she passed it, she led the Chawners along the hall to the kitchen, where a lively discussion of health and safety was in progress, featuring accidents to friends and families, and celebrity disasters and death. It tailed off as they entered.

There was no need for introductions. Condolences had long since been offered and accepted. There was nothing left to say.

Lisa, whose seat was closest to the Rayburn, jumped to her feet. 'Come and sit down and warm yourself, Eve love. 'Tis perishing cold.'

The others nodded and muttered.

Eve took a step backwards, as if repelled by Lisa's tattooed arms. Her husband guided her to the head of the table, where Gaynor surrendered her own chair before going to search the oubliette for anything that might bear Ray Chawner's weight. She returned a couple of minutes later with a dusty dining-room chair, hoping for the best. Ray pulled it over to his wife's side and sat down. It squeaked but held firm. Claire moved discreetly to one side in order to avoid contact with his fleshy left leg.

Ray took custody of Eve's shoulder bag, dumped it on the floor between his legs, and pulled out a box from which he extracted a wad of A5 leaflets. He passed them round the table.

Above the photograph of a handsome clean-cut teenage boy was a heading in big red letters, WHO KILLED JASON CHAWNER? Underneath, in smaller red letters, was the legend: *We demand the owners of Crubscombe quarry takes responsibility*! Below this, in black, was, *Public meeting. Sunday 17th March 7.30. Crubscombe village hall.*

Heads bowed and voices murmuring, the committee studied the leaflets.

'Good,' said Lisa.

Mrs Edwards nodded.

Vicky frowned. 'Could be libellous.'

Gaynor scanned the text with a schoolteacher's practiced eye. 'Should be, *take responsibility,* not *takes,* she thought, but eventually said,' I shouldn't think they'll take us to court.' She shifted the committee's pile of leaflets behind a row of empty wine bottles. Though headed with the environment group's logo suggesting green hills and butterflies, and definitely more tasteful than the Chawners' effort, they were unlikely to have as much impact. 'If anybody wants to sue us, Vicky, they'll have to establish that they actually own the quarries.'

'If we use these,' Vicky pointed out, 'we'll have to reprint them with our logo. If you publish something you have to put your name and contacts on it. It's a legal requirement.'

Ray stirred, challenging the stability of his chair.

Gaynor skimmed through one of the leaflets. 'There's a bit of space at the bottom. I've got a kids' printing set somewhere. We can do it by hand.'

'Do what?' demanded Ray.

'How about, *pp Crubscombe Environment Group?*'

The committee concurred.

Ray's chair creaked ominously.

'You don't want to get on the wrong side of your employers do you, Ray?' Gaynor said, with an almost imperceptible flicker of an eyebrow.

'I'm an independent contractor, my love.'

'But you have a contract with Aggrementos, don't you?'

'I'll take my chances, love. I lost my boy.' He looked at his wife, who raised her head and glanced round the room with watery eyes.

'We still need to know who's legally responsible.' Gaynor reminded everybody.

Ray spread his legs. Claire shifted hers sideways. 'Archbold,' he said. 'His Lordship's not short of a bob or two, is he?'

The meeting contributed its own observations.

'Got that big posh house up in Marley Combe.'

'Can't be arsed with Crubscombe now.'

'Or Earwick.'

'Dug it all up, haven't they?'

'And buggered off.'

'More interested in his pretty young wife,' Ray suggested, leering.

Lisa swallowed a mouthful of crisps and washed them down with a large gulp of white wine. After a moment's thought she added: 'Lady Alexandra. Huh! My auntie Jen was at school with her mum. Fur coat, no knickers.'

Everybody joined in the laughter apart from Gaynor, who was trying to stay awake. She managed a smile. 'We still need to know...' she began.

Ray scoffed 'We know, my love.'

Gaynor gave up. 'OK. We'll need another meeting to discuss strategy – decide what we're going to say to the public meeting.' She looked enquiringly at the Chawners. 'And to the village and to the press. We've got very little time.'

Again, she wished that Jimmy was there. He always had the right information, or, at least, gave the impression that he did. He also knew how to sort out overbearing fools with a mixture of emollience and banter, and always had a plan. Her mounting anger found its mark. *Damn Jimmy*. He ought to be here. She shouldn't have to rely on him, but she did. *He'd better be at the next meeting, or else.* This, of course, ruled out Thursdays. As everybody's other weekday nights were taken up with essential dates and duties, they settled on a week Saturday, grudgingly giving up a small portion of their weekend shopping and television.

'Date of next meeting,' Gaynor finally announced, 'Saturday the sixteenth of March, four pm.'

'The day before the public meeting?' Stella asked, sounding far from convinced.

'It'll have to do,' sighed Gaynor.

Ray stood up and helped his wife to her feet. 'Don't worry, ladies! We'll sort them out.'

Courteous to the last and radiating sympathy, Gaynor escorted them to the front door. When she returned to the kitchen, she poured herself a large measure of red wine, ripped open another bag of crisps and crammed a handful into her mouth.

III

At the folk club, the interval had just begun. Miles and Jimmy migrated from smokers' corner to the bar, followed by Luke, who had noticed that his glass was nearly empty and remembered that it was his partner's turn to drive the van. Inside there was a frantic scrum. The little hut seemed to be bulging at its ferro-concrete seams. Hopes and expectations were rising, as well as thirst. Miles' set was to take up the whole of the second half and at the edges of the seething mass of slightly damp humanity occupying the space around the bar there was intense, but mostly polite, jostling for the best seats.

Luke pulled off his hat and placed it on the counter, carefully avoiding pools of spilled beer. It was a bell-shaped thing with an upturned brim and a green band securing a single pheasant's tail feather, which he habitually wore above his left ear.

'Should I get that thing a saucer of milk?' Miles asked, amiably.

'Ah, Miles. You can get him a pint of ale if you like.' Luke studied Miles' glass of lime and lemonade with sharp hooded eyes. 'He'll be sure to drink it.'

Miles, who had been leaning on the bar, stood up straight and glanced over the top of Luke's close-cropped head, greying hair thinning slightly at the crown. 'How's life been treating you, Luke?' he drawled. 'Still playing with … er … "Below The Salt"?'

Luke nodded.

'How's it going?'

Luke shrugged. 'Ticking over.'

'That reminds me,' Miles said, 'Alex, my delightful hostess…

Jimmy picked up a refilled mug of beer, which Terry had slid over the bar in his general direction, and turned to join in the conversation. 'Lady Alexandra?'

Luke raised an eyebrow.

'She's been let down. The top-notch ceilidh band from London she engaged for the Aggrementos staff's St Patrick night's ceilidh has pulled out. Got a better offer from some hostelry in Donegal, apparently. Everyone's so disappointed.'

'Really?' Jimmy frowned, concentrating for the moment on not spilling his beer. 'I didn't know they cared.'

'Who?

'Aggrementos' staff, about St. Patrick.'

'They don't. It's a free booze-up. Alex's idea, of course – morale booster for the retainers. She asked me if I knew of anybody who might be able to help out.'

Jimmy and Luke exchanged looks.

'She's offering good money, and all the free booze you can drink, obviously.'

'How much?' said Jimmy.

'Fifteen hundred.'

Jimmy and Luke tried, without much success, to hide their astonishment.

'Paddy's Night, then,' Jimmy said, 'Week Sunday?'

'Saturday the sixteenth. Can't have a works' do on a Sunday. Would you be available?'

'Definitely,' Jimmy said. 'It's short notice, but we should be able to get enough musicians together for that money.' The band had been inactive recently, its members distracted by births, deaths and the other social engagements that attend family life. The Thursday-night sessions at the folk club had been the only thing holding them together.

'Great!' said Miles. 'I'll tell Alex you're on.'

'Better not mention me by name,' Jimmy suggested.' George Archbold has gone off me a bit since we closed down his quarry.'

'He won't know. It's Alex's project. She organises social events, and runs the charities. Typical rich wife. She's into folk music, or so she tells me.'

Jimmy laughed. 'Sounds like you haven't lost your touch with the ladies – I mean women – Miles.'

Terry, who had been making sure that his duties as a barman kept him as close to Miles as possible, interjected: 'Lady Alexandra? Lisa Coles' auntie went to school with her mum…'

Sensing danger, Jimmy gave his old friend a discreet nudge. 'You're on in five. Better get ready.' He took Miles gently by the elbow and manoeuvred him through the crowd to the kitchen where his guitars and other musical instruments had been carefully stacked in the gap between the fridge and a redundant cooker. After making sure that Miles had everything he needed, he returned to the bar to discuss logistics with Luke.

'Will we have a quorum?' Jimmy peered through the crowd and spotted the other members of Below The Salt wandering back into the hut from smokers' corner, but was unable to catch their attention.

'Nobody's playing anywhere else this year. Family stuff, y'know?

It'll be three hundred quid each. That'll be worth dumping the kids on the granny for.'

'Not to mention all the free beer we can drink.'

'It'll be good to start gigging again.'

'Absolutely.' Jimmy raised his glass, then lowered it again. He'd seen a possible flaw in the enterprise. 'We'll need a driver.' He considered this for a moment. 'How about your Liam?'

Luke shook his head. 'He's off to Bristol with his mates.'

'I could ask Catrin,' Jimmy suggested tentatively. Catrin was being difficult at the moment.

Luke understood. 'Not Daddy's girl anymore?'

'Nothing I said. She's upset about something.' A possible explanation crossed Jimmy's mind, 'Are they still an item, Catrin and...?'

Luke shook his head. 'Liam's been a naughty boy.'

Jimmy's face assumed an expression of disappointment. Gaynor, he thought, would be pleased to hear this. In her view boyfriends, especially local ones, were an impediment to the progress of a young woman's academic career. 'Gone off men, then?'

'She wasn't very happy, Jimmy. I thought you knew.'

'She never tells me anything these days. Kids, eh?' Jimmy looked at his watch. 'Time to get moving. I'll offer her some cash,' he added. He started to edge his way through the crush towards the kitchen to give Miles his final call.

IV

'With her apron wrapped around her, he took her for a swan,
    And it's oh and alas it was she Polly Vonn...'
    As the last notes died away Miles picked up his guitar and shook

it as if to scatter the last scraps of tragic beauty into the laps of his enraptured fans. His second encore, and they still wanted more.

He had triumphed. The audience loved his songs about Nicaragua, Chile, Palestine and Bosnia. He'd been there, seen it all with his poetic heart. They'd laughed at 'Clarence the Rat', joining in riotously with the chorus. They'd even received 'The Little Dancer' with friendly applause, though, at the time of its release, it had been frowned upon by the intelligentsia.

'Just one more then,' he told them huskily, but still maintaining the slight West-Country burr which his voice had acquired when he'd first stepped out under the light. He lifted his guitar over his head and propped it against the bar. 'I'm sure you'll be able to help me out,' he twinkled at them, launching into an a cappella version of 'Wild Mountain Thyme', a favourite folk club closing number which had become the code for *that's all folks, time to go home*'. The crowd sang in gusty harmony. Some swayed, while others looked down, misty-eyed into their drinks.

He was back, fingers wrecked, voice almost spent, soaring over his home domain on a current of adulation. The applause was thunderous. There was stamping and yelping, American-style, like the cries of startled puppies. Miles Hollowtree was sailing round the final headland on his way home. Exhausted, but exultant, he waved to the fans, applauded them, returning their love, and stepped back to lean on the bar where a delighted Jimmy was waiting for him. They clapped their right hands together.

The good times are back, Jimbo.'

'Twenty-five years,' Jimmy sighed. 'Let's have a party!'

'Sure. When?'

'Easter Saturday. That's when we started, Easter Saturday 1988. You up for it?'

'Yeah. Don't think I've got a gig. Have we got time to tell everyone?'

'I'll tell them now,' Jimmy said. 'That'll get the bush telegraph going.' He walked out into the spotlight and called the celebrating mob to order.

Miles leaned on the bar, laughing.

Almost blinded by tears, Terry slipped a cool, heavy, glass mug into Miles' free hand. Beer. Chedgy's original. 'Go on, mate. Have one on me.'

He sniffed at the edge of the sweet, brown, foam-flecked pool and then he dived in and drank. This, he speculated, like a conquering general returning to ancient Rome, might be the appropriate moment to drop dead.

V

Shortly after the departure of the Chawners, Gaynor slid the massive steel kettle on to the hot end of the Rayburn and made a pot of tea, both for sustenance and as a hint. The attendees supped up gratefully, and most then left in ones and twos. A few stalwart committee members lingered to attend to specific issues, including the last of the wine and crisps.

Claire, the vicar, stacked used glasses and plates in the sink and started on the washing-up. 'You sit down,' she'd insisted, when Gaynor had tried to help, 'you look done in.'

Gaynor sat down and passed round the last of the open wine bottles.

Stella grabbed the red and poured some into her glass. 'Oh, God! I was on the white!'

Vicky, who was studying one of the Chawners' leaflets with hostile intensity, looked up. 'You shouldn't mix them, Stella.'

'All goes down the same way,' Lisa said, cheerfully. 'Thanks Gaynor, I'll have some more of the white, if you don't mind. No point going home sober. Brian will be pissed as a fart when he gets back from the club.'

'Will he be violent?' Vicky asked, with fascinated horror.'

'No. He just falls over.' Lisa raised her glass, offering a toast to equal opportunities.

'What about the kids?' Vicky persisted.

'Off out somewhere.'

'Don't you know where?'

'Course not. You don't seriously think kids tell you where they're really going, do you?'

'I'm sure mine do.' Vicky looked at Gaynor for confirmation.

Lisa chuckled. 'They'll be back when they get hungry.'

Gaynor did her best not to look censorious.

Vicky returned to the leaflet. 'I'm concerned about this, Gaynor. It's defamatory.'

'I honestly don't think there's anything to worry about, Vicky'

'She'm a worrier, aren'cha love?' Lisa said. She looked at Vicky and shook her head.

Having washed all the dirty dishes she could find, Claire gave up looking for a dry tea towel and left them to drain. She said good night and headed for the door to the utility room, followed by Stella and Lisa. Gaynor showed them out.

As she returned to the kitchen, she thought she could hear a faint crunching sound, and that of a bowl rattling on the wooden tabletop. Vicky, sitting alone at the table, desperate and wild-eyed, was guzzling the remaining crisps. She reached for a bottle, filled her half-pint water glass with the last of the red wine, and would have knocked it back in one if Gaynor hadn't restrained her.

'I don't know why I bother, Gaynor. Nobody listens to me.'

Gaynor lifted Vicky's hand-spun woollen jacket from the back of her chair and helped her into it. Taking her arm, she led her gently out into the utility room.

'Stop worrying,' she coaxed, as they made their way towards the outside door. 'I'm sure if there are any problems Jimmy will be able to sort them. He'll be at the next meeting.'

She ushered Vicky firmly out into the yard and closed the back door. No need to lock up. Catrin should be home soon, held by a solemn promise always to be in bed by midnight, at least until the exams were over. As for Jimmy, he might or might not stumble in through the back door sometime before dawn. Neither could be relied upon to remember their keys. She wasn't unduly worried. Crubscombe, though resolutely down-market, was still surprisingly free of crime. Burglary, in particular, was thought to be unprofitable.

She left the kitchen light on and went upstairs to bed. Little had been resolved apart from the date of the next meeting.

VI

In the event, Miles got dead drunk. His liver groaned, his kidneys protested, but these were probably matters he could deal with tomorrow. Autographs had been signed, CDs sold. *Better try and get it together to record a new one sometime. Not now... later...*

That scary woman who had given an in-your-face and raunchy rendition of 'I'm getting married on a Monday morning', received a plastic tumbler of white wine from Terry.

'Sorry, my love. We're running out of glasses.'

'No worries,' she said, dropping coins into his outstretched hand.

She turned to Miles, but instead of congratulating him for his set, eyed his long- abandoned lime and lemonade with disgust. 'Filthy stuff. Dries out the kidneys and wrecks the bowels.'

He raised his fourth – *or was it his fifth?* – glass of beer and smiled at her. As she returned to her seat he scanned her body with a practised eye, mulling over her recent performance as he did so. Not his type, obviously, but all women were up for it, even those who claimed to be feminists. His head was spinning. He needed to lie down. *It's just a matter of asking them nicely* he concluded, as he swayed and tottered in the direction of the benches which lined the back wall near the door to the Gents.

The third half was now well under way. Most of the punters had gone home. The Bristol crowd had left at midnight after retrieving their coach driver from the interesting conversation about the sewers of ancient Rome which had taken possession of smokers' corner.

Only serious musicians and drunks remained.

Below The Salt were leading the session, jamming with anybody who could still stand up. They'd got through all the reels and the jigs and the slides at least twice, ripped through some klezmer, and now, sentimental and drunk, they'd moved on to the French café waltzes.

Collapsing on to the narrow bench, Miles grasped at fleeting memories. The question of overnight accommodation floated into his conscious mind. *Archbold's... Alex... Bath... car... oh, shit...*

The musicians started another waltz, 'Les Amantes Infideles'. Should he attempt to join in? *Better not.* He seemed to be losing control of his limbs. Thank God he hadn't had to follow this lot...

Frankie strode past him. Pausing to shoot a withering glare in Miles' direction, he loaded a tin tray with dead glasses and headed for the kitchen, where Mary was doing the washing-up and Terry now hovered, wafting a damp tea towel.

'Wasn't he just fucking brilliant – 'scuse my French?'

'Lovely,' Mary said, gently teasing a paw-marked tumbler from his sweaty hand and re-washing it.

Frankie arrived, fixing him with a disapproving frown, and he scurried back to the bar with a tray of newly washed glasses.

Having rounded up the Bristol contingent and watched their coach lumber up the track from the car park to Crubscombe Hill, its wheels skidding in the damp gravel, Jimmy wandered over to smokers' corner. The brief exposure to fresh air had induced sober reflection. So far, the evening had been an outstanding success and it might be wise to make sure that nobody, propelled by euphoria or drink, spoilt it by blundering over the edge into the Lower Pool.

As he approached, Cyril stretched and leant backwards in his chair, almost toppling over.

'Careful,' Jimmy chided him.

'Hah! That's all I ever hear these days. The wife, the job, even the bloody pub. Can't take a glass out into the garden in case somebody breaks it and cuts themselves. Gotta drink out of one of those plastic things.'

There was a general rumbling of agreement and the conversation moved on to a discussion of medieval toilets before mounting another one of their favourite hobby horses.

Jasper, a painter, who lived in a stone cottage he and his wife had renovated with their own bare hands, and whose surname Jimmy had forgotten, stared out of the gap between his up-turned collar and bushy eyebrows at the mysterious deeps beyond the fence.

'Sublime,' he muttered, raising his glass to the void.

'It's turning into a nature reserve.' Cyril added. 'The English countryside is filling up with agri-business and housing developments, little boxes and pesticides. Wildlife is being driven to the margins.'

Brian, the rabbit slayer, who had been dozing over a half-consumed pint, woke up and added some inside information. 'They want to turn it into a country park so it'll all be nice and safe. Won't be able to shoot rabbits no more.' A shotgun lay at his feet.

Cyril shifted in his comfortless seat. 'What? Like a play-pen?'

'Something like that. Our Lisa's on the committee,' he sighed. 'That right, Jimmy?'

Jimmy inclined his head, then added: 'I think it might be a good idea if you left that gun in your vehicle, Brian.'

''Tis only a shotgun. I was showing it to Cyril here.'

'Better not bring it to the club in future, mate.' Jimmy pleaded. 'Some people don't like them.'

Brian picked up his gun and, escorted by Jimmy, walked over to the car park where he found his Land Rover. He left the offending article on the back seat.

'Shouldn't you lock it up?' Jimmy reminded him.

'Lock's broke, Jimmy. Can't afford to have it repaired.'

Jimmy gave up and headed for the comparative warmth of the clubhouse.

Time for another? he asked himself as he made his way over to the bar. *Well, why not?* He handed his glass to Terry.

'Just give us a half, Tel.'

Terry filled the glass to three-quarters and handed it back.

Jimmy took a big, gratifying gulp of beer. *One too many perhaps, but hey...*

He was joined by Luke, who fished some pound coins out of a leather purse and asked Terry for a shot of Jameson's.

'It's been a great night, Luke – magical.'

'You could say that, Jimmy.' Luke nodded in the direction of the bench at the back of the room where Miles was now lying like a dead thing. 'What you going to do with the left-overs?'

At about three, the musicians decided to call it a day. Some, waving and staggering and calling out their thanks for a great night, gathered up their instruments and crammed themselves into Luke's van, marshalled by Jen, Luke's wife, who had remained dutifully sober. Others dispersed, shouting, laughing and stumbling into the village streets and by-ways, a few brave souls risking the treacherous pathways through the quarries to the neighbouring village of Earwick.

Mary hung up the final tea towel and slipped daintily out into the night.

Frankie permitted himself the briefest of frosty smiles in her direction and then appraised the evening's unfinished business. 'Leave him here,' he said, sweeping the recumbent Miles with a baleful stare.

'We can't do that,' said Terry, 'he'll freeze to death. There's no heating. The gas...' he indicated a portable gas heater, 'have run out.'

'I can't, 'said Jimmy. Really, I...'

'Can't leave him here, Jimmy,' Terry insisted.

Frankie snapped shut the fastenings of his guitar case and stumped out.

'I can't do nothing,' Terry said, 'We only got a little house. There's me and the wife, and our Christopher and Tanya, and their Sam. We got no spare bedroom. You got a big place, Jimmy.'

This, Jimmy conceded, was manifestly true. He'd look like a complete bastard. Miles was an old mate, for God's sake. Perhaps he could smuggle him up the back stairs to the third spare room – the old servants' bedroom at the back of the house – then lock him in for the night, with a bucket. Nobody ever went in there these days. Certainly not Gaynor – not first thing in the morning. Gaynor's morning routine never varied, shower, coffee, piece of toast, gather up the books and out the door to the Citroen estate standing in the front drive. Jimmy knew its every detail, to the minute.

It seemed the only decent thing to do. Jimmy's personal jury was still out on the case of Miles versus the moral majority. *It wasn't all his fault, surely. Relationships break up all the time; usually six of one and half a dozen of the other.*

VII

Dragging and steering Miles' semi-comatose body between them, Jimmy and Terry approached the farmhouse through the orchard. Skirting round the edges of the farmyard, out of sight of occupied bedrooms, they headed for the back door.

A waning moon, fully risen, floated between banks of clouds, allowing some intermittent light. Jimmy held his keys up to it, searching for the right one.

Temporarily propped against Terry's shoulder, Miles stirred.

'Where's my guitars?'

'Sshh!' Jimmy whispered.

'We left your stuff in your car,' Terry said. 'It'll...'

'Sshh!'

Jimmy tried successive keys in the lock, but none would turn it. He tried the handle and the door flew open, bouncing off the corner of the chest freezer.

The utility room was in darkness. The washing machine, several recycling bins and random deposits of brooms and old hoovers were among the obstacles around which they would have to navigate before reaching the light switch. As they crept through the door, Jimmy thought he heard a sound coming from the downstairs toilet, a small square cubicle which had been partitioned off from a corner of the room sometime in the 1970s. He stopped dead, then sprang across the room to switch on the light, colliding with an old hoover en route.

'Ow! Oh, sh...!'

'Quiet!' Terry said loudly.

There was a barely perceptible movement behind the frosted glass door of the toilet.

'That's all we need,' muttered Jimmy. 'A bloody intruder!'

Terry took his mobile out. 'Do you want me to get Brian up

here with his gun?'

'No thank you, Terry, I do not!'

Jimmy advanced to the toilet door and pulled it open, whispering as loudly as he dared, 'We know you're in there. Now why don't you just come out and bugger off, and leave us alone.'

'Dad?'

Catrin stepped out into the utility room dressed in an enormous and rather smelly dressing gown which Jimmy vaguely recalled had been hanging on the back of the toilet door for some years.

'I was going for a pee.'

'All the way down here?'

'Mum's in the other one.''

'Really?'

'You know she's always wanted an en suite.'

The bottoms of a pair of dampish jeans were visible below the hem of the noisome dressing gown, and under them, a pair of sopping wet trainers. Surely even teenage girls didn't wear wet jeans to bed, though experience had taught Jimmy that one can never be quite sure.

Miles, suddenly awake, decided to make the most of the situation. 'Who's this?'

'Shut up, Miles!' Jimmy hissed.

'Picked up another derelict dipso at the club have you, Dad?'

'Catrin!'

'Catrin,'' said Miles, advancing, delighted. 'The last time I saw you...'

Catrin backed away.

Jimmy and Terry dragged a protesting Miles back into custody.

'Is your mother still in the bathroom?'

'Ah Gaynor, lovely Gaynor!'

This was met with a three-part chorus of hisses.

'Shut up, Miles!'

I think I heard her going back to bed,' Catrin whispered. 'She'll be out of it by now. She gets so tired these days.'

'Better not mention any of this to her, then. She'll only worry.'

'Better not say anything, yeah?' Catrin agreed.

'OK,' Jimmy said.

Catrin helped her father and Terry haul their startled guest across the kitchen and up the back stairs to the servants' bedroom and then left them to it.

VIII

The moon sank into a cloud rack, giving up any further thoughts of illumination for that night. Its last rays momentarily lit up the shards of glass and twisted metal in the space that used to be Frankie Dando's lawn. But the sofa had vanished. Mice, as Gaynor was wont to remark to shifty larcenous children, must have come in the night and nibbled it all away.

CHAPTER 6

I

The following lunchtime Jimmy and Luke sat in the bar of the King's Arms in Chine savouring their meagre alcohol allowance. When they'd both worked for the local authority drinking in a generous lunch hour had been a daily ritual. It was only Fridays these days, and the session was usually dedicated to the business of the ceilidh band. They faced each other across a distressed wooden table, of the kind that could be found in every back parlour in the 1950s. The pub had once been genuinely scruffy, but the new management had scoured everything from flagstones to oak-beamed ceiling and covered the walls and woodwork in tasteful shades of pale grey.

'How much longer do you think you're going to get away with this, Jimmy?'

Get away…? Jimmy sampled his precious lunchtime pint – three pounds eighty-five in this fashionable country pub – ruinous. A man could be bankrupted by beer without drinking enough to lose his driving licence. He answered his friend's question with a shrug and focused his mind on that morning's encounter with his wife and daughter.

It had been a bit hairy. An image presented itself of Gaynor, gulping down coffee, slice of toast in one hand, swearing at the cat, 'I've just fed you… bloody thing must think its name is Bugger off.

Jimmy? Where did you sleep last night?'

'Spare room. The back one,' he'd said. 'I didn't want to disturb you with my snoring.'

'That was considerate of you, dear.'

Footsteps sounded overhead! Jimmy had forgotten that the back bedroom was immediately above the kitchen.

'Who's that?'

More footsteps followed, then the sound of some heavy object being dropped and a muffled scuffling.

A long, tense minute or so later Catrin strolled into the kitchen carrying a dust-encrusted paperback.

'Was that you in the back bedroom?'

'Yeah. Went to get this.' She held up the book. 'Harry Potter and the...' He couldn't quite read the smaller print.

'Comfort reading,' Catrin said, slumping dramatically into a chair. 'I need to be in another place.'

'Are you all right, love?' Gaynor asked her.

'Course I am!' Catrin visibly pulled herself together and said, 'Mum? Did you know the kids call you Bellatrix?'

Gaynor shrugged. 'Used to be Maleficent.' She gathered up her books and baggage. 'Don't be late!'

'Haven't got anything till after break. See you in French.'

'...and,' Gaynor shouted after her, 'tell Rosie I need to have a word with her – not in school – here, when she's got a moment.'

As soon as he'd heard Gaynor's car leaving, Jimmy galloped up the stairs and tore into the back bedroom. It was empty. Nothing remained but a draught from the open window and a faint whiff of tobacco smoke.

He returned to the kitchen and found that Catrin had set aside the comfort reading and pulled her copy of *Paradise Lost* out of the heap of books and paper at her end of the table. She was muttering to herself, trying to commit the verse to memory.

English Literature, according to Gaynor, was her weakest subject.

'Down he fell...' she intoned

'Catrin?'

'Oh...! Try clicking on refresh.'

'It's not about the computer,' he'd reassured her before proceeding cautiously with, 'Are you free a week Saturday?'

'I don't think so.'

'I need a lift to Bath in the afternoon, and one back...er...late.'

She raised her eyes from her book and looked at her father, scornful and impatient. 'Off with your piss-head mates then, Dad?'

'Working actually. The band's playing at the Aggrementos St Patrick's Day ceilidh.'

'And being paid with beer, obviously.'

'I'll give you fifty quid for a lift.'

She held his eye for a moment. 'Hundred.'

'I don't know what your commitments are on that day of course,' Jimmy said, affable but calculating.

'All right! Seventy-five.'

'Seventy-five it is then.

Catrin returned to her book. 'Down he fell...' she declaimed.

'Are you enjoying that?'

'Bit long-winded and weird. Love the palace in hell.' She looked round the kitchen in a pointed manner.

He went outside to get in the coal.

'Well, Jimmy?' Luke said, breaking into his recollections.

'Close one,' Jimmy admitted, 'I had to put Miles up last night.'

'Really?' Luke seemed taken aback. He and Jen had not regretted moving out of the farmhouse and away from the malign influence of Miles.

'Gaynor doesn't know. For God's sake don't tell her. She wouldn't understand.'

'Actually, I was thinking more about the club, Jimmy.'

'Oh? They loved him – most of them.' Jimmy couldn't quite work out what the problem was. It was a great night, wasn't it?'

'The club, Jimmy. It's a fucking tip, man.'

'Who cares?'

'The council?'

'It's the craic that counts, mate.'

'Yeah! The cracks in the walls, the floor, the ceiling…'

'Very funny, Luke.'

'The wiring…' Luke continued. 'Christ knows, Jimmy, I'm not a spark, but it's out of the ark.'

'1960s, probably, before they extended the quarry. You're talking like a structural engineer.'

'I am a structural engineer.'

'How's business these days?'

'Never busier, since I got made redundant. Working for councils all over the country now, not just the one. You should try it yourself, Jimmy. Set up your own business.'

'Too much paperwork. I'd rather work for somebody else's company. Let them do it.'

'Jen does all that, bless her heart.'

'Nice,' said Jimmy, imagining what might ensue if he asked Gaynor to take on such a role.

'I've got a family to keep.' Luke swallowed a mouthful of Guinness and wiped the foam from his lips. 'For God's sake, Jimmy, stick to the point. What if…if a bit of that rotting plasterboard falls out of the ceiling and brains someone for example?'

'Is it likely to?'

'I don't know, I haven't looked that closely.'

'You're the structural engineer.'

'Well…it probably won't happen; not in our lifetime. It was just an example; that's not how they think, though.'

'They?'

'The local authority. You worked for one, Jimmy, you should know. They'll send somebody round.'

'Who?'

'I don't know – some contractor. Me even.'

'Better make sure it is you then. Put in a nice low tender.'

'Jimmy!'

'They're not going to ask you to inspect the place, Luke – you or anybody else,' Jimmy said, faintly amused, 'because it doesn't exist.'

'Go on, Jimmy! Don't tell me; it's in a parallel universe.'

'That's one way of looking at it, I suppose.' Jimmy sank another self-satisfied mouthful of beer. 'The quarry closed in 1992. They'd completely forgotten about the social club, so we just carried on using it. There's no paperwork or any computer records that I know of. All that ancient software, if they had any, perished in 2000. Anyway – who's going to bother to rewrite the software for a business that's been closed down? They were all too busy panicking about the emergency services and the collapse of international trade. The company's gone, swallowed up by mergers and takeovers. Even if they still own the quarry the Aggrementos lot won't want to know, will they? Someone might ask them to clean up the mess.'

'I thought you were, Jimmy.'

'I'm on the committee.'

'Well then?'

'Best place to be if you don't want to get something done.'

'But you'll do as Gaynor says, won't you?'

'Her heart's not in it, mate. Duty calls, you know? What she really wants is a quiet life. It'll all blow over.'

Luke chuckled grimly. 'Some of the walls might.'

'Best to leave things as they are,' Jimmy said. 'I mean, Terry'd like some more kit for the bar and a cold cellar for the beer in the summer, but I've told him we haven't got the money. He does perfectly well with those wet tea towels anyway. Everybody's happy.'

Luke sucked Guinness foam from his bottom lip, then started chewing it.

'Half of Somerset must know about the club, Jimmy – all those 'great nights'...'

Jimmy floated back to earth for a moment. 'Could be a bit awkward, I grant you. It's been all right so far. Nobody's going to say too much, are they, not with good beer at one pound fifty a pint – not to mention Terry's mum's cider at sixty pence.'

Luke sighed and shook his head.

'It's a private party, Luke, what can they do?'

'Bust you for criminal trespass, with recklessness?'

'I was hoping,' Jimmy reminded him, peevishly, 'to talk about band practice and the anniversary bash. We've arranged it for Easter Saturday. Only a few weeks to get it together. The bush telegraph's humming already, plus a few discreet ads in *Folk Times*. Miles says he'll come back and give us some songs. Everybody will be coming.'

'What about Gaynor?'

'Gaynor...?' Something stirred in Jimmy's memory. *Ah yes. Brittany*. He'd have to deal with that at some point.

'Gaynor will be in France. She's meeting up with...' Remembering Jen's strictures about Bron's style of housekeeping and parenting, he decided to phrase this carefully, '...some old friends. And don't worry about *Folk Times*– nobody reads it, except folkies.'

'You're in denial, Jimmy.'

'Yep!' Jimmy sank the last of his pint and slapped the glass mug down on the table. 'Stout denial! Never fails; got me through my school career without being beaten to death. Thing is Luke, life is for living, and our little club has been alive and well for twenty-five years. I think that's worth celebrating. And after that... we could all be dead.

II

'Bellatrix!'

Elliot 'Priceless' Price raced from his post at the classroom door into the seething mill that had once been 8H's French lesson, cheeks flushed with excitement, eyes wide with fear.

The rest of the class, having enjoyed the riotous moments immediately following the trainee's tearful flight to the staffroom, had now gathered in a circle at the back of the room to watch while Jordan Fishlock, seeking revenge for some insult, or perhaps, simply because he could, was in the process of tearing out Lucy Venning's hair.

The kids scattered to their desks exchanging whispered imprecations. They stood silently to attention as Gaynor swept into the room.

'I am appalled!' she told them quietly. She wasn't, of course. It was the default behaviour for this particular shower of young thugs. She took the class register out of her bag and began reading out names. She did not permit them to sit down.

'Very well,' she said, finishing the roll call and sliding the mark book back into her bag, 'We shall meet again – Monday – three forty-five, detention. How dare you let me down like this!' Her steely eye roved among the guilty faces and rested for a moment on the tearful form of Lucy Venning.

'Lucy?'

'Miss.' Lucy tried to supress a sob.

'Is everything all right?'

'Yes, miss,' she gulped.

'Hmmmm,' Gaynor said, and addressed the class. 'Sit down! Page fifteen in your text books, exercise three, translate into English.' She noticed Jordan Fishlock shiftily stuffing a fistful of golden hair into his trouser pocket then turning round and attempting to catch Lucy Venning's eye.

'Do it now please, Fishlock.'

Jordan Fishlock noted the use of his surname and flipped anxiously through his dog-eared textbook.

'You will all sit in silence and work. I shall be back soon. If Mr Jenkins,' she inclined her head in the direction of the next-door classroom, 'tells me he's heard a squeak out of any of you, there'll be consequences. And if you dare to mess about in Miss Phipps' class again, I will know all about it. Got that? Fishlock?'

The boy trembled. Consequences might involve telling his mum. 'Miss!'

'Good.' Gaynor walked calmly out of the room. As she strode down the corridor the bell went for the end of lesson. Oncoming children swerved out of her path. She owned the space. Reaching the staffroom, she found the trainee, red-eyed and huddled in a corner, and made her a cup of coffee.

III

Rosie Dando stood in front of her grandparents' headstone silently reading the inscription on the plain grey slab: MICHAEL FREDERICK DANDO 1925 – 1996… ROSE DANDO 1930 – 2012

She knelt to arrange a vase of gaudy supermarket flowers. If the weather had been better, she might have been able to bring something from the garden. There was still a forsythia bush and some obdurate daffodils, but nothing else had dared showed its head yet this year. As she worked, she complained to her grandparents about her father's latest outrage.

'Stupid old twat!' she muttered, 'Dipstick.' She'd had a trying day and she hadn't even got to school yet.' Sorry, Nan' she sighed.

Over what passed for breakfast in the Dando household, she'd raised the matter of the damaged bedroom window with her dad. Failing to receive a sensible explanation, she'd dismissed him with the words, 'Bugger off to work and I'll sort it.' She'd collected as much of the shattered glass and metal as she could find in the garden and scattered it round her father's bedroom and then gone round the remains of the window frame with a lump hammer, knocking the jagged edges inwards. It wouldn't convince an expert, she supposed, but some jobsworth from the housing association might be persuaded that it was an unfortunate accident.

At 9.30am a nervous young man in a suit had knocked on the front door. He was hugging a padded laptop bag to his hip as if the envious and grasping underclass of Crubscombe might suck out its contents and spirit them away as he stood there.

Lisa stuck her head out of her living-room window. 'They'm out. Whatcher want?'

The man jumped, eyes darting here and there, looking for cover.

Better get him in here, thought Rosie, *before he runs away*. She wrenched the front door open.

'Good morning. Don't worry. Dad's at work and...' she jerked her head in the direction of Lisa's house '...she's all right. Come in please. I'm Rosie Dando.'

She showed him the damaged bedroom window while he tapped the keyboard of his laptop.

'Must have been a meteorite, or a block of ice from an aircraft or something.'

·

His face registered nothing as he added this information to the electronic record. When he'd finished, he told her that somebody would come round to assess the damage properly and make sure there were no structural problems.

After he'd gone, she had phoned Jimmy Sullivan.

'Stupid old bugger.' She inveighed against her father to the gravestone once more.

Her grandparents were in the non-conformist burial ground, a kind of annexe to the parish churchyard. They'd been Methodists, her nan a devout and sincere believer all her life, despairing of her son's aversion – and, later, her granddaughter's indifference – to God in all His manifestations.

Over in the church section a new, expensive monument caught Rosie's eye: marble, the best the local undertaker could provide, with ornate carvings of angels and an inscription picked out in gold.

JASON RAYMOND CHAWNER 24TH OCTOBER 1995 – 5TH AUGUST 2012

ASLEEP WITH THE ANGELS

Highly unlikely, Rosie thought, even if there actually is a God. The real Jason Chawner was a bully who delighted in picking on any sort of perceived weakness and worrying at it, scratching and taunting until his prey snapped and retaliated. His victims often got a reputation for being troublemakers, or retreated into the once-safe haven of their bedrooms till Jason's girlfriends got at them on some troll-infested social media platform.

When picked on by Jason Chawner, Rosie had resolved to go down the former path. In the end, she hadn't had to. Frankie had gone to have a word with some people down the pub, reinforced with a diplomatic squeeze of selected windpipes, and the trouble had ceased forthwith. She understood, too, that Gaynor had held her corner against more sophisticated oppressors in the staffroom, while Jimmy Sullivan had negotiated the continued liberty of her father with the local police.

As for social media, Rosie and her select group of friends had decided some time ago that it was for saddos and people who need to get a life. Half their parents were on Facebook and Twitter, for god's sake! One needed these things for communication, of course, but Rosie and her friends did culture. They read books, went to the cinema, listened to their dads' prog rock albums. They were the 'snobs'. The others were the 'smelly boys' and their doxies.

But even a 'smelly boy', Rosie had to admit, didn't deserve what had happened to Jason Chawner. Staring at the cold, white memorial which neither shone nor cast a shadow in the grey gloom that passed for daytime at the moment, she shuddered. Her Nan, frail and sick, supported grudgingly by her son, had tottered up the road to pay her respects to the horse-drawn, flower-studded hearse, but Rosie had stayed at home.

There were prayers and stuff in school assemblies. Counselling was offered, and taken up by anybody who fancied missing maths, and then the kids had moved on.

The smellies and their dickhead doxies were planning their leaving do, a prom. A dozen or so year eleven 'no-marks' had even hired a stretch limo.

American crap.

'We don't like Americans, do we, Nanna?' Rosie said aloud, wondering if her mother had taken part in a prom. *Did African Americans do proms? Bet she did,* Rosie thought.

'Gaynor says she wants to see me,' Rosie confided to the headstone. 'Gaynor thinks I ought to go and meet her. What do you think, Nanna?' A light gust of wind wafted round the graveyard ruffling the flowers in the vase. 'Nah? Thought not.'

She never wanted to know me before, Rosie thought bitterly. Gaynor had tried to explain that her mother had gone back to the States to finish her degree; that she couldn't take Rosie with her. But she'd never said why. *No room in her life for a grubby kid, presumably.* She had been deserted.

'She cares about you,' Gaynor would insist. One of those meaningless mantras that adults broadcast, giving no comfort and clarifying nothing.

Now Gaynor was consorting with the enemy, supporting the vile, ignorant Chawners.

A loud motorbike came to a halt beside the churchyard gate and a tall figure in black leathers got off it, unstrapping his helmet and releasing a headful of golden curls onto his shoulders. He leapt over the low wall into the non-conformist plot, bent over Rosie and kissed the top of her head.

Charles – not quite the right name for the coolest, most intelligent and talented man she'd ever met. His friends and admirers called him Chaz. The bitterness departed. Her face lit up with an adoring smile.

'Your taxi awaits, madam!'

She looked at the grave once more. It was a little bit tatty compared with the others, in all their regimented devotion, but her dad could deal with that. He'd always been a dutiful son. *Rose Dando.* Everybody thought Rosie been called after her nan, but actually she'd been named Rosetta, after Sister Rosetta Tharp.

Time to go! *French in twenty minutes, though Chaz's bike would probably do it in ten.* She took the spare helmet and jumped on the back.

Rosie had found love.

*'An outlandish knight came from the north lands
And he came courting of me...'*

Gaynor used to sing that when they were kids and they all used to go to the folk club together.

IV

At two o'clock, or thereabouts, Jimmy reluctantly returned to his office at Chine Manor. He looked over the open lid of his laptop, a compact dark blue slab with integral screen equipped with the latest software – Windows 10 or maybe that was something called the operating system? He could never remember which was which. There'd been training sessions, but any useful knowledge they might have attempted to disseminate had passed him by. He could open and send emails, generate Word documents and access websites. Anything else he left to his assistant, the youthful but super-competent Suzy. She was sitting at her desk in the neighbouring office, suit jacket draped carefully over the back of her ergonomically designed chair, blonde hair tied back from her pale, serious face and secured at the nape of her neck by something Catrin had informed him was called a scrunchie. He could hear a faint rattling sound as her fingers flew over the keys of her laptop with the assurance of a concert pianist, navigating the portal to some distant planet that Jimmy had no wish to explore.

Feeling his eyelids droop, he leant back in the faux leather armchair he had purloined from the social interaction space. His own ergonomic office chair, a thing of wheels and levers, which had the capability to collapse or send him flying across the room without prior warning, had been pushed to one side.

The building had been renovated, brought up to modern health and safety standards with double glazing and a central heating system controlled by incomprehensible thermostats and timers. The effect was both spartan and stuffy. In order to mitigate the general sense of austerity, the management had encouraged the introduction of plants. Two had been allocated to Jimmy's office where, nurtured by Suzy, they flourished in the warm stale air. Some sort of creeping vine was climbing up one side of the window frame and cascading over the edge of its pot onto the floor while a massive rubber plant stood behind the door, giant leaves thrusting upwards and sideways like an Amazonian tree. Not for the first time on a Friday afternoon Jimmy peered round his own little shop of horrors and wondered how he'd managed to get there.

He'd joined the local authority in a bygone age to work on the structure plan – something vaguely related to his degree in geography. Those were the days of lassitude and long lunch hours. Colleagues and managers said he was 'outgoing and sociable', translated by Gaynor, the linguist, as 'drunk and disreputable'. After the structure plan had bitten the dust, sometime in the 1990s, he floated upwards through the various restructurings. He must, he supposed, have kissed the right sets of buttocks at the right time.

Jimmy pulled a face. The thought of his various bosses and their cheap-suited buttocks made him wince; except for Jenny de Torey. *Better not go there, not very PC. Must be dozing off again; age, probably, or boredom.* He'd always been faithful to Gaynor, a good, loyal husband. He was a virtuous man damnit! Never screwed around and never stolen a penny, though he could have, and he knew, through all those years of comradeship and lunchtime drinking, all the people who had done either or both. Office wits, he'd once heard, called him the 'chief archaeologist', because he knew where all the bodies were buried.

He preferred to think that it was his experience, from his university days onwards as a music promoter and performer, which had enabled him to transfer to the Events and Entertainment section. In 2011 it had been outsourced in a management buyout. They'd called the new company 'Asteroid', relocated to a renovated bothy at the back of Chine Manor, a neo-gothic mansion owned by the county council, and taken Jimmy with them under the new title of 'cultural resources and publicity co-ordinator'.

Something pinged into his inbox. He sat up straight and read the title, 'Management briefing'. The usual list of pointless meetings to discuss 'blue-sky thinking' initiatives that would never happen because there wasn't enough money. Whatever it was, it could wait till Monday.

He looked at his watch: three thirty – the doldrums. If he'd still smoked, it would be time for a fag. If it weren't for Catrin's education he'd pack it all in now. His grasshopper mind alighting briefly on the younger generation, he remembered Rosie's phone call and shook himself awake. He reached for the landline, tapped in a number, and was put through to Geordie Edwards, an ex-colleague now working for Careall, the Crubscombe and East Somerset Housing Association. He put on a stage, Welsh accent:

'Starboard Lookout yere, CRAP Coordinator Sullivan chatting.'

'Jimmy?'

'My new title – like it?'

'Sounds relevant.'

'What are you doing these days?'

'Still Contracts and Commissioning Officer, last time I looked. What can I do for you Jimmy?'

'You know Luke Connelly? Irish Luke?'

'Yes. Does a lot of work for us. Good bloke. Played at our Hannah's wedding. Your band, isn't it?'

'Below The Salt? Yes.'

'Great band.'

'I think Luke could be just the man you need to look at number ten Apple Close – you know – Crubscombe? Broken window, I believe...'

'OK. Noted and filed'

'Thanks, Geordie.'

Jimmy replaced the phone in its cradle. There were one or two things to do then he'd be able to get off home, where he had, he recalled from his early morning conversation, a difficult meeting in prospect. *Six pm, prompt. Row with wife*, he thought miserably.

He returned to his laptop and brought up some files relating to The Anglo-Irish Friendship Festival, an event which he had inaugurated and which took place in the beautiful but underused grounds of Chine Manor every March.

Everything was in order, meticulously researched and typed up by Suzy. After skimming through licences, permissions and lists of potential hazards – the tidal waves of paperwork that threatened to overwhelm any event these days – he added a note to the thirty-five-page risk assessment:

In the event of an asteroid striking the site, customers, or remains thereof, will be removed to the company's safe storage facility on Pluto.

It would be interesting to find out if anybody actually read these things.

Moving on to artists' contracts, it occurred to him that although he had managed to engage some very distinguished Irish musicians for the Friday and Saturday shows, the Sunday lunchtime concert would benefit from a more popular English headline act. He picked up the phone again and after enjoying a long gossipy chat with Miles Hollowtree, offered him the gig. It was gratefully accepted and he sauntered into the next-door office to ask Suzy to draw up a contract.

There was just one more little job to do. Before closing down the laptop he emailed *Sad Folk*, the Somerset and Dorset Folk website, with a discreet text for its listings:

Jimmy's 25th anniversary party, Sat 30th March (Easter Saturday). Crubscombe Folk Club 8pm. Usual place.

He added his mobile number and clicked on 'send'.

On his way out, he wished Suzy a happy weekend and told her that he had to leave early to deal with a family crisis. At the car park he got into his elderly but reliable Peugeot estate and set off for Upper Crubscombe and the pub.

V

Darkness had long since fallen by the time Jimmy walked down Crubscombe Hill to the old Manor farmhouse. His stomach felt uneasy, but this might have been because he'd consumed three pints of beer, a pork pie and a pickled egg. He'd worked out that if he entered through the front door, he might make it upstairs to bed before Gaynor, who was likely to be in the kitchen, noticed his arrival. After that, he could pretend to be asleep.

The door creaked, but he flitted guiltily towards the foot of the stairs anyway.

'Jimmy?'

The voice, although filtered through ancient oak, could not be mistaken. He went down the hall to the kitchen door, opened it a crack and put his head round it.

Gaynor was sitting beside the Rayburn in an old armchair which she had dragged in from the sitting room, as she always did on a Friday night. She was drinking red wine and he noted that the bottle she had placed at her feet was half empty.

'I was just on my way up to bed,' he said hopefully.

'Been to the pub, have you?'

'Ermm…'

'Where's your car?'

'In the pub car park. I don't drink and drive… Oh!' Jimmy gave up. He shuffled across the kitchen looking, he hoped, suitably apologetic.

'We've left you some supper. It may or may not still be edible. It's in the bottom oven if you want it.'

Jimmy grabbed a tea towel and pulled his dinner out of the

bottom oven, having decided that he had better accept it, edible or not. He sat down at the table and set it before him, wondering where the first salvo would come from. There were a number of possibilities, but the worst-case scenario would be that she had somehow found out about Miles' overnight stay in the back bedroom. He braced himself.

'I wanted to talk to you about Rosie.'

Jimmy relaxed. Rosie, as far as he could tell, was not a major cause for concern. She was successful, seemingly confident, a credit to them both, Gaynor in particular.

'And Frankie.'

'Is Frankie a problem?'

This was met with exasperation. 'He could be. Rosie is eighteen, and Estelle is coming over to the UK. We need to discuss this. I thought you would be coming home early this evening.'

Jimmy attacked a shard of caramelised gravy with his knife. It flew off the plate, scattering pieces of brown shrapnel across the table.

'Sorry,' he mumbled. 'I had to go to the pub to meet Luke. Last-minute thing. We've got a gig – Paddy's night ceilidh, next Saturday, the sixteenth.'

'What!'

The vehemence of her response was alarming. For some reason things had suddenly taken a turn for the worse

'They're paying us fifteen hundred quid,' he reassured her.

Gaynor's pent- up anger burst upon him. Unreasonably, he thought.

'Jimmy! We've got an emergency meeting of the environment-group steering committee on the sixteenth. You said you'd come.'

'No, I didn't.' Jimmy was sure of his ground on this one. He chewed a mouthful of crispy cottage pie, swallowed and continued, 'How can I have agreed to come to a meeting when nobody told me it was happening?'

She thought for a moment and then changed tack. 'You're supposed to be a member of the committee. We need your input – you have information, contacts, friends in high places…'

Jimmy shrugged.

'A lot of people in this village look up to you.' Her tone was sceptical. 'People I can't reach.' She sounded cross. 'Especially the men.'

'OK,' Jimmy said, 'I'll talk to the men – see if I can persuade them to come to the public meeting. Got any leaflets?'

'On the table in front of you. There might be some that you haven't spattered with your gravy.'

He reached across the table, pulled a handful of leaflets from the bottom of the pile and stuffed them into his coat pocket.

Gaynor watched him. She seemed unconvinced. 'I sometimes wonder if you have any commitment to the village these days.'

An unjust and provocative slur, Jimmy thought, but decided that to mention it would be an unnecessary escalation. 'Of course I'm committed to the village. Our folk club is a village institution.'

Gaynor looked at him pityingly.

'It's as much a part of the village as any of your committees, and much more real, I might add. Things happen.'

'Like booze and dope…?'

'Like great music.'

'…and adultery.'

'I beg your pardon?'

'I wasn't talking about you personally, Jimmy.'

'These things happen. It's life. The only place around here where you can find any these days.'

'It's a magnet for anybody who wants to get pissed for one pound fifty a pint,' Gaynor countered.

Something, as far as Jimmy could see, that would appeal to most villagers if offered committee meetings as an alternative. 'It's a magnet for gifted musicians and singers,' he reminded her.

'That would include Terry Mivart?'

'You have to take the rough with the smooth I grant you, but that's democracy. I thought you approved of democracy.'

Gaynor made no response. She appeared to be sulking.

Deciding he must have won the exchange of fire, Jimmy charged forward from the trenches to what must surely be the commanding position on top of an unassailable hill. Dramatically pushing the remains of his dinner to one side he declaimed, 'Do you know who'll be playing at our anniversary party? We've had promises already – Pete Coe, Martin Carthy...'

Gaynor looked up at him, frowning. She did not capitulate. 'What anniversary party?'

'The club's. It's twenty-five years old this...' Too late he realised he'd blundered into no-man's land and got tangled up in the wire. 'Easter...' He'd forgotten about Brittany. Head bowed, eyes down and looking at his hands – which, for some reason, were picking at the edges of a place mat they'd encountered without his noticing – he waited for the storm to break. He prepared himself mentally for a night in one of the spare bedrooms.

Gaynor put her wine glass on the floor next to the half-empty bottle. She looked across the room at him, staring intently into his eyes as if searching for clues, but she said nothing.

Jimmy looked back at her, waiting, puzzled.

The silence, which continued for half a minute or so, seemed to Jimmy to last for half a century.

Finally, Gaynor found some words, a wail of disbelief. 'Oh Jimmy! How could you?'

'Twenty-five years,' Jimmy mumbled. 'You should know. You were a founder member. So was Bron, come to that.'

'You are impossible!'

Every muscle in Gaynor's body tensed up. She appeared to be grinding her teeth. Her right foot found an empty tin and kicked it across the room. It came to rest under the table. After that all the fight seemed to drain away. Her shoulders slumped. She bent down, picked up the bottle and filled her glass.

'Catrin doesn't want to come either,' she said miserably.

Jimmy was not surprised. He couldn't see how any of their old friends would interest their daughter, even if she remembered them. 'You can't make her, she's eighteen.'

'She's still young. Oh Jimmy, I was counting on you to talk her into coming.'

He shook his head. The inevitable bribe, he reckoned, would probably cost nearly as much as the holiday. 'She's a mystery to me these days.'

Gaynor took a gulp of wine. She looked utterly defeated and demoralised. His heart went out to her, but there was no way he could cancel, or even postpone, the party.

'Couldn't we do it after Easter?' he suggested brightly.

'I'll be back at school. Catrin's got her exams.'

'Half term, maybe?'

'It's all arranged, Jimmy – has been for months. You know it has.'

'Tell you what,' he suggested generously, 'You go. Have fun with our…your…old mates. I'll stay here and keep an eye on Catrin.'

Gaynor hesitated. She eyed him suspiciously for a moment. 'Make sure you do,' she sighed. 'Don't get so involved with your party you forget about her.'

'Of course, I won't,' Jimmy said indignantly. 'She's my daughter for heaven's sake.'

'She says she needs to finish her coursework,' Gaynor said mournfully. 'I wish she'd get herself organised. Rosie handed everything in days ago.' She straightened up suddenly, causing the wine to slop over the top of her glass. 'Oh God! Rosie!'

'Well?' said Jimmy.

'Not now!' Gaynor snapped. 'I've had enough. I'm off to bed.' She stood up.

'I'll do everything I can to help,' Jimmy pleaded.

She raised her eyebrows.

'I'm sorry about the gig, but I can't get out of it now. The band needs me too. I'll come to the public meeting, obviously.'

'Yes?' Her face was grim and judgemental. He was reminded of Sian Phillips in the role of the Empress Livia. 'OK, Jimmy. First, you can bring us any information you have garnered from those shifty suits you used to drink with about what, if any, obligations Aggrementos might have towards the ongoing maintenance of Crubscombe and Earwick quarries. Second, you can bring with you any villagers over whom you have influence.' He was beginning to feel dizzy. 'Third, you can tell the meeting everything you know.' She paused. Jimmy waited. 'Also,' she said. 'You can apply your so-called gift for strategy and bring us a plan.' That had to be it?

'Oh, yes,' she added. 'You might like to join us in the afternoon to help set up the village hall.'

She strode across the kitchen and wrenched open the door before turning with a parting shot. 'Sunday the seventeenth of March. Don't forget, or, so help me, St Patrick's Day will be the day of your martyrdom too.'

'Yes, miss,' Jimmy muttered as the door closed behind her. He went over to the Rayburn and picked up the glass of wine she had left on the floor. *No point wasting it.*

VI

Jimmy walked briskly up Crubscombe Hill, turning up the collar of his jacket to fend off the damp evening air. He could have done with a woolly jumper, but such things were for old men.

Sunday lunch, prepared by Gaynor and Catrin, had been a chilly affair. He was not forgiven. Evidently, he needed to demonstrate to his wife that he was genuinely committed to the villagers and their concerns. At the top of the hill, he turned right, heading for the pub. This, he knew, was where on a Sunday evening he would be most likely to find the people Gaynor said she could not reach.

A lazy wind got up, nipping his ears as he approached the warm glow that poured out of the windows of the Jolly Collier. He stopped, looking around him, contemplating what exactly to do next.

On the opposite side of the road to the pub there was a gap between the new private houses and the council estate which was yet to be swallowed up by developers, and which, in daylight, afforded an expansive view over the valley. Now it was a dark lake lying between Upper Crubscombe and the ghostly shadow of Earwick Ridge, picked out against the fading sky by patches of brilliant white light that flared upwards and outwards from the working quarries. Usually these could be further located by a continuous rattle and hum, but on Sundays the machines were idle and the workings silent.

Finding no inspiration in his surroundings and suffering from the cold, Jimmy decided to play it by ear. He pushed open the door, entered the corridor that ran through the centre of the building and turned left into the bar.

The Jolly Collier was at least a hundred years older than its name. A solid and severe structure of grey stone, it had been built to serve the first coal miners of Upper Crubscombe and called the New Inn. Long after the last mine closed, Ivor, the current landlord, took it over, smartened it up, installed a kitchen that dispensed simple English cuisine, including curries and spaghetti bolognaise, and gave it its new name. Apart from a skittle alley, which had been built on to the back during the 1960s, the original layout, dating from the Napoleonic wars, had been retained. There were flagstone floors and the internal walls had been stripped back to grey stonework, décor which Ivor insisted was tasteful and modern.

Ivor himself appeared to be the only barman on duty that night. Short, bald and flushed with exertion, he hurried between the taps and the pumps, the optics and the till, occasionally pausing to run round the tables to collect empty glasses. A dozen or so customers sat at heavy wooden tables watching a football match on an outsized TV screen and a young couple embraced in the window seat, whispering and laughing.

'All right, Jimmy?' Ivor called across the room, looking up from a carefully measured pint of lager.

Jimmy strolled over to the bar. 'OK. How's yourself, mate?'

'Mustn't grumble.' A stock answer; Ivor listened, exchanged witticisms and banter, but he never grumbled. He and Jimmy had an understanding. The club lured beer drinkers from the Collier on Thursday nights, but rarely opened at any other time.

Ivor closed the till and turned his full attention to Jimmy. 'Usual?'

'Yes please.' Jimmy slipped a note out of his wallet and handed it over before placing a wad of leaflets on the bar.

The landlord looked across at them as he pulled Jimmy a pint of Chedgy's. 'I seen them already, Jimmy. Ray Chawner was in lunchtime.'

The two men exchanged looks of understanding and pity.

Ivor sighed. 'Poor sod.'

Jimmy nodded.

'Eve's took it bad, mind.'

Obviously, Jimmy thought, but what else could one say.

The football disappeared to be replaced by advertisements for men's toiletries and fast cars and the drinkers drifted over to the bar. Some picked up leaflets, studied them for a moment and put them back on the pile. There were expressions of heartfelt sympathy.

'A tragedy,' they all agreed.

'Scandal, innit.'

'Should've done something about it years ago.'

'Anybody thinking of coming to the meeting?' Jimmy asked.

'Yeah.'

'Maybe.'

'Probably.'

'Dunno.'

'The wife'll be there,' somebody volunteered.

The young man from the window seat took a leaflet, skimmed through its text and dismissed it. 'No point bothering, is there? They won't listen, will they? Nobody listens to us.'

'Have you ever tried actually telling them?' Jimmy asked.

The boy frowned, but he folded the leaflet and put it in his pocket.

'Come and have your say.' Jimmy picked up his pint and carried it towards the door where he turned to deliver a parting shot. 'The press will be there. I expect they'll be interested in your views.'

A buzz of conversation followed Jimmy out into the corridor, the football momentarily forgotten. He walked along the corridor, past the door of the deserted dining room to the back bar where he expected to find his own social circle.

Sometimes known as the snug, the back bar was a small room. There were two long tables set against opposite walls and the Sunday crowd had filled the space between them with chairs dragged in from the dining room. The only entertainment offered was a shove halfpenny board which had been pushed into a corner. Jimmy spotted Frankie sitting at one of the tables with three of the stalwarts from smokers' corner. Opposite them sat a row of elderly men who had, as young lads, worked underground in the Radstock collieries, the last of the Somerset pits to close. The Upper Crubscombe pits were ancient history, largely undocumented and forgotten.

The two rows of men stared across at each other, stony-faced. The old coal miners' closed fists rested on the table in front of them. They were playing 'tip it'. Jimmy knew better than to interrupt them. He chatted instead to the other occupants of the room handing out leaflets and canvassing their views.

Many of them were newcomers, inhabitants of renovated stone cottages or new houses in the private estate who had frequently been denounced by Ray Chawner and his acolytes as snobby bastards who 'can't afford to buy in Bath or Frome'. Not unreasonably, the snobs had gravitated towards the back bar and the company of old men, who fascinated them with their stories of times long gone, and their strange traditional pastimes. A lot of them were people he knew well from the folk club. There was one noticeable absentee.

'No Terry, then?' Luke enquired, weaving through the crush and arriving at Jimmy's side.

'No,' said Jimmy, remembering for the first time that night his latest morsel of hilarious gossip. 'No more drinking on a Sunday for Tel. It's his family day. Karina's put her foot down.'

Luke spluttered on his latest mouthful of beer. 'How long's that going to last?'

'Dunno. Maybe we could run a book.'

'Fiver says two weeks.'

'OK,' Jimmy said.' You're on. I'll give it one.'

They shook hands.

'Coming to the meeting?' Jimmy asked, remembering his mission.

Luke sighed. 'Yeah, probably. Jen thinks we ought to.' He ran his eye over their fellow drinkers. 'I guess most of them will pitch up. They like to get involved, you know? I think some of them are on Gaynor's committee.'

Jimmy looked round the room. He noticed Stella Palmer and her husband standing talking to a group of people near the door. Judging that he could leave her to whip in her friends and neighbours, he turned his attention to those Gaynor considered to be unreachable.

The game of tip-it moved towards its climax. Frankie sat straight-backed in the wooden settle, scanning the row of fists on the table before searching the faces opposite for signs of duplicity. Cyril was on his left, Brian and Jasper to his right. The scores stood at six all. A tense silence spread to the rest of the room. Selecting the right fist of the man sitting directly opposite him, Frankie reached across the table and tapped it with his finger.

'Tip it!'

The hand opened to disclose a fifty pence piece and the whole room cheered. The opposing side conceded graciously. Even Frankie permitted himself the faintest of smiles.

Jimmy waded in with the leaflets.

Frankie glanced at his copy and scowled but Jimmy felt sure that he would be able to rely on his old friend's loyalty after a bit of calculated persuasion.

Brian scanned his, turning it over and over as if searching for some mitigating points that he had missed the first time. 'Lisa's all for it,' he said wistfully, 'but I prefer it as it is. Great place for hunting. No old farmer to chuck you out for trespassing.'

Cyril, too, was sceptical. 'They'll build on it, of course. Lots of little boxes or –' he lowered his voice as he conjured up even worse horrors – 'an industrial estate.'

Though broadly sympathetic, Jimmy steadfastly did what he could to honour his promise to his wife. 'The committee was thinking of something like a country park. They just want it to be a bit less dangerous,' he explained.

Jasper scowled at him. 'I don't want safety. I like it as it is. I'm an artist, a bohemian! I don't want to spend my life in a bloody playpen.'

'So why don't you come along?' Jimmy insisted. 'It's a chance to have your say.'

The unreachables heaved a collective sigh.

'All right, Jimmy,' said Cyril. 'If you insist.'

With little enthusiasm, the others agreed. They shrugged and went out to the bar to replenish their glasses. Jimmy resisted the temptation to join them. He would have to get home early to inform Gaynor of his triumph before she went to bed. Then all he had to do was to work out some means of pleasing everybody. He needed a plan. Time was pressing. St Patrick's Day and then the public meeting was only a week away, and most of that week would be spent working and rehearsing with the band for the Saturday night ceilidh.

CHAPTER 7

On the south side of Crubscombe Brook the old workings opened out into a wide, flat, dry-floored amphitheatre known as Earwick Quarry, where, in the 1980s, the quarry company had helped itself to thousands of cubic metres of limestone hillside, hauling it away to Twyford Down or the M25. The brook was long gone, having been diverted into an underground pipe.

During the twenty years since the quarries closed, the hoppers, lifting gear, conveyor belts and spoil dumps had been colonised by oak and ash and assorted rank underwood plants. The dusty floor, edged for two-thirds of its circumference with sheer cliffs, remained clear of vegetation.

At the Crubscombe end, where a tree-covered spoil dump met the edge of the workings, there were more recent colonists.

A kind of bower had been created by suspending tarpaulins and camouflage netting between the taller trees. Beneath it, Frankie's old sofa had been placed before a roaring brushwood fire. A standard lamp stood close to one end. There were armchairs of differing ages, fashions and states of repair and an occasional table on top of which cans and bottles of cider had been dumped around the base of a lava lamp. The lamps and a sound system were powered by car batteries from which electric wires spread out across the ground like plant suckers. Just outside the circle of light and warmth a young woman wearing ragged jeans, a puffer jacket and a head torch was studying and assembling bits of machinery.

Over by the sheer cliff on the far side of the quarry the light from another head torch bucked and winged as a lad in a paint-spattered hoodie sprayed his master work on to one of the smoother sheets of limestone. Under the title, 'The Drowning Boy', he had painted the image of a young lad. His foot was trapped in a metal claw, shackled to the bottom of a pool, and the whites of his eyes were blazing with terror. A speech bubble screamed 'Help Me!' in comic-strip 3D.

It was Saturday, late evening. The moon sulked behind dense cloud cover.

Catrin sat on the sofa next to Rosie. Around them, draped over or sunk into armchairs, or sitting on the floor as close to the fire as they could get without singeing their clothes, world-weary teenagers drank cider, smoked weed and chatted. They were dressed in an assortment of hoodies, puffer jackets and ripped jeans. Their trainers and boots were cheap. Most of them were not made of leather.

Led by Rosie, the Hales Mead Comprehensive intellectuals were discussing 'Promdemonium', the year thirteen alternative prom.

'Di's on the electrics.' She nodded in the direction of the girl with the head torch who was too absorbed with her task to reply.

Rosie sipped cider from a can and passed it on to Catrin, who shook her head and handed it on. 'You all right, Catrin?'

Catrin scowled. 'Can't have any more, can I? I've got to go back to Bath to pick up the ancient piss-heads from their Paddy's night ceilidh.' She fell into gloomy introspection, listening with half an ear while Stuart Fleet, a tall, muscular youth with spiky bleached hair, explained how he was going to build the stage.

She'd driven Jimmy, Luke and Jen over to Bath that afternoon.

Four twenty-pound notes sat in her wallet as a result, but they had come at a price. She had missed band practice. This mattered, as she was the lead singer and they were headlining the alternative prom. When she had explained to the other band members that she needed to humour her father for security reasons they had understood, but she didn't want to push it too far.

It was Chaz's band. He was lead guitarist and wrote most of their songs. But its name, 'Hell's Delight', had been Rosie's idea. *Spot on*, Catrin thought. She had a feeling that it might have been pillow talk by Rosie that had got her the gig.

On top of these anxieties, she had more bad news. During the drive into Bath her father had dropped another bombshell. She'd have to tell the others about it, and soon.

Stuart continued to enlarge upon his plans. 'We can get all the stuff we need from the old buildings.' He waved his hand in the direction of the ruined plant and offices. Bricks, breeze blocks, metal sheets and wooden pallets lay strewn under a covering of nettles and brambles. 'It'll take a while to drag it all over there.'

Everyone looked across the quarry at 'The Drowning Boy', the intended backdrop for the stage.

'I don't know why Mikey's done that,' Rosie said. 'He couldn't stand Jason Chawner. He was always getting duffed up by him and his gang.'

'Statement, innit,' said Jodie Baker, a student of English Literature, erratically bespectacled and stoned. 'We're all chained to the burning lake.'

The other intellectuals mulled this over, sipping booze and sucking on spliffs.

'Jason Chawner was a twat,' Stuart concluded finally.

Rosie nodded.

Sensing that he was under scrutiny, the artist looked over his shoulder at the censorious gathering round the fire.

'All right, Mikey!' Stuart shouted, then turned to the others. 'Thinks he's Banksy.'

'Maybe he is,' said Rosie.

They all stopped talking and looked across at the painting, different bits of it dipping and flashing in and out of sight as the torch beam played over its surface.

A hoodie spoke up from the depths of his armchair. 'We could sell it then, couldn't we?'

Rosie snorted. 'Can't get it off that. It's not like a wall. It's solid limestone.'

The hoodie, accepting a new joint, drew on it too deeply, gasped and guffawed. 'Get your dad to do it, Rosie. He's got the bang.'

'He can't do that, you dill. He doesn't bring it home. They keep it locked up in the quarries. Don't want him down here anyway, he'd...' As her speech faltered she turned and looked at Catrin. They both shook their heads. There were any number of things, Catrin knew, that Rosie would rather not share with her father.

Catrin pulled herself out of her reverie and decided she must now tell them the latest bad news, but her attempted intervention was swept away by a tide of repartee.

'He could do it with his teeth.'

'Yeah! He's a monster.'

'Frankie...Frankenstein.'

This traducing of her friend's dad was too much for Catrin. 'Frankenstein was the scientist,' she said primly, 'not the monster.'

'What's it to you?' asked the hoodie.

'She's my sister,' Catrin said, putting her arm round Rosie's shoulder.

'No she isn't!'

'We're twins,' said Rosie. 'Can't you tell?'

'Yeah right.'

'Gurt lesbos,' the hoodie explained.

Catrin and Rosie looked at each other with exaggerated despair, while the social liberals present, a clear majority, picked up empty cans and dog-ends and threw them at the hoodie.

'When the hubbub subsided, Catrin raised her voice. 'For fuck's sake! Listen! We've got a problem,' she yelled with as much dramatic presence as she could muster. This time they listened. 'My dad's not going away for Easter. He's staying here because the poxy folk club's having a gig on Easter Saturday.'

The hubbub rose again.

'Easter Saturday? You said it's always on a Thursday!'

'Twenty-fifth anniversary,' Catrin tried to explain.

'At the old clubhouse?'

'Yeah!'

'Shit!' they all said in unison.

'Same night as Promdemonium.'

'Shit!'

'There'll be gazillions of old farts up at the clubhouse,' said Rosie, 'but we can't change it, can we? All Chaz's mates are coming from Bristol.'

Catrin elaborated, 'There's a man coming to hear the band. He used to be an A and R man from a record company.' He was a friend of Chaz's dad, but he could still have contacts. It was an opportunity not to be missed.

She hoped she wasn't being overambitious. Rosie and Chaz kept assuring her she had a great voice, but deep down she wondered. Was she pretty enough? Chaz and the other boys in the band, mates of his from Bristol Uni, had told her she was talented. Sometimes they even let her write a song or play her flute.

A miserable silence fell.

At the other side of the quarry, Mikey ran his torch over his painting and, satisfied for now at least, gathered up his spray paints and shambled over for a drink.

'What's up?'

They told him. He took a can of cider and paced around the quarry floor, scanning the horizon. 'Can you see it from here?'

'What?'

'The old social club? Miles away, innit? I can see the Boundary Stone look, 'cos it's high up, but not the social club. It's lower down and there's all those old apple trees and stuff in the way. If we can't see them, they can't see us, can they?'

'What about the music and the light show?' said Rosie.

'Bank holiday, innit? There'll be loads of stuff going on. They won't know it's us, will they?'

'They'll make me go to the club,' Catrin said. 'My dad wants me to give them a song.'

'At the folk club?' said Stuart, aghast.

'It used to be compulsory. Me and Mum and Rosie – we all used to go.'

'What's it like?'

'Appalling – grungy old gits singing long, boring songs about bribing parrots and stuff.'

'No way?'

Catrin put an exaggerated finger in one ear and started to sing:
Don't you prattle, don't you prattle my pretty Polleee
And tell no tales of me
And your cage will be made of the pure beaten gold
With a door of white ivory.

Stuart was duly appalled. 'Right! What happened next?'

'Stupid, fucking parrot fell for it,' said Catrin.

Even Rosie, reliably the woman with a plan, was thoughtful. 'We can't let them find out. They'll take all our stuff away and stop us coming here.'

'They mean well,' Catrin sighed. 'Just don't trust us.'

'They'll think we're doing drugs,' said Stuart, casting the roach into the fire.

Voices of doom chimed in on all sides.

'We'll have nowhere to go.'

'Except that seat outside the church.'

'They've taken it away...'

'...because we were sitting on it.'

Diana, putting the finishing touches to her work, stood back to look at it for a moment. It had assumed the shape of a diesel generator. 'I wouldn't worry about the folk club,' she reassured them. 'Mikey's right. If you can't see something, it can't see you. Physics,' she intoned, as if this were a shamanic belief system.

The hoodie stirred. 'It can if you're an ostrich.'

Diana favoured him with a long disbelieving stare. 'Sheep shagger,' she concluded eventually and turned her attention back to the generator, polishing it tenderly with an oily rag. The Carnival club had given it to her father, owner of the village garage, to repair, but he'd said it wasn't worth his time, so he'd given them another one and left it lying around his yard. It had taken meticulous planning, involving the theft (borrowing) of Frankie's van on a Thursday night, to remove all the bits from Mr Osborne's yard to the quarry.

'Your dad's all right, isn't he?' Rosie asked Catrin, 'He's not likely to give us any grief.'

After a moment's thought, Catrin agreed. 'He's likely to be off his face.'

Diana sighed. 'My dad'll go mental if he finds out. He wants me at home revising all the bloody time so I can go to uni.'

'Can't you just work at the garage?'

'No. The boys'll inherit the firm. He wants me to go to uni and be a teacher.'

'Fail your A levels then,' said Stuart. 'Easy.'

'Can't do that. I want to go to Rolls Royce and get an apprenticeship.'

'In Bristol?'

'No, Derby. I want to build jet engines.'

Jodie Baker sniffed. 'That's not very good for the environment.'

They were interrupted by the sound of a powerful bike threading its way towards the far side of the quarry between spoil dumps, then tearing across the flat floor before skidding to a halt inches from the fire.

Rosie leaped off the sofa, gazing upon the rider, love light in her eyes.

Diana, in a similar condition, eyed the bike.

Chaz got off, removed his helmet and unstrapped a heavy can from the back of it.

'Diesel,' he said, wrapping his free arm around Rosie's waist and kissing her.

Catrin watched them, envious in spite of loyalty to Rosie. She wished she had a boyfriend, but since she'd caught her latest love, the perfidious Liam, snogging Verity Pennels in the year twelve recreation area, the hunt had not progressed well. She looked at her phone. *Almost midnight, time to head back into Bath.* 'See you tomorrow,' she said, getting stiffly to her feet and, momentarily, distracting the young lovers.

Diana pounced on the can and bore it away to the refurbished generator. After a few minutes' pouring and tinkering, she cranked the machine into life. It spat uncertainly for a moment then roared away. As the assembled kids cheered, she messed about with plugs and wires and switches until skeins of previously invisible fairy lights, draped and wound around the remains of the quarry plant, lit up, twinkling in reds and blues, greens and yellows and oranges.

She curtsied to the cheering kids and, looking up at the veiled and surly moon, muttered, 'Fuck the environment. I want to build Trent engines.'

Catrin, walking past her, gave her a comradely grin and began trudging up a steep bank behind the bower, heading for the hidden pathway to the Lower Pool and Crubscombe.

CHAPTER 8

I

Sitting on a stool next to the bar at the back of an elegant Regency ballroom clutching a pint and surveying the wreckage, Jimmy reflected that the Aggrementos workers' ceilidh had, for the most part, been a success. Dead bread rolls and cardboard plates soaked in coleslaw, accompanied by empty lager cans, lay in unruly heaps on and below tables, which had been carefully arranged around the perimeter of the dance floor. Paper streamers were strewn around pillars and furniture or floated in abandoned beer mugs. Couples pressed into shadowy enclaves snogged and fondled. Someone had been sick all over the floor in the Gents and there were rumours of a punch-up in the car park. Jen, returning to the stage from a comfort break, had reported from the Ladies that a young woman whose boyfriend had deserted her for another was sitting in the end cubicle, drenched in tears and gin and barricaded against the world, while her friends, yelling and fussing like demented geese, attempted to break down the door.

A good and profitable night.

Jimmy was the caller. This involved standing in front of the band explaining the choreography of the sets to a largely untutored audience, encouraging them to join in and calling out each move as the dance progressed. The results were often chaotic, but that was part of the fun. He was a master of the art, adept at persuading self-conscious punters, with a mixture of humour and cajolery, to leave their inhibitions in the shadows at the edge of the floor. He'd done well tonight. The workers had participated with gusto.

He looked out over the softly lit ballroom. Bar staff had already started to move through the disordered furniture scooping the food waste and beer cans into black bin liners, but there were still several people resolutely, if unsteadily, dancing. For their benefit, and for their own pleasure, the band was playing a medley of jigs and reels.

The Archbolds, after an hour or so of dull formalities, appeared to have fled the scene. His Lordship, much to Jimmy's relief, retreated to a private bar with some self-important bloke who might be a fellow member of the Upper House or his gamekeeper. Whoever he was, he was wearing a lot of tweed.

More suitably attired in jeans, grey shirt and his caller's waistcoat, adorned with green satin shamrocks, Jimmy wondered at the dress codes of the upper classes and their retainers. He was interrupted by the approach of Lady Alexandra.

'Jimmy?'

Jimmy focused. She was small and slight. Her skirt wafted just above her knees, a haze of bright blue. Sequins glinted as she walked. Her low-cut bodice was so tight that he wondered how she was managing to breathe. A thick rope of red-gold hair hung down her back.

'I'm so sorry!' the vision breathed. 'I had to deal with an incident in the Ladies.'"

'Ah! Lady Alexandra?' Jimmy sprang to his feet and offered her his hand.

'Alex, please! That was a wonderful evening, Jimmy. You really took them out of themselves. Thank you so much.'

'All part of the service,' Jimmy said modestly, but loudly. The band was still playing.

She unhitched a chunky leather bag from her shoulder and rummaged around in the bottom of it, producing five thick rolls of bank notes. 'Cash all right?'

'Cash is good.'

'I hear you were at Glanafon College with my husband.'

'I didn't know him very well,' Jimmy said smoothly. 'He was in the year above me.'

'You were in the same year as Miles, weren't you? George got on well with him.'

'Miles was always the outgoing one.'

'George says he had a way with the girls.' She arched an eyebrow.

'Oh yes, even as a kid.'

They laughed. Jimmy looked into the sparkling blue eyes and glanced down at the shapely legs. She was cute but, he told himself sternly, not his type. He thought of Gaynor, stuck at home, probably still arguing with her committee about tomorrow's public meeting. In a guilty moment he recalled that he had made no effort to find out more about the recent history of the quarry companies.

He smiled warmly at Alex. 'I'm glad you've enjoyed yourself.'

'Oh, I do so love folk music,' she sighed, 'especially if it's Irish. I've got an Irish granny.'

'A lot of us have,' Jimmy said, then added casually, 'but you've always lived in Bath?'

'Yes.'

'How long have you known George?'

'We've been married for sixteen years.'

Jimmy hid his astonishment behind a swig of beer. She couldn't have been more than thirty-five.

'Our son, George, started at Glanafon last September.'

Suppressing a pang for George Junior, Jimmy got down to business.

'So, you're working for the company now?'

'God, no! I just organise events for the staff. George would never think of it. And, of course,' she confided happily, 'I've got my charities.'

'Good for you,' Jimmy said. He smiled at the pretty face. Nothing to see there, it would appear.

They both turned to look at the dance floor. The band had started playing the French café waltzes and those couples who had retained any mobility were clutching each other and swaying to the music.

'What a lovely tune,' Alex sighed.

'*Les Amantes Infideles*,' Jimmy informed her.

Something in the shadows at the edge of the ballroom caught her eye. 'Lovely talking to you, Jimmy, must dash!' She picked up her bag and tripped lightly away.

The words of a popular Irish folk song floated through Jimmy's mind as he stuffed the bank notes into the pockets of his jeans and waistcoat:

She stepped away from me and she moved through the fair...

He finished his pint and asked the barman for a refill.

The barman obliged. Jimmy could not fault the Archbolds' generosity. He sipped with deep contentment. Gaynor's public meeting was tomorrow's problem. Looking over his shoulder, he noticed the lovely Alex waltzing daintily, but somewhat intensely, with a tall, handsome young man.

II

The following morning, Jimmy got up late, as was his custom on a Sunday. He could dimly remember Gaynor rolling him over in bed and hissing into his ear, 'See you later, OK,' before sweeping out of the house to supervise the setting up of the village hall. Since he'd reported his efforts in the pub the previous Sunday, she appeared to have relented. Civilised discourse had been restored. He considered getting up and offering to help, but drifted back to sleep instead.

It was nearly midday by the time he was shaken awake by a barrage of prog rock from Catrin's bedroom. He rose painfully, dressed, and shambled down to the kitchen where he shoved the kettle to the hot end of the Rayburn, attempting to marshal his thoughts as he did so. There were seven hours left to come up with a plan. He needed more information, but the previous night's conversation with Lady Alexandra, hazily recalled, had proved fruitless. He fussed fretfully over the cafetière, discarding the soggy remains of Gaynor's coffee and ladling in fresh grounds: *one spoon? Two? Three?* No, Four. Heavy-duty cerebral stimulus was required.

A search through the cupboards and fridge yielded muesli and skimmed milk.

Jimmy cleared a space on the kitchen table, gathered up a mug, the cafetière, a bowl of muesli and his laptop, arranged them on the table in front of him and chewed miserably on the unyielding grain and dried fruit. In a moment of weakness, he thought of going to the pub for a bacon bap and a hair of the dog, but virtue prevailed.

Resolutely masticating, Jimmy reached across the table and switched on the portable radio. A familiar voice addressed him, but it wasn't the usual radio Somerset DJ.

'The Anglo-Irish friendship festival,' it said, speaking against a soundscape of distant music and revelry, 'brings together musicians and singers from the UK and Ireland. I'll be batting for England, so to speak, drawing on the old songs my granny taught me when I was a kid in Oxfordshire and contributing some of my own material.'

It was Miles of course, giving a quick interview before going on stage. Jimmy noted, with a sense of self-satisfaction, that the press releases, written by him and circulated by Suzy, had landed in the right place. He couldn't recall Miles ever mentioning his granny as a source of old songs... *Oh well...whatever it takes...*

'You've been away for a while, Miles,' the interviewer said, fishing for sensational revelations.

'I was burnt out, touring twenty-four seven. It destroyed my home life. I just had to let go for a while. Start afresh...you know...?'

Jimmy knew some of it. Bron, the other half of that home life, had somehow managed to take him for a fortune in 'palimony', threatening legal action. Miles had paid up and decided to rebuild his life overseas, eventually finding sanctuary in a distant cousin's music shop in L.A. Poor sod deserved a bit of a break after that, surely?

He switched off the radio in case Gaynor decided to come home for lunch and, pushing aside the bowl of muesli, opened up the laptop, sinking a deluge of strong coffee while it booted up. It seemed to work. A plan was starting to form.

Aggrementos, he reasoned, could probably be shamed into spending a few grand repairing fences and blocking entrances but Gaynor's committee would be unlikely to find any legal means of compelling them to carry out major restoration of the landscape. He would point this out as gently and diplomatically as possible to the public meeting and suggest that the best course of action would be to work out their own plan for improving the safety of the old quarries and then to apply to charities for funding. A workable strategy, but it would take time, years probably, and, in Jimmy's experience, community campaigns rarely had that much staying power. People moved away, had children, sick relatives and other family or work responsibilities. It was one thing to get a quarry closed down, quite another to raise the money to make good. *If Gaynor's heart was really in it, it might be possible...* In his bones he felt that it wasn't. He clicked on Google and forced himself to concentrate.

After an hour of clicking, surfing and typing he had compiled a list of local charities whose declared purpose was to help communities improve their environments in various ways. By now he was nursing a slight headache, brought on, he was convinced, by staring at the screen. He picked up the laptop and took it across the hall to the back parlour Gaynor used as a study in the warmer summer months, where there was a printer.

Strange music drifted down the stairs. Catrin appeared to have dispensed with Jethro Tull and was now practising weird arpeggios on her flute. *Teenage angst,* he assumed, wondering vaguely if he should go and ask her if she was all right. *Best leave her to it,* he decided as he wriggled the laptop into a space on Gaynor's desk and plugged in the printer. He checked the paper feed and clicked on the icons and drop-down menus Catrin had shown him after a previous debacle. To his surprise and delight the printer, after emitting a series of alarming noises, actually worked. He picked up the printed sheets from the out-tray and returned to the warmth of the kitchen to study them and work out exactly what to tell the meeting. On the face of it there appeared to be enough alluring offers to keep the committee occupied for months, or even years. He sat down at the table and reached for the dregs of his last cup of coffee. Everything was under control.

His phone, which had been lying on the table, black and apparently switched off, buzzed and sang its horrid little tune.

Work?

Jimmy groaned, picked up the phone and prodded the green telephone icon a few times until it made a connection. As he clamped it to his ear Miles' jovial voice boomed out:

'Jimmy?'

'No, it's the burglar.'

'Ha! Ha! Cheer up, mate!'

In the background Jimmy could hear uninhibited jigs and reels. 'Is everything OK?'

'Certainly is. All the tourists and the fancy suits and chains have buggered off. The Irish lads are still here, and...'

'And?'

'There's free beer.'

'What?'

'Don't worry, mate, your lot's not paying. The barman's tapped more barrels than he can sell so he's giving it away. If we can't get rid of it, he'll have to tip it. I should get your arse down here pronto if I were you.'

Jimmy demurred. 'I don't think...' He could hear the distant wail of Irish pipes. 'Is that Dezzy McGuire?'

'It is,' Miles assured him. 'Best piper in Ireland. Davey Sugru is still around too.'

'The harper?'

'The very same.'

Jimmy's resolve crumbled. He'd called in a lot of favours to get those guys, and other distinguished Irish musicians, to fly over. Surely he'd earned the right to hear them play? There was still time to slip away for the afternoon. 'See you later,' he said, rapidly turning over the logistics in his mind as he stabbed the red telephone icon.

He tapped in another number.

'Terry?'

'That you, Jimmy?'

'I believe it's your alcohol-free day,' Jimmy said approvingly.

'Arr. Sober as a judge, Jimmy.'

'Good man. Would a lift be possible?'

'I got the grandkids here, Jimmy. The wife's down the village hall with Gaynor and them.'

'It's the Anglo-Irish Friendship festival down at Chine Manor. Miles is there. I'm sure he'd love to meet up with you again.'

Terry hesitated, then turned aside from the phone to address one of the teenage members of his numerous family, 'Mand! Can you mind the kids for a couple of hours. I got to go out urgent like.'

A female voice responded, 'Oh, all right.'

Terry returned to his phone. 'Where do you want picking up then, Jimmy?'

'I'll come round to yours if that's OK.'

'Yeah, fine. Gotta be back for the meeting, mind, wife's orders.'

'Me too,' said Jimmy. 'I've just got one or two things to sort out. Be with you in ten minutes.'

He went out into the hall, lifted his old anorak off a coat hook and, stuffing the list of charities into a pocket, headed off in the direction of the village hall.

III

Crubscombe village hall was an old but enduring building, made from local stone just after the First World War. Its porch, embellished with carved wooden boards, gave it an air of rustic charm. Inside it smelled slightly damp and musty. The frosted windows admitted much outside air but little light and the kitchen, housed in a corrugated-iron lean-to, was always cold. The floor of the hall itself consisted of solid oak blocks stained with dark brown varnish: a handsome investment from long ago, made for dancers.

Gaynor looked at her watch. Time for lunch. She could dash home for half an hour and see what Jimmy was up to or retreat briefly into the kitchen to raid the tea and picnic food supplied by Mary and other thoughtful members of the committee. All around the hall, under two bars of fluorescent strip lighting, dedicated helpers were getting down to work.

Vicky, clipboard in hand, was searching for trip hazards and inspecting the out-of-date electrical fittings. She jotted down some notes before making her way to the front of the hall where Stella's husband, Pete, was assembling the PA. system he had been persuaded to lend for the occasion. He paused, exasperated, while she issued him with instructions. *Not much point,* Gaynor thought to herself, *until the stage has been set up.*

There had been a performance of a children's play the previous afternoon, after which the stage (comprising four lengths of steel-deck, commandeered years ago from a defunct municipal theatre by Jimmy and some of his mysterious acquaintances) had been left in the middle of the room. Each of the hefty components measured four by one metres.

Ray Chawner had lifted up the end of one and, in his attempts to drag it to the front of the hall, narrowly missed dropping it on his toe. He cursed furiously and then asked the ladies to excuse his French, whereupon Lisa abandoned her allotted task of sweeping children's sweet wrappers off the floor and disappeared for a while to return with Frankie, whom she had somehow persuaded to help.

The two men were now glaring at each other across four metres of steel-deck. Ray pushed his end, digging Frankie in the stomach and ribs. Frankie pushed back.

Gaynor decided it would not be possible to return home for lunch. She texted Catrin, asking her to put some ready meals in the Rayburn at five o'clock and went into the kitchen where she found Mary distributing sandwiches and sausage rolls. She put the kettle on, leaned against the counter and bit into a warm sausage roll. It was soft, succulent, home-baked heaven.

'Thank you, Mary,' she murmured.

Vicky strode into the kitchen, steely-eyed, clipboard clasped to her bosom. 'Gaynor! We've got a health and safety situation. They won't listen to me.'

Gaynor dumped the remains of the sausage roll on the kitchen counter and returned to the hall to find that Frankie had pinned Ray Chawner against the wall and was now crushing his ribs with the steel-deck. Ray, gasping and snarling, managed to articulate, 'To you, you pillock!'

He was rescued by Mary, who had followed Gaynor out of the kitchen to see what the commotion was about. She rushed over to Frankie's side and had a quiet word. He relented, backed off and the steel-deck fell to the floor with a terrifying crash.

After a moment of tense silence, Gaynor heard the door at the back of the hall open and turned to look as Jimmy strolled in. He stood still for a moment, assessing the situation, then approached her bearing a sheaf of printed notes.

'A list of local charities,' he said. 'I've been working on it all morning.'

'Thanks,' Gaynor said distractedly. 'I'll pass them on to Stella.'

Jimmy looked from Gaynor to the two angry men and the steel-deck. 'Would you like me to take Frankie away?' he asked quietly.

'Would you?'

'My pleasure,' Jimmy said with a kindly smile.

'Thank you,' Gaynor sighed, then, pulled herself together. 'Don't take him to the pub!'

'Absolutely not,' Jimmy reassured her. He wandered nonchalantly over to Frankie, put a comradely hand on his arm and, making a suggestion that seemed to meet with the big man's approval, led him out of the hall.

She watched them leave, wondering what her husband had

in mind. There was something about that smile. She decided to catch up with him later and turned her attention to more pressing issues.

Mary took over Frankie's end of the steel-deck.

'You sure you can manage, my love?' Ray asked.

'It's a matter of balance, Ray,' Mary said sweetly. 'Brute force and ignorance don't get you anywhere.'

They lifted the steel-deck.

'To me!' said Mary.

Gaynor returned to the kitchen to claim her half-eaten sausage roll.

IV

In a spacious marquee under Union Jacks and Irish tricolours, which hung damply in the still air, the Anglo-Irish Friendship festival was officially winding down. Energetic jigs and reels leaked into the grounds of Chine Manor as the survivors, happy and mostly drunk, played on.

Terry, acting on Jimmy's directions, drove round to the back of the stone mansion into the staff car park. There'd been a short delay en route while they picked up Luke and Jen, who after a brief discussion had decided to dump the younger kids on Liam, their eldest, for a consideration, up front, in cash. Jimmy sprang from the car and helped his companions unload musical instruments. He'd decided to avoid the main entrance and led them round the side of the manor house, across the terrace that fronted it and over a slippery wooden bridge that had been thrown across the ha-ha, to the parkland and the marquee.

Inside, they found a sweaty mass of bows and boxes, bodhrans, bagpipes, guitars and tin whistles. Plastic chairs which had originally stood in rows were now being drawn into an ever-widening circle of musicians. There was a platform at one end decorated with green flounces and bunting; shamrocks were much in evidence. At the other end was the bar, longer and deeper, but less ornate. The beer, standing in a row of massive wooden barrels on trestles, had not run out, but the glasses had.

They toured the bins and retrieved the least sordid-looking plastic beer glasses. Then, having wiped them with anything more or less suitable that came to hand, they presented themselves at the bar.

'I'll just have the one,' Terry said as they lined up with their recycled beakers.

Out of the corner of his left eye, Jimmy spotted a disturbance at the far end of the bar. A knot of women, mostly middle-aged, had gathered around something – or someone. They were clutching CDs and scraps of paper. Miles Hollowtree, the object of their attention, who had been leaning against the bar signing autographs, straightened up for a moment. He noticed Jimmy and waved, a cool dandy indulging his public with all the practised ease of one of the younger members of the Royal family.

Jimmy picked up his beer and moved through the crowd to join him. Frankie headed for the musicians' circle and agreed to play them his crowd pleaser, 'St James' Infirmary Blues'. Luke and Jen, meanwhile, placed their drinks on the nearest chair and lifted a box and a fiddle out of their cases.

'Jimmy!' Miles exclaimed, smooth and expansive.

They raised their glasses and drank.

'How's it going chez George and Alexandra?'

'Fine! I'm not there all the time, of course. The gigs are coming in thick and fast now, Jimmy.'

'Has George forgiven us then?'

'For…?'

'Closing down his quarry.'

'Water under the bridge, Jimmy. I never had much to do with that anyway.'

'Too busy getting pissed in that club in Bath with dear old George?'

'Campaigning was always more your thing.'

Jimmy smiled and shrugged. He let his friend ramble on. The groupies and autograph-hunters, realising they had lost their idol's attention, gave up and threaded their way back through the crowded bar towards the entrance.

'The Boquerie,' Miles said dreamily. 'You should have joined us. It was fun.'

'Not my kind of music.'

'They had folk nights.'

'So called.' Remembering that his friend had occasionally headlined there, Jimmy continued, 'We had Catrin to look after.'

'The ever-uxorious Jimmy.' Miles sighed and shook his head in mock reproof.

'What's George up to these days?'

'Hard to say. You know these businessmen…'

'Conquering the world of roadstone aggregates?'

'Possibly. Alex says she hardly ever sees him.' Miles drained his glass and handed it to a passing barman. 'She was impressed with you, and the band.'

Jimmy chuckled. 'She didn't look much like a folkie. Pretty gir…woman.'

'More like a well-preserved thirty-five. They've been married for sixteen years.'

'A pretty good innings, I gather, for one of George's bits of… er…wives.'

'She was one of the office girls,' Miles said, taking delivery of his refilled glass. He held it up to the light. 'This stuff really is excellent.'

'Not thinking of climbing back on the wagon then, Miles?'

'St James' Infirmary Blues' wound on to its doleful conclusion, to be received with enthusiastic applause.

The musicians, tuning and tinkering with their instruments, fell into a discussion of whether the song was African-American or Irish. Frankie nodded his thanks, picked up his beer and sat down next to Luke and Jen.

Over by the bar Miles shook his head and shrugged. 'It's only beer, Jimmy.'

'Only beer!' Terry approached them carefully guiding his glass through the crush, treading on toes and jabbing arms with his bony elbows as he did so.

Miles received him gracefully. 'How you doing – er – Terry?'

'Not so bad. How's yourself? I heard the gigs're going well.'

Miles told him that they were and then began to elaborate. He was always glad of an audience, especially one as respectful as Terry.

One of the Irish musicians stood up and hollered over the heads of the rollicking crowd:

'Jimmy! Good to see you! You gonna give us a song?'

It would be rude, Jimmy felt, to refuse such an honour, and, in all honesty, he could live without the minutiae of Miles' comeback tour. Terry was gobbling up every morsel like a puppy at its dinner plate. Miles' reminiscences should keep them both happy for a while.

Luke found another chair and Jimmy wandered over to join the musicians, shaking hands and slapping backs as he went. He decided to give them something jolly. 'The Ballad Of Drum Snot' suggested itself, if he could remember all the words. To improve his memory he collected a refill at the bar.

The song went down well. There was laughter and lengthy applause, even a few cheers. Jimmy leaned back in his chair causing its back legs to drill deep into the soggy ground. He sank the rest of his pint and gave the glass to Frankie, who was on his way to the bar.

A mysterious bottle wrapped in a plastic carrier bag was being handed round. Jimmy took a swig. It tasted pleasant, some sort of apple brandy. Once past his lips it kicked him in the teeth, exploded up the back of his nose and hit his stomach like a depth charge. He choked discreetly behind his hand, expecting to see smoke wafting out of his ears.

'Applejack,' the bottle's owner told him proudly. 'Like it?'

'Goof!' whispered Jimmy. 'Yeah...' He took another sip for courtesy's sake.

Frankie returned with his refill and he took a large gulp, hoping to restore his powers of speech. The chair tilted slowly backwards into the mud and Jimmy with it. Music and the lively banter of old friends wrapped themselves around him.

The music was really what it was all about, he told himself, sipping beautiful ale from a container he'd rather not think about. Irish pipes, flutes, accordion and fiddles wove intricate patterns out of ancient melodies. This was a gathering of the elite, famous in their own land and among the folk cognoscenti, but little known in the wider world. They'd bothered to hang around for the survivors' session. Jimmy felt honoured and moved. He closed his eyes. Everything was beautiful and good.

Sometime later Jen fished out her clarinet and led the musicians into a melange of riotous klezmer. The conversation at the bar grew louder, there was shouting and the occasional scuffle where the less inhibited were attempting to dance.

Jimmy woke. He became aware of a disturbance somewhere by the bar. Looking more closely through the gaps between the supping, swaying people, he saw that Terry was trying to waltz with Miles, who didn't seem to be quite as keen on the idea. They were both plastered.

Panic rising, Jimmy looked at his watch. *Six o'clock! Jesus!*

Giving up on Miles, Terry was now gyrating on his own and, excruciatingly, singing along with the music. There was something long and cylindrical clutched in his sweaty right hand. As he jigged and spun its plastic wrapping detached itself and fell to the ground, disclosing a bottle of home-made applejack, now almost empty.

Jimmy reached for his mobile, stabbed the its shiny face repeatedly and desperately until it made a connection and a disgruntled female voice responded.

'Catrin?'

'What?'

There were electronic noises in the background, a band setting up perhaps. Who on earth was she going out with now?

'Your Daddy needs help.'

'We all know that. What do you want?'

'A lift.'

'From?'

'Chine Manor, work.'

'You've been working?'

'Yesss,' Jimmy said carefully, hoping he sounded sober.

'Where to?'

'Home. Now. Please, Catrin, or I'm a dead man.'

'Fifty quid.'

'Done. Better bring my car. There's a lot of us.'

The phone went dead.

Jimmy rounded up his companions. They found Terry lying on the ground next to the bar, Miles attempting to drag him to his feet.

'I think we might have to carry him.'

Frankie glowered over the stricken Terry. He looked as if he might prefer to break a few of his bones.

'I'm sorry Jimmy. I have got a bit...'

'Pissed?' Luke suggested.

'Dis...combobulated...talking to Miles here, see...putting the world to rights.'

Miles leaned across what was left of the bar – the other end had already been dismantled– and called to the barman, who was busy taking down the optics.

'Would a coffee be possible?' he asked in his best condescending artiste's drawl.

The barman, unimpressed, summoned a flunky and issued her with the necessary instructions. 'Would throwing up be possible?' he asked, favouring Terry with a calculating stare.

'Perhaps we'd better get him outside,' Jimmy said. He and Luke took an arm each while Jen scurried away to pack up the musical instruments.

Miles backed away. 'Bad back, I'm afraid. It's been playing up ever since I fell down the back stairs at the farmhouse all those years ago.'

Jimmy nodded sympathetically. He still had vivid memories of that particular party.

'Sorry,' said Miles

Frankie favoured him with a death stare but, with an air of pained reluctance, picked up the other end of Terry.

'How are you getting home?' asked Miles.

'I phoned Catrin. She'll be here in a minute.'

Miles decided he could manage to support Terry's head and the four men carted the sometime chauffeur out into the cold, cheerless dusk, dumping him on the grass where he sat in a shivering heap.

'I'm all right, really, Jimmy.'

The coffee arrived, followed about five minutes later by Catrin. She seemed to be dressed for a night out, tight blue jeans, high-heeled boots and a glittery top under an open jacket that couldn't possibly be warm enough. She picked her way towards them through damp tussocky grass.

Miles sprang forward to greet her. 'Catrin!'

Catrin hooded her eyes.

Jimmy introduced her: 'You remember Miles, don't you?' He shot a meaningful glance from one to the other, emphasising the last bit of the sentence.

Miles beamed. 'You've grown since I last saw you. Don't suppose you remember me?'

She sidled over to her father's side and whispered, 'The ancient piss-head I let out of the back bedroom a couple of weeks ago, right?'

Miles took her by the shoulders and kissed her on both cheeks.

'I have to be back home in half an hour,' she informed her father, pulling away from his friend's embrace.

'What are you up to these days?' Miles asked her.

'Studying for my A levels.' She looked at him as if from a distance, keeping her cool. She did not return his smile. 'Come on, Dad!' she said to Jimmy.

They dragged and hustled Terry across the grass and over the bridge to the terrace.

'Nice to meet you, again,' Catrin said to Miles once they'd reached the car park, and turned swiftly away.

The drive home in the over-loaded Peugeot estate was quick, probably too quick, Jimmy thought, clutching the sides of his seat as they swung round corners and overtook various assemblages of farm machinery. He wondered vaguely why Catrin was in such a hurry to return to her books on a Sunday night; homework deadlines perhaps. Gaynor had said something about her being behind with her course work. Closing his eyes and gritting his teeth he hoped she wasn't cracking under the strain. He hoped

Terry, who had been wedged under the hatchback next to Frankie's guitar, would manage not to throw up.

They arrived outside the village Hall at 7.31. Catrin put out her hand.

'Fifty please.'

He dug out some notes and handed them to her.

'Oh, and by the way...' She reached across him into the glove compartment and took out a packet of extra strong mints. 'Whatever you've been drinking smells like paint stripper.' He handed a mint to each passenger as they struggled out of the car, slammed the doors and went round to the open driver's side window to return the package.

'Keep it,' she said, 'I suggest that whoever keeps farting sticks it up his arse.'

The car pulled away, almost dragging him along the street.

Sucking on mints, the men walked up to the hall entrance, Terry now more or less upright.

'That your Catrin?' asked Pete, who was standing in the porch handing out leaflets.

Jimmy told him that it was.

'She's a lovely girl. Going to university, I hear. What'll she be studying?'

'Modern Languages,' Jimmy said grimly.

V

Jimmy stood at the back of the village hall, an inevitable consequence of his late arrival but, as any experienced political activist knows, a useful place to station oneself at a meeting. From this vantage point he could study the movements and interactions of those present without being noticed.

It was a good turnout; upwards of a hundred people filling all but a few scattered seats, chattering, greeting one another and scraping chairs. A sizeable proportion, he judged, would be sensation-seekers, likely to be swayed by the drama of the moment. Looking down the length of the hall he noted a long trestle table had been set up on the stage with photographs of Jason Chawner stapled to display boards at either end. Behind it sat prominent committee members. Gaynor, in the middle, was flanked by Stella, the secretary, and the proprietorial bulk of Ray Chawner. Her eyes swept over the crowd a couple of times until she located Jimmy and held his gaze.

So glad you have graced us with your presence, they seemed to be saying. *Why don't you come and sit nearer the front?*

He returned her gaze, raising his eyebrows a little. *I know what I'm doing.*

Ray Chawner said something to her and she looked away.

Jimmy cast his eyes about discreetly. His appeals to the Sunday-night drinkers at the pub, reinforced at the folk club on the following Thursday, appeared to have borne fruit. The ratio of men to women among the interested parties had risen noticeably as a result of his efforts. She should be grateful to him for that. Smokers' corner was well represented. Some of the men were sitting demurely in the main body of the crowd, safe in the custody of their wives. The rest, gravitating towards Jimmy, stood at the back.

The press occupied seats reserved for them in the front row, apart from a photographer who strolled around the space between the stage and the chairs raising a camera now and again, looking for angles. The rest of the Chawner family sat on the opposite side of the aisle, Eve perched nervously on the end next to her sister, who had her arm around her. Further along the row Jimmy recognised the jaunty blonde ponytail of Jason's older sister,

Rachel and, behind her, a group of teenagers, mostly girls, Jason's friends and admirers. Some were holding up phones, filming and photographing the event.

Behind the press and the main actors in the drama were the interested villagers who had arrived early to claim the best seats. Jimmy identified them as residents of the new Upper Crubscombe estates and old villagers from the council houses whom he had encountered occasionally in the pub or, less often, the Co-op, likely to sympathise with the Chawners. Between them and the unregenerate standees at the back there were other representatives of Bohemia, painters and potters, the Sullivans' nearest neighbours who lived in lovingly restored stone cottages on Crubscombe Hill, many of whom had enthusiastically supported the campaign to close the basalt quarry. Older and greyer now, they could still be found at weekends or on summer evenings perched on rocky outcrops sketching the upended landscapes of the old workings. Loyalty to Gaynor had most likely dragged them from their firesides on this chilly Sunday evening. None of them, Jimmy noticed, had brought their children. He wondered for a moment which way they would jump, then turned his attention to more immediate anxieties.

He was developing a headache, but at least his wits were recovering from the cider brandy hooch. Further along the back row, Luke swayed. Jen grabbed him by the elbow and held him upright. Terry had cleaved his way unsteadily through the crowd to claim a seat which his wife had been keeping for him. He'd left a wave of curses and crushed toes in his wake but was now resting quietly in the bosom of his family.

But Frankie, standing rigid and inscrutable between Luke and Jimmy was a cause for concern. Jimmy turned to his friend and whispered, 'Are you OK, mate?'

Frankie nodded, expressionless. His cold eye ran along the

front row until it reached the faded blonde head of Eve Chawner. 'I feel sorry for *her*,' he said at last.

The sound system fizzed and crackled. Pete fussed over leads and plugs and Vicky frowned at him from her seat on the platform. Gaynor leaned into the mic and called the meeting to order.

'Good evening, everybody, thank you for coming.' The crowd fell silent. Jimmy watched and waited.

Gaynor invited Ray Chawner to speak, informing the crowd that, as a well-known member of the community, he would need no introduction. Jimmy approved: *smart move. Let the bastard bang on a bit before the meeting gets down to business.* Reproaching himself for his cynicism, he tried to listen to Ray Chawner's eulogy for his son, a sad mixture of media-inspired clichés, half-truths and inarticulate grief. Jason had been a dutiful son, popular at school, 'a loveable rogue with a cheeky smile and a winning way, especially with the ladies.'

In the front row Eve Chawner and her sister clung to each other. Rachel sat with her head bowed. Her friends shuddered and reached into their sleeves for tissues. Jimmy spared them a morsel of sympathy. *If it had been Catrin...*

The photographer paced softly, flashed and snapped.

'The old quarries,' Ray Chawner concluded, 'were an accident waiting to happen.' His mouth tightened. He blinked and then swept over the whole assembly with a challenging glare which intensified as it moved towards the back of the hall.

'Thank you, Ray,' Gaynor said softly. 'We are all truly sorry for your loss, but now we must turn to the question of what, as a community, we can do about it.' Her voice as she turned towards him was warm and sympathetic, but the steely blue eyes brooked no argument. She swung round and addressed the secretary.

'Stella?'

Stella flicked through a pile of notes, stacked neatly on the table in front of her. 'As far as we know,' she began nervously, 'the land still belongs to the original quarry company, which is now a part of Aggrementos, owners of half the working quarries around here.'

'So they can afford to sort it,' interrupted a voice from the audience.

The crowd seethed and muttered.

Gaynor stared it down. 'Absolutely,' she said, looking towards the back of the hall and Jimmy. 'But the problem is we're not sure if they are legally obliged to do so.'

Jimmy raised his hand. He cleared his throat, running swiftly through his plan in his head before saying. 'If I may...?'

'Please,' said Gaynor.

Heads turned and scrutinised Jimmy. Some looked eager to hear what he had to say, others evidently suspicious.

Choosing his words carefully he outlined his plan. First, he suggested that Aggrementos could probably be persuaded to improve the security of the site, repair fences, replace gates, and so forth to deter trespassers, but to restore the whole landscape would cost millions. He pointed out that fencing off the Boundary Stone would be controversial as it was on an ancient right of way. However, it might be possible to get permission for minor improvements of the area around it. The space could be cleared, the footpath surfaced and made safe, attractive shrubs planted. It could be made into a garden dedicated to the memory of Jason.

The audience stirred. Suspicious bottoms shifted in plastic chairs.

'The Boundary Stone,' Jimmy reminded them, 'has always been an unofficial viewing point from which those willing to risk the existing path can look out over a magnificent vista of the Mendip hills.' *But not,* he might have added, *the old quarrymen's social club.* 'We could transform it into a more congenial and accessible beauty spot. More people would go there more often and this would deter youngsters from going there to engage in… er…dangerous activities.' Marvelling at his own inventiveness, he added seductively, 'This could be done for a relatively modest sum of money. There are local charities which fund environmental improvements and local amenities in areas which have been adversely affected by quarrying.'

This seemed to go down well with the majority of those present. Jimmy looked over the heads of the buzzing crowd, seeking approval from Gaynor. She nodded graciously and with a quiet 'Thank you Jimmy', turned and asked Stella to read out the list of potential funders.

The crowd listened. Terry, Jimmy noted with some amusement, was whispering animatedly in his wife's ear while she took notes.

Once Stella had finished Gaynor opened the meeting to the floor. She pointed to a hand waving eagerly from one of the front rows.

'We need to put a fence round the Boundary Stone,' it pronounced. 'Stop people from going too close to the edge.'

Scattered voices agreed.

'They ought to have done it years ago.'

'Should be a new fence all along the edge of that blasted quarry.'

'Thank you,' said Gaynor and nodded to Stella, who was taking the minutes.

Jimmy looked across at Gaynor, raising his eyebrows. He knew, and so did she, that fences could be cut. But his main concern was that now might be a good time to wind up the meeting with promises of action, while the mood remained largely positive. Some of his friends in the back rows were turning towards him and grumbling. It would be too obvious to run his finger across his throat so he raised it and revolved it, the folk singers' signal meaning 'last chorus'. She ignored him and selected a man with a beard and bushy eyebrows who had been waving at her for some time. Though he could only see the back of his head Jimmy recognised him as Jasper from smokers' corner.

'I'm sorry for your loss,' Jasper said in the general direction of the Chawners, 'but...

Jimmy's heart sank. He willed Jasper to turn round so that he could somehow warn him off.

Ignorant of political necessity, Jasper addressed the meeting. 'I think we should leave the old workings alone. They're part of our history, industrial archaeology if you like and, in their way, they're beautiful.'

A tide of anger started to build among the Chawners' supporters and the sensation-seekers.

But Jasper persisted, raising his voice above the growing hubbub: 'Walking in the quarries is a matter of choice, with all due respect...'

Oh God! Jimmy thought.

'...the boy chose to jump off the Boundary Stone Rock.'

Irrespective of its views the entire audience gasped.

Eve Chawner rose to her feet and rushed up the central aisle towards the exit like a pheasant breaking cover. Her sister and daughter took off after her and her husband turned over the table in front of him and jumped down from the platform to join the pursuit.

As she approached the back of the hall, Eve raised her head. Her eyes darting from Jasper to Jimmy and to the cold impassive figure of Frankie, she spoke, quietly at first:

'How...how...' She turned her tear-stained face towards Frankie, choked and then raised her voice: 'How dare you! You don't know what it's like to lose a child. My boy never got the chances some people get. Some people are teachers' pets,' She glanced over her shoulder at Gaynor, who was standing on the platform with other members of the committee watching the developing scene intently. 'Because...I'm not a racist, but it's because...'

Jimmy moved quickly over to her side. 'I'm sure you're not, Eve,' he said softly, 'but don't forget the press are here. We wouldn't want them to get the wrong idea, would we?' He looked past her to where enterprising journalists were trying to elbow their way through the Chawners' friends and supporters, and whispered urgently to her sister and daughter, 'Take her home.' They each took an elbow and propelled Eve towards the exit.

As soon as the heavy door had swung shut behind them Jimmy returned to look for Frankie. He found him standing in the centre of the aisle confronting Ray Chawner. His eyes were glittering. 'My Rosie,' he said slowly, dragging the words up from the deeps, 'is clever and she works.'

There was a shimmering silence interrupted by scuffling and whispering at the back of the hall as Mary and Lisa outflanked the crowd and manoeuvred around its edges to approach Frankie.

'Time to go home,' Mary told him firmly.

'Come on, love,' Lisa coaxed.

He looked down at Mary for a thoughtful moment, turned and let her escort him out of the building.

Lisa followed them, announcing reassuringly, 'Brian's outside with the Land Rover.'

Jimmy hoped he'd put his shotgun out of sight.

Eric Adams of the *Somerset Free Press* interrupted his thoughts. 'Hi Jimmy! How you doing?'

'Never better,' Jimmy said, noting with alarm that Ray Chawner was also bearing down upon him.

The photographer sauntered over to join them. 'Wotcha Jimmy! Great weekend over at Chine,' he said, referring to the long-forgotten Anglo-Irish Friendship Festival. Jimmy looked from the angry father to the hungry reporters, swiftly weighing up his options. He favoured them all with a bland smile, introduced them to one another and suggested that they should all meet up in the pub for lunch tomorrow.

'Ray's wife,' he informed the news hounds with an air of saintly concern, 'is in great distress. He needs to be at her side right now. This evening has been a terrible strain for the whole family. They have all been very brave.'

Ray looked doubtful, but he decided to leave. As he passed Jimmy, he pulled him aside and whispered: 'You're in with them, aren't you?'

'I hope so,' Jimmy said pleasantly. 'They're great guys but they can be dangerous. Think very carefully about what you're going to tell them.'

As Ray pushed him aside and stomped out of the hall, Jimmy called out to the reporters, 'Twelve o'clock tomorrow, then. At the Jolly Collier?'

'See you then, Jimmy.' They gathered up their notebooks and cameras and left. *Probably heading for the pub now*, Jimmy thought. He could have done with a pint himself but realised he'd better run this past Gaynor first.

All around him the last traces of the meeting were disappearing as the remaining committee members gathered posters and leaflets into a cardboard box or stacked chairs into neat piles against the walls. He could see Gaynor prowling round the front of the hall looking for something, clearly something which had displeased her. Noting his presence, she advanced into his personal space.

'Jimmy!' She wrinkled her nose. 'You took Frankie to the pub, didn't you?'

'No, I didn't.'

'You've been drinking.'

'I got a call from work.'

'Don't lie to me, Jimmy. Where did you go – to the club?'

'To Chine Manor.'

She raised her eyebrows.

'I had to sort out an incident at the Anglo-Irish Friendship Festival, which, you may recall, I set up on behalf of the local authority for the Regional Arts Development Board.'

'An incident?'

Jimmy decided to change the subject. 'It wasn't my fault that tactless prat Jasper decided to shoot his mouth off.'

'He's your friend, Jimmy.'

'He's an acquaintance,' Jimmy conceded. 'Nor is it my fault,' he added, 'that the Chawners are racist bigots.'

She looked at him with a mixture of amusement and contempt. 'I know how you operate, Jimmy.'

'Not on this occasion,' he insisted. 'I outlined a plan. It went down well, remember? Tactless outbursts from the audience were not part of it, trust me.'

'Can I?'

'You're going to have to,' he answered, calm, but inwardly seething at the injustice of her implied accusation, 'because someone's got to deal with the press.'

'Off to the pub then, are you?'

'That's where they'll be.' Her attitude was incomprehensible. As far as he could see, he'd just dealt with a very tricky situation, saved the day even. He looked round the hall, making sure the other committee members were out of earshot before adding, 'You should have closed the meeting while the majority of the people there were happy.'

She turned away from him and swept out of the hall. He followed her into the street, calling after her, but she started running.

Reassuring himself that he was as much in need of congenial company as drink, Jimmy stole away to the pub.

VI

Gaynor ran down Crubscombe Hill, past her own front gate and the junction with the track that led to the old quarrymen's social club and its truncated playing field. Scrambling over a wooden stile, she took the path up to the Boundary Stone Rock. She needed solitude and fresh air. How could he? How dare he dismiss her in that way, as if he were in charge of the situation and the whole debacle was her fault? Who the hell did he think he was? It seemed that he was not the man she'd married.

She stumbled on up the path, no torch, unsuitable shoes, but she wasn't bothered. She'd been up here in the dark before, many times, happier times, walking up here with Jimmy after the folk club, to see the moonlight over the wild alien landscape, the legacy of their triumphant campaign, where the dust was settling and life beginning to recolonise the shadowy spoil dumps and inclined planes.

She reached the top cursing and gasping, almost colliding with the stone itself.

Around its base plastic-wrapped bouquets of flowers grown in faraway lands fluttered and decayed.

'Stupid kid!' Gaynor said, aloud. 'Poor, stupid kid. Poor, stupid kids all of them… I do what I can. For God's sake! I do what I bloody well can! And nobody gives a shit!' She realised that she was shouting.

'He doesn't care any more!' she yelled, searching the dark sky for the invisible moon. 'He's living in a fantasy world. He's a one-eyed king, worshipped by a bunch of pathetic quarrelsome drunks and social misfits who imagine themselves to be artists.'

The moon paid no attention.

Gaynor reached out a hand to the stone, leaning on it to restore her balance as her fury abated like a passing squall.

As husbands go, she thought miserably, Jimmy wasn't that bad.

'Your Jimmy,' Mary the postmistress had once confided, 'is a diamond.'

This was probably true, but the competition wasn't strong. A dismal parade of her friends and associates and the various impositions that men had brought into their lives, flashed past her mind's eye: life-draining tedium (Estelle), infidelity (Bron), control (Eve Chawner), cruelty (Mary). Mary disclosed little about her past, but there had been rumours.

Then there were things she'd seen, or half seen, at school, hiding in the shadows behind truculent children, sometimes the subject of staffroom gossip. She'd reported her suspicions to Al Messenger, Deputy Head, whose duties included discipline and welfare, to be dismissed with a casual wave of an authoritarian hand.

'Better not to get involved. Leave it to Social Services.'

The only thing that senior management ever wanted to involve themselves in, as far as she could see, was the imminent transformation of humble, bog-standard Hales Mead Comprehensive into an academy, with smart new uniforms and a modern building, including an IT centre, designer classrooms, an atrium, and debts going forward into the next Ice Age.

If Jimmy was a diamond, then half the world were shards of glass and base metal, plastic waste and other flotsam. Whatever they were, they made the rules.

She stood up straight again, looking beyond the Boundary Stone, staring into the black wilderness. In spite of its strange glamour, she knew that most of the villagers felt they deserved better. Crubscombe had been neglected, by employers, by local and national government, by everyone. It hadn't been an issue when there were jobs. But the working quarries in the area had mechanised, hardly anybody worked in them any more; the companies made huge profits and gave little in return.

The residents, old and new, had had enough. It wasn't just about poor Jason. People wanted a fight, needed to land a blow on something, anything, with their tiny fists.

Even the moon, she felt, was failing in its duty, skulking somewhere up there behind a mass of cloud.

'Come out!' she shouted into the lowering sky. 'Come out, you bastard, I know you're up there somewhere. Show yourself! I need to bay at you!'

'It's not fair!' she declaimed. 'The world is run by men in pubs!'

Somewhere over at the Earwick end of the workings, in the old limestone quarry, she could see little pinpricks of coloured light. They twinkled at her for a moment, as if in jest, and then went out. *I must be losing it*, she thought.

CHAPTER 9

I

Jimmy waved to the departing press corps and walked up Crubscombe Hill, phone held up in front of him looking for a signal. Behind him, reporters and photographers were loading their gear into cars and vans, slamming doors, revving engines and taking off up the narrow lane to meet their deadlines.

As far as he could tell, the press briefing had been worth an afternoon of his precious annual leave. The story had grown overnight and they'd been joined by a woman from 'Points West' who had spent the morning coaxing an interview out of Eve Chawner.

'Did she say anything?' Jimmy had asked her, as he escorted the party up the slippery path to the Boundary Stone.

'She talked about Jason, mainly. Enough, I hope, to shame the quarry company into doing something.'

He sensed a faint light of kindness flickering under the professional armour and nodded sympathetically.

She responded with a calculating frown. 'Do you know her husband, Jimmy?'

'Not really,' he replied, 'I see him around the village now and again.'

When they emerged into the rough, bramble-strewn grass around the Boundary Stone, he moved away from her to tell the whole group about its history. The journalists and BBC cameraman advanced to the edge of the rock. Marvelling at the length of the drop, they filmed and photographed and talked to their recording machines.

Jason wasn't the first to jump, Jimmy told them. It was a popular sport among some of the local youth. The boy had been unlucky. They shook their heads, sighed and tutted, and applauded the villagers' campaign to make the place safer. Then, observing that it was getting cold, they packed away their kit and allowed Jimmy to lead them back to the road. He was relieved that they had shown little interest in the wider environs of the rock.

Near the top of Crubscombe Hill, the phone finally picked up a signal. Screwing up his eyes to read the tiny print on the screen he found Gaynor's number. There was still about five minutes of her school lunch hour left.

Her voice, when she answered, was rushed and muffled. 'Jimmy! I've only got a couple of minutes and I'm trying to eat my lunch.'

At least she was speaking to him. 'Hang on,' he said urgently, and told her how he'd dealt with the media.

She did not appear to be grateful. 'Yes. Thanks. I've got to go now, Jimmy. I've got years nine and ten this afternoon, fifty books to mark, and a meeting with the deputy head.'

Jimmy tried sympathy. 'Never mind, love. It'll be Easter soon and you'll be off to France.' A thought crossed his mind. 'When, exactly, are you leaving?' He heard the grinding rasp of the school bell in the background.

'Thursday – day before Good Friday. As soon as we've broken up. Now,' she lowered her voice, 'bugger off, Jimmy, I've got to go.' She cut the call.

Bugger off? Jimmy sighed from the depths of his wounded soul. His status had sunk to the same level as the cat's. He scrolled down the list of contacts and called Miles.

'Jimmy!' At least Miles sounded pleased to hear from him, 'What can I do for you?'

'Still up for the anniversary party on Easter Saturday?'

'I certainly am. I've got a gig at a festival in Devon but it's not till the Monday.'

'Well why don't you come and stay at the farmhouse for the weekend. There'll be a crowd, lots of old friends. I'll reserve you the best spare bedroom.'

Miles chuckled. 'How can I resist?'

Jimmy sensed that he was no longer alone. He looked up and saw Catrin sauntering down the hill towards him. 'Sorry, mate, got to go. See you then.'

'Looking forward to it,' said Miles as Jimmy prodded the red telephone icon.

'Dad?'

'Why aren't you in school?'

'I don't have any lessons on Monday afternoon.'

'How did you get here?'

'Tekky Di borrowed the courtesy car from the garage. Why aren't you at work?'

'I've been showing the ladies and gentlemen of the press around.'

'Around?'

'Just the Boundary Stone.'

'Oh right,' Catrin said, with an exaggerated air of unconcern.

Up to something in the quarries then, he thought, *Earwick, probably.* He'd always thought Earwick Quarry, with its wide but enclosed space, had considerable potential for creative teenage miscreants. 'They didn't go anywhere near Earwick,' he volunteered.

Her eyes widened momentarily. 'Earwick?'

'Nothing to see down there, is there?'

'No. No.' She looked him in the eye. 'Off to the pub then, Dad?'

'I don't think so. It's alcohol-free Monday.'

'OK,' she said and strolled on down the hill.

He watched her disappear into the farmhouse drive. As he turned to resume his progress to Upper Crubscombe and the pub, the sirens at Broxcombe Quarry wailed around the valley, accompanied by a series of detonations. Good to know, he reflected, where Frankie was and what he was doing.

II

By the time Thursday evening came round again Jimmy's plans appeared to be maturing. The media were browbeating Aggrementos, who were looking into the possibility of doing something about the old fences, and the Crubscombe Environment Committee was busy googling and downloading forms. He sauntered down the informal path leading from Upper Crubscombe to the old quarrymen's social club, pensively chewing a fried fish. *Should keep them all happily occupied for a while? In due course leading lights, moving away or just overtaken by life and its unpredictable events, would drop out and nothing would change. Only ten days to go now until the twenty-fifth anniversary of the great invisible folk club. Artists, some of them quite famous, and punters, had been phoning from all over the country.*

But there was still cause for anxiety. Gaynor had not forgiven him for the events of the previous Sunday. He could see no reason why this was. He'd sorted it all out, hadn't he? His reward had been exile to the best spare bedroom, and they seldom spoke.

Unable to face another family mealtime navigating his wife's silent reproach, he'd decided to pick up some fish and chips and dine at the club. As he reached the edge of the car park, he heard footsteps running towards him and looked up. Terry was charging through the equinoctial dusk in full panic mode.

'He've gone mad, Jimmy! He've took all the bottles from the rubbish and he's smashing them up!'

'Who?'

Terry gasped and spluttered. 'Frankie.' He waved a long, bony arm in the direction of the clubhouse.

Jimmy listened.

The sound of shattering glass was accompanied by an impact which caused the building to shiver. It was repeated about thirty seconds later – and a minute or so after that. Jimmy swallowed his mouthful of fish and made his way cautiously to the scene of the action, where he found Frankie methodically working his way through a line of empty optic bottles, inserting the ring finger of his left hand into the neck of each one. Some he merely cast aside. The ones which sat most comfortably on his finger he smashed against the corner of the building before throwing the main part of the bottle on to the reject pile and adding the neck to a collection of jagged-edged weaponry at his feet. A few yards away, at the edge of the car park, Brian was leaning against the side of his Land Rover calmly observing. He was holding a blowtorch.

Keeping a wary eye on Frankie, Jimmy sidled over to him. 'What?'

'It's our Lisa's fault,' Brian observed nonchalantly.

Jimmy's jaw dropped. A couple of chips fell out of his rapidly cooling fish supper.

'She tidied his house, didn't she? She meant well. You know how women are.'

Jimmy wasn't sure, but he nodded anyway.

'That poor little Rosie haven't got time with her exams and that. Lisa said she'd do the hoovering for her and went in there with all her cleaning stuff, and she found all his bottle necks and threw them in the recycling.'

'Of course,' Jimmy sighed, intensely relieved. 'I can't see why he doesn't buy them in a music shop like everybody else.'

'Frankie i'n't everybody else, is he? He's...'

'Authentic?'

'Reckons the glass ones is traditional, and they do sound better,' Brian explained. 'You done then, mate?' he called over to Frankie, who was now resting from his labours.

Frankie responded with a curt, barely perceptible inclination of the head and Brian strolled over to him. He ignited the blowtorch and gave it to Frankie, who started blasting the bottle necks, melting and blunting their jagged ends.

Jimmy left them and rescued Terry, who had gone into hiding in the scrub behind the clubhouse. They went inside to make final preparations for the evening. Cars were starting to crawl down the track to the car park, tyres crackling on the rough gravel.

'Got something to tell you, Jimmy,' Terry announced. He'd recovered from his recent trauma and was fussing over his pipes and taps as the first customers arrived, demanding beer. 'Tell you later,' he added with a cheery wink.

'Give me a pint would you, Tel.' Jimmy found a beer glass and waited while Terry filled it. He gobbled the last of his fish and chips, then pulled his notebook out of his pocket and started threading his way through the gathering crowd to make a list of performers.

A careful balance had to be maintained. The feminists didn't like the sexist songs, the old-fashioned, 'Men with Guitars' didn't like the feminist songs (unless they'd written them themselves), the traditionalists didn't like guitars, or anything involving electric amplification, and nobody liked that woman who cupped her hand behind one ear and sang interminable ballads, many verses of which she had personally rediscovered after hours of research at Cecil Sharp House. She invariably delivered them in a low, pitiless, expressionless drone, which even the purists found trying.

They were all entitled to a spot. The main thing, Jimmy reckoned, was not to put too many similar acts on one after the other. He studied his growing list and shuffled names around, concentrating. It would change over the course of the evening as people arrived and left, and there was always the possibility of the unexpected, but he enjoyed a challenge.

He started the proceedings in the time-honoured manner of all MCs by singing a song himself. 'The Sheep Stealer' was a cheery account from Somerset of a poor man who rustles sheep, involves his children in cutting up the evidence and gets away with it. After that, came the usual procession of the gifted and the dreadful, all receiving enthusiastic or dutiful applause.

An underlying sense of friendship or, at least, camaraderie, triumphed as usual, balm to Jimmy's troubled soul, and the first half flowed on until he decided it was time for a beer break.

'Ten minutes,' he warned the happy participants, moving swiftly ahead of the stampede for the bar to get his order in. 'Top me up would you, Tel?'

Terry filled up Jimmy's glass and leaned over the bar to hiss, 'Got something to tell you, Jimmy,' in his ear. Before he could elaborate, they were both swept up by the needs of the performers and drinkers.

Jimmy's well-honed antennae picked up a frisson. Something was going on in the car park. Slipping out to investigate, he found Brian selling rabbits to foodies and impoverished carnivores from the back of his Land Rover. Jimmy asked them to stash the stiff, furry little corpses in their cars or under a pile of stones at the back of the clubhouse. 'Don't bring them inside,' he insisted. 'A lot of people are, you know, vegetarians.'

Brian looked cross. 'Vegetarians,' he said with a disgruntled shrug, and slammed the door of the Land Rover.

'I don't mind what you do out here, Brian,' Jimmy said, 'as long as you do it quietly. Now why don't you come in and give us one of your brilliant poaching songs?'

He let Brian start the second half. His poaching songs were loud and rousing and could be relied on to get the proceedings going again. In spite of the slaughter of wildlife portrayed in the verses, even the most dedicated vegans would side with a poacher against the gamekeeper. Besides which, Brian had a true and powerful voice. The whole audience cheered and clapped.

Frankie followed him. Having carefully selected one of his new bottle necks, he played 'Mississippi Delta Blues'. The audience wouldn't let him go without an encore. Listening to 'Catfish Blues', Jimmy wondered why his friend wasn't interested in professional work. Doing the bang for the quarries was, presumably, more lucrative.

Once the third half had begun and his responsibilities as a host were over, more or less, Jimmy felt he could relax. Formality was dispensed with as the survivors gathered at the bar to gossip or tuned their instruments for the jam session. He leaned against the bar listening to the stories and banter.

Rob, the mandolin player, was missing. As Luke approached the bar to buy more Guinness, he made enquiries.

'He's had to go to Birmingham to see a client,' Cyril explained.

Jimmy knew that Rob was a social worker and, as such, often went on mysterious errands.

'He's got a new client. A remittance man. They're paying him four hundred pounds a month to stay away from Bristol.'

Those who'd overheard were impressed.

'I'd do that for two hundred,' someone said.

'One hundred!'

'Fifty!'

And so the Dutch auction progressed.

Jimmy drank on and sighed with contentment while the musicians got stuck into a bit of klezmer. He looked over the bar to where Terry was still tending the beer. Currently he was testing the weight of the barrel and inspecting the bung.

'You're doing a grand job there, Terry!'

''Tis a pain keeping good beer in this tip. But,' Terry's eyes lit up, 'it won't be for much longer. You know I got something to tell you?'

'Go on,' said Jimmy, indulgently.

'I have applied for a grant.'

Jimmy spilt some beer. 'What?'

Terry was barely able to contain his excitement. 'There's this charity in Bath that gives money to places that have been affected by quarrying and suchlike. They told us about it at that meeting, about improving facilities in Crubscombe. I thought we ought to grab some of that money before anybody else thinks of it, so me and the wife went home and googled it. She helped me fill the form in. We done it, Jimmy. Trouble is,' he finished, somewhat deflated, 'we couldn't do the submit bit, so we had to print it out and put it in the post.'

'You did what?'

'We put it in the box this afternoon Jimmy, first class. It'll be there by tomorrow. We'm in with a chance, in'us? I think you could say that this is a community that has been affected by quarrying.'

'Oh Christ, Terry! You… you…'

'Have I done something wrong?'

'No! Yes! You should have asked us first!'

'Asked who? I'm the Honourable Secretary.'

'Us…the membership!'

'Don't you want the money?'

'How much did you ask for?'

'A thousand pound.'

'Have you any idea,' Jimmy said, 'how many thousands of pounds it would cost to make this place legal?'

'Thousands?'

'Hundreds of thousands, probably. We've only survived this long because nobody's noticed we're here.'

Terry finished his pint and took his jacket from a hook behind the bar.

'I'm sorry, Jimmy, if I done anything wrong.' Dignified and downcast, he walked out of the clubhouse.

CHAPTER 10

I

Frankie and Terry sat on a slimy log near the top of Hammering Batch, the last visible remains of the Hammering Deep Mine, which loomed over the north side of Upper Crubscombe. The pithead buildings had long since been demolished, the headgear had been sold for scrap, and the exact location of the access and ventilation shafts had become the subject of debate among industrial archaeologists and anxious owners of the elegant new houses on the Ashgrove Heights estate. Behind the two men, rooted in fine black soil, there was scrubby, bramble-infested woodland. Before them lay a wide and unrestricted view of the whole of Crubscombe, the new estates, rows of old stone or brick cottages, the abandoned stone quarries and woodlands as far as the Boundary Stone, and beyond.

They were looking for Mary from the Post Office, who lived in one of the miners' cottages at the foot of the batch. It was eight o'clock in the morning. The sun was up, somewhere, but in the grey and grudging light of seemingly endless winter, the whole splendid panorama resembled Eeyore's Gloomy Place.

Terry clapped a pair of binoculars to his eyes, sweeping the back garden of Mary's cottage.

''Tis a pity she did go home early from the club last night.'

Frankie shrugged. He was not required at any of the quarries until the afternoon. He had better things to do with his morning off than babysit Terry. But Jimmy was worried, and Jimmy was a mate, and Jimmy was expected to be in his office this morning to deal with some sort of pointless management rubbish.

Try to stop him from putting his foot in his mouth, Frankie.

Frankie could imagine all sorts of effective, and enduring, ways of achieving this, but Jimmy would be unlikely to approve. So, he watched and waited, the model of restraint.

They'd been dismissed at the Post Office counter by that cheeky Wallace girl who had informed them that Mary didn't come in till ten on Fridays, and where she was now was none of their business. Terry, undeterred, had set off to talk to the post mistress herself accompanied by his dutiful minder.

The back door of the cottage opened and Mary appeared carrying a basket of washing.

Terry watched intently through the binoculars as surprisingly dainty bits of lace and Lycra emerged from the basket, to be firmly and cheerfully pegged to the line, where they seemed to dance and float.

'She'm hanging out her smalls.'

Frankie wrenched the binoculars from his trembling fingers, 'You're disgusting!' He got to his feet and started walking down the batch. With a swift, imperious glance, he instructed Terry to follow him.

Terry followed, skittering down the path, eyes still fixed on Mary's back garden. 'Ooer!' he jabbered, 'She'm putting out her judo kit!'

Mary had pulled some more substantial garments from the basket – white baggy trousers and tunic in a heavy cotton material, followed by a strip of black cloth. Long divorced from a man she never discussed in public, Mary had filled her leisure time with many different interests, including folk singing and the occasional stray dog or cat, but she had pursued her judo lessons with particular dedication. Though kind, she was no longer trusting.

'You talk to her, Frankie,' Terry said, quailing before the strip of black cloth.

'We'll go round the front like gentlemen.'

They were met at the front gate by an overwrought Cairn terrier, all bared fangs and pulsating pink throat. Frankie leant over the gate and tickled it behind its affronted ears.

*I should watch out, mate,' Terry advised, 'She've got terrible little teeth.'

'Would that be me or the dog?' Mary was standing just inside the open front door. 'Can I help you gentlemen?'

The dog sniffed Frankie's hand.

'Er,' said Terry, glancing sideways and catching Frankie's eye.

Frankie, leaving the dog to its own devices, stood up straight. He was struggling, every word locked in by shame and embarrassment. He thought of Jimmy and the long years of what posh people called support. Jimmy had always been a cheery drinking companion and could be relied on for timely intervention whenever things got out of hand.

'Thing is Mary, we'd like to ask you a favour. My friend...'

'I posted this letter, see,' Terry interrupted, anxious to get to the point. 'By mistake.'

'He posted it yesterday, to a place in Bath.'

'Yesterday, that's right, for the five o'clock post...only we got it wrong.'

'We were wondering if...'

'We got to have it back, see.'

Mary shook her head. 'I'm sorry, boys, once it's in the post, I can't do anything. It would be stealing from the Royal Mail.'

'Who's to know? We i'n't going to tell nobody'

'Sorry.'

'But...'

Mary sighed. 'It's gone anyway, my love. It'll be in Bath by now.'

'Thank you for your time,' Frankie said, with as much dignity as he could muster.

'I'm really sorry, boys. Why don't you come in for a cup of tea?'

But Terry was off, seized with panic-stricken resolve and galloping down the street towards some new objective. Frankie watched for a moment, then despondent, but mindful of his responsibilities, he made to follow, glancing over his shoulder at Mary's inviting cottage door.

'Sorry, I got to go.'

Baking smells wafted after him as he ran.

II

A holiday, a holiday, and the first one of the year...

Friday morning, eight fifteen. In the faux-jasmine-scented bathroom of number 34, Smollett Close, Sam Beresford pulled a comb through his spiky brown hair, this way and that, checking the effect of each subtle stroke in the mirror. Then, nervous and hesitant, remembering, he stared into the deeps of his own pretty brown eyes. Downstairs, his mother, having packed his father off to work, was listening to one of her favourite records.

Lord Donald's wife came into the church the gospel for to hear.

She'd retired from teaching the previous summer and more often than not these days her hands went to the stack of old vinyl before the Hoover. Though she'd never been near a festival, and hadn't been to a live concert since marrying his dad, she liked those old sixties folk groups – sweet tunes and sad stories, a little bit of rock and roll even, but nothing too industrial. Apart from paying for guitar lessons for her son, old records by Fairport

Convention were as far as it went. Sam had done quite well really; got his degree and now he was working for a prestigious local company.

And there she saw little Matty Groves walking in the crowd.

Sandy Denny's golden voice rocked on, propelling the poor country boy and his upper-class mistress towards their doom. Looking into the mirror, Sam conjured up a vision. She was small and slender; she had long red-gold hair and a laughing face.

By the rings on your fingers I can tell you are Lord Donald's wife.

'Alexandra Archbold – Alex.' She'd smiled at him, red lipstick and sparky blue eyes.

It was at the Aggrementos International Aggregates' St Patrick's Day staff dance at the Oldland Manor Hotel. He'd joined them four months previously as a graduate trainee in the Estates Office, and she was the CEO's wife.

The evening had begun with a ceilidh. Her idea, she'd said. She'd told her husband it would encourage the workforce to bond.

'I just love Irish music,' she told him, arriving at his side after some manoeuvre called a ladies' chain.

Sam decided that he did too. He told her that he was a folk singer, in his spare time.

'Isn't the band marvellous?'

'They're great,' he said. 'Really authentic.'

He wasn't lying. They were accomplished musicians, engaging and friendly. The caller was a bloke with longish curly hair called Jimmy, bit old, but funny. He'd got them all on their feet dancing and clapping to the rhythm, and made them laugh by demonstrating the moves with the man who played the box.

'They're from Crubscombe,' she said. 'Who knew?' And she winked at him as she danced onwards to the next set.

As the night was drawing to a close, she asked him to dance again. The Irish jigs and reels had come and gone. The band, fed and drunk, waiting for resentful loved ones to collect them in family saloons, were playing French café waltzes.

And he and Alex had bonded.

Smiling, Sam turned away from the mirror. He went into his bedroom, pulled a set of workmen's overalls from a box in the bottom of the wardrobe, folded them and stuffed them into his briefcase. It was Friday.

He ran down the stairs.

'Hurry up, love,' said his mum, intercepting him in the hall with a kiss, 'you'll be late.'

'No, I won't!'

He danced out into the chilly morning air, down the concrete path, through the little steel gate and into the close.

Square, seventies houses, built of breeze blocks, grey bricks and clapboard, clung incongruously to the hillside. Below him, the city of Bath lay in a hazy bowl of rush-hour traffic fumes. Up here on the hill, the wind whipped over the rooftops and eddied through the tree-lined streets and lanes. But Sam barely noticed. It was Friday. She did her voluntary work on Fridays, in the office of a charity sponsored by the company. Officially he was supposed to be doing site visits, checking security at the disused quarries round Crubscombe. The company were carrying out urgent repairs to the fences and gates, but he could drive down there tomorrow morning to check it all out and have his report on the boss's desk by Monday morning. Who'd know?

There were other risks. Lord Archbold was a jealous and bad-tempered man. His spies, human and automated, were everywhere. But in a small yet tasteful apartment, two floors above the charity's office and occupied by an old friend of Alex's in exchange for discretion and a low rent, they would sport and play.

Lord Donald's not at home.

III

Telephones didn't interest Frankie. He was vaguely aware that sophisticated mobile phones were essential for the kitting out of the modern teenage girl and funded them accordingly. Every so often, a hand-me-down would come into his possession.

You need it Dad, for your business!

This puzzled Frankie. All the quarry managers he knew drank in the local pubs. He was an artist. He was widely known to be able to drop an old chimney inside its own length in any direction he chose. Blasting away a limestone quarry face was a piece of piss. Apart from the years of his youthful adventures in the US, he'd been doing it all his life – learned it from his dad, who'd set up the business when he came out of the army. He was the best. If anybody wanted him, they knew where to find him.

Mindful of the urgency of this particular occasion, Frankie fumbled with Rosie's latest cast-off, pressing the tiny button to switch it on, just as she'd shown him some months previously. Brightly illuminated pictures and symbols darted across the screen, sliding away as he tried to trap them. Occasionally a keyboard floated by. Now you see it, now you don't. After a while he gave up and drove home to investigate the landline, which, though not the same as the old phones, had seemed more biddable last time he looked.

It was in a corner of the living room next to some gadget called a hub. Frankie picked it up gingerly and pressed the button with the green telephone on it. This yielded a dialling tone. So far so good. At least this thing had a real keypad. He tapped out a number and waited, pacing and fidgeting until he got a response.

IV

In the 'little shop of horrors' Jimmy sat at his desk, doodling on the back of a piece of paper from one of the drifts that regularly accumulated in his 'paperless' office. He was brooding on the great matters of the day. He would prefer to evade the management briefing, scheduled for ten o'clock and now rapidly advancing upon him. It promised to be a pep-talk from the usual phalanx of New-Age dickheads who, driven on by self-generated flatulence, had floated over the ruined lives of honest workers to senior management posts.

Hoping to learn more, he looked at his inbox – a depressing experience, usually, and nearly always pointless. The relevant email was from something called New Dawn, which had recently been pestering him with daily reminders. So far, he had resisted the impulse to mail the Chief Executive to ask if the firm had been taken over by Greek Nazis. Inspection of the small print revealed that they were consultants who had been brought in to manage the downsizing of the office facilities. Working practices were being reviewed, working from home was under scrutiny, hot-desking was being considered, and – horror of horrors – a questionnaire had been circulated to all members of staff. His hand hovered over the mouse while he considered his response. He could tell them he was busy right now.

To some extent this was true. The company had been commissioned by some government-sponsored group called 'The Local Environment Initiative' to organise a reception for the stakeholders, whoever they might be. So far, he had asked Suzy to book a room in a smart hotel and look around for suitable caterers. A decent spread would keep everyone happy for a while. Miniature scotch eggs and stringy bits of indeterminate white flesh fried in breadcrumbs and welded to short sticks cost money, but not nearly as much as cleaning up rubbish dumps and polluted rivers.

Suddenly another idea took hold of his wandering mind. *Might voluntary redundancy be in the mix?*

He'd been dreaming of early retirement in recent years. If he could persuade Gaynor to do the same, they'd be free. They could paint the house, do the garden, run a few sheep under the apple trees, make the state pay for Catrin's education. They could even revive their folk-singing careers. But he knew that Gaynor would never agree.

What was it all for? Responsibility? Jimmy thought. *Educate your kids, give them a good start in life and then leave them to do the same for their kids, and so on and so forth until, as some old song put it, the sun dries up the sea. The world had become mercenary, embittered and joyless. We're free to spill our guts, but we daren't have fun, not even the rich, who appeared to pleasure themselves by hoarding more stuff than anybody could use in a lifetime and hanging out with other boring servants of mammon – the bored boring each other to death or, at least, into expensive private clinics.*

And lately, it seemed to Jimmy, the advancing tide of regimented tedium was invading every public and private space, except Crubscombe, where there were still pockets of resistance. Despised, downmarket Crubscombe was still home to artists and musicians, people who valued life above possessions. 'The Lost World' Gaynor called it. Perhaps she was going over to the other side ... borne away by the material tide? As he picked up the mouse to open the email, the phone rang. He reached across the desk and picked it up.

'Frankie?'

'He's gone to Bath.'

'Why?'

'To get his letter back.'

For a moment Jimmy was too appalled to think. 'We'd better stop him,' he said, 'before he gets into serious trouble. Did he tell you who he'd sent it to?'

There was a long pause while Frankie searched his memory. 'Restoration.'

'I'll meet you in Bath – the car park down by the bus station – if it's still there.'

Before leaving the office, Jimmy googled the charity 'Restoration' and then consulted an old edition of 'Who Owns Whom', years out of date but still useful sometimes. He opened the email from New Dawn and clicked on Reply…

I am sorry and disappointed to have to tell you, he wrote, *that I have been called out to inspect a potential venue in Bath. The owner flies to Canada this afternoon and, therefore, has only a few remaining hours in which to meet me. This means, sadly, that I shall not be able to attend this morning's briefing. Kind regards, Jimmy.*

V

In the sixth-form block at Hales Mead Comprehensive the consequences of the public meeting were being felt.

'They're putting up a fence!'

'They can't be!' Hugo Lennox's eyes widened with horror.

'They're having a bloody good try,' said Tekky Di. 'Our dad was called out this morning to pull one of their piledrivers out of a ditch.'

Supposedly preparing for a French lesson after break, the year thirteen modern linguists, all six of them, were gathered in the Senior Students' Recreation Area. There were padded benches and coffee tables, a few scattered armchairs, a coffee machine, rows of lockers along one wall and a desktop computer which had recently been jettisoned by the IT department. The carpet was cheap and, in spite of nightly hoovering, perpetually grubby. Envious lower-school wits called it the 'Care Home'.

Rosie withdrew her nose from a French edition of *Les Misérables*. 'They're replacing all the gates too. Chaz and I rode past the one down Earwick Bottom on our way here.'

'The get-in?' Catrin said. 'Shit! Have they dumped any boulders in front of it?'

'They will do. Chaz was well pissed.'

Tekky Di frowned, making calculations, 'Most of the kit's already in.'

'What about the guests?' said Catrin, 'They're not all from Crubscombe. They'll be driving.' She was incensed. Not all the guests would be schoolkids. The band was getting noticed. 'What the fuck are they doing it for? The quarry company doesn't give a shit. Why now?'

'It's because of what happened to that … to Jason Chawner.' Rosie flicked over a page of her novel in a detached manner.

'You actually reading that?' asked Hugo.

'When I get the chance.'

Tekky Di was still considering the logistics. 'They can't do it all. They won't be able to get access to the whole perimeter, not with their kit. Anyway, fences can be cut.'

But the mood did not lighten. The bell went and they headed for the door, complaining and debating. Much more needed to be discussed, but Madame Sullivan would be pissed off if they were late. In spite of being sophisticated seniors, they still feared her wrath.

In the corridor, Rosie took Catrin to one side. 'We need information. Your mum will know what's going on. Let's ask her.'

VI

After half-an-hour spent wandering round the tall terraces of central Bath, bickering over a threadbare copy of the relevant 'A-Z' and accosting wary passersby, Jimmy and Frankie found themselves in an elegant and secluded street of refined Georgian residences. The two opposing terraces were precise and impenetrable constructions of steam-sawn ashlar, fronted by wrought-iron railings and stout, wooden doors. Archbold Terrace had been named after one Henry Archbold, whose once modest holding in Combe Down had supplied the stone for this and many other developments all over the city.

The two men stopped in front of number 1A and loitered outside.

There were four floors and a basement, all discreetly barricaded against the living world. The front door was locked, and the basement, once the domain of cooks and maids and accessible to tradesmen and other riff-raff, had been sealed. The gate at the top of the area steps had been secured with an elegant, but serviceable, black-painted padlock and chain.

Jimmy advanced to the front steps for a closer look. It was clear that the charity's offices were on the ground floor. Posters depicting vivid blue lakes, green woodland dells, picnic areas and sailing boats had been placed in the window, beneath a sign which read: 'Restoration. Making good the land. Life! Leisure! Communities!'

Beside the front door, there was a small, polished-stone plaque, daintily carved with flowers and some sort of vine which resolved itself into the word 'Restoration'. There seemed to be no way in.

Eventually Jimmy found a strip of labelled doorbells attached to the stonework on one side of the doorway, almost out of sight: Restoration ... Flat A ... Flat B ... Flat C ... Basement. Above them was an intercom speaker. His hand hovered over the bottom bell. He'd assumed he had a plan, but, turning over all the possibilities in his mind, he found that he hadn't.

Where was Terry? Presumably not inside; the place looked too calm. He backed out of the doorway, looking up and down the street. *No sign of him.* He collided with Frankie, who appeared to have frozen in the middle of the pavement, eyes turned upwards, apparently fixed on some celestial object. 'There's a camera.' Frankie nodded to the top, right-hand corner of the doorway where, secured to the stonework on a slowly gyrating bracket, a security camera, its little red eye winking at them intermittently, was sweeping the doorway and the street in front of it, observing their shifty presence, recording every move, loyally feeding every detail to its master, like Lord Donald's servant.

'I think there's a pub just round the corner,' Jimmy suggested.

Frankie nodded.

'We need to make a tactical withdrawal.'

Frankie didn't argue. He was thirsty.

They walked down the narrow lane along the side of number 1A, and found that the terrace backed on to a park, on the opposite side of which stood the Archbold Arms, set in the middle of another golden terrace. A muddy path, of the type known in the landscape-gardening trade as a desire line, led straight across the park to its front door. The path skirted a deserted children's play area and ploughed through ornamental shrubs which, naked and bitter, were hanging around in their artfully placed clumps waiting for spring.

Jimmy and Frankie followed the path, slithering now and again on its greasy surface, and emerging from the ornamental shrubs onto the road outside the pub. There, to their astonishment, they found free parking spaces. Sitting in one of them was Terry's family saloon.

'Six-pound-fifty,' said Frankie, between gritted teeth as they walked past a board offering *real ales, fine wines and locally sourced, traditional English cuisine* and entered the bar, 'is what I paid for the multi-storey.'

'Let's not make a scene, eh, mate?' Jimmy counselled him.

Though they searched every space – the bar, the lounge, the skittle alley, the restaurant and the snug – startling customers and attracting suspicious glances from the management, they could find no sign of Terry.

'He's bound to come back to his car, isn't he?' Jimmy reasoned, 'Might as well stay here for a bit.' He sent his friend to a table by the front window and bought them each a pint of Chedgy's. He brought the beer to the table with a warning. 'Don't spill any. It cost four pounds fifty a pint.'

Clenching his hand into a boulder-like fist, Frankie gripped the handle of his beer mug and raised it to his lips.

Jimmy drank and tried to concentrate. The situation, he realised, was absurd, embarrassing even. Stopping for a drink, he had to admit, had done little to improve matters. Nothing to do now, he supposed, but wait. In the old days he'd have sailed in there and talked his way out of it. He seemed to be losing his touch. Frankie, he noted, was beginning to simmer. Nothing visible yet, but to the trained observer...

Frankie held his glass up to the light. 'Better kept at the Collier,' he observed, 'and cheaper. And we wouldn't have to drive.'

'We can't just go home and leave him. He might...' Jimmy paused, trying to imagine the consequences of any action Terry might take, '...get himself arrested.'

Frankie took a carefully calibrated swig of his beer, about twenty pence' worth. 'He could ask them to give him his letter back ... be polite?'

They looked at each other with mutual despondency. 'This

is Terry we're talking about,' said Jimmy. 'Whatever he does, he's likely to draw the attention of the wrong people to the club. This charity is connected to Aggrementos. I think it would be better if Aggrementos didn't know we were trespassing on their land.'

'Hasn't your friend told Lord Georgy Porgy?'

Jimmy realised he was talking about Miles. 'Good God, no! I've asked him not to.'

Frankie looked him in the eye, long and hard. His lips twitched a little before he took another mouthful of beer.

'Who calls Archbold that?' Jimmy asked.

'People in the quarries.'

'Why?'

Frankie seemed to choke on his beer. 'Kissed the girls and made them cry.'

Jimmy studied his friend's face closely and spotted a glimmer of mirth in the habitually dead eyes. 'All right, mate, point taken.'

After that the conversation died.

'I enjoyed your songs last night,' Jimmy said eventually.

'Thank you.'

The beer levels sank low in their glasses.

'Fancy a top-up?' Jimmy asked.

'Driving. Gotta keep my licence.'

'Oh yes…sorry. Bag of crisps?'

Frankie shook his head.

Jimmy tried once more to lighten the atmosphere. 'I hear your Rosie's got her scholarship for Cambridge,' he said. 'You must be really chuffed.'

Frankie swirled the remains of his drink round the bottom of his glass. 'It's in East Anglia.'

Jimmy gave up.

A young man dressed in spotless workmen's overalls and carrying a hard hat and a briefcase emerged from the Gents.

Jimmy looked up as he passed their table, heading for the door. The youth, who looked vaguely familiar, didn't appear to have noticed the two middle-aged men sitting at the table by the window. Once outside they watched him put on the hard hat, cross the road and start following the desire line across the park.

Having nothing better to do, Jimmy followed the boy's progress towards the back of Archbold Terrace. Like the backs of many Bath terraces, it was constructed from inferior decaying rubble and adorned with metal fire escapes – health and safety winning out over Georgian elegance. Jimmy noticed for the first time that there appeared to be some sort of building work going on at the back of numbers 1 and 1A. Hardly surprising, he thought. Georgian Bath was a harbinger of the new world: spec-built, fancy Palladian facades tacked on to cheap rubbish. The whole thing was probably falling down. The young man, he supposed, must be the project manager.

Idly, Jimmy scanned the back wall of flat 1A, then stopped abruptly and paid attention. The door giving access to the second-floor flat had been propped open and a couple of feet below it, climbing nimbly up the fire escape, was Terry. He glanced nervously over his shoulder and then, reaching the second-floor landing, slid through the door, disappearing into whatever lay beyond.

Nothing happened. Whatever Terry had encountered on his burglarious entry into 1A Archbold Terrace, it retained a serene and, it seemed to Jimmy, menacing calm. 'Drink up!' he said. Frankie engulfed the remains of his pint in one mighty swallow, like a blue whale feeding on krill. 'Four pounds fifty,' he muttered as he surfaced. He followed Jimmy to the door.

They ran as fast as they could along the slippery path, eyes fixed on the door to the second floor flat. Still no response. They might be in time; might be able to remove Terry from the scene before he was apprehended. They were halfway across the park when Jimmy saw the young man running eagerly up the fire escape, following in Terry's footsteps. Kicking aside whatever was holding the door open, he went through it into the second-floor flat. The door snapped shut behind him.

VII

It was Gaynor, rather than the students, who was late for the sixth-form lesson. She had spent the period before break patrolling the corridor outside the classroom where the hapless trainee was having another go at subduing 8H. The rebellious mob inside could see her through the glazed upper half of the door, but she kept out of sight of the trainee.

'Can anybody,' Gaynor heard her shout, loud and clear, 'tell me the French word for a box?' They were discussing Easter eggs, in as much as 8H could be said to discuss anything. 'Jordan?'

That's right, Gaynor thought, *home in on the troublemakers*.

The Fishlock jaw dropped.

'La boite,' a neighbouring girl hissed.

Fishlock appeared to mishear. 'La twat, Miss.'

Uproar.

Gaynor entered the classroom quietly and ordered Fishlock to follow her out.

First came the bollocking. 'How old are you? Thirteen or three?'

'Thirteen, Miss.'

'And…?'

'It wasn't my fault, Miss. Krista Lewis told me to say it.'

'Nevertheless, Fishlock, I am holding you responsible.'

'Miss! You got it in for I,' he ventured bravely, trembling in the blast from her manufactured anger.

She fixed him with a terrible glare, hoping he hadn't noticed her suppressed laughter. 'I have you in my coils, young Fishlock.'

'Miss …?'

She stood him up outside the staffroom door with a list of simple French words to learn. Five minutes before the end of break she made him repeat what he'd learned – very little – and then released him.

By the time she'd gathered the sixth formers' latest essays and got her head back into their revision programme, she had been five minutes late. She found the class angry and restive. *Not them too?*

'Bonjour,' she greeted them, with as much positive energy as she could muster.

Gaynor and her daughter had an agreement that domestic issues were not to be discussed in school, but, when Catrin asked in perfect, flawless French why Aggrementos had suddenly decided to repair the fences round the old quarries when they must know it would not do anything to improve their safety, she decided to engage in the discussion. Catrin was particularly good at the conversation and language side of the subject and to hear her daughter speaking French with such ease and fluency lifted her mood. She knew, and Catrin knew, that she had some experience in the matter of fences, but that it would be better, in their present surroundings, not to go there. She informed her daughter that it was a political gesture and they'd probably just replace the gates and the most accessible and visible bits of the fencing.

Then she got down to handing back their essays.

VIII

The flat felt chilly. Any heat remaining after its tenant's hasty morning exit was now hovering around the moulded plaster in its lofty ceilings.

Sam went into the kitchen. Carefully setting his briefcase down on the work surface, he took out a bottle of fizz – Prosecco, which she had assured him, was much nicer than all but the most expensive champagne – and a box of chocolates. He put the fizz in the fridge and then went into the spare bedroom, a normally sunny little room overlooking the park, and placed the chocolates in the middle of the double bed. *No sun today.* The back yard appeared to be deserted. Presumably the workmen had gone over to the pub for an early lunch, but he put the blind down anyway, just in case. He gave an involuntary shiver. *Better find the central heating and turn it on.* He went out into the hall, wrenched open the door to the cupboard which housed the gas boiler and various other bits of household flotsam, and found himself staring down at a shabby, denim-clad backside.

Sam froze. What was a man, a workman apparently, doing fiddling with something at the back of the utility cupboard – *fitting something? A listening device?* Maybe Lord Archbold suspected. Could this be a private investigator? The backside quivered slightly, but its owner remained silent.

Terry, meanwhile, was searching the cavernous halls of his mind for an explanation. On hearing someone enter the flat from the fire escape he had bolted for this door, hoping it was the exit to the stairs. Then, realising he was trapped, he had crawled as far into the darkness as he could and cowered, like a dog in a thunderstorm, hoping the danger would pass without further incident.

'Can I help you?' said Sam. The ice broken, both men spoke at once.

'I'm from…err…British Gas…right?' Terry stuttered.

'I'm from English Heritage,' Sam said. 'There's a problem with the…' He had never actually studied architecture, but the place looked vaguely like a listed building.

' … been called in to check for a gas leak.'

'… I'm looking at the … er … architrival stanchions in the ceiling joists. They might fall down and…'

Terry backed out of his hiding place and stood up. The lad looked much younger and stronger than he was, but he seemed nice enough. 'There could be an explosion see?' Terry explained.

IX

Jimmy and Frankie ran round to the front of the building. This time Jimmy pressed the bell.

'What you going to do?' Frankie asked.

'Don't know yet. Drag him out one way or another, preferably dead… Sorry. Forget I said that. OK, Frankie?'

The intercom buzzed. A cheery, but slightly impatient-sounding voice said hello.

Jimmy told it he was an events' organiser.

A long, sustained buzz invited them to push open the door and enter.

The office was strictly informal; a wide desk by the window, the rest of the space mostly taken up with scattered armchairs. Behind the desk stood Lady Alexandra Archbold. She had placed all the paperwork into neat piles and relevant trays, switched off the computer and pushed it to one side. Clearly, she was ready for an early lunch, but she favoured the visitors with a warm and welcoming smile.

Jimmy strode over to the desk, hand extended, mind blank.

'Lady Archbold?'

'Jimmy, isn't it? Please call me Alex.'

'This is Fr... er... Hezekiah Dando.'

Frankie grunted.

'What can I do for you, gentlemen?'

'I'm so sorry to trouble you, Lady Alex.' Looking straight into her sparkling, blue eyes, Jimmy leapt in, feet first, hoping that his natural buoyancy would eventually bring him back to the surface. 'Unfortunately, I have to advise you that there is an intruder in the building.'

'There can't be! We have security cameras.' She seemed anxious, nevertheless.

'My friend and I saw him on the fire escape.'

'It's not possible. There are men working at the back.' She appeared to be panicking.

'You see, we know this man.'

'Do you? It's probably just the project manager. He likes to check things, you know?'

'We know him,' said Frankie. '

'He's...learning disabled,' Jimmy explained. 'He's obsessed with writing to charities and asking them for money.'

'The project manager?' Evidently Lady Alex was losing her grip.

'No, not him, our friend. We need to get him back home before he gets into trouble. He sent you a letter, and now he's afraid that he'll be in trouble and he's trying to get it back.'

'A letter?'

'He needs help. Mr Dando here...' Jimmy could hear the babble of his own voice as if from a distance, '...is his carer.'

'I see.' She turned to Frankie. 'You're a nurse?'

Frankie assembled his features into a sinister and forbidding expression that was, Jimmy supposed, meant to look caring.

Alex rested a hand on the edge of the desk as if trying to steady herself. She appeared to be thinking. 'Was it something to do with a folk club?' she asked.

'It was just a begging letter really. He had no authority to send it. The matter has not been discussed by the committee.'

'I see.' Alex tripped daintily round the desk on very high heels and rifled through the contents of a plastic tray. Producing a large brown envelope, she handed it to Jimmy. 'I don't think it comes within our remit.' She spoke kindly, but Jimmy found her air of efficiency and acuity alarming.

'There's two of them,' said Frankie.

'Two?'

'Two men.'

Alex wobbled on her heels.

Jimmy pulled himself together, remembering. 'Yes, two, your project manager and our friend. They'll both be in there somewhere...'

Her eyes widened. 'Is your friend violent?'

'Oh no,' Jimmy said. 'Just...disabled.'

'Don't worry, madam,' said Frankie, getting into character.

They raced up the stairs to the second-floor flat. Alex pummelled the solid but tasteful security door.

'Sam! Sam! It's Alex! There's an intru–'

The door opened revealing Sam, unharmed but confused. Behind him, apparently hiding, was Terry, who, seeing Jimmy, leaned round the young man's elbow and winked.

'I'm from British Gas. I was just telling this young man...'

'Come on, Tel,' Jimmy said gently. 'Time to go home.'

Terry pointed at the young man. 'He's from English Heritage.'

Jimmy looked more closely. The young man still looked familiar somehow. In his head, he could hear the French café waltz 'Les Amantes Infideles'. *Ah yes! The pretty boy from the ceilidh.*

'We have been havin' a interestin' conversation.' Terry sounded a tad put out at being interrupted. Jimmy suspected that he must have noticed something in Frankie's expression that did not bode well and decided he might be better off staying in the flat with this nice young man.

'Sam,' said Alex, her voice full of tender concern, 'This man's not very well. He needs to go home with these people.'

'There's nothing wrong with me!'

Carefully sizing up Terry's potential for mayhem, Alex approached her beloved and whispered as loudly as she dared, 'He has a learning disability...'

There was nothing wrong with Terry's hearing, however. 'No I haven't!' he shouted, outraged. 'I have got a job...' He pushed past Sam to confront his accuser, 'And a wife and...'

Frankie flashed out a massive paw, laid hold of Terry by the collar and hauled him through the doorframe and onto the staircase. Then, pulling one of his prisoner's hands behind his back and pinning it there, he marched him down the stairs and out, more or less in one piece, to the street.

Particles of Victorian dust and eighteenth-century plaster floated down and settled delicately on the remaining protagonists. Unable to contain herself, Alex put a comforting arm around her sweetheart.

Jimmy, still hanging around on the staircase, watched the scene with polite detachment.

Alex smiled. 'So, you have a folk club, Jimmy?'

He looked from Alex to her pretty young man and back again. 'Yes.'

'I hope I'll be able to hear your lovely band again soon.'

'Excuse me,' said Jimmy, 'Must dash. Better get our friend home to his family before he has a relapse.'

As he emerged into the street Jimmy could hear Terry's loud

complaints. 'She said I was disabled, Jimmy. She said I was...'

'Nobody really said anything much,' Jimmy told him. 'It's the traditional, English way.'

Frankie stood over Terry, toe to toe, looming and simmering like Vesuvius. At last he found some words. 'You need to see a chiropractor.'

'Chiropractor?'

'Yes! Right!'

Terry trembled. 'Why?'

'See if he can insert your head into your anus.'

X

Later, in the warm, post-coital luxury of the back bedroom, Sam drew circles on Alex's shoulder blade with his fingertips, targeting a favourite dimple, which he kissed.

'Do you know anything about a folk club in Crubscombe?' she murmured.

CHAPTER 11

I

A decision would have to be made. Gaynor sat on the bed in the second spare bedroom, brooding. In the middle of the floor lay an open suitcase: too small. Around the room, covering every available surface, were clothes, shoes, underwear, toiletries and small packages for long-missed friends: too much. She was sure she shouldn't put the Crème Eggs in with her best party dress. They would be bound to get squashed and leak. Perhaps she could take them in her handbag. Perhaps she needn't take them at all. Though a quintessentially English delicacy, adored by her French friends, they were probably available in Carrefour these days.

Meanwhile, there was no way she'd have room for both the red and the green boots. Decorated with buckles and glitter, armed with four-inch stiletto heels, totally unsuitable for work – she wanted them both

She was going on holiday, but she wasn't quite sure she should be. There was too much going on.

The quarry campaign was going well, on the face of it. Aggrementos had been goaded into action. Broken fences had been replaced and all the entrances sealed with steel gates festooned with padlocks and barbed wire. The lay-bys were now blocked with massive boulders, which prevented everyone, including dog walkers, from parking their cars, causing friction and debate in the village pub. The kids were annoyed too. Strange, but she'd noticed through long years of working with them how the young hate change nearly as much as they insist on rejecting old-fashioned values. *Oh well ...omelettes and broken eggs, or whatever the old saying was. It wouldn't work anyway. At least the Chawners were happy, for now.*

The black dress, boring, would go with both red and green boots; the blue dress, vibrant and new, with neither. She gave up and stared aimlessly into the middle distance, stymied. It was Wednesday evening. School broke up the next day and Jimmy had agreed to pick her up and take her straight down to Castle Cary. He'd see her on to the train for Plymouth. Had she been too hard on him? Recent experience suggested that he was probably just making sure she was leaving.

He was around, somewhere, in and out, messing about with his computer and his mobile phone, knocking on Catrin's door and bleating for help every time something went wrong, which was frequently:

'No! Not there...*there*...look!' Catrin sounded as if she was addressing a small child. 'Leave it alone! It's an app. You don't want it. There you go. Now bugger off! All right? I'm trying to study!'

He said thank you and Catrin's door slammed behind him.

She shouldn't be talking to her father like that.

Gaynor wondered in a detached manner what he might be up to. Arranging his wretched folk club anniversary she supposed, whatever that might entail. Should she worry? Probably, but she was too weary to care. It would almost be better if he was having an affair. Then, at least, she could throw him out into the street, followed by his unpleasant laundry. She could gather up the broken guitars, busted bodhrans, tin whistles and all the festering mementos that lay gathering dust in the dining room and burn them under the old apple trees in the orchard. But there was little chance of that. Jimmy loved her, she was sure, like a big smelly old dog that insisted on swimming in foetid ditches, rolling in unmentionable substances and, returning home to shake the foul deposits all over the furniture; then, hoping to make amends, slinking out into the garden and digging up a festering fragment of bone to lay it tenderly at her feet.

Loud angry music featuring thunderous bass and strange arpeggios on the flute exploded from Catrin's room. It was vaguely familiar, Jethro Tull? *Prehistoric! Well, 1970s.* Why on earth was her daughter digging up those ancient fossils? She couldn't possibly be studying, not with that racket…

Gaynor threw a pair of black shoes into the bottom of the suitcase. Her thoughts raced, bouncing from one source of anxiety to the next. Should she be leaving Catrin alone with Jethro Tull, let alone her father and his louche associates? Musicians; bums and scallywags someone had called them, but she couldn't remember who. *Just idiots really. Oh for God's sake, the girl was eighteen, grown- up, nearly.* When Gaynor was eighteen, when not diverted by Plogoff and Greenham Common, she'd wanted to be a folk singer. She had a lovely voice, everybody said so. Later, at uni, she'd gone round the folk clubs singing to Jimmy's accompaniment on the guitar: Jimmy and Gaynor Sullivan, like Richard and Linda Thompson, only not quite. They'd been wasting their time. *Musicians were fun…twenty-five years ago…*

Catrin could sing too, but that had been very firmly shoved on to the back burner, in spite of her father's protestations.

Then there was Rosie, Frankie's responsibility really, but… Hidden in a folder on her computer was the latest email from Estelle, who was coming over to the UK shortly after Easter, ostensibly to launch a book she'd written, but also, Gaynor knew, to reclaim her lost daughter. Rosie had done well, brilliantly in fact, and she had been such a good friend to Catrin. They were lovely girls, and they had the sense to understand that they could not change the world.

Gaynor was looking forward to seeing her old friend, and dreading it. What would Frankie do? Estelle had always insisted he wasn't a bad man, but, with Frankie, who could tell?

She picked up the blue dress, then sat down heavily on the second-best spare bed, a tired, creaking divan, and stared out of the window watching the apple branches swaying back and forth against a darkening sky. The farmhouse had held so much promise when they'd first bought it, a great place to bring up kids, wild and remote, away from the dark desperate struggle for survival that their city lives had become. Once they'd forced the quarry to close, it should have been an earthly paradise. But Crubscombe had proved to be a trap, a sad remnant of a forgotten world. Anybody with anything about them got out.

Old friends, Breton farmhouse cooking and French red wine wafted into her conscious mind, dispersing the fog of indecision.

Gaynor got to her feet. 'I need a rest,' she said out loud. 'A bit of me time I think they call it these days.' It was all booked anyway, she reasoned. If she didn't go, she'd be letting the others down. She sprang into action, made decisions, finished her packing and then concentrated on the essentials: passport, tickets, money... She reached across the bed to her open laptop, still online in case of unforeseen developments, closed it down and, once all the pings and chirrups had finished, wedged it carefully into a shoulder bag. She could Skype Catrin from France.

II

PC Paul Edwards swung his patrol car into the sodden dust that lay in drifts outside the main entrance to the old workings at

Earwick Quarry, wildlife scattering as he skidded to a halt in a manner reminiscent of the inhabitants of Hazard County.

Lifting a large torch out of the boot, he left the car and wriggled between two of the smaller boulders that now barricaded the lay-by. He strode up to the gates. *Boring stuff really*, he thought, a bit beneath him these days. He'd been seconded to the helicopter crew, but it would only be a very small part of his duties. He shone his torch over what had been the main entrance to the quarry. This, sadly, was the real business of policing. The gates gleamed in the torchlight, new and magnificent, ten by three metres of toughened steel bristling with spikes, garlanded with coils of barbed wire, secured with a padlock the size of his own head and a chain strong enough to lift an engine block out of a truck. The site was impregnable. Just a routine visit, then, but important.

A boy had died in these quarries. It was necessary, his sergeant had told him, for the police to maintain a high profile, be seen to be patrolling the perimeter of the whole complex. Plus, he could call on his nan, who lived in one of those nice old miner's cottages near the top of Crubscombe Hill. She'd make him egg and chips, with fried bacon if he was lucky, and a mug of builders' tea.

III

'There's no cameras, no alarms,' Tekky Di pronounced, after a cursory inspection of the rusty mesh.

The organisers of Promdemonium stood in the bottom of a narrow, rock-cut gulley between Earwick Quarry and the Boundary Stone Rock. Here, hemmed in by alder, brambles and blackthorn, was a section of the older perimeter fence, which had been constructed before the quarry closed.

'You sure?' said Catrin.

'They haven't even looked at it.' Rosie rattled the fence. Though covered in a film of rust it was still solid. 'Too mean. They're not going to spend money if they haven't got to. Nothing's been down here, look.' She shone her torch over the fence and the surrounding scrubland. 'No vehicle tracks, are there? And you're not going to tell me those lazy gits walk anywhere, are you?'

Catrin opened her rucksack and produced a pair of bolt cutters. 'My mum's,' she said with a hint of pride. 'She was at Greenham.'

'Cool,' said Hugh Lennox.

Diana examined the bolt cutters. 'Bit small.'

'She had to hide them from the cops and the bailiffs.'

Diana wrinkled her nose. 'They'll have to do. I couldn't get anything from the garage. Our dad was working late. He'd ask questions, nosey bastard.' She selected a section of the fence and started to cut.

CHAPTER 12

I

Terry and Frankie arrived early at the club to install and tap a new barrel of Chedgy's. Leaving it to rest for a while, they put out the motley seating and the rickety tables, placing a wax-encrusted wine bottle in the centre of each one, ramming fresh candles into the remains of old ones.

Then they inspected the Gents, half flooded, as usual, and generally beyond redemption.

''Tis Maundy Thursday,' said Terry, 'there'll be a lot in.'

Frankie shrugged. He lumbered out into the comparative civilisation of the bar to sample the new barrel.

Outside it was chilly, but less musty. They leaned over the fence at smokers' corner, craning their necks to observe a kind of ritual going on around the Boundary Stone.

Terry watched intently through his binoculars. 'Vicar's up there, and some kids.'

A faint tinkling and a few chords of clunky accordion music floated down on what Pink Floyd might have described as a steel breeze.

'There's two Morris sides an' all. 'Tis ancient tradition, see, taking the choirboys up to the Stone, turning them upside down and banging their little heads on it, bless 'em, so they never forget where the parish boundary is.'

A shaft of light escaped briefly from the sinking sun, catching a shiny object which bounced up and down just above the Boundary Stone. 'The cross,' Terry said, eyes glued to his binoculars. 'The vicar's banging it on the Stone. Don't bang the kids' heads any more, see? Can't get choirboys no more anyway.'

'Not surprised,' said Frankie, surfacing for a dutiful moment from some distant realm of gloom.

'They do use the Boy Scouts.'

'Humph.'

'Everything changes, dunnit? Nobody goes to church no more. I reckon nowadays more people do worship Elvis.'

Frankie took down a long draught of beer.

'He's been seen. People think he have risen from the dead.'

'You mean they think he didn't die.'

'No! Seriously! He'd be a very old man by now if he hadn't died. They seen him, looking young and handsome like. They think he's risen – thousands of them. Maybe that's gonna be the new religion, in the twenty-second century – Elvisism... Elvistianity. Could be a bit awkward, mind.' He looked through his binoculars at the bouncing crucifix. 'Died on the toilet, didn't him?'

Noticing that his glass was nearly empty, Frankie stumped back into the bar to get some more beer.

II

Something to do with Catrin, or was it Rosie? Gaynor was worried about them, but Gaynor worried about everything these days. Her last words to him as he dropped her off at Castle Carey station had been...Oh God! He couldn't remember... Oh yes...the Rayburn, *don't let it go out.* Or maybe she was talking about Catrin...

Jimmy's hand hovered over the gearstick of the Peugeot estate. He was wondering if the car would make it to the top of the hill in fifth. It had a good engine, always started first kick, but it was old, had been even when he bought it, from a mate of Terry's for fifteen hundred quid – *bargain!* Gaynor hated it, of course; said it was like riding in a shed with square wheels. It was reliable though, more so than her newer, smarter, cleaner model, with all those exciting computer-driven gadgets that invariably, in his experience, cause trouble, and had soldiered on through numerous MOTs. Admittedly, it had, over the years, developed a wide repertoire of disconcerting noises; but you could only hear them when the windows were open.

Women, thought Jimmy. He was no sexist – far from it – but this was most assuredly true: women always seemed to be worrying about the small things, always fortifying the watchtowers, maintaining a garrison against troubles which, left alone for long enough, might just creep into the shadows and slink away.

He marshalled his wandering thoughts. It was Maundy Thursday. Folk club tonight. Like the Windmill, they never missed a gig. It was a damn nuisance that Aggrementos had taken it into their corporate heads to include the entrance to the club car park in their health and safety drive and replaced and padlocked the gates, but he'd managed to make other arrangements, and to get Gaynor out of the way before their impact became apparent.

There was plenty of room in the farm yard, which had been designed, after all, to accommodate herds of animals and farm machinery. If he opened up all those redundant farm buildings, he'd be able to squeeze in more vehicles. Gaynor had no reason to complain, surely, but he knew that she would. Accessing the club through the orchard might prove to be a challenge for some of the ageing survivors of the folk revival; but there was the secret path through the gap in the perimeter wall where he had been quietly encouraging the surprisingly unstable stonework to collapse since Catrin and her friends started the process some ten years ago. The rest of tonight's arrangements he'd had to leave to Terry and Frankie. Who would come? One never knew. Lots of Morris men, probably, and the Vicar, taking a quick break between symbolically banging kids' heads on the Boundary Stone and her other, more spiritual, Easter duties. He caught himself hoping that the 'Strong Wimmin' would take a rain check. They'd be out in force on Saturday, but that wouldn't matter so much. They'd be outnumbered. Everybody was coming on Saturday, as far as he could tell. The bush telegraph had done its work: who needed the worldwide web?

Nevertheless, it always paid to be thorough. Exploiting a quiet spell at work, he'd gone through all the relevant websites, putting up his coded message:

Don't forget! Jimmy's anniversary party. Easter Saturday, 8 till early... Bohemia... Somewhere between Rome and Shepton Mallet.

Several members of the folk aristocracy had told him they would be dropping by – Martin Carthy, no less, and Pete Coe, among others. Miles, now riding high on a wave of renewed popularity, would be arriving at the farmhouse tomorrow afternoon, along with many other old friends. Luke and the rest of the band and all the other local musicians would be there as usual. A worrying thought flitted briefly through Jimmy's mind: would there be enough beer? Of course there would! Terry could always be relied on in respect of beer.

Some of the old crowd would be missing. Exploring the Somerset folk website *Sad Folk* in search of news he'd found another death! Fred Page, cheery, chubby fool of a Morris man, never had a bad word for anyone; sudden heart attack. He can't have been more than sixty. A wave of sadness washed over Jimmy. The 'Woodstock Nation' was getting old, past it, way over the hill; winnowed away by day jobs, family stuff, and now death.

The car roared and spluttered into the sinister defile through the middle of Barrow Wood – supposedly haunted by the ghost of a wronged woman; she only appeared to women, so no worries there.

Gaynor's bitter commentary seemed to float out from the trees:

Irresponsible fools; they refuse to grow up, they've fried their brains and their livers, and now their booze-fuelled spaceships are crashing to Earth.

'All spaceships crash in the end,' he said aloud to the gathering darkness, 'so what's the point of worrying?'

Gaunt tree boles stood along the roadside. One by one they flashed past, picked out in turn by the car's headlights, forbearing to comment, but censorious.

Why was she like this? She never used to be. They'd been friends once, agreed about things, worked together against the forces of oppression, made each other laugh.

The day they met was as clear in his memory as if it were yesterday – clearer, in fact. Yesterday was frequently a bit of a blur these days, if he was honest.

He'd been sitting at the back of a student conference about Cruise and Trident, listening with mounting despair and boredom as one delegate after another from IMG, YS, SWP or some other such association of dickheads seized the mic in order to bang on about 'seizing the commanding heights of the economy'. Their remarks had nothing to do with disarmament, nuclear or otherwise. Moved by the pointless tedium of one speaker's relentless, but limited, phraseology and the forceful blows of his right hand, which struck the air in front of him like a jackhammer, Jimmy made a fundamental and lasting political decision. He left for the bar.

And there she was. He'd seen her earlier, sitting near the front, the beauty with the long black hair, who had vanished half an hour ago. He hadn't expected her to hang around.

She was sitting on a high stool at the bar, blue jeans, blue eyes, sparkly blue stuff smudged over their heavy lids, draining a glass of red wine. She had a long, slender, elfin – he thought that was probably the right word – figure. He hoped she wasn't taller than he was.

But Jimmy had status. He was Entertainments Secretary for the Students' Union. He decided to give it a go, approaching the bar with a cool and, he hoped, purposeful stride.

She looked past him, through the door of the meeting room: 'Fourth International hacks!'

He smiled at her; she was witty too. 'Probably working for MI5.'

She laughed. 'Wouldn't be at all surprised.'

'Can I get you another one?'

'Oh, yes please.'

'Another red wine please, Alan, 'Jimmy said to the barman, 'and a pint of Skull Attack.'

They lined them up and knocked them back, putting the world to rights. He couldn't work out why he hadn't met her before.

'I've been in France. I'm a mod...' She was on her fourth red wine. Articulation was becoming a challenge. 'Modern linguist. Year abroad... Was at university...'

'Paris?'

'Rennes...Brittany.'

'Ah, yes, Brittany! Been there. The Inter-Celtic festival!'

He asked her if she'd like to hear some folk music.

'I love folk,' she said. They seemed to agree about everything. 'I used to sing when I was at school,' she confided, sliding unsteadily off the bar stool.

'Where was that?'

'Caernarfon.'

She was from North Wales – he had a fleeting moment of

doubt. Jimmy had no truck with racism of any sort, but North Waleans are strange... 'I'm from the South,' he confessed.

'Siarad Cymraeg?'

'Er...dipyn bach...'

She laughed. 'They all say that.'

'I'm a Cardiff Irishman. Give me a chance.'

'You don't sound Cardiff.'

'I went to boarding school.'

'Oh dear! Ah well. Dim ots!' Leaning against him rather heavily, she allowed him to escort her from the bar.

He found an Irish music session. There was always music somewhere in Cardiff if you knew where to look. Luke, then studying for his degree at UWIST, was there with the rest of his band, plus Miles, in his Irish personification. Jimmy shared a greasy chicken-in-a-basket with Gaynor, and they decided to wash away the taste with more alcohol. Then they fell into each other's arms and danced to the French café waltzes.

The rest, Jimmy supposed, was history. Bit of a bitch, sometimes, history.

The car trundled out of the wood and down the hill towards Lower Crubscombe. Strings and clusters of orange sodium lamps reflected off low-hanging cloud. Somewhere behind the swirling mass one could just detect a full moon.

Estelle! That was what she'd been on about... Estelle's visit to the UK was imminent, a book-signing tour apparently. He saluted her success – good for her. It would be great to see her after all these years. Perhaps it would be better not to raise the issue with Frankie, not very tactful. She would be coming to Bristol, sometime after Easter. They could meet up with her there, couldn't they?

III

Catrin sat at the top of the bank overlooking the makeshift bower in Earwick quarry. 'But I can't!' she wailed at her mobile. 'Don't you understand? I'm the lead singer!' The phone went dead.

She tapped the screen with her forefinger, got the keypad up again, connected, but there was no response. Dumped again. What was their problem? All the boys liked her – well, some of them. They asked her out and then… maybe she looked too much like her mum, the dreaded Bellatrix, but she didn't really; her eyes were brown and her long hair was chestnut and curly. 'You're not like your mum', was, in fact, their favourite chat-up line, along with 'you're cute'. She wasn't sure about 'cute', but they meant it to be a compliment.

They all wanted to take her out on Saturday night, that was the problem. The band was getting gigs now, scuzzy dumps mainly, some downright dangerous if you looked behind the furniture, but they'd also been booked for Glastonbury. Cynics had taunted that this was because Chaz's dad knew Michael Eavis, to which Diana, chief roadie, had retorted, 'Everyone's dad knows Michael Eavis. Got a farm just over the hill, hasn't he?'

'Your dad know him?'

'Yeah, a bit. My mum's his third cousin.'

They'd sent a DVD and they'd been booked. Now they had to practise, and they needed all the gigs they could get. Catrin always invited her boyfriends to the gigs, but they weren't interested, except for that time the band had supported Shazzmania, the latest multi-hit, mega YouTube phenomenon to invade London from Bristol, boring 'slap yer ho's bass bang boot boys', one of whom was the second cousin, or something, of the Bishop of Bath and Wells. Tony Badcox had agreed to accompany her to that one, and had spent all night trying to get into the Shazza's dressing room – *wanker!*

She was the lead singer, *for God's sake*, not some pathetic groupie. She had status, and she wasn't about to miss a gig or even a practice night for anyone. It was bad enough keeping up with the boys on stage, making sure they got to play some of her stuff, getting a chance to play the flute, like Ian Anderson (*Respect!*). She stuffed the phone resentfully back into a front pocket of her jeans. She ought to be more careful with it really, but – *oh, sod it!* Right now she hated the fucking thing.

Better go and help the others set up. She stomped down the slope into the quarry with as much offended dignity as she could muster without losing her footing and rolling to the bottom in a heap. The generator was working. Powerful lights had had been attached to an overhead trelliswork of scaffold poles and gantries, which Diana had acquired from the Carnival Club. Their many coloured beams washed over the pallet-and-breeze-block stage, where Diana, assisted by a coterie of spaced-out, but aspirational, road crew, was setting up the mics, blowing into them from time to time and muttering 'one two, one two.'

'Bring us some tape!' she commanded. 'No, not that…gaffer.'

One of the stoners picked up a roll of gaffer tape and pottered over to the centre of the stage, where Diana was holding a mic in one hand and a stand in the other. He put the roll of tape in her mouth.

'Kanksh!' she said, looking on him kindly. It was Justin Hughes. He would be accompanying her to the gig. Even Tekky Di had a boyfriend – probably hadn't dared say no.

Behind the stage Rosie and Chaz were unloading guitars and amps from the back of Frankie's van, borrowed for the evening, one way or another. Wouldn't matter anyway. He'd be getting pissed down the club by now with her dad and that stupid old twat, Terry Mivart.

Surrounded by make-do, mend and chaos, Rosie and Chaz worked calmly together; he pulled her to him and kissed the top of her head as she walked past with an armful of leads; they exchanged loving glances, laughed at each other's jokes.

Rosie always seemed to fit in. She was better-looking than Catrin – more striking anyway, more modern somehow, cleverer. She'd had stick from the smelly boys for sure, when they were all younger, but at least she never had any from the teachers. They all thought she was wonderful. She got 'A's in everything. She'd even got an AS in Maths. She actually enjoyed doing homework. Catrin was aware that she was able herself, or so she'd always been told. 'Able, but lazy', that stupid, meaningless schoolteachers' label. It didn't come as easily to her as it did to Rosie.

Schoolwork was always a chore. She'd rather make it all up herself, write her own songs and musical arrangements. Music was the only subject she'd ever really enjoyed, apart from the theory, but at least that had its uses. Things might work out OK, she supposed, if they both got into Cambridge... if... They'd be in different colleges, but at least Rosie would be around.

It wasn't that Rosie actually did her homework for her – her mother would have been straight on to that, no messing! But Rosie always gave her a steer. Their homework sessions together were like seminars, and Rosie was always the tutor. She'd read out Milton's interminable and intricate sentences and explained to her what the poet was on about. Mind you, she'd had all that God stuff from her nan, had been carefully, if ineffectually, instructed to fear the devil and all his works. And now she was loved, adored by the beautiful Chaz.

Catrin wondered if there was any boy she could beg or even bribe to accompany her to the Prom. Irving Mottishead? He was known to be a transvestite, but, what the hell? She wouldn't even mind if he wore his best dress.

God! She admonished herself, *What are you thinking of? He might be gay, not trans, or he might be both. He'll probably be bringing a bloke! It was supposed to be the alternative prom, for Christ's sake!*

She tried looking on the bright side, *Mum's halfway to France and Dad will be getting pissed with his scuzzy friends all weekend.* She'd had to agree to sing during the first half at his poxy club reunion, and to bring Rosie, but after that the night would be theirs, and he would be drunk.

She walked towards the stage humming the tune of her latest composition, well arrangement really, 'Seafaring Girl'. It was essentially, she had to admit, based on a folk song her mum used to sing, 'William Taylor' – the tale, in fact, of his sweetheart who dressed herself in man's apparel and followed him to sea, found him consorting with another woman and shot them both. When the captain of the vessel discovered both her gender and what she'd done, he promoted her to captain of a ship from the Isle of Man. *How cool was that?* Bit folky, but Led Zeppelin *(Huge, mega respect!)* had been known to dip into the folk canon on occasion… *Dally dally dum dally dum dum di do…*

What was she going to wear? That was crucial. She had to find the look.

IV

Jimmy checked his watch; ten o'clock and all was well. His decision to open tonight had been justified. There were a fair few in. As the Easter holidays had begun, the numbers had been swelled by the quiet types: earnest young(ish) couples, some of whom lived in the new houses in Upper Crubscombe. Many just came to listen, but there were plenty of regulars to keep them entertained. They'd start drifting away soon, their children and their time in the hands of teenage babysitters. They were gentle souls, quietly supportive of all village activities, and Jimmy valued them, always engaging them in pleasant conversation, and buying them drinks, on the rare occasions when they ventured out to the pub or club.

The Morris men, released from their ceremonial duties at the Boundary Stone, were imbibing large amounts of Chedgy's under the watchful gaze of Frankie, who was manning his station by the door. A couple of them were buying drinks for the vicar, hoping to chat her up.

'Must be hard work banging little boys' nuts on the Boundary Stone,' observed a grey-whiskered, bell-encrusted, tabarded old fool, high on Chedgy's and hugely entertained by his own wit.

The vicar raised a censorious eyebrow, a useful talent, and one not taught at theological college. She was not her usual cheery self this evening. Tradition required her to carry out the ancient ceremony at the Boundary Stone. The diocese had asked her to fill in a ten-page risk assessment. 'We don't bang little boys' nuts, or any other part of their anatomy on the Boundary Stone any more, Clive, as you should know,' she said sternly.

'Little boys' nuts! Ooh ar, vicar!' Terry seemed to collapse under the impact of his explosive repartee.

A loud whisper blew over from somewhere in the audience. 'Shut up, Terry. There's a lady trying to sing.'

A good night, mused Jimmy, *calm and steady, as long as the Morris men behave.*

The door flew open and a couple entered, right in the middle of a powerful rendition of the doom-laden ballad 'Sheath and Knife', a salutary tale of royalty, incest, suicide and murder. The singer had gone to some considerable trouble to discover several previously lost verses. Her moment destroyed, she glared at the intruders. Disapproving susurrations rose from the traditionalist wing.

'Oh! I'm so sorry!' Lady Alexandra exclaimed.

'Welcome,' Jimmy said pleasantly. 'Please sit down.'

Her young companion was carrying a guitar. They struggled through a gap between two tables and sat on a chewed-up bench at the back of the room, looking shifty. Lady Alexandra eased a bottle of Jameson's out of her elegant, but capacious leather handbag, unscrewed the lid and sucked on it like a bottle-fed baby.

'Leonora,' Jimmy said to the singer, 'please carry on. And then,' he informed the rest of the gathering, 'I think we'll have a beer break. Take your time, Leonora. Start again, if you like.'

Leonora started again. There was a discernible wave of resentment from the more degenerate drunks and modernisers. They'd thought the ballad was nearly over. When it was, Jimmy moved swiftly to the back of the room.

Lady Alexandra shrugged off a loose woollen coat revealing a tight upper garment of the sort that Catrin, as far as Jimmy could recall, described as a vest. Constructed from shiny velvet patches, it hugged her ladyship's tiny waist, while managing to contain – just – her surprisingly ample bosom, which strained against a row of pearl buttons. There were gaps between the buttons. Jimmy tried to look her in the eye: 'Lady Alex... Alex! Good to see you and...?'

'Sam,' said the Buildings Inspector.

'Has your friend recovered?' Alex enquired, looking over towards the bar.

'Oh yes, fine now, taking his meds, and... He's very good with beer. Tends it as if it were his own precious child. It's in the family, you know.' Jimmy could hear himself babbling again.

'Is he still working for British Gas?'

'Would you like to give us a song?'

'Yes, please,' said Alex and Sam in unison.

Jimmy added them to his list. 'Can I get you anything?'

'No need! Thank you! I've brought my own.'

'A glass of water perhaps?'

'I'm fine, thank you. Sam's done this sort of thing before. He's almost a professional, but I am a bit nervous. Does it show?'

Jimmy gave her his warmest smile. 'Nothing to worry about. The natives are friendly.' He decided to have a quick word with Frankie and eased his way through the crowd in the direction of the door.

Sly glances flitted across the room, accompanied by mutterings:

'Lady Alexandra?'

'Oh, yes?'

'Lord Archbold's wife?'

Snorts and guffaws issued from somewhere near the bar, but the crowd was too dense for the perpetrator to be identified.

Sam, shutting out the hubbub with intense concentration, tuned his guitar.

Terry leaned over the bar passing on everything he knew to anyone who'd listen. He had a number of fascinated takers.

Frankie, propped against a doorpost, arms folded, paused in his conversation with Mary to listen to Jimmy's concerns and raked the assembly with the death stare. Feeling a sudden draught, people turned towards the door. Even Terry faltered.

Time, Jimmy decided, to start the second half. He moved towards the performers' end of the hut, consulting his list. The space next to the bar cleared as punters and artists returned to their seats. Expectant faces turned towards him; people who had sat patiently and, for the most part, silently, through the first half, enduring even Terry's assault on the Bob Dylan classic 'Lay Lady Lay', and who were expecting to take their place under the spotlight sooner rather than later.

At the back of the room Lady Alexandra knocked back another mouthful of whiskey and tried a few tentative notes. If he put her and her paramour on now, they might just leave immediately afterwards and, with any luck, never return. It would be worth giving offence to the regulars, who were, at least, paying less than half price for their beer. He made the decision.

'Have we all had enough to drink?'

'No!' the crowd roared.

'Ah well, there's always one.'

The crowd laughed, and then became calm and quiet.

'We've got a real treat for you tonight. I'd like you to give a very warm welcome to a couple of newcomers. All the way from Bath, we have Sam and Alex!' He led the applause as the couple came forward to take their positions under the little spotlight which shone over the space in front of the bar, Alex still sucking desperately on the whiskey bottle.

Jimmy whipped the bottle from her hand as she passed. 'Shall I take care of that?'

Sam shot him a grateful look. The remaining whiskey sloshed around and found its level well down the bottle. Clutching it, Jimmy backed away to perch on a stool beside the bar, from which he would be able to supervise artists, audience and, if necessary, Terry, who was leaning forward over the light lager tap, his gaze fixed upon the velvet-sheathed bosom.

Sam played an introduction, 'Fotheringay', by the late, still much-lamented, Sandy Denny. *Ambitious,* mused Jimmy. *Oh well, at least the boy could play.* Guitarists all round the room looked up from their drinks and whispered conversations; even Frankie looked impressed. Alex took a deep breath, Jimmy braced himself, and… *She wasn't bad, tuneful even. A bit breathy perhaps, but for a first effort…* The audience paid attention. When the song ended, they applauded with genuine enthusiasm. Jimmy nodded to Sam, indicating that a second song would be welcome.

Alex, beaming at the audience, relaxed and launched into a long low, powerful version of 'The Last of the Great Whales'.

Young Sam joined her with a sweet tenor harmony. It was awesome, but, alas, too powerful for the velvet patchwork bodice. The audience, deeply moved, had joined in with the last lines of the first verse when, with a delicate pinging sound, a dainty pearl button flew across the performance space and bounced off a pint mug belonging to a retired dentist sitting in the front row. Alex clutched at the gaping hole and soldiered on. Trying to pretend that nothing untoward had occurred, the audience carried on too. But the physics was against her. There was no way that antique velvet and delicate pearl could contain a size thirty-six F cup, half a bottle of whiskey and 'The Last of the Great Whales'. Clasp her bosom as she might, buttons flew in all directions, rolling into the dingy shadows beneath the tables, bouncing off chair legs and glasses. Terry's eyes boggled; his jaw rested on the top of the light lager tap. Several Morris men were similarly affected, but Alex, still clutching at her wayward garment, would not be stopped, nor would the audience. The applause, when she finished, was wild and passionate. There was cheering and stamping as Frankie, stepping swiftly under the spotlight, dropped her loose woollen coat around her shoulders and, just as quickly, disappeared back into the shadows, like Sir Walter Raleigh protecting his queen.

This, Jimmy realised, would be a hard act to follow. He summoned Below The Salt, his ever-reliable ceilidh band, to the spot to play some tunes while he circulated, informing the other hopeful participants of their place in the revised running order.

The second half passed without further incident. Jimmy chatted between the acts and drank freely with no thought for the consequences. *Good Friday tomorrow.* He'd have to sort out beds for his weekend guests, but not till the afternoon at the earliest. He was sure that Catrin would help out, albeit with suitable financial inducement.

As the surviving musicians were getting themselves together

for the third half Jimmy realised that Alex and Sam were still around. The club's regulars, in festive and cheerful mood, had taken them to their hearts, a circumstance that Jimmy found disquieting. Young Sam had been eagerly invited to jam with the other musicians, leaving Alex to mingle. She appeared now at his elbow, mercifully wrapped up in her woollen coat and holding a mug of coffee which Mary had shoved into her hand as she passed the kitchen door. Jimmy looked round in vain for some means of escape, but there was nobody about; they were all detained elsewhere, playing or having a drag and a gossip in smokers' corner. Frankie was in the kitchen helping Mary with the washing-up. Jimmy considered the Gents, but courtesy, and its dismal ambience, deterred him.

'So you managed to find us then?'

'Oh yes. Sam knows all the folky people, and, of course, he knows Crubscombe.'

'Does he?'

'It's part of his job, looking after the old quarries. He works in the company's head office. I don't know what they do all day really. It's supposed to be a graduate trainee scheme. Sam's the only one who's got any sort of brain. My husband –' she fixed Jimmy with a slightly cross-eyed stare – 'likes blondes, girlies. He's filled up the office with girlies, tall, thin girlies with pink skin and golden hair. It looks like a shed full of forced rhubarb.' She giggled, 'I'm afraid I'm a bit drunk and –' she cast a sideways glance at her young paramour, now happily joining in with 'O'Carolan's Argument with the Landlady' –'I hope you don't mind me talking to you like this.'

'Not at all.' There was no escape.

'You're a nice man, Jimmy,' Alex said. She wrapped her coat closely around her and gazed into his eyes, seeking a reaction.

Jimmy remained aloof.

'I need your help.'

Terry materialised, as if from nowhere, and stood behind the bar. Frankie, advancing suddenly from the kitchen, pulled him away.

'Is there somewhere we can talk?'

Behind the old clubhouse, screened off by brambles and nettles and the occasional wild apple tree, there was a grim bower, a sad trysting place for club members engaged in adultery or the consumption of illegal substances. Jimmy led Alex there and, in the company of the rotting corpse of some unidentifiable wild animal they got down to business. Sweet music drifted out of the clubhouse, where, tiring of O'Carolan and the like, the musicians had started on the French café waltzes.

'Sit down,' Jimmy invited her, indicating an up-turned oil drum.

Alex perched cautiously. Though she must have been in her early thirties, at least, she looked like a wayward teenager, lost but defiant.

'Well?' he said indulgently.

'This place is illegal, isn't it?'

'It's a moot point.'

'You're trespassing.'

'Which is a civil matter.'

'It's a great club, Jimmy. Sam says it's the best he's ever played at. It's got –' she paused and pulled the woollen coat more tightly round her – 'soul; and the music's just gorgeous.'

Jimmy wondered where all this was leading. He leaned against the back wall of the clubhouse wishing he had been drinking less generously. 'And…?'

'You and George go back a long way, don't you? You were at school together.'

'He was older than me. A prefect who liked to push the small fry around.'

'Did he bully you?' she asked eagerly.

Jimmy chuckled. 'He would have liked to, but Miles was my best mate. He liked Miles.'

Her eyes widened, 'They weren't…?'

'No. Much too fond of girls, all of us, when we could find any. Miles was good at that.'

'So's my husband. He can have what he wants. He's got money and power.'

The great blue eyes fastened on him again. They were full of tears. 'I want a divorce, Jimmy, only I can't afford it. I love Sam. He's the only one. I was loyal to George all those years… All those little mistresses he's had…'

'The forced rhubarb?'

She sniffed. 'All kept in the dark, like me. He cheats on me again and again; I know he does, but I need proof. He takes them to that club of his.'

'The Boquerie?'

'Yes. He never lets me go near the place'

Jimmy was sympathetic, but his feet were beginning to freeze. He wanted to be in the warm and he wanted more beer. 'I don't think I can help you.'

'It would be awful if your lovely club had to close.'

He agreed with her, but had to insist that he knew nothing about Lord George's love life.

'What do you know about the Boquerie?'

'Very little. I only went there once when Miles was playing.'

'If he finds out about me and Sam,' Alex pleaded, 'he'll throw me out without a penny.'

'He'll have to give you something, surely.'

She glared at him, welling up with bitter bile. 'I want more than something. And –' she bit her lip – 'I want my boy. I want my son out of that horrible school.'

Jimmy genuinely regretted that there was little he could do. 'Ask Miles. He used to go to the Boquerie.'

'He won't say anything to me. He and George are like that.' She linked two fingers, then lowered her voice to a dramatic undertone. 'Public school omerta. You talk to him, Jimmy. You find out, for me.'

'I doubt he'd be any more likely to tell me.'

The wayward teenager pouted. She reminded him of a fourteen-year-old Catrin receiving the news that she must finish her homework before going out. 'If the landowners find out what's going on here they might chuck you out.'

Jimmy considered this. If anything, he had more to fear from the local authority, the health and safety police. 'I shouldn't think George would do that to me. As you say, us public-school chaps stick together. For all I know, Miles has already told him about the club.' This might be stretching the truth but it appeared to have the desired effect.

She chose her next words carefully. 'I think that would depend on whether his company actually owns this little shack.' She prodded the wall of the clubhouse with a bright blue fingernail. 'Sam and I think it belongs to whoever bought the Manor farmhouse.'

'I beg your pardon?' Jimmy wondered if his years of drinking had finally done for him. Could it be that he had fallen over and, like so many of the folk club's clientele, was now lying on one of the rat-eaten benches unconscious and dreaming?

'Sam's been going through all the documents he can find about the Crubscombe quarries. He's found maps and deeds that go back to when the county council owned it.'

Jimmy tried shaking himself awake, but the strange dream persisted. 'It was a council farm,' he said, feeling slightly dizzy. 'The old family died out, sons killed in the war, or something, so the council bought it ... sold it to Archbold's in the 1960s.'

'We haven't found out who owns it now,' Alex continued.

'My wife and I do,' Jimmy said, finding solid ground at last. 'We bought it off the quarry company. Miles and your husband did the deal.'

Alex gave him a knowing and extremely irritating smile. She stood up and walked over to a naked tree which grew at the edge of the clearing, its branches leaning over the roof of the clubhouse, and snapped off a twig. 'Apple, I think.' She handed it to Jimmy. It did, indeed, look like apple.

'How strong is your orchard wall?'

'Blow on it and bits of it will fall down. The foundations are shot.'

'Suppose it's got no foundations? Suppose it's been moved? I think we have what businessmen call a quid pro quo, Jimmy. You get proof of my husband's adulteries from Miles and I'll get Sam to give you a copy of the documents.'

Jimmy thought for a moment, then smiled and shook her hand. 'Of course,' he said smoothly.

As he escorted her out from behind the clubhouse, Alex caught her foot in a trailing bramble and he took her by the arm to steady her. Over in smokers' corner heads turned.

'See you later, Jimmy,' she called cheerfully before stepping lightly back to the club to retrieve her sweetheart from the session.

As her watched her go, tripping daintily, if a little unsteadily, over the uneven ground, Jimmy weighed up the possibilities. If he actually owned the clubhouse he could do what he liked in it and nobody could evict him or the folk club. On the other hand, he and Gaynor would be joint owners and she would be likely to raise objections. She'd worry about the possibility of their being sued if anybody was injured on the premises, and other unlikely scenarios. But that could be dealt with later. The first step would be to find out where he stood.

He could try to persuade Sam to show him what he'd found, but he had little currency. Miles would probably be happy to tell all sorts of racy tales, but for most of the duration of George and Alex's marriage he had been in California. After about five minutes' desperate thinking, it occurred to Jimmy that, if the documents under discussion related to a purchase from the local authority there would probably be a copy somewhere in the council archives, many of which had been moved for storage to the basement of Chine Manor. *Worth investigating, and as soon as possible, ideally before Gaynor gets back from Brittany.* Tomorrow morning he would have to go into work. So much, he thought sadly, for his Good Friday lie-in.

He trudged round to the front of the clubhouse. Sweet singing greeted him as he entered the porch. The musicians were resting and Mary was giving them a song:

Here's a health to the bird in the bush, a health to the bird in the bush.

And we'll drink up the sun and we'll drink down the moon.

Let people say little or much.

CHAPTER 13

'Morning, Jimmy!'

Jimmy started as if he had been shot in the back. He turned and found he was confronting a security guard. He needed to pull himself together, clear his head and find a plausible explanation for his presence in front of the door to the basement of Chine Manor on Good Friday. The security man, shirt pressed, boots polished, uniform neatly buttoned, advanced, permitting himself to smile. 'Good to see somebody takes their work seriously, Jimmy. 'S'not a real bank holiday see, 'tisn't mandatory, but they all do bugger off and lie under their duvets. Idle sods!'

'Ah, Barry!' Jimmy beamed at him like a duplicitous Westminster politician. 'So much to do, so little time. I need to look at some plans.' He turned back to the door, waved his pass at it and, diving through, found himself under the startled scrutiny of the County Archivist.

'Debs?'

'Jimmy?'

She seemed to be doing some kind of stocktaking, moving along the shelves, picking out selected files, inspecting the spines and replacing them, not always in the same place.

'Good day to get things done, isn't it?' said Debs. 'No one chasing you with random requests from the general public, or our political bloody masters.'

'All skulking under their duvets apparently,' Jimmy said.

'Can I help you, Jimmy?'

'I have an event to stage, an arts thing, you know – Art and the Environment?' Jimmy was amazed by the depth and elasticity of his own imagination. 'I need to look at some plans of the old quarries.'

'Haven't they been digitised?'

'Not all of them. Couldn't find anything suitable on the GIS.' The mention, Jimmy felt, of some new-fangled bit of software would add plausibility to his case.

'Quarry stuff's in 42Q,' Debs said absently before returning to her picking and placing. Quarries, being largely post-medieval, didn't interest her. 'Be careful with the light switch, Jimmy!' she added as an afterthought. Her voice drifted behind him down a narrow stone stair that long pre-dated health and safety regulations and had somehow managed to elude the repeated refurbishments to which the venerable building had been subjected over the past thirty years. 'I don't think anybody's been down there since about 1972,' she added.

Perfect, Jimmy thought. His head hurt and he wanted to be alone. He really shouldn't have helped Luke dispose of the rest of Lady Alexandra's bottle of Jameson's. His fingers groped along the damp, gloss-painted brick wall until they came to a metal box, about the size of his palm. There was a bobble-shaped thing wobbling around in the centre of it, which he took to be the light switch. He flicked it downwards with a swift, defensive movement of the index finger, stepping backwards as he did so and colliding with a steel bookshelf. Startled neon strip-lights flickered into life, illuminating what appeared to be miles of Meccano shelving. Cardboard files, and books bound with stiff linen fabrics in sober browns, faded greens and maroons, had been arranged according to some outmoded filing system. They contained obsolete reports, discredited science or biographies of forgotten civic dignitaries; rank upon rank of them, all reeking of neglect. Jimmy wondered how long it might be before the whole lot turned to compost. He walked down the nearest aisle peering at faded, sticky labels.

42Q occupied a dark recess at the far end of the cellar. It contained a plan chest, yet more shelves of boxes and books and a poisonous air of decrepitude. 'A fine and private place', thought Jimmy, *like the grave. No questions asked, at least not recently.*

He wrenched open each drawer of the plan chest in succession and scanned the contents; ancient estate maps that told of an era before the mines and quarries. They'd been commissioned by proud landowners, before the profitability of mining and quarrying had become apparent. Fascinating relics, but they yielded no useful information about the extent of the Manor Farm orchard and nothing at all about the sale to either the local authority or the Archbolds. With a sigh he closed the last drawer and looked around.

Tucked away at one end of a Meccano shelf he found a stiffly bound book whose surviving dust cover depicted the headgear of a vanished colliery beneath the title: 'Crubscombe, the history of a Mendip parish', by Joseph Archbold, Lord George's father, he supposed.

He skimmed through its pages, curious and then drawn in. Lord Joseph seemed to have been quite a nice old boy: distinguished war service, wounded at Monte Casino. There was a sense of real affection, love even, for the wild plants and creatures of the valley, and for its history. The narrative contained touching descriptions of boyhood walks over a landscape that Jimmy had never known because much of it now lay on the surface of a hundred airport runways. He flicked through more pages and found an old photo, taken from the Boundary Stone. It looked over the bottom of the valley at what had then been a small working quarry. Next to it was another faded snap of the quarrymen's clubhouse in 1962, tidy and proud, playing field still intact, hosting a team from Bruton for a game of cricket.

Jimmy crashed back into the present. It was getting late. He'd been wasting time! The weekend's guests would already be arriving at the farmhouse. Terry would be there soon with a polypin of Chedgy's, five gallons of good beer, drawn off bright. The party was about to begin.

Turning to leave, he noticed a filing cabinet in the far corner standing in the right angle between two sets of shelves. *Might be interesting.* Why was he bothering? Time was getting on, but documents relating to old land sales and purchases might be in there. His own copy of the deeds relating to the farmhouse were held by the bank, which was closed until Tuesday. He wanted to gather as much information as possible and he wanted it now.

After a quick glance at his watch, he decided there was time to check it out. He flicked through hundreds of tightly packed files, until his fingers ached, but found nothing. Perhaps Lady Alexandra had been trying to stitch him up. Another hour and a half ticked by before, emerging dusty and empty-handed from the basement, he'd been obliged to ask Barry to let him out through a side door.

II

Warmth!

Overwhelming, blood-sucking heat from a log fire burning like a blast furnace in a grate the size of a small bedroom.

Granite walls and old sofas, deep and soft and covered with faded throws; a place furnished for comfort by a retired hobby farmer and a some-time hippy activist.

Gaynor sniffed, then gulped down the red wine. Bordeaux. The one all the locals had been buying at the supermarket. She tore a light, crispy chunk from a passing baguette, real French bread, baked that afternoon: *A jug of wine, a loaf of bread, and thou...* No 'thou' of course, Jimmy was actually on the other side of the Channel singing in a distant wilderness and Gaynor was finding this unusually relaxing.

Bron was sitting to her left, Isolde to her right; Eli and Marianne had commandeered the armchairs. They toasted their feet in the blazing heat from the fire, passed round old photo albums and chatted in a mixture of French, Breton, Welsh and English.

The men were cooking dinner, giving rise to some anxiety among the women.

'It's all right,' Bron said. 'Darren used to be a chef.'

'They'll use every pot in the place and we'll have to wash them up,' Eli scoffed.

'There's a dishwasher,' said Bron.

'Yeah, us. It's woman's lot, my dears. We have advanced from chief cook and bottle washer to sous chef and...bottle washer.'

Bron laughed. 'Don't be so cynical, Eli!'

Gaynor smiled at her. It was good to see Bron looking so bright and positive. Maybe she'd been on another of those ghastly courses. Assertiveness, self-awareness, anger management, she'd tried them all. Her blonde hair had faded to premature grey and her face was thin and lined.

Her daughter, Eirlys, flitted between the kitchen and sitting room maintaining the supplies of bread and wine. She was blonde and pale, like her mother, and even thinner. All traces of the vibrant, rebellious teenager had gone, leaving behind an air of controlled calm; an exoskeleton constructed by years of intensive therapy. Gaynor suspected an eating disorder, but dared not ask.

'So what's Jimmy up to then?' Good vibes radiated from the surface of Bron.

Gaynor took a large gulp of wine 'He's organising an event,' she said carefully, not sure which relics of their past lives could be safely resurrected.

'Still working for the council then?'

'What?' Gaynor dragged herself away from her thoughts. 'Oh, Jimmy? Not exactly. He's been outsourced to a company called Asteroid. He's Cultural Resources and Publicity Co-ordinator, apparently.' The joke passed unnoticed.

'Local authorities still have enough cash for jollies,' Gaynor added, hoping to steer the conversation into the comparatively safe waters of politics, 'and Jimmy's contacts are cheap. Folkies are grateful for modest accommodation and they don't demand expensive riders in their contracts.'

'Are you still singing?'

'No! No time. Too busy. You know how it is?'

Actually, Gaynor thought, she probably didn't. In recent years she'd been pampered and supported by the kind and stalwart, but boring, Darren.

'How about Catrin?'

Oh God! Gaynor felt cornered. Couldn't they just slag off the government, or complain about austerity and privatisation? French or British, either would do. The comparison between Catrin's brilliant prospects and the diminished Eirlys would surely cause terrible pain. Looking wildly round the room, she spotted her salvation in the form of her tablet, which she'd dumped on the window sill and forgotten about. She dragged herself off the sofa and retrieved it. 'We could Skype her now if you like.'

'That would be lovely,' Bron said.

Gaynor reclaimed her seat between Bron and Isolde and woke up the tablet.

Bron leaned over her left shoulder to look at the screen while she searched menus and tapped icons.

'I haven't seen Catrin since she was a baby.'

'Pwot!' said the tablet.

III

The doorbell grumbled again. It was old, pre-dated the Sullivans, and had not been replaced. With its moving parts housed in a damp corner of the front hall, it had developed some sort of electronic laryngitis.

Catrin dragged herself away from her dressing-table mirror once more and clumped petulantly down the stairs. She seemed to have spent most of the afternoon admitting old friends of her parents, her father's mostly, showing them to their rooms, making tea and listening to them as they informed her, in more or less patronising terms, how much she'd grown up. They would then ask her enervating questions about her future plans. Some she knew already. Terry and Frankie had turned up, lugging something called a polypin, full of beer, followed in quick succession by that hideous old letch, Miles Hollowtree, who'd made all sorts of warmish observations about her appearance.

Once pots of tea and coffee had been provided, she informed them that she was going out to a party at seven o'clock, had coursework to finish first, and left them to amuse themselves in the kitchen.

Sounds of intensive, blokeish jollity slid under the old oak door and between the floorboards, while, in her bedroom, Catrin put the finishing touches to her costume for tomorrow night's gig. The alternative prom was, suddenly, an imminent reality.

She was wearing fishnet tights under cut-off leggings and a

tight velvet bodice, laced up the front, but only so far. This revealed a low-cut, frilly blouse. With her hair tied back in a glittery headscarf, she wore shiny hooped earrings, vivid eye makeup, glitter scattered across her cheekbones, and lipstick a terrifying shade of dark blue. It was her 'Seafaring Girl' look, the image she had finally settled on as lead singer of the band. There was a touch of Weymouth on New Year's Eve about it all, a kind of psychedelic pirate. She had felt obliged to point out to her father's guests that the party was fancy dress.

Reaching the front hall, she entered polite hostess mode and opened the front door. It was Rosie.

'Wow Catrin! Cool!

'They're in the kitchen,' she whispered. 'Come upstairs quick!'

They legged it up the stairs, swift and silent, and burst through the door of Catrin's bedroom, consumed by a fit of giggles.

Rosie sobered up first. 'You look amazing, girl! You're an artist!'

'You think so?'

'Yeah! So will Chaz. He rates you, you know?'

'He does?'

'As a singer.'

Catrin looked in the mirror at the scary mask she had created. 'We all need to be rated by men, don't we?'

'No. Course not.' Rosie chose her next words as carefully as she could, 'Did Jonathan, di… Is anybody, taking, going with you to the prom?'

Catrin felt the shaft, not unkindly meant, but hurtful. But the mask said, 'Fuck it!' She studied her reflection in the mirror, 'I don't need an escort. I'm the lead singer.'

'True.' Rosie decided to change the subject: 'Is my dad here?'

Catrin nodded.

'We ought to go downstairs,' said Rosie. 'We should be keeping an eye on them.'

They both sighed.

'That man, Miles Hollowtree's there, isn't he?' Rosie asked. 'I don't want my dad doing time for GBH. He's got a down on him for some reason.'

'Yeah? Why?'

'Dunno. He takes against people sometimes, never says why. My dad, in case you hadn't noticed,' Rosie elaborated, 'suffers from verbal constipation.' To illustrate her point she hunched her shoulders and lurched around the room muttering. 'Don't like him. Don't you go near 'im…needs a kicking…where it hurts. It's not funny.' She ended her performance on a note of dark menace.

Catrin's lip trembled. 'No,' she said, ''s'fucking hilarious!'

They collapsed onto the bed in a bundle, sobbing with uncharitable mirth.

'I bet he'd escort you to the prom.'

'What? Your dad?'

'No! Miles, you dill!'

'Shut up!'

'Sorry,' said Rosie. She'd gone too far.

Not very sisterly, Catrin thought. *Something's wrong.* There was a long, awkward silence during which she scrutinised her friend from behind the mask.

'What's up?'

'Nothing.'

'Bollocks! There's something going on. We're sisters, right? I can tell.'

Rosie reached across the bed, dragged her rucksack over and pulled out an envelope, a dainty thing, expensive and tastefully decorated in one corner with a tiny pastel drawing of forget-me-nots. It was addressed to Ms Rosetta Dando.

'Your mum gave it to me,' said Rosie. 'She's tried to write to me before, but Dad must have found them. I expect he burnt them.

It's from my mother.' With studied nonchalance she flipped the envelope across the duvet. 'Want to read it?'

'No…I… It's private, isn't it?' Catrin longed to drag the neatly folded paper out of the envelope and devour its contents, but she had a feeling she probably shouldn't.

'Go on. We're sisters, aren't we? It's about how she's sorry she left me and how she'd like to meet me, so she can explain and… and all that shit.'

Catrin pulled the paper out of the envelope and read the letter, slowly, nervously, as if she were defusing a bomb. 'She keeps saying your dad's not a bad man.'

'Don't think I need her to tell me that.' Rosie sat up, straight and stiff. 'There were reasons, apparently.'

'At least she's been thinking of you.' Catrin replaced the letter in the envelope and handed it back. 'Do you want to meet her?'

'Not really. Hasn't been arsed to come looking for me until now, has she?'

Rosie clenched her jaw and put the letter back in her rucksack. Her eyes were as hard and blank as her father's.

'Finished with my copy of *Les Miz*?' she asked, trying to sound casual.

Catrin put her arm round her and she burst into tears.

'Hey!' said Catrin, 'They're idiots aren't they, so-called grown-ups. Can't let them out on their own, can you?'

Rosie sniffed. Catrin delved into a drawer and found her a tissue

'Thanks.' Rosie dabbed her eyes and blew her nose. 'Your mum's all right.'

Catrin thought about it. 'Actually,' she said earnestly, 'there's something I've got to tell her.' She sighed, keeping Rosie in suspense for a moment. 'I can't stand Molière, I mean he's just not funny, or Flaubert.'

'Rosie rubbed her eyes with the tissue and grinned. 'Oh, I dunno. The death of Madame Bovary's a hoot.'

'You heartless git! I thought you liked French literature.'

'I can read it,' Rosie said without undue modesty. 'Doesn't mean I like all of it. *Les Miz* is good.'

Catrin nodded.

'You haven't finished it yet, have you?'

Catrin admitted that she hadn't.

The sound of male voices uplifted in raucous song drifted up from the kitchen.

How we huddled roon' that wee pot stove
That burnt oily rags and coal...

It was accompanied by a whiff of burning paraffin.

Catrin strode across to the bedroom door and wrenched it open. There was a slight wuffing sound from below and wisps of blue smoke curled under the kitchen door into the hall.

'They're trying to light the Rayburn!' she yelped.

Putting their troubles behind them for the moment, they raced down the stairs.

IV

In the kitchen, the singing gave way to coughing and choking and the occasional chesty guffaw.

Terry, standing on a chair, leaned precariously over the sink and pushed and battered the window which eventually creaked open, rocking on its rusty hinges.

Frankie strode over to the Rayburn and opened the top damper. He then inspected the contents of the firebox, now roaring away like a jet engine. Seizing the hod in one hand, he threw in a load of coal before closing and fastening the door. The smoke thinned and then blew away through the window as Catrin, followed closely by Rosie, entered the kitchen.

It was a big room, but it was crowded. The numbers had been swelled by folk- club regulars who, escaping from domestic chores and Easter shopping trips, had slipped in through the back door. They had swooped on the polypin which had been carefully set up on the old Welsh dresser, the coldest corner of the kitchen and as far as possible from the Rayburn. Their glasses primed, Luke and the band were gathering between the table and the dresser taking musical instruments out of their cases and pulling chairs into an approximation of a circle, preparing to start a session. Mary and Jen, hovering over the electric kettle, were making tea.

Terry jumped off the chair, wobbling as he landed. Normally, he would have stationed himself beside the polypin, dispensing good cheer, but he was shadowing Miles. Along with other seedy habitués of smokers' corner, Miles had migrated from the perishing cold utility room to which the smokers, by common consent, had been banished, to the anticipated circle of warmth around the Rayburn, intending to restore his insulted lungs.

The degenerates, energetically wheezing and coughing, launched into a discussion of farts. Her mother, Catrin recalled, used to refer to them as 'The Brains Trust'.

''Tisn't methane,' observed one authority, 'that is animal, see? And cattle. Humans do fart hydrogen.'

Terry was impressed. 'Can you still light un then?'

'Oh, yeah. He'll burn. Bend over and drop one, Tel!' The lecturer flicked his lighter.

'Taxi!'

It was at this point in the experiment that, disturbed by the draught from the opening door, they looked up and noticed the presence of Catrin and Rosie.

'Hold on!' bawled Terry, 'There's young ladies present.' Clearly tea makers and musicians did not qualify for such an accolade.

'It's all right,' Catrin said sweetly. 'We used to do that in year seven.'

There was a momentary silence. Catrin and Rosie took in the scene. The scene, in return, took in Catrin and Rosie, most notably Catrin's more-than-festive attire. Old family friends looked at the two young women with a mixture of shock and admiration. Could they really be Jimmy's and Frankie's little girls?

Miles rose from the scruffy armchair, in which he had been seated by a solicitous Terry, and bore down on them, arms held wide.

'Catrin!'

She backed away.

'You look rather fetching.'

'Fancy-dress party,' she said, sliding through the crush in the random direction of the polypin.

'Would you like a beer?'

She shook her head. On the other side of the room, she could see Frankie watching the proceedings closely.

Rosie threaded her way through the underbrush of drunks and assorted chairs to intercept him.

'I'm sure I can find a glass somewhere,' Miles offered.

'I know where the glasses are kept, thank you. I live here.'

He laughed. His eyes twinkled at her. Was she being presumptuous, or was this old man actually chatting her up? He had, according to her father, a bit of a way with the ladies. Try as she might, Catrin could not begin to imagine how any woman could find this repulsive old husk attractive. She dodged away from Miles, who, citing long years of friendship with her parents or some other such guff, continued to insist on invading her personal space.

Thoughts of her lost, much-lamented, love invaded her mind. The perfidious Liam. How she wished he was with her now to hold her and comfort her. *How absurd! Men never do that.* But he'd see off this hideous reptile.

'Are you all right?' the reptile asked her kindly.

Oh God! Hadn't her silence driven him away? She looked Miles over, from the twinkling eyes to the sharp blue jeans and smart suede shoes. Could there be any body fluids remaining inside that desiccated insect?

The mask indicated that it would like a quick word. 'Tell him to fuck off,' it counselled her. *But,* her inner self reasoned, *he's an old mate of Dad's.* Neither love nor filial piety figured in her calculations. Her dad knew or suspected what was going on in the quarry. He could tell Mum. She loved her mum, really she did, but she wouldn't understand…

'I'm fine, thank you, Miles,' she said, cool, but polite. She moved away in the direction of the table. 'I think I'd better make sure there's enough tea and coffee.'

Miles followed her.

A soft Irish voice interrupted her thoughts. 'You all right there, Catrin?'

Liam's dad. Oh shit! 'Yeah! Fine thanks, Luke.' Catrin looked round the room desperate for some means of escape, and spotted her laptop at the far end of the table, still open, but snoozing. 'There it is!' she cried, falling upon it as if it were a lost child. 'I need to go online. Now. Got an essay to finish by…Wednesday!'

'What are you studying these days?' asked Miles, still in attendance.

'Tell him to sod off,' said the mask.

'Er,' Catrin said. Out of the corner of her eye she could see Frankie hovering at the other end of the table, inscrutable but still watching, while Rosie tried to distract him with a chicken drumstick she'd found at the back of the fridge. A deeply buried part of her mind wondered if it was still safe to eat.

'Still studying music?'

'Yes. I'm still having flute lessons.'

'Good girl! Maybe I could give you some advice?'

Catrin hesitated. It was possible that the old git might be useful. She wondered if he really did have significant connections in the business.

Rosie's voice cut across the hubbub. 'Come on, Dad! I expect you forgot to have your tea, didn't you?'

The mask was becoming restive.

'Are you sure you're all right, Catrin? Come on. You can tell me. I'm your dad's oldest friend, and your mum's. Shame they've left you here all on your own, isn't it? Would it help if we went somewhere a bit quieter?'

'There's no need' Catrin said. She turned her attention to the computer, rousing it from its slumber.

'We could have a nice, private little chat.'

The mask prevailed. Catrin turned away from the computer. Engaging the twinkling eye, she curled an indigo lip: 'You might as well do it in the road.'

Miles looked hurt, but before he could reply the computer interrupted them.

'Skype!' said Catrin. Turning away from the annoying gadfly, she clicked on the link and the screen filled with her mother's face and that of a pale, fair-haired woman.

'Hi Mum.'

'Gaynor!' cried Miles over her shoulder, 'Great to see you!'

Catrin could see her mother and Bron. They could see her and Miles. They heard as Terry, bowling across the kitchen, scattering drunks and chairs, yodelled, 'That Skype you got there, Catrin? That your mum? Hullo, Gaynor!'

The faces on the screen froze, without any help from unreliable technology.

The back door opened and Jimmy bounded in clutching a large paper parcel. 'Fish and chips anybody?'

On screen, Bron sat motionless, goggle-eyed.

Gaynor's lips moved. 'Jimmy!'

Catrin shut down the computer. While the guests fell upon Jimmy, scrumming down on fish and chips, she and Rosie fled from the kitchen and up the stairs to lock themselves in her bedroom.

Downstairs the festive spirit quickly reasserted itself. The session had begun. This time they started with the French café waltzes.

CHAPTER 14

I

She's called for a brace of pistols
That were brought at her command,
Fired and shot her false Willy
And the bride at his right hand.

Catrin sang a vehement but dutifully traditional version of 'William Taylor'. The anniversary party joined in with the chorus. *Dally dally dum, dally dum dum di do...*

Jimmy sang too, proud but puzzled. She was a gifted singer. He couldn't understand why it had been so difficult to persuade her to come along. In the end a reference to their quid pro quo arrangement had inveigled her into dropping in on the first half, en route to her second fancy-dress party of the weekend.

He was starting to unwind. The tribulations of Good Friday, the pointless search in the basement of Chine Manor, and Gaynor's furious face glaring at him from Catrin's laptop were receding into the far distance like the view at the wrong end of a telescope. There would be repercussions, but *sufficient unto the day...* Tuesday, probably, when Gaynor was expected to return.

Now it was Saturday night and the faithful had answered the call, parking in a haphazard and muddy caravanserai in the orchard, filing through the hole in the wall and marching along narrow, paths between encroaching briars, like an army of ants. They followed a trail of tea lights, suspended in jam jars from trees and bushes, through the scrub and old apple trees to the clubhouse. Some carried their most precious possessions on their heads or shoulders, out of reach of the grasping brambles: musical instruments, cushions, handbags, party food and the occasional paranoid dog.

The bar was rammed, standees six deep at the back, all cheerfully ignoring the sour odours which, in spite of Mary's intensive campaign with bleach, infiltrated from the Gents. She and Frankie had been stalwarts. They'd spent the whole day cleaning and clearing everything out of the bar that wasn't actually a serviceable seat or table, stripping out anything combustible and heaping it onto a massive bonfire at smokers' corner. Mary had brought sausage rolls and an enormous birthday cake.

Lisa and Brian had turned up during the afternoon with offers of help and a rabbit pie. Mary issued them with J-cloths and disinfectant and instructed them to wipe down the kitchen. Then they'd opened the hatch, which had groaned and resisted until Frankie battered it with his fists. The splintered edges left by his exertions were concealed behind a skein of Christmas tree lights which Jimmy had found in a box under the dining table in the farmhouse oubliette. All was set fair.

'Dally dally dum dally dum dum di do...'

Luke sidled up to Jimmy and whispered in his ear. 'Just as well our Liam's not around to hear this.'

Jimmy smiled at the joke. Projected from Catrin's navy-blue lips, 'William Taylor' had acquired a certain edge.

In spite of the heat generated by tightly packed bodies, he noted that she had not taken off her fleece. Underneath it was the skimpy top half of her pirate-wench costume; below it, fishnet tights. Cold knees seemed to be an alien concept to young women.

Rosie, who refused to sing but had joined her friend to support her, and to humour her own father, was wearing a very short skirt and a puffer jacket, but didn't appear to be in any sort of fancy dress. She was hanging around near the door trying to look interested.

Whatever they were up to Jimmy felt sure that both she and Catrin were old enough and sensible enough to look after themselves. He should probably have a quick word with her later.

Right now, though, he had a large crowd to manage. Between the acts, people squeezed past one another. Shuffling in their seats and retracting arms and legs the audience allowed other merrymakers to collect plates of food from the hatch and drinks from the bar. Some wandered out to an impromptu instrumental session which had started up at smokers' corner. Jimmy wondered if this could be seen as disrespecting the performers, but it solved the overcrowding problem. He was no fan of excessive regulations, but there were limits and the old building was straining at its seams.

From behind the hatch, Mary was watching, ready for action if anybody blundered into a musical instrument or knocked over a candle. Frankie kept to his place by the door. Between them they had it covered.

Terry's efforts on the other side of the bar were no less than heroic. He'd thrown out the cabinet under the optics, along with its long-forgotten contents, and filled the space with extra barrels of beer, now standing ready on a row of trestles. He was cheery, welcoming, and in his element.

Catrin's song was received with whoops and cheers. The crowd moved again. Other dads, on their way to the bar, shook Jimmy's hand or clapped him on the back:

'Great voice!'

'She's a lovely girl!'

'A credit to you, mate.'

'You must be so proud.'

He was. Clever, talented, confident, what else could a man ask of his daughter? *Perhaps she'll join a folk club when she goes to Cambridge.* Young people were getting into folk these days, or so he'd heard. He accepted the compliments graciously.

Catrin and Rosie headed for the door, making polite excuses to the group of well-wishers who had gathered round them congratulating Catrin and asking them both what they were planning to do with their lives. One of the group was Miles, who popped up suddenly at Catrin's side. He handed her a card. She smiled, thanked him and tucked it into a pocket before Rosie bundled her out into the porch.

'Bye, Dad!' Rosie called over her shoulder to Frankie, who had been quietly absorbing everything. He nodded to her, then stepped into the space between Miles and the door.

Jimmy looked at his list. Brian, already hovering at his elbow, was on next. He moved carefully into the spotlight to give the company one of his usual songs about poachers and their guns and the merry slaughter of wildlife. Lisa, helping Mary in the kitchen, glanced at him through the hatch, rolled her eyes and carried on with her task of filling bin liners with used paper plates. As soon as her husband had finished his song, she beckoned him to the hatch and handed him two full bags of rubbish, indicating that she wished him to take them out to the bonfire.

'Another pint then, Jimmy?'

Jimmy turned and found Miles leaning on the bar next to him. He swallowed the remains of his drink and pushed his glass across to Terry, scanning the room as he did so. Sam and Alex were on next and he'd no idea where they'd got to. After a longish pause, during which he considered changing the running order, Alex emerged from the crush.

'Hello, Miles,' Alex said.

'All right, Alex?' said Jimmy.

'I'm just waiting for my accompanist,' Alex said primly, as Sam and his guitar came into view, weaving their way towards the spotlight. He had spent most of the evening at smokers' corner.

Alex introduced Sam to Miles.

'Miles Hollowtree?' Sam exclaimed, apparently overcome.

Miles preened. 'Hi there, Sam.'

'His mum was my teacher when I was a kid,' Alex explained. 'She's a big folk fan.'

'She's got all your albums,' Sam insisted.

Jimmy assessed the situation, then, without comment, addressed the audience. 'And now we have an exciting new act. Please give it up for the wonderful Sam and Alex!'

The audience cheered as Sam and Alex took up their positions under the light.

'Already got a following then?' Miles whispered to Jimmy.

'They're really rather accomplished,' said Jimmy.

This time the couple stuck to 'Fotheringay' and Alex's top was disappointingly zipped up at the back.

As soon as the song had concluded, Sam retired as swiftly as he could to smokers' corner and Alex returned to the bar, where Miles offered her warm congratulations, adding: 'You're full of surprises, Alex.'

He turned to talk to Jimmy but he had disappeared, gone to ask Below the Salt to close the first half with a few Irish tunes. On his way back he was waylaid by old friends and collaborators.

Miles was not the only member of the folk aristocracy to have made good on his promise to appear. Mighty giants of the genre, some of whom occasionally merited recognition from the national media, had arrived without ceremony, joining the ant trail, entering the battered clubhouse and hailing Jimmy as a long-lost friend. Taking advantage of the beer break, they surrounded him, buying him drinks, gossiping and reminiscing, pausing now and again to exchange greetings with their devoted fans. In this world, Jimmy reflected, sinking a mouthful of Chedgy's, the stars mingled freely with ordinary mortals. Heaven on Earth.

II

Catrin and Rosie picked their way up the lighted path to the farmhouse carefully avoiding any brambles or thorns that could damage their party clothes, Catrin paying particular attention to her fishnet tights. They negotiated the broken-down wall, ran through the orchard, across the farmyard, past the outbuildings and through the front gate on to Crubscombe Hill, where they stopped and waited.

A short-wheelbase Land Rover, past the first flush of its youth, but tidy, drew up beside them. The window slid down and Tekky Di stuck her head out, grinning.

'Done your set for the old farts, then?' she asked Catrin.

'Aced it!'

'Don't worry about them,' said Rosie, 'they're all pissed.'

Di was impressed. 'Already? What are your dads like?'

'Pissed,' said Catrin.

They climbed into the passenger seats. 'This your dad's?' Rosie asked Di.

'It's his third best limo.'

'Cool,' said Rosie. 'Can you get it into the quarry?'

'Easy,' Di reassured her. 'Me and the lads have made a big hole in the fence by Green Lane.'

'That's not a road,' Catrin pointed out.

Di crunched the gears and started off down the hill. 'No problem. This thing's been driven across Siberia.'

III

Jimmy had decided to give most of the second half to the professionals. Anticipating greatness, the majority of the party-goers crammed themselves into the clubhouse.

'I hope you can still breathe,' Jimmy warned his old friends. They laughed. Terry offered them free beer, but most declined. They would have to slip away early to headline paid gigs in Bath or Bristol or Chippenham, or to drive overnight to concerts and festivals further afield. Jimmy felt deeply honoured.

'Wouldn't miss this for anything,' an old pro enthused. 'It's one of the best clubs in the country.'

'Authentic,' another concurred, looking round at the primitive furnishings and unprepossessing décor. 'Not many clubs like these left anymore.'

There was a general shaking of heads.

'You're doing a grand job, Jimmy.'

Jimmy looked at his watch and called for quiet. 'And now, in no particular order, as I believe they say in 'Strictly Come Dancing', we'll kick off the second half with Danny Donellan!'

Rotund and cheery, Danny Donellan moved into the spotlight. 'You going to join me in the dance-off then, Jimmy?'

The crowd laughed and cheered.

Jimmy executed an ill-advised pirouette and crashed into a table. Miles grabbed him by the collar, pulling him upright and preventing any further damage.

The second half flew on blissfully towards midnight, surfing a tide of old favourites: raucous crowd-pleasers, tragic ballads and tender love songs.

Carla James, dropping in on her way to The Cause in Chippenham, temporarily subdued the masses, stunning them to silence with 'The Riddle Song'.

My head is an apple without any core.
My mind is a room without any door.
My heart is a palace wherein she may be,
And she can unlock it without any key

Gaynor used to sing it too. A man's song really, but she'd sing it anyway because she loved the tune and the mysterious lyric. Jimmy put a hand over his mouth, hiding any embarrassing signs of emotion. *Must be getting sentimental in my old age*, he told himself. Reviving, he looked round from one enraptured face to the next, all evoking different images and dreams.

At midnight, Jimmy finished off the second half in traditional style by leading a passionate rendition of 'Wild Mountain Thyme':

And we'll all go together
To pick wild mountain thyme
All among the purple heather
Will ye go lassie go.

The whole party swayed and roared in happy harmony. When the last chorus ended with a long diminishing note, they cheered and stamped till glasses bounced on the table tops and the windows rattled. It was a triumph.

Jimmy thanked everyone for coming and announced that there was plenty of beer left and that the third half would begin after a short break.

A heaving mass of people pressed in on him, shaking his hand and hugging him. They thanked him for a brilliant night before gathering up their outdoor clothes and leaving. They were replaced around the bar by dedicated musicians, refuelling for the third half, and unregenerate late-night drinkers.

Alex made her way through them, approaching Jimmy and indicating that she wanted a word.

'Wonderful night, Jimmy,' she gushed. 'It must have brought back some memories.' The big blue eyes twinkled. 'Youthful indiscretions?'

'Not on my part,' Jimmy said sternly. 'I'm a one-woman man.'

'But you know about people, don't you, Jimmy?'

'I'm afraid your husband's world and mine haven't overlapped for more than thirty years.'

'You sure, Jimmy?'

Jimmy thought it best to change the subject.

'Where's your boyfriend?'

'Over there, with the musicians. We can't…you know…?' Her eyes filled with tears; her rosy lips quivered.

The musicians were gathered into a circle in the middle of the room. Led by Luke, they started playing the French café waltzes.

'Why don't you go and have a chat with Miles?' He put an avuncular arm round her shoulders intending to steer her towards the back wall, near the entrance to the Gents, where Miles was chatting to his fans. 'He's well pissed. You never know what he might let slip.'

They were distracted by a scuffling sound coming from the porch, then a voice called out, something indistinct. The door burst open.

There were gasps and exclamations as Bron charged into the crowd wild- eyed and vengeful, like the monster Grendel's mother. A heartbeat behind her was Gaynor, breathless and agitated. She caught sight of Jimmy and Alex and stopped.

With a guilty start Jimmy let his arm drop.

Alarm swept through the room.

Bron was carrying a shotgun. She took another step forward and halted. The nearest partygoers stepped back. She grasped the weapon tightly in her right hand and slowly moved her gaze left and right, raking the ranks of the merrymakers with a fearsomely concentrated glare

Then, locating Miles, she put the gun to her eye, levelled it and took aim.

It took a while, or so it seemed, for those at the front of the room to grasp the reality of the situation. 'Les Amantes Infideles' ran down like a watch with a broken spring, stopping finally when the last box player, jabbed in the ribs by Luke, looked up and squeezed his instrument into an involuntary rasping death rattle. Conversation thinned and died, leaving only Terry, jocund and flowing freely as the chestnut-coloured beer he was drawing off the latest barrel of Chedgy's, to observe to Jimmy: 'You watch her Ladyship here don't burst her buttons again.'

Jimmy, meanwhile, was thinking, trying to lay out a plan in nanoseconds. He caught Gaynor's eye fleetingly. It said 'See me!' in bright red ink. Quailing, but not, he hoped, visibly, he filed it under 'later'. He stared at Bron and the gun. *How much damage could it actually do, and at what distance?* As far as he knew these things were designed to kill smallish birds.

'Hello Bron,' he said, trying to sound calm.

Bron swung round, training the gun on him. Somebody screamed, then somebody else. People shouted, grabbed one another and dived under the nearest available item of furniture. Those closest to the door fled out into the night and the confusing, tangled byways of the quarry, apart from Frankie, who stood motionless, watching, waiting for his chance.

Exploiting the distraction, Miles did a bunk into the Gents. Bron careered after him, singers, musicians and drinkers scrambling away from her like small animals in the path of a forest fire. Jimmy sprang after her. Gaynor sprang after Jimmy.

'Jimmy! Stop! You idiot!'

Spotting the fury in her eyes, he wondered why she was bothering about his safety.

'What are you doing here?' he said, keeping his voice as low as possible in the midst of all the shouting and shrieking and the crashing of overturned furniture.

'She wants to kill him!'

'How did she get that gun through customs?'

'She found it...you...you idiot! It was on the back seat of a Land Rover belonging to one of your damn fool friends. It was in our orchard!'

Jimmy stopped for a moment, trying to think of something to say. Finding nothing, he slid round the door into the dank passageway that led to the Gents. Gaynor followed him, then Frankie, then Terry. Trembling, but stealthy, he waved his phone around looking for a signal.

Shouts and imprecations could be heard emanating from the urinal. Light escaped round the door, which had not been properly closed for half a century. They crept towards it, froze as if in one single, solid mass, and listened.

'You evil, rotten, incontinent, manipulative, shagabout bastard!' Bron shrieked.

Jimmy pushed the door.

'Don't!' Gaynor hissed.

'She's not going to do it, is she?' whispered Jimmy. Peering round the door he could see Miles with his back pressed into the jakes, white shirt absorbing mossy slime and other more recent deposits. His eyes flitted leftwards now and again towards the rotten door of the fire exit, while Bron glared over the top of the shotgun with narrowed eyes.

'Can you actually kill somebody with one of those?' Jimmy asked. He turned, looking for a response, and saw Frankie for the first time. Frankie nodded, but said nothing.

'You ruined Eirlys. Wrecked her life...my little girl!'

'Bron?' Miles' voice, hoarse and sepulchral, echoed round the bleak, damp cavern.

'Oh Christ, Miles!' Jimmy murmured, 'Don't argue with her.'

'You raped her!'

'She was sixteen. It was consensual.'

'You don't get it, do you?' Bron's voice had become calm and level as the shotgun. 'This isn't about the law, Miles.'

Desperately, Miles tried sweet reason: 'It was a commune. Open relationships? It's what we all believed in, free love. That's how it was in those days.'

Silence.

Miles pursued what appeared to be his advantage. 'I still think about you, Bron, and Eirlys. I loved you, you know? Both of you. It was fun, wasn't it?' The old charm seemed to be working. Miles decided to press home his point with a little philosophy: 'The world's changed, Bron, and not for the better. People have become mean-spirited and narrow-minded.'

Bron's jaw tightened. 'Save it for your phoney song lyrics, Miles. My…my …little girl…you broke her heart. She was a child. She was infatuated, like they all are, and you're not going to do it again.' She took aim, carefully, coldly.

Jimmy pushed the door wide open, distracting Bron as her finger squeezed the trigger. The report seemed to fill the available space, crashing through Jimmy's eardrums, temporarily emptying his mind of all thought, while Miles, lunging and ducking to his right, reached the emergency exit. He kicked it then put his shoulder to it. The rusty iron bar suddenly gave way, tipping him out into the tangled mess behind the clubhouse. Bron fired again at the Miles-shaped hole in the shattered door, but he'd gone. The air was thick with smoke and fragments of vitreous china.

Jimmy and Frankie rushed in to the urinal and fell upon Bron before she had a chance to reload. Terry, fiddling with his phone, retreated to the bar.

Frankie wrenched the shotgun from Bron's right fist. Breaking it swiftly, he hurled it to one side. Then he took off his coat and wrapped it round Bron, who had sunk to the floor in a sobbing, quivering heap. He raised her gently to her feet and handed her over to Gaynor, who directed an ice-cold parting glance at Jimmy which seemed to promise vengeance and death. She took her friend's arm and led her away. The others followed them through the now deserted and wreckage-strewn clubhouse.

Terry was standing on the bar talking into his mobile phone. He broke off briefly with reassuring news: ''Tis all right. I have called the police.' He turned again to the phone. 'Yeah! Yeah! We'm at the old quarrymen's clubhouse in Crubscombe.'

'For Christ's sake, Terry!' Jimmy yelled, 'There's no need...'

'She've got a gun,' Terry advised the operator.

Frankie, crossing the intervening space in one bound, hauled Terry off the counter, twisted the phone out of his hand, threw it on the ground and stamped on it.

The three men stood like statues, dumbstruck.

'Look what he've done to my phone,' Terry wailed.

IV

Miles stumbled.

Panic and darkness had caused him to lose his bearings. He'd crashed out of the fire door and bolted across the car park in a straight line until he found a path. Soon, he realised his route to freedom was coated with slippery mud and strewn with loose branches, stones and brambles. Seemingly guided by some malevolent intelligence of Middle Earth, sharp prickles tore at his clothes and hair and tried to wrap themselves round his ankles. He couldn't see any of it.

Above him, a pale glow indicated the presence of a waning moon behind the cloud cover. Otherwise, there was no light. The earth beneath him lay somewhere at the bottom of a fathomless black pool. His ears were ringing and he wasn't quite sure that Bron's second fusillade hadn't hit parts of his fleeing extremities. No time to check, only to hope that he wouldn't bleed to death before re-emerging into civilisation. He appeared to be going downhill, descending into God knows what.

Attempting to right himself, he planted his free foot on what should have been the next step on the path. There was nothing there. He grabbed at dry brambles which pricked his fingers and instantly tore away from their shallow moorings, pitching him head first down the invisible slope. He rolled, he bounced, he grabbed and slithered, until, after a moment, or more, of oblivion, he found himself lying on a level area of damp gravel.

He reached out a hand and swiftly retracted it. *Water!* Slowly, he raised his spinning head and peering through the minimal light afforded by the cloud-covered moon realised that he was lying on the edge of a hellish mere which, though there appeared to be no winds to drive it, lapped against the shore as if something large and hostile was awakening in its oily deeps. To his left he could just make out sheer black rocks, like knife blades. The cliffs of the Boundary Stone Rock.

His heart thudded, driven on and on by some external rhythm that was no part of him. His head, having apparently doubled in size, throbbed. Surely it, or possibly his chest, was about to explode. He groaned, closed his eyes, but the darkness kept spinning. Perhaps he was dead, lying in the pit of hell?

He patted his head, neck, ribs, abdomen, limbs, buttocks, but though there was mud and vegetation attached to him in various places, he could find no potential sources of blood. He opened his eyes, tried to focus, and raised himself tentatively into a sitting position. Somewhere on the horizon there were lights; gold, then red, then orange. A woman's voice, in his head, or outside it, he wasn't sure, started to sing. It bounced off the cliff and floated back and forth across the lake:

Down...Down...Down he fell
From the soaring heights
To the pit of hell.

She was singing about him! He must be dead. They were welcoming him to hell. It was so unfair. He hadn't been a bad man, not really. Women liked him. He was kind to them. He made them happy. It was unfortunate that they all wanted a piece of him. This, he reasoned, was the price of fame. Better get on with it, he supposed, find out where he was exactly, He rose to his feet, still trembling. His head weighed a ton and he couldn't be entirely certain if he was operating inside it, or merely balancing it on his shoulders. He put up his left hand to support it in case it decided to drop off and roll away into the hostile vegetation.

Down... Down... Down... mocked the voice. It was followed by a deep rumbling roar, rhythmic, penetrating every bone in his body. The wrath of God was in it.

Somehow, he made his way round the edge of the lake until his feet found another path leading in the general direction of the voice. He staggered forward, supporting his aching head with one hand and fending off vengeful, clinging plant life with the other. Might as well present himself to whoever was in charge. The path widened and flattened. The vegetation receded. Corroded steel rails appeared at his feet and the occasional half-buried wooden sleeper lay in muddy hollows waiting to trip him up.

The air pulsated with insistent rhythm as the rails guided his feet onwards, to stop abruptly at the top of a steep gravelly slope. Below was the floor of the dry quarry where he could see the denizens of the after-life sitting around on old or improvised furniture or queuing at a barbecue. On the far side of the quarry, a small crowd had gathered in front of a makeshift stage, rigged with impressively professional-looking banks of lights, flashing gold, then red, then orange, where a pretty girl was singing to a heavy menacing beat, embellished with drum rolls, sinister wailing guitar riffs and general weirdness from an electronic keyboard.

It seemed to be a rock gig. Not his field of expertise, but an explanation of sorts. The girl had a terrific voice but she was doing some strange and terrible things with it in a way that that seemed to be the fashion these days. The voice swam round in his inflated head. The bass jarred his spine. Suddenly, the song crashed to a halt in a single juddering chord.

The girl breathed into her mic through indigo lips, 'Cool Milton.'

She looked familiar. Which of the hideous modern rock 'n' roll pantheon had died recently?

Miles tried to get a grip. He knew about music, for god's sake. It was prog stuff, early seventies. The keyboard player clearly wanted to be Rick Wakeman. Was this his punishment, to be marooned in a prog rock gig for all eternity? The girl was dressed like some sort of pirate. The fog that had become a permanent feature of his vision lifted momentarily. It was Catrin. Jimmy's Catrin.

He tottered over the edge of the slope, tripped and slid down it, arriving in a filthy, undignified heap beside the barbecue. After a moment spent attempting to salvage his wits and his dignity, he looked up and saw a young black girl who was talking to the proprietor of the barbecue. She seemed to be ordering food for the band. His mind reverted to default. His eyes ran up her legs, nice! Her face swam into view. Very pretty, familiar somehow, with some association of danger which he could not quite pin down. Intrigued and, by now, barely conscious, he reached for the forbidden fruit. He smiled.

The girl favoured him with a hard stare which, for some reason, reminded him of Frankie Dando. 'Just dropping in then, Miles?'

'Rosie?' He knelt before her and tried to take her hand. 'What you doing in hell?'

Rosie forked a charred sausage off the barbecue and dropped it on to a cardboard plate. 'Bugger off, Miles!'

A cheerful stoner, who had been standing behind Rosie in the food queue, took an interest at this point. 'Hey Rosie – that's a bit harsh!'

'Huh!' said Rosie.

'He's just an old man.'

'Beautiful voice, Catrin,' Miles observed genially, hoping to strike the right note.

Gently, the stoner helped him to his feet, 'Here, mate, have some of this.' He waved a fat, sweet-smelling joint under Miles' nose.

Miles accepted. Taking a grateful drag, he looked at his rescuer. Huge, kind, concerned eyes gazed out at him from rings of glittering mascara. Very pretty, but it seemed to be a boy in a dress. Miles was beyond asking questions.

Rosie shoved her face into his: 'Don't you even think of going anywhere near Catrin.'

'My dear, as if I...'

'You degenerate old nonce!'

Miles swayed in the arms of his rescuer. His eyes scanned the horizon, searching for a fixed point with which to steady himself. His headache was easing, but the lights on the periphery of his vision seemed to be turning blue.

V

As smoke and unpleasant airborne particles cleared in the shot-up urinal, Jimmy and Frankie returned to view the damage. Through the broken fire door, they could hear faint cries and retreating footsteps fanning out from the scene of the crime. Gaynor, Bron and the remnants of the folk club were fleeing, groping their way through the woody scrub behind the clubhouse, seeking the path back to the orchard. The tea lights were long dead.

'Best to be somewhere else,' Jimmy suggested.

They went back into the bar, where Terry had picked up the remains of his phone and was trying to put them back together. 'I expect the coppers will be here soon,' he reassured them.

Frankie glared at him.

'Not a good idea really, Tel,' Jimmy said gently. 'You overreacted a bit there, didn't you?'

'But...?'

'They'll be tooled up like the Los Angeles Police Department. They'll shoot at anything that moves, and ask questions later, especially when they see all this evidence.' He looked round at the overturned and destroyed furniture and spilled drinks. With difficulty he held down the imprecations that were threatening to break through his outward appearance of calm. 'Better get out of here before they arrive,' he said grimly, before finding his coat and going out into the car park.

Frankie followed him, but Terry stayed where he was, still trying to repair his phone. 'I'll give them another call shall I, Jimmy?' he shouted after them, 'Tell them not to bother?'

Frankie took a small but powerful torch from one of the pockets in his padded jacket. Its beam swept over the car park, the smouldering remains of the bonfire at smokers' corner and played along the length of the rotting fence at the edge of the quarry.

'What about *him*?' Frankie said.

'Miles?'

Frankie nodded.

'He'll be long gone,' Jimmy said. He didn't know what to think about Miles, or who to believe.

The torch beam moved on to the end of the fence and lingered on the gap where its final section had long since been torn aside. This was the access to an informal path which intrepid explorers had made over the slumped and scrubbed-up edge of the quarry down to the Lower Pool.

Frankie strode across the car park to take a closer look. 'Somebody's been down here.' He trained the light onto recently snapped branches and trampled mud. 'It wasn't like that before.'

Jimmy thought he could see the imprint of Miles' elegant and distinctive leather boots.

'We ought to find him. Give him to the police,' Frankie pronounced.

'He hasn't done anything illegal, mate. Appalling, but...'

'I'll sort him out then.' Frankie pushed through the gap in the fence, splintering twigs of elder and bramble.

'No!' Jimmy cried. 'For Christ's sake, man! Do you want to be done for assault and battery?'

Frankie shrugged.

'They'd arrest Bron as well,' Jimmy wheedled.

'She hasn't done wrong.'

'I know. It's not fair, but it's the law.' Jimmy put a restraining hand on his friend's arm. Frankie shook it off and started walking steadily but cautiously down the path with an unexpected agility and turn of speed.

Heart thumping, beer still sloshing round his guts, Jimmy slithered after him. His eyes were trained on what he could see of the slippery path, his mind searching for any possible means of preventing one old friend from murdering another.

From somewhere in the direction of Earwick Quarry, there came a deep, repetitive, pulsating thud. Looking up for a moment Jimmy thought he could see flashing lights. His foot slipped and he was obliged to grab the back of Frankie's jacket to steady himself.

Back at the clubhouse Mary, who had taken refuge in the

kitchen, emerged. Picking her way through the bar to the door, she saw the two men's headlong flight into the bushes and stood, watching their progress until they disappeared from view and their voices could no longer be heard. Then she went back into the clubhouse, took her coat from the hook on the kitchen door and followed them. '*Stupid bloody men!*'

VI

The police operation was not progressing well. Excited and prepared, firearms issued to certain personnel, helmets, visors and bullet-proof vests allocated to all, they advanced upon the scene of the crime. The helicopter was circling the target area, probing it with a powerful searchlight. Satnavs primed, but weirdly inoperative, the crack troops had eventually arrived at the entrance to the old clubhouse car park, to find it locked. The gates were secured with a hefty padlock and topped with rolls of barbed wire. A row of massive limestone boulders, each of which might as well have been a separate mountain peak, had been placed in front of them.

The helicopter circled low. All over Crubscombe people woke and rose from their beds to watch the unfolding drama. It circled again, its formidable searchlight picking out a row of solid grey miners' cottages where an illuminated window had been flung open and an elderly woman, partly covered by a red dressing gown, was leaning out at a terrifying angle.

Lights came on all along the row. More windows opened.

Gazing up into the blinding white light, the woman in red waved and cried out to the downdraught, to her neighbours and to anybody else who might be listening, ''Tis our Paul! Hello Paul! What you'm up to then, love? 'Tis the Police helicopter,' she informed them. 'Our Paul's one of the crew.'

Inside the aircraft, Paul Edwards informed his superior officer that he thought he could see signs of suspicious activity down in the old quarries, somewhere near Earwick. The helicopter wheeled and departed.

On the ground, the armed response unit dropped shoulders and charged one of the recently fortified gates. They bounced off it. Determined to defuse a nasty public relations issue, Aggrementos had not stinted on materials. Though fully armed and expensively accoutred the doughty coppers could not raise a set of bolt cutters between them. They debated the possibility of shooting off the lock, but desisted, repelled by the possibility of the resulting paperwork. As they regrouped for another charge, a lowly crime car drew up among the gleaming armoured minibuses. A world-weary sergeant got out. Swiftly appraising the situation, he fished a bundle of felonious-looking tools out of the glove compartment. He pushed his way through the confused mob of space cadets to the gates and picked the lock. Pulling the massive chain away from the fence with one long, slow, scornful movement of his left hand, he pushed the gates gently inwards.

'After you, boys and girls.'

'What about the vehicles, sarge?'

'You'll have to walk, you lazy young bastards.'

Bereft of its shell, the armed response unit advanced cautiously through the gates into the blackness beyond. They trained the beams of their powerful torches on the writhen thorn trees and brambles which grew along the edge of the quarry pit. The eyes of startled beasts flashed, sudden pinpricks of green or blue light, as their owners slunk away into formless thickets.

Used to operating in the mean streets of Easton or St Paul's, or even Twerton and Snow Hill, the squad was becoming nervous. Nevertheless, they pressed on, whispering among themselves as they followed the track to the clubhouse car park.

'Where the fuck are we?'

'Are we still in the UK?'

'Christ knows! Are we still on Earth?'

The clubhouse, when they eventually found it, was illuminated from insanitary kitchen to shattered urinal but completely deserted. Returning to the car park from a cautious search of the premises one of the officers remarked: 'It's like the bleedin' Marie Celeste.'

Before the mystery could be investigated any further, an urgent call came over the radio. 'Large crowd of people in Earwick Quarry, looks like a rave, calling for back-up.'

This was more like it. 'The squad raced back up the track and sprang into their vehicles. They might not need their shooters, but at least they'd see some action.

VII

Frankie and Jimmy arrived on the stony beach beside the Lower Pool. Miraculously, both were still on their feet. Frankie shone his torch over loose stones and shingle, looking for footprints, but there were none. He stood still for a moment, reviewing his options, then took off for the abandoned track to Earwick Quarry, the only other way out. Jimmy followed him round the edge of the pool, lurching over jagged shards of rock and sliding scree, until he reached the comparatively smooth surface of the old railway. By this time, Frankie was well ahead of him, loping forwards like a big cat scenting its prey.

Jimmy ran, stopping now and again to catch his breath and rub his knee. In the middle distance, and by his hazy calculations the bottom of Earwick Quarry, he could see coloured lights flashing and dancing to the rhythmic thuds that were now resolving themselves into some sort of music. He thought he could hear a woman singing. The voice was familiar. A picture of what might be waiting for them at the end of the track began to form in his mind.

'For God's sake, mate,' he shouted after Frankie. 'Calm down!'

Often, in the past, this sort of timely advice had worked, but this time Frankie would not be deflected from his purpose. He rushed onwards.

Gulping in air and ignoring his aching knee, Jimmy ran faster. He thought furiously, but to little effect.

Miles was a bit of a tart, everybody knew that, and it was possible that Bron had been exaggerating, imagining things, even. She was a catastrophist, informed by the sort of crazy ideas people now described as conspiracy theory. Eirlys had been wild, impossible. She had bunked off school, going to hang out with a bunch of junkies in some rat-infested den in Bath. It was Miles who'd brought her back to the farmhouse, chastened and repentant. And then... Jimmy stopped running. He bent double, gasping...and then...? *Surely not...not under my roof...!*

As oxygen returned to his circulation, he began to think more rationally. If anything had happened, Gaynor would have known. Of course she would. Whatever the truth of the matter, violent reprisals would not be helpful.

He straightened up. He could now see the far end of Earwick Quarry in some detail and the music was becoming clearer. Someone was singing a song from an ancient album by Jethro Tull. Staring intently into the multicoloured lights he recognised his daughter.

What was a kid doing singing this? Perhaps what had attracted them to the song was an opportunity for the lead guitarist to show off, and for the crazy flute solo that Catrin had now started playing. Jimmy listened, lending his daughter and her band a professional ear. They were a bit rough – young and amateurish – but they were promising, especially Catrin. Jimmy was entranced. He looked round the quarry, at the lights, sound system and mixing desk. They'd put all this together from nothing. 'Respect' as the kids said nowadays. A crowd of youngsters, gathered in what he understood was called the mosh pit, seemed equally enraptured. Some swayed, some embraced and all seemed to be holding a small brightly lit rectangle above their heads. Their phones, Jimmy saw. They were filming the performance, themselves and each other. He looked again at the stage and the young woman singing behind all that terrifying makeup and realised that it was possible he no longer knew her.

He caught up with Frankie at the top of the gravelly bank where the ground had slumped to the quarry floor, abruptly shearing off the railway line. Below it, in a pool of light created by draping skeins of electric bulbs over the encroaching bushes, there was a trestle table covered in cans and bottles, various kinds of seating (including Frankie's old sofa) and a barbecue. In the centre of this space, clearly lit by gently swaying light bulbs, was Rosie, apparently engaged in conversation with a strange-looking youth and Miles.

Frankie grunted and started down the slope. Jimmy grabbed his arm. He dug his heels into the gravel, but the forward motion of a large and very angry man could not be resisted. Jimmy was dragged along like a piece of light luggage, his flailing feet trying to maintain contact with the ground. Eventually he let go. Momentum carried him down the bank until he landed on his knees at the bottom. His ears picked up the whining chuckle of an approaching helicopter. Suddenly alert, he stood up and looked around. On a distant horizon, somewhere in the direction of Earwick village, he could just see flashing blue lights.

A chill wind blew suddenly over the alternative prom, fingering the crowd in the mosh pit, whipping round Diana and her acolytes at the mixing desk, and moving on to the performers on stage. Phones were lowered and clamped to anxious ears. All along the little watchtowers the messages spread. The band stopped playing with a kind of truncated thump. Panic set in. The party broke up, scattering into the wooded spoil dumps and scrubbed-up pathways. Diana jumped into the Land Rover, roared through and round the fleeing fans until she reached the stage, where she picked up all the band members, apart from Chaz, who ran towards his bike. She drove away from the advancing blue lights, towards the Crubscombe end of the quarry, disappeared into the bottom of a worked-out lava flow and stopped the engine. Jimmy could hear doors opening and slamming as the kids got out and fled into the labyrinthine workings.

None of this had any impact on Frankie, who, intent on protecting his daughter and administering justice for Eirlys, bore down upon Miles.

Noticing the disturbance, Rosie looked over Miles' shoulder.

'Dad!'

Frankie closed in.

'No…don't…Dad…for Christ's sake…!'

Reaching out one massive hand, Frankie grabbed Miles by the collar of his sodden white shirt. His grip tightened as he drew back his free fist, trying to decide which bone to break first.

Miles choked.

A small figure careered down the gravel slope. Skidding to a halt at Frankie's side, it seized the upraised arm and, using all the force of the intended blow, sent him sprawling onto his face in the dirt, releasing his grip on the astonished and terrified Miles as he fell.

Miles took his chance. He tottered away in the general direction of the fleeing teenagers until he reached the middle of the quarry floor. Here, stumbling on a half-buried iron rail, he fell into a low pile of damp scalpings and gave up. In as much as decision was still possible, he decided to wait and see what might happen next.

Frankie raised his head. He glared through a red mist at his departing prey and then turned to identify and deal with his assailant. He rose to his feet and, stooping upon a small person in a long woollen coat, found himself taking aim at Mary. He bit his tongue instead.

Mary folded her arms, wishing to indicate disapproval. 'Behave yourself, Frankie!'

'Arrrgh!' said Frankie.

'The police are on their way, my dear.'

'You?' whispered Frankie.

'I've been studying the martial arts for more than ten years, Frankie. I hope you didn't mind.' She took hold of his arm again, this time tenderly.

Jimmy stood on the sidelines following his friend's every move with rising anxiety. He wouldn't, would he? No. He would never hit a woman. He was looking down at Mary completely tongue-tied. Nothing unusual there, but there was something unfamiliar in his expression. Respect? Humility, even?

'I didn't knock you down, my love. Your own anger did that.'

Frankie stared at her. It was all too complicated.

'Come on,' Mary said.

Frankie turned to talk to Rosie.

A motorbike was approaching across the floor of the quarry. Roaring and puttering, it pulled up at Rosie's side, the rider holding out a helmet. Rosie hesitated for a moment and then, love triumphing over filial piety, put on the helmet and sprang onto the back of the bike.

'Rosie!' Frankie's cry was drowned out as the bike tore across the quarry, bouncing over tussocks and small dirt heaps and the half-buried remains of dismantled industrial plant. It raced towards hidden paths and trackways, looking for a hiding place or a way out.

Mary took hold of Frankie's arm and led him gently up the gravel slope as the police, finding one of the breaches in the fence made earlier by Diana and her crew, started pouring onto the site of the doomed Promdemonium.

Jimmy reckoned that it was time for him to make his own escape. He guessed that Catrin and the other youngsters would be making their way home through the wooded canyons and hidden tracks of the old quarry workings and decided to do the same. The prospect of what might await him at the farmhouse filled him with dread but he needed to get there in time to intercept Catrin before she was interviewed by her mother.

When the police reached the crime scene, they found it deserted.

VIII

Blue lights flickered and swirled in the road in front of the Old Manor Farmhouse, raking through the orchard, picking out the ruts and mires from which most of the erstwhile folk-club patrons had reclaimed their vehicles. The police seemed to be everywhere. Mary had said goodnight in front of the deserted clubhouse and had taken Frankie away to a cup of tea and a bowl of warming soup at her place, leaving Jimmy to negotiate the path to the orchard alone.

He clambered through the gap in the wall, ducking away from the lights. The orchard itself was quiet. There were still one or two abandoned cars, but no one seemed to be around. He could see a light on in the kitchen and flashes from a television screen. Hopefully Catrin had got home safely.

Jimmy crept through the trees towards the blue lights, then stopped abruptly. He thought he could hear voices coming from the front of the house. He wasn't quite sure at this stage if he was a wanted man, so he decided it would be best to keep out of sight. Creeping out of the orchard and across the farmyard, he took refuge in an outbuilding, from which he could see a squad car parked in the front drive and a couple of vans loitering in the road, emergency lights revolving in an idle manner as if someone had forgotten to switch them off.

The front door opened.

'Thank you, Gaynor,' said a formal-sounding voice. Jimmy was sure he'd heard it before, but discretion prevailed. He needed to know what Gaynor had said to the police before he talked to them himself. He stood still and listened.

'Goodnight.' Gaynor's voice. It sounded cross and tired.

The front door slammed shut and the crash of three huge iron bolts being rammed home followed. Jimmy hadn't realised they still worked. She must have smashed them out of their corroded beds with a hammer.

The copper, a senior-looking type, definitely officer class, put on a peaked cap and headed towards the car. Then both he and Jimmy became aware of a rustling in the vegetation under the trees behind the house, sounds of ineffectual creeping. Something large and confused, and very stupid, was lurching towards the back door of the farmhouse, where it stopped.

'Jimmy,' it croaked, in what it seemed to think was a discreet undertone.

Jimmy turned. In the light from the kitchen window, he could see Terry. He was carrying the shotgun. Jimmy broke cover and ran across the yard frantically signalling to him to ditch the gun.

'I have got the gun, mate,' Terry whispered proudly. 'Didn't think I ought to leave it at the club. Someone might of found it. I was going to put it back in Brian's Land Rover, only...'

'Shuttup!' hissed Jimmy. He grabbed Terry by the arm and dragged him towards the back door, fishing in his pockets for his keys with his free hand.

'...it's gone.' Terry concluded, 'He must of come back and drove it home.'

Jimmy found his back door key, shoved it desperately into the lock and turned it. The door wouldn't budge. She'd bolted that one too. He hammered on the door, 'Gaynor! Catrin!'

Powerful torch beams surrounded them.

'Armed police! Throw down your weapon!'

Terry felt this was a tad unjust: ''Tisn't mine,' he protested.

'Do it! Now!'

Guns were closing in on them in a tightening circle. *Some sort of automatic rifles*, Jimmy speculated, but the distraction of near panic made him unsure.

'Throw them the gun, you pillock!' Jimmy advised Terry.

'Oh, all right then.' Terry threw the shotgun on to the ground.

'Lie down!'

'What?'

'Lie down!' Jimmy hissed.

They lay down flat on their faces while visored policemen felt them up, not sparing even the most intimate places, looking for concealed weapons. Satisfied at last, they hauled Jimmy and Terry to their feet and handcuffed them.

The man in the peaked cap advanced into the torchlit circle to inspect his catch. He frowned and, after a moment's thought, said, 'Hello, Jimmy.'

'Colin?' Jimmy said. 'Detective Inspector Jameson?'

'Commander,' Colin informed him, with just a hint of smugness, Jimmy thought.

'Still playing the box, Colin?'

The commander became uneasy, 'Now and again, Jimmy, er, duties permitting. You know how it is.'

Jimmy smiled. 'I don't think I've seen you since the CID annual dinner dance in…oh… Great night, wasn't it? Exciting.'

'Great band, Jimmy. You still gigging?'

'When was that, ninety-one…ninety-two…?'

'Another time Jimmy. Another county.'

'It was on a boat, wasn't it?' Jimmy reminisced. 'On the Thames because, as I recall, the event had been banned by every pub in the district.'

The Armed Response Unit turned to look at their commander, helmeted ears cocked.

'It was quite a hooley,' Jimmy prattled, chuckling at the memory, 'the Thames Valley Cops…'

The commander ordered the handcuffs to be removed.

'All a complete misunderstanding of course. As your colleagues realised as soon as…'

The commander told his men to put Terry in a squad car. 'Find out where he lives and take him home,' he instructed them. 'Tell him to stay there.' Then he and Jimmy sat down on a low wall in the cowshed to reminisce and look for a solution to the present misunderstanding.

IX

Miles opened his eyes hoping to see some improvement in his immediate environment, but, if anything, it had got worse. His head still ached, the lights were still there, yellow red and orange and now they had been joined by blue and white ones. Through the incandescent mists a hulking humanoid figure, helmeted, his visored face reflecting red and orange light, clothed from head to foot in what looked like black leather, was coming for him. The devil himself! It reached out a gauntleted hand and attempted to raise him to his feet. It said something about Nick.

Old Nick? At last he might find out what fate awaited him for all eternity.

'You do not have to say anything,' the Devil informed him, 'but anything you do say may be taken down and used in evidence against you.'

X

Alone once more in the cowshed, Jimmy reviewed his triumph. The coppers had departed. Colin, the commander, apparently satisfied with his explanation.

As Jimmy understood it, somebody, kids probably, had broken into a vehicle which had been parked in the farmyard and stolen the gun plus a few rounds – probably wanted to have a go at shooting rabbits in the quarry, but they had been disturbed by his wife and her friend, returning from an Easter break in France, and had dropped the gun and legged it. Gaynor's friend had picked up the gun and brought it to the club for safekeeping, not realising that it was loaded. Women, Jimmy pointed out, don't know anything about guns. His old friend had agreed. Unfortunately, Terry, not the sharpest knife in the box, seeing the woman with a loaded gun, had panicked and called the police. Jimmy had taken the gun into the Gents to keep it away from the crowds in the bar and, would you know it? The damn thing had gone off, twice! Naturally, the sound of gunshots had caused panic in the bar and during the ensuing stampede to the exit drinks and furniture had been upended. Some had been damaged beyond repair.

The Commander had not been convinced, initially, but once Jimmy had invited him to revisit the incident with the CID annual dinner dance and the Thames Valley Drugs Squad, he loosened up a bit. After a while he started laughing.

'What was happening in the quarry then, Jimmy?'

'Kids' party.'

'Ah yes, rock 'n' roll?'

'Something like that.'

'Sex?'

'Possibly'

'Drugs?'

'No! They're the swotty set – nerdy intellectuals, bless them. You're no more likely to find drugs there than at the CID annual dinner dance.'

And so they had parted, best mates once more, agreeing to meet up again sometime over a pint.

Congratulating himself for his victory, Jimmy got to his feet. He was stiff, cold and tired. Time to be inside, tell Gaynor he'd sorted it all out and get some well-earned sleep. He went round to the front door and pressed the bell. There was no response. He tried again. The old bell was getting a bit sclerotic. She probably hadn't heard it. Still nothing. He went round to the back of the house and shouted up at their bedroom window. She can't have slept through all that commotion. He shouted again and then started searching the ground at his feet for loose stones.

'Gaynor!'

The window opened wide and a large suitcase flew through the air. It landed on the path behind him, where it bounced, coming to rest under an apple tree.

The window banged shut. Splinters from its wooden frame pattered down into the yard. Jimmy stared up at it for a while, shocked and hurt. *What was this about?* Hadn't he just saved the situation? The police had all gone away. He walked over to the apple tree and retrieved the suitcase. Turning it onto its back, he opened it. It contained a selection of clothes, his toothbrush and his underwear, most of it unwashed.

He ran to the kitchen window. Inside, the telly, forgotten but clearly audible, blared out into the unresponsive night. The BBC News Channel was informing insomniacs of an incident in a disused quarry in Somerset, before returning to scenes of warfare and misery in some faraway country.

CHAPTER 15

I

*Swinging on the gallows wit
Arse-cheek England
You must be joking mate...*

It looked like an attempt at a song lyric. What on Earth did it mean?

Gaynor sat down on Catrin's bed. She rubbed her eyes and her forehead, aching and defeated. Around her, on the bed, the dressing-table top and any other available surface, lay loose pages or scraps of discarded paper. It must be somewhere. Everyone wrote down their password, didn't they? She reread the strange lines of what? Poetry? Not a password clearly, much too long.

She'd been through everything: school files, books, flute music, the bin, but all they'd yielded were A-level notes and similar fragments of verse – very blank. She'd even taken down the posters and looked on the backs of them, but there was nothing. They were an odd assortment for a teenage girl, now that she 'd found time to look more closely; abstract patterns and arty images advertising gigs and bands she'd never heard of, alongside photographs of the artistes, including the seemingly eternal images of Bowie and Freddy Mercury. There was also a mad-looking hippy standing on one leg playing the flute – *Ian Anderson?*

Vinyl discs and their covers littered the floor. She'd been through Catrin's stash of prog rock like the drug squad, wrenching the albums from their sleeves and casting them aside. They'd disclosed nothing, apart from Jimmy's name, school house and room number neatly inscribed on sticky labels attached to the covers.

Next, she'd poked gingerly and guiltily through the contents of the top drawer of the dressing table, the usual repository of teenage secrets. There was nothing in it but makeup, some of it old and decaying, much of it impregnated with glitter, a box of cheap, but shiny, jewellery and wraps of what turned out to be sugar-free gum. The key had been left in the lock. For a teenager with no apparent secrets Catrin had become utterly mysterious. Her laptop sat on top of the dressing table, open but black and inscrutable. Beside it was Gaynor's mobile phone, which now accompanied her everywhere. She reached for it, opened the text she'd received that morning and studied every word again and again:

OK. Me & Rosie staying with friends. Pl don't let Dad call the cops again

What was all that about? She'd have to talk to Jimmy. A picture from the previous Saturday night invaded her head and danced before her mind's eye: Jimmy and that blonde woman whispering…sharing secrets. She really didn't want to talk to Jimmy – ever. It was the ultimate betrayal. She'd thought she wouldn't care if she found out he was carrying on with another woman, but now she'd seen the evidence for herself, she felt deeply hurt. If it wasn't for the all-consuming fear for her daughter she'd find time to cry.

What if…? What if Bron was right? Gaynor still felt affection for her, and loyalty, but these days she seemed to have lost her mind. It wasn't her fault, of course. She'd been dealt a terrible hand, but she wasn't reliable, or was she?

Darren had arrived that morning, having paid a fortune for an early flight from Rennes on Easter Monday, to retrieve his ailing wife. He had gently confiscated the keys to their car and installed her, sobbing and shivering, in the passenger seat. Turning the ignition, he'd looked round and caught Gaynor's eye.

'Bastard!'

Gaynor nodded. 'Thanks, Darren.' She hadn't been able to think of anything else to say. Then the car had shot up the drive, turned into Crubscombe Hill with a roar and a crunch of expensive tyres on damp gravel and vanished. All she had felt, at the time, was relief.

Bron had warned her. It happened to her Eirlys. It could happen to anyone, though, thinking about it, Gaynor wasn't quite sure of that. Years of working with teenagers had shown her that Eirlys was fragile. She'd never quite worked out why, and it had seemed a betrayal to think that her old friend's daughter could turn out like that, but... She always thought it was the sort of thing that happened to deprived children on sink estates. Was Eirlys deprived? Her mother had always loved her, but she hadn't always been there, not until the awful truth had been coaxed out of a heart-broken child – who had once seemed so strong and independent.

Gaynor slumped forward, put her head in her hands, fingers ploughing through the roots of her hair: 'You think you know people,' she informed her kneecaps, 'but you don't.'

She'd seen it on Skype: Miles Hollowtree hovering over her daughter, like Count Dracula. She leaped to her feet animated once more by despair. *Where was Catrin? With friends – what friends? Where was Miles Hollowtree?*

She paced round the room, tripping over a drift of fashionable shoes and colliding with the open dressing-table drawer. Passing the bed, she picked up a pillow and hurled it at the smug, silent laptop. It bounced off the blank screen and landed among the shoes, harmless and impotent. But the action brought a measure of calm. Surely Catrin had more sense. She was putting down her own daughter, seeing her as a malleable child. She went back to the dressing table, picked up her phone, woke it up and stabbed in a series of numbers. She would have to talk to Jimmy – not that he ever answered his wretched mobile, or even switched it on. The usual automated message responded.

'Jimmy! I need to talk to you now, about Catrin. Don't think I'm about to forgive you, because I'm not, ever! Call me back as soon as you get this message, will you!'

As if she had conjured him using some magic spell, a voice floated up from the orchard. It sounded a bit hurt, which only added to her fury.

'Gaynor?'

She pushed open the window and leaned out, staring for a moment at the top of his head: dark brown curls, speckled with grey, but not thinning, yet.

He looked up at her. 'I've been ringing the front door bell,' he explained. 'It seems to be broken.'

'I disconnected it.' In fact, she'd kicked the bell housing in a fit of rage, shortly after the departure of the police. Her left big toe was still bruised from the impact.

'Can I…?'

'No. We can talk here.'

'Like this?'

'Yes. Do you know where Catrin is?'

'I thought she'd come home.'

'She's moved out, apparently. Moved out, Jimmy, six weeks before the most important exams of her academic career, exams that will define her entire future. She texted me. She's staying with friends.'

'She's safe, then?'

'Who knows? She won't say where she is.' Gaynor's tone was controlled and icy.

Jimmy felt like some year eight miscreant who had been caught chewing in class.

She read out the end of Catrin's text: *Don't let Dad call the cops again*. 'What would that be about Jimmy? What exactly has our daughter been doing?'

Jimmy was not keen to discuss this in any detail. He could feel his status sliding from year eight miscreant to that of whatever it might have been chewing. 'I don't know. Why don't you ask Rosie?'

'Rosie's gone too. Frankie came round with Mary. He's beside himself. Stupid kids!' Gaynor's voice cracked. 'They're throwing their lives away!'

'I'll find her,' he said, trying to sound reassuring. 'Have you asked…?'

'Everybody? Yes. I hear there was a rave or something of that sort down in the quarry.' Gaynor leant on the window sill, arms folded, calm, taking her time. 'What was Catrin doing at a rave, Jimmy?'

Jimmy seized the opportunity to turn the conversation away from anything that might later be used in evidence against him. 'She was singing, I believe. She's very talented, you know?'

Gaynor's eyes drilled into his. 'Where's Miles Hollowtree?'

'I don't know, honestly. Last time I saw him he was in Earwick Quarry trying to run away from the coppers.'

'Ah yes, the police. What were they doing down there? Why weren't they up at the club arresting you and your damn fool associates?'

This offended Jimmy. He felt inclined to remind her that it was neither he, nor his 'damn fool associates' who had turned up at the club with a loaded gun, but that would be unlikely to further his cause. He held his tongue and, with what he hoped was a bitter and tormented sigh, he turned away.

'I'll find her,' he threw back up at the window before walking towards the hole in the wall at the bottom of the orchard.

'Try asking your friend Miles Hollowtree!' Gaynor shouted after him before slamming the window.

II

The hotel stood before her, a Georgian building of some importance whose elegant front porch had been replaced with massive sliding glass doors. Behind the tall windows, muslin curtains reflected light back into the street while, high above them, flags of many nations broke and fluttered over the rooftop. Every now and then, super-confident people, suitably and immaculately dressed, trotted up the steps and floated through the plate glass which gave way before them and then closed with a neat, self-satisfied clunk.

Rosie rubbed the toe of her trainer along the edge of the bottom step. They'd cost a lot, six months ago, but it occurred to her that, even as accessories to the best of her Primark finery, they might not make the grade in this establishment. She wriggled out of her backpack and took out her mother's letter, checking its contents again. This was definitely the right hotel. Her mother's itinerary, it seemed, was a busy one: the morning spent in Waterstones signing books, followed by a lunch and civic reception at the hotel. In spite of initial resistance, Rosie was intrigued. Gaynor had told her that her mother was a university lecturer in English Literature.

'She always had her nose in a book,' Gaynor had insisted, looking deep into her eyes. Another adult trying to prise open a door that Rosie kept securely bolted and barred.

Five days in a sordid squat somewhere in the vicinity of Stokes Croft had persuaded Rosie that she did not like poverty. Love had not triumphed over filthy damp bedding and a stinking lavatory which leaked. Her father's house, though sometimes sparsely furnished, had always been clean and warm. Even more corrosive was the fact that all the other female residents of the squat, apart from Catrin, were hangers-on, groupies, actually.

She had almost certainly alienated her father and Gaynor, had effectively dumped Chaz and fallen out with Catrin, who seemed these days to take up much more of her ex-boyfriend's time than she ever had. When she had taken her friend, her only sister, to task about this, she was told that it was just about the music, but she hadn't believed it…

'I am no man's groupie,' she said out loud, and looked around to see if anybody had heard. But the city moved on around her, noisy, polluted and unconcerned.

Looking up again at the overbearing façade of the hotel, she considered sneaking in round the back, through the tradesman's entrance. Then she put her shoulders back and marched up the steps. Having no interest in dress codes, the glass door admitted her and she stepped inside, noting the plush fixtures and fittings as she did; curious, but trying to look cool.

There was carpet, rose-coloured and unfeasibly clean, stretching as far as the eye could see. Plump armchairs and sofas were gathered around what her nan used to call 'occasional tables', where neatly folded copies of the *Financial Times* and the *Daily Telegraph* had been placed for the perusal of the passing executive. But what held her eye was a flyer which someone had left on one of the tables. She picked it up.

On the front there was a picture of a book cover depicting an elegant black woman viewing sinister, low-lying marshy wasteland through the scope of a rifle. 'Swamp Life' was the title and below it was the legend, 'A new Martha Ann Davis mystery'. There followed what Rosie, as a student of literature, recognised as promotional guff, plus an invitation to the book-signing event. She turned the leaflet over and studied a photograph of the author, who appeared to be receiving some sort of award.

Meet the latest US best-selling crime writer, Dr Estelle Clements, said the leaflet before adding the time and date, and the address of Waterstones in Bristol.

Rosie could only speculate as to where the 'Clements' or the 'Dr' had come from, but the author, leaner, cooler, more handsome and certainly better dressed, was the young woman she had seen in Gaynor's 1990s snaps.

A receptionist, who had been watching the young intruder from behind a long, curved desk of highly polished oak, moved forward to deal with the situation.

'Can I help you?'

Rosie looked her over. 'Yes, please. I'd like to see Estelle Clements.'

The receptionist's eyebrows rose into the roots of her coiffed and sculpted hair. She was tall and fashionably slim and dressed in some sort of tailored uniform. Sheer tights flowed from under its hem into five-inch heels which, Rosie noticed, were made of red leather and matched the chiffon scarf neatly tucked into the top of her blouse. Every fingernail was an identical masterpiece of precision filing and crimson lacquer.

'Do you have an appointment?'

'No.'

'Dr Clements will not be receiving visitors without a prior appointment. She has, as you will appreciate, a very busy schedule.'

'I think she'll want to see me,' Rosie said, not, she thought, unreasonably.

'If you want a selfie…?'

'I don't think so.' Rosie stood up, rising to the full height of her intellectual indignation.

The receptionist took a phone out of an inside pocket and, passing immaculately manicured fingers over it, summoned security.

'Do you think you could tell her please that Rosetta Dando is here to see her?'

'Who? No! Of course I can't!'

Rosie took off her rucksack and opened it.

'You can't stay here!'

She took out a couple of crumpled pieces of paper. 'You know you said did I have an appointment?' She handed the letter to the receptionist.

The receptionist sighed, glanced over the bits of paper and then, backing away so that her side of the conversation would be inaudible, spoke to her phone. She looked at Rosie, spoke to the phone again and then scrutinised her over the top of it before saying: 'Would you take a seat please? Somebody will be down in a minute.'

The receptionist put her phone away and retreated to solid ground behind the oak desk.

Rosie snuggled into the armchair and then leant forward to pick up a copy of the *Financial Times*.

III

I'm good, said the text, followed by a little circular thing that Jimmy, from his limited acquaintance with the young, understood to be a smiley face. *Pl stop fussing. Love 2 Mum.* Lots of crosses and a heart, but no address.

Teetering dangerously on top of the bar, Jimmy cursed mobile phones. They were familiar but anonymous. You knew where you were with a landline. More specifically, you knew where the other person was, or at least you could find out. Landlines could be traced, if the police could be persuaded to co-operate, which, in this case, Jimmy reflected bitterly, they couldn't. Catrin, the police had informed him soothingly, was eighteen and she was keeping in touch with her mother. She wasn't a missing person. But she was young, Jimmy had insisted, she was vulnerable. There was nothing anybody could do, not even his old mate Colin Jameson. 'She's all right, Jimmy. She's with her friend, isn't she? They'll probably get fed up and come home when the money runs out. Keep texting.' So he had, but, so far, he'd only received these two cryptic lines in reply.

Fearing the worst, he'd texted Miles, but had heard nothing from him either.

His arm ached. He put the phone back in his pocket and climbed down from the bar. Texting from the sometime Quarrymen's Social Club involved a great deal of tiresome physical effort. He stretched his stiffened limbs and stamped around the floor for a bit. Then he selected a chair, carefully, testing its legs and joints before slumping into it. Previous spontaneous gestures of despair had ended in collapse (of the chair) and injury (to his nether regions).

The chair didn't suit him; it was too low. He fidgeted, stretching his legs out in front of him, leaning forward, leaning back. The partially foam-covered benches were no better. They were too narrow and slippery, like the seats grudgingly provided in modern bus shelters, designed specifically to discourage vagrants. Jimmy had usually been on his feet at the folk club and had never fully experienced the discomfort endured by its clientele. He returned miserably to the chair.

After his first night in residence, he had been obliged to go to Lidl and purchase a sleeping bag and an air bed.

Food wasn't a problem, really, just a bore: mostly fish and chips, and sandwiches from the Co-op. If he fancied home cooking, there was something in the kitchen called a Baby Belling, two crusty hot plates and a grill which might or might not catch fire when switched on. *Beans on toast, then, at some point,* once he'd summoned up the enthusiasm.

Washing, though, remained a challenge. He needed a shower; in all honesty he couldn't return to work without one. He had explored the rusted and lichen-coated contraptions that had once been the cricket club's showers. There was water, but he couldn't be sure he wouldn't emerge dirtier than when he'd gone in; plus it was cold.

Maybe he should ask for help – Luke perhaps, but his place was already crowded with boisterous teenagers, who, as well as taking up space, would tell all their friends. Frankie's place was locked up and deserted and, as for Terry…it would be all over the county within hours if he found out. He'd looked in earlier to check the beer for the folk club. Jimmy had explained that there would be no folk club that night, and possibly never again, and that he was only there to clear the place up.

'Life do have to go on, Jimmy,' Terry lectured him with an air of bracing certainty.

'Not in the present circumstances.'

'You'm going to get depressed if you're not careful. I heard Catrin's gone off somewhere.' Clearly Terry was genuinely concerned for his friend.

Jimmy had been unable to think of any relevant or even reasonable reply.

'Don't you worry, mate,' Terry reassured him, making his way towards the door. 'I got contacts with all the young people. I'll find her.'

Jimmy remembered asking him if that was a threat or a promise as, blithely unaware of any censure, Terry left the clubhouse to get on with his uncomplicated life. Jimmy reflected grimly that the best news Terry had given him was that he would be unable to help today, as he had to go out in the van delivering beer, somewhere or other; elsewhere, fortunately.

Oh well, perhaps it would be over soon. He'd find Catrin, persuade her to come home, and then he might be forgiven.

He rose from the chair and walked behind the bar to the beer barrel, his only friend, reached for a glass and opened the tap. It was getting low.

How had he got here? He hadn't done anything wrong, well not much, really. The house was a bit of a mess. There'd been a lot of drinking. They'd all been having a good time. Gaynor never used to mind that, she'd even been known to join them before the walls of respectability started closing in. And it wasn't him who'd grabbed a gun and taken potshots at people. It wasn't his fault that Bron was unstable, was it? Why was Gaynor so angry with him? He took a long, soothing draught of beer.

'Women!' Jimmy shook his head, offering the accumulated wisdom of all human experience to his beer glass. 'They make such generalisations.' He loved her, nonetheless. She had many qualities. She was strong, determined, principled, hard-working. She kept the home together. Of course, he loved her. She was his rock. One didn't mention it, no need. *These things are understood.*

He'd worked and played with so many blokes, metrosexual types, who banged on about how they loved their wives, adored women, then had affairs and betrayed them. The more they rhapsodised on the subject of their precious wives, the grosser the philandering. Jimmy had never been like that. He'd never let her down. Miles, of course, had always insisted that he adored women.

Staring across the room at the clubhouse door he remembered the last time he'd seen his daughter. She was pocketing a card which Miles had given her. What if…?

Jimmy dragged a wooden chair up to the bar, climbed up on to it again and waved the mobile phone over his head. It chirruped.

A call?" No! A text. Catrin?. He lowered the phone a little and read:

Any info yet? I have something that might interest you. Meet me at the Jolly Collier 2night 8pm. Alex.

This was all he needed. He decided to ignore it. The woman was a pain, hanging around, haranguing him about her husband's infidelities. *As if I care.*

It dawned on him, suddenly, that Gaynor had seen them in what could have looked like a compromising situation. Surely she didn't suspect him and Alex of having an affair? She'd seen them talking in the club, the night of the great disaster, but that was nothing, they were just chatting. There was nothing going on, well nothing of a sexual nature.

He returned to the recent calls list, then held the phone above his head for what seemed to be at least ten minutes, until his arm went numb.

There were three missed calls from Terry and a text: *In pub bed down foul catering.*

Jimmy could not imagine why Terry thought he would be interested in his accommodation problems. The man was an idiot.

Still nothing from Catrin. He climbed down from the bar again and returned to his glass of beer. A wave of misery swept over him and he sat in his uncomfortable chair, motionless, his mind blank, frozen in stasis on some alien planet, a pathless wilderness in which there were no familiar landmarks. He knew nothing any more, did not even know himself. He was lost.

He was brought back to what passed for solid earth by the

sound from outside of approaching footsteps. Jimmy sprang out of the chair, knocking it over backwards, raced round the room gathering up bedding, and any other evidence of occupation he could find and threw everything into a heap behind the bar.

Miles sauntered in from the porch. There was a fading bruise on his forehead and he was favouring his left leg a little. Otherwise, he looked pretty chipper. He was wearing clean clothes and smelled of recently applied aftershave.

'I called at the farmhouse,' he said airily. 'Nobody at home.'

'I think Gaynor's in school,' Jimmy explained. 'Inset day or something.'

'Well, I've found you anyway.'

'Beer?'

'Yes please. Your home from home, eh Jimmy?'

'You could say that.' Jimmy went behind the bar, found a clean pint glass and stooped over the barrel, coaxing a thinning stream out of the tap.

Miles leant on the bar and surveyed the mess behind it. 'You all right, mate?'

Jimmy stood up and held the half-full glass up to the light. 'Living my best life, as the young people say.'

'Oh dear.'

Jimmy placed the glass in front of Miles. 'I think you'll find that's all right. Where have you been?'

'The cops arrested me, kept me in a cell overnight and booted me out the next morning.'

'Still living dangerously then, Miles?'

They didn't charge me with anything and I have returned to the bosom of George and Alex. I'm a law-abiding citizen, Jimmy.'

'Really?'

Miles stared into his beer as if it were some sort of witches' brew showing him images from a forgotten past. 'She was sixteen.'

'Eirlys?'

'Yep, Eirlys. Sweet girl and, trust me, mate, she was up for it.'

Jimmy was beginning to feel light-headed. He walked unsteadily from behind the bar, picking up his drink en route, and sank down into his chair. He glanced up at Miles, who was still standing, resting his drinking arm on the bar, looking casual and unconcerned.

'Are you telling me categorically, without anybody actually pointing a gun at your head, that you seduced your girlfriend's daughter?'

Miles flinched, as if hurt by the faint note of censure in his oldest friend's remarks. 'If you put it that way.'

'Is there any other way of putting it?'

'You must have known, Jimmy.'

'No, mate, I didn't.'

'Miles laughed. 'Everybody knew.'

'We didn't, neither I nor Gaynor.'

'Oh Jimmy!' Miles shook his head, chiding him for his innocence. 'It's not as if there was any wrongdoing involved.'

Jimmy would have liked to have vented his disappointment and anger, but he had more immediate worries. He needed to keep a clear head. 'You've been staying with George and Alex since last Sunday?'

'Yes, of course.' Miles chuckled. 'They're not bothered. Alex told George all about our evening in the folk club. George knows all about Eirlys anyway, always has and I can assure you…' At this point Miles was overcome by a laughing fit. He shuddered, pressed his hand over his mouth and, finally giving up, let out a guffaw. 'It's not as if he's in a position to cast any stones, is he?'

'Isn't he?'

'Nah. He's always been a regular customer of the notorious Boquerie. Helps that he owns the place, obviously – gives him ample opportunity to sample some of the younger, prettier clientele. He's got a little love nest above the shop, so to speak. It's got a jacuzzi and a four-poster bed. Wealth and glamour, Jimmy. The girls really go for that.'

Jimmy wondered if he was experiencing the early symptoms of a stroke. 'When did you last see Catrin?' he asked, and held his breath

'Catrin?'

Jimmy nodded.

'I haven't seen her since last Saturday, trust me, mate.'

'Can I?'

'Whoa!' Miles stood up, wide-eyed, shocked. 'I didn't...I wouldn't try anything with her. She's my oldest friend's daughter.'

'And Eirlys?' Jimmy heaved himself out of his chair and stood up as straight and steadily as was possible in the circumstances.

'Catrin is talented. I wanted to help her, give her some advice, you know, about the business? But...' His mouth twisted. Jimmy sensed that he was floundering. 'She'll go far. She's a hard case, Jimmy, like her mother.'

Dumbfounded, Jimmy took in every word and weighed it carefully. Even if the bastard had not succeeded with Catrin, he had almost certainly tried it on. His oldest friend had betrayed him. His staunchest ally was a thoughtless, callous, shallow, self-serving mountebank. Gaynor was right. She'd tried to warn him, but he'd just dismissed it as nagging. He'd got it all wrong, completely, totally, utterly. She was kind and good, always loyal, and he'd driven her away. He'd lost her, and Catrin. He knew it was all his own fault, but looking at Miles, his long lean frame resting once more against the bar, lips curved in that ironic smile he'd once found so amusing, all Jimmy's wit and urbanity deserted him. Hot blood thundered in his ears.

'You bastard,' he croaked, 'how dare you talk like that about my daughter, my wife.' He bunched his right hand into a fist and lunged forward, aiming for Miles' sneering lips. He missed, fell to his knees and hit the bar instead.

'Get out!' he gasped, rubbing his hand and rising painfully from his battered knees.

Miles stayed where he was. He was smiling. Jimmy looked for his drink, intending to do some damage to Miles' teeth with the heavy glass mug, but was deflected from any further attempts at assault by the sound of voices in the porch.

Frankie stepped into the room, followed by Mary.

Miles got out, skirting nervously past Frankie and bolting for the exit. But Frankie did not pursue him. Instead, he walked over to Jimmy and gently took his arm.

'Are you all right?' he asked stiffly.

Jimmy hung his head. 'Dunno, mate.'

'Has he seen Rosie and Catrin?'

'Hasn't been near either of them as far as I can tell.'

'Thank goodness,' Mary said.

'How much of that did you hear?' Jimmy asked.

'We heard,' said Frankie.

'You're not going to give him a kicking?'

'No point,' Frankie said with an effort.

Mary looked at him approvingly

'No,' Jimmy sighed. 'Too late. I've messed up. I'm sorry.'

Going over the recent conversation with Miles in his mind, an idea occurred to Jimmy. His life was destroyed but there remained a small opportunity for vengeance. He found the wooden chair he'd been using as a ladder, dragged it across the room and, in spite of anxious looks from Frankie and Mary, climbed up on to the bar. He took his phone out of his pocket, found Alex's text and replied to it:

Have info re Boquerie. See you later.

As Frankie and Mary were helping him down from the bar,

a loud and familiar voice drifted down from the path to Upper Crubscombe. It was Terry, addressing the fugitive Miles: 'Hello there, Miles, Good to see you!'

There was no reply.

Jimmy, Frankie and Mary exchanged despairing looks.

Moments later Terry arrived. 'What's up with him then?'

Nobody said anything.

Terry appeared to give up, and changed the subject. 'I have been trying to phone you, Jimmy, and I sent a text. Bit difficult,' he added, shooting a reproachful glance at Frankie, 'because I am still learning to use my new phone.'

Realising that Terry was not going away until he had received some sort of acknowledgement of his presence, Jimmy opened the enigmatic text and showed it to him. 'Frankly, Tel, I've got more important things on my mind right now.'

Terry read the text. He frowned at it: '*Foul...?* That should of said found Catrin.'

Jimmy dropped the phone. 'What?'

Terry shook his head. 'It's that productive text.'

'Where is she?'

'Bedminster Down, like I said in the text.'

They hustled Terry out of the clubhouse and ran with him up the path to Upper Crubscombe, where he'd left his van.

'I was delivering beer to this pub, see,' Terry puffed as he ran. 'The Jolly Roger on Bedminster Down. They got a festival on this weekend and...'

'Terry, please,' Mary said gently, 'get to the point.'

'Give me a minute, will you?' Terry stopped to catch his breath. 'Your Catrin's there,' he said to Jimmy, 'with her band. They got some funny name.'

Frankie and Jimmy took an arm each and propelled him up the path to the road.

'Best take my van,' he advised them once they'd arrived. 'I can park by the back door of the pub. You can go anywhere if you're delivering beer, even in Bristol.'

He held the nearside door open for Mary and installed her in the passenger seat, while Jimmy and Frankie wedged themselves in the back between beer barrels and crates of bottles and cans.

'Good ale is the stairway to heaven!' Terry crowed, revving up the engine. He took off with more speed than accuracy in the direction of Bristol.

IV

They found the band rehearsing in a pub outhouse that had been converted into what is known in the theatre world as a black box. At the far end of the room was a stage where a terrifying red-haired fiend breathed adolescent poetry into an over-wrought sound system backed by raucous but mathematically calculated guitar, bass and keyboards, and lively percussion. In spite of the urgency of his mission Jimmy could not help being interested. It was a kind of fusion: early Pink Floyd, Jethro Tull and, perhaps, a bit of late King Crimson. It was bone-crushingly loud, but quite accomplished, in its way. He looked around, taking in the whole set-up.

Strip lighting, suspended from a high sloping roof still caked with brown stains from a distant geological era before the smoking ban, disclosed patches of greying plaster where the black paint was flaking away. The dirt-encrusted floor was strewn with cables connecting the many amps, mics, speakers and other electronic paraphernalia on the stage to a mixing desk which stood on a low podium at the back of the room.

Jimmy leant against it, wondering what to do next. Long

ago he'd been familiar with this kind of scene, but no more. The place resembled a snake pit, managed by officious teenagers. He recognised one of them as Diana, daughter of the Crubscombe garage proprietor. She glared at him.

Frankie, with Mary's restraining hand on his arm, turned towards him. 'Pop,' he mouthed through pursed lips, in a manner that, had he been able to listen to himself, would have reminded him of his mother.

'They're good musicians,' Jimmy shouted back, but nobody heard him. He remembered that Gaynor had once told him he was so broad-minded you could land a wide-bodied jet between his ears.

'Noise!' said Frankie, loudly.

Mary patted him gently on the arm, trying to introduce a note of calm, but he broke away from her and, bore down on the nearest teenager like a Kansas tornado.

'Where's my Rosie? Where's Catrin?'

'That is Catrin!' yelled Jimmy, breathless, catching him up.

They watched as the red-headed fiend raised a flute to her lips and blew into it with ferocious intensity, staring back at them all the while.

What on earth, Jimmy wondered helplessly, was Gaynor going to make of all this? It would be on Facebook by now, or Instagram, or some other inescapable mass medium. It would be all over the bloody school.

The band rocked on, propelled by a tremendous onslaught from percussion and growling bass. The guitar wailed, the flute squeaked and gibbered. *Like the sheeted dead*, thought Jimmy. He'd heard that somewhere, in school maybe…Shakespeare? His mind was becoming swamped with mathematical progressions of overwhelming sound.

She'd asked when she was little, about six or seven, for a flute.

They'd told her it would be difficult to play, that they'd make her practise, and they had – well, Gaynor had mostly. The music screamed at him from all directions. Where had they got all this kit?

He tried once more to concentrate and found himself scrutinising Catrin's costume. What there was of it seemed to be a variation on the 'Seafaring Girl' theme of the previous weekend. It looked very tight. One could count her ribs. Jimmy squirmed. He was sure he must be blushing. The bass lodged itself in his coccyx and then crawled upwards, taking over his heartbeat and making his teeth rattle. He seemed to be spinning on the edge of a black hole.

At the edge of it he could see Frankie advancing, scattering officious teenagers to right and left. Some, briefly, considered remonstration, but mostly they backed away, looking for somewhere to hide.

He vaulted up on to the stage with sudden agility, and stood over Catrin,

She held her ground, looking him straight in the eye, fingering the flute as if considering what she might usefully do with it in the event of physical violence.

Jimmy and Mary picked their way through the nests of cables and stood at the foot of the stage. The music died, tailing off into a patter of cymbal and snare drum until somebody caught the attention of the drummer.

'Frankie!' Mary admonished him.

He paid no attention. 'Where's my Rosie?'

The fiend looked at him from under hooded green eyelids. 'She's not *your* Rosie.'

Mary climbed up on to the stage. 'For God's sake, girl, she's breaking his heart!'

Frankie looked as if he would like to lay violent hands on Catrin but he managed to contain himself.

'Your mother's worried about you,' said Mary.

Jimmy, who had been listening to these exchanges trying to form a plan, made his way to the foot of the stage. 'She's right, Catrin. Your mother needs to know you're all right. She wants to see you.'

The band were getting impatient. They'd been standing around listening, fascinated at first, but they were becoming restless. The lead guitarist spoke up.

'Rosie's gone,' he said morosely. 'She went to see her mother.'

There was a pause.

Officious teenagers began to whisper, the Crubscombe contingent enlightening the city sophisticates.

'Where?' enquired Frankie, with agonised restraint.

'Dunno. Some posh hotel.'

Frankie took a step towards the miserable-looking youth.

Catrin relented. 'The Ivy Lodge,' she told him.

Frankie leapt from the stage and headed in the direction of Terry, who had been hiding behind the mixing desk, shouting to him as he approached.

'Do you know where it is?'

'What?' Terry asked nervously.

'The Ivy Lodge?'

Jimmy could see from Terry's inaudible response that he did. He beckoned to Catrin to join him and asked Mary to go and tell the others to wait for him while he had a word with his daughter.

With a visible display of weary obligation, Catrin came over to the front of the stage and sat on it next to her father.

'You must come home with us,' Jimmy pleaded. Out of the corner of his eye he could see Frankie looming over an anxious-looking Terry, while Mary did her best to restrain him. He appeared to be keeping his cool for now. Jimmy felt he had minutes, seconds perhaps, to reach a settlement before the grief-stricken father and Bristol collided. 'Your mother...'

'I can't. We've got a gig.'

'Your mother is desperate to see you.'

'We're committed, right? You should know. So should she.'

'You owe her an explanation, don't you think?'

'I'm sorry if I've hurt her.'

'You need to tell her that yourself.'

The band was becoming increasingly restive.

Catrin glanced up at the clock on the wall above the exit sign. In spite of the mask she was beginning to look anxious. 'Is she all right?'

'Of course she's not.'

Catrin made up her mind. 'All right. We're on first. I'll come after we've done our set. OK?'

Jimmy turned to go and then turned back. 'There aren't any buses.' Now was not the best of times to launch into a discussion of rural bus services, but he persisted. 'The last bus to Crubscombe's already gone. I'll have to come back and fetch you.'

'You can't!'

'Why not?'

'You're pissed.'

He had to admit that this was true.

'Don't worry. I'll get there,' Catrin reassured him.

'Can you?'

'Yes. Just don't tell Mum where I am. I don't want her coming after me as well.'

'Chance would be a fine thing.'

Catrin studied his face closely. 'What?'

'She's chucked me out, Catrin. I don't know why.'

She sighed, expressing a mixture of exasperation and forbearance as if she were the long-suffering parent. 'Oh Dad, you're hopeless. Don't phone her, right?'

'Why not?' Jimmy asked.

'She'll call the cops.'

'The cops aren't interested.'

'The cops are always interested in busting young people. Like they were when you told them about our party?'

'What do you mean, *I told...*? Oh, never mind. For God's sake, Catrin, you're not exactly keeping a low profile. She's bound to find out eventually.'

'Don't phone her, right. I'll come home as soon as I can. Don't make any promises.'

Jimmy walked away from her, far from convinced that he'd made any impression. He'd give her till tomorrow morning.

V

As Terry's van stopped and started with the traffic flow into the centre of Bristol, Jimmy braced himself, trying to avoid colliding with its cargo. He contemplated the disastrous consequences of what he had done, or not done, and viewing in his mind's eye the creature his daughter had become.

Her mother's heartbroken.

Visions of the past rose before him. Wrapped in a blanket before a cold untended Rayburn at a table piled high with blue exercise books and folders, Gaynor sat reading, checking, correcting, her frozen fingers wrapped around a red ballpoint pen. Then a flickering series of tableaux: Christmas and birthday gifts of money from relatives and friends, all presented to a disgruntled child as a line of print in a cardboard bank book.

You'll need it – Gaynor's voice – *when you go to university.*

The little bank book swam before Jimmy's eyes, faithfully topped up at the end of every month, on pay day; fifty pounds originally, a bit of a struggle in the early days, then a hundred as the salaries increased, an almost religious ritual, grimly presided over by the high priestess Gaynor. No holiday, excursion, festival or concert could ever provide an excuse to avoid it. And Gaynor, he suspected, had added more whenever she could.

On her eighteenth birthday they'd taken Catrin to the bank. Smiling and proud, showing off their clever daughter to the staff, they had turned everything over to her, title, book and debit card.

Shunting and sliding round him, advertising strap-lines printed on boxes of beer seemed to be mocking Jimmy: *Chedgy's original... fine real ales... the stairway to heaven...*

VI

Hesitating at the entrance to a well-appointed meeting room, Rosie stared at her mother, disbelief, for the moment, the overriding sensation. All the writers and artists she had ever known or read about had been poor, from Crubscombe's shabby intelligentsia to the African Americans of the Deep South.

She looked taller than the sweet-faced young woman cradling a tiny baby in Gaynor's old photos. The hair was close-cropped, emphasising big eyes and even features. Her clothes – Rosie wondered at her own shallowness – were boring but expensive; loose trousers made of soft green jersey wool and an asymmetric top whose uneven hemline hung down below the hips, cleverly designed to hide the shortcomings of the middle-aged woman's figure.

All around them the remains of the reception were being cleared by hotel staff with discreet efficiency.

Rosie eyed the leftovers. There were tall thin glasses full of white fizz arranged in geometric patterns on long tables at the edges of the room and between them wide salvers of *canapés* and petits fours, many of them untouched. Evidently, the literary glitterati of the West Country were too elegant to eat. Rosie hadn't eaten for hours. She dragged her attention back to her mother, wondering what to say.

Estelle cracked first, advancing on Rosie and wrapping her in a tight, tearful and scented embrace. Taken aback by such a violent demonstration of affection, she wriggled free.

'Sweetheart!' cried her mother.

Rosie stood apart from her, cold and aloof, still desperately seeking words.

'Why?' she managed eventually, and then gave up.

Her mother tried again. 'You know your daddy really loves you?'

Rosie couldn't quite see how this was relevant. Admittedly it was true, though she had often felt over the years that she had not so much been parented as minded by a large and ferocious dog. She looked hard into her mother's troubled, slightly damp face, trying to read it. The room had gone quiet. Rosie realised she had become the star of her own personal soap opera.

'Why did you leave me, Mother?'

They were interrupted by Jimmy and his entourage, who appeared suddenly and unceremoniously, like a haunting. Each of them was carrying a box containing what appeared to be large quantities of alcoholic drinks. Mary, a wary embodiment of their conscience, hovered at the rear. She slid into a chair next to the nearest wall, looking quietly apprehensive.

For a long moment nothing much happened.

Terry, buckling under the weight of a polypin, dumped it on the ground. He grunted and massaged his hands.

Comfortably folding his arms round a case of cans, Frankie stared at his estranged wife. His brow creased, but he said nothing.

Jimmy, who seemed quieter than usual, decided to take charge of the situation. 'Estelle!' he exclaimed warmly, accompanying this utterance with a friendly and inclusive sweep of his left arm. A beer can detached itself from the broken box he had been clutching to his chest and, bouncing off his foot, rolled away under a table, where it rocked gently. Jimmy, cursing under his breath, slackened his grip even further, allowing a number of its companions to wriggle out of the torn cardboard to join it. They lay in the rose-coloured shagpile like unexploded bomblets.

'Well, Jimmy,' Estelle enquired, after a moment's thought, 'you sure you guys have enough to drink there?'

Terry tried to explain. 'Hello Estelle! All right? We had to bring all this beer in, see love, or they wouldn't of let us in. We're delivering for Chedgy's.'

Jimmy dug him in the ribs.

Rosie felt aggrieved. Sensing that the moment had slipped from her control, she took in the newcomers one by one: her father and protector, her mentor's husband and family friend and their faithful companion. They were disgusting, utterly appalling – the three musketeers, Athos, Porthos and Bathos. She smiled inwardly at her own wit.

Suits appeared from an inner chamber; lean, sharp business suits, burly suits with muscles bulging beneath dark blue serge, and a female suit with very high heels and heavy, thick-rimmed glasses.

Estelle addressed her former husband, 'Hezekiah.'

Frankie started at the unfamiliar mode of address.

'Rosetta. '

With a slight inclination of the head, Estelle instructed them to follow her into the inner chamber. She turned to whisper something to the female suit and walked through the open door. Rosie followed her, and then Frankie, with a swift backward glance at Mary, also complied. The door closed behind them.

The suits, male and female, melted away into the background.

Terry picked up one of the fallen cans and opened it. It popped and gushed over the carpet.

'Anybody like a beer?'

CHAPTER 16

I

Gaynor opened the firebox door and chucked in a hod full of coal, enough she hoped to keep the recalcitrant Rayburn going until morning. It was April, but still too cold to let it go out.

She'd left the school's pre-term briefing early complaining of a headache, not telling them that if she was obliged to sit through another minute of Al Messenger's strategy for the future of Hales Mead Academy she would be likely to suffer some kind of physical or mental collapse and have to be removed from the premises feet first. School was becoming a bore but, right now, it was all she had left. Behind her, on the table, the paraphernalia of teaching was strewn about; exercise books, folders and her laptop. Life must go on.

For some reason the computer had refused to boot up. She sat down in front of it and fiddled with the mouse. Catrin would have made sense of it. Where was Catrin, what was she thinking of?

'I should know,' Gaynor bitterly informed the blank screen of the laptop. She thought of her own youthful exploits at Plogoff and Greenham and her delusional attempt to find fame as a folk singer, accompanied by Jimmy; a triumph of misplaced hope and ambition, fuelled by love. How could she have been so reckless, so thoughtless, such a disappointment to her parents and, ultimately, to herself?

Gaynor rubbed her eyes. Scenes from her distant past flashed before them. An old man propped up on white pillows in an old-fashioned bedroom stared into the coal fire in a hearth made of Welsh slate, coughing and wheezing in a terrifying struggle for breath: the last time she'd seen him before he died. He was her grandfather and, though he looked to a frightened child like the ancient of days, he was fifty-seven. He had dust disease from years of working in the quarry sheds splitting slates.

Like all the remaining quarry workers he'd been promised compensation, but the government had fallen and the whole issue was pushed aside by its successor. The quarries were long gone, closed even before her grandfather had fallen ill, leaving nothing but water-filled craters, disease and inadequate pensions. The injustice had burnt itself into her soul.

'Radicalised,' she murmured sadly to the moribund computer. 'Anybody's for a just cause. Still at it, must be an addiction.'

Catrin wasn't like that, was she? She was sensible, cautious, non-political; like most of the kids of today, focused and studious, wasn't she? *Could she have been seduced?*

Her laptop screen had filled with the image of Miles' avuncular face, old and lined, but charming, leaning over her daughter's shoulder. In the background there had been what sounded like a riotous drunken party in her kitchen. And, in the middle of it all, Jimmy blithely handing out fish and chips. *Could he possibly have condoned it?* She held her head in her hands, staring at the rows of random letters on the keyboard. No, he wasn't like that. He probably hadn't noticed anything untoward. He was an easy-going, amusing and, she conceded, loveable prat. No wonder the blonde floozy had taken a fancy to him. *Whatever.* She'd lost him, and Catrin too. Even clever, sensible Rosie, the ablest pupil she'd ever taught, had deserted her.

Somewhere under the pile of books and papers her phone

chirruped. She scrabbled through the detritus and seized it. An unknown number. She looked at the name.

Estelle!

Coming by Crubscombe later... Bringing... 'Part of message missing', the phone informed her. Then, as often happened in Crubscombe, the signal died.

Gaynor got to her feet, then careered round the room waving the phone over her head. She ran out into the hall, heading for the stairs. Halfway up the signal started to revive and the battery gave out.

'Ooooh!' Gaynor raved at the unresponsive slab of priceless rare earth metals, prodding the screen here, there and everywhere, leaving nothing visible but fingerprints.

The charger! She ran back into the kitchen. *Where was it?* She remembered chucking it into one of the drawers in the dresser. One by one she turned them out, but the charger was nowhere to be found.

Jimmy! He'd nicked it, of course. They had identical obsolete models. He'd lost his charger years ago – *typical!*

Gaynor resumed her miserable station at the table fretting over what she could remember of the truncated message. Why was Estelle coming over now? As far as she could recall, they'd made an arrangement to meet up after the weekend.

The book signing! She'd been invited. She'd completely forgotten about it. How rude! She must have been forgiven and instead Estelle was coming to visit. It was seven thirty. Would she want to stay the night? The place, to put it mildly, was a tip. No time to hoover or clean the bathroom, not even for the customary lick and promise.

Panicking, Gaynor filled the sink with hot water and started on the washing-up. There was too much of it; she'd never get it all done and put away in time. She found an empty cardboard box in the utility room, filled it with dirty dishes and headed for the oubliette.

It was hopeless. Everything was filthy. There were cobwebs that Gaynor felt sure Estelle would recognise from her last visit some seventeen years previously. You could plough the dust and put in potatoes. Strewn about the hall was an assortment from Jimmy's random hoard, which she had in her rage hurled from the dining room with a view to putting it out for the next rubbish collection. She picked up a mouldy trainer – it didn't seem to have a pair – and, in a futile gesture, returned with it to the oubliette. There she sat on a wooden dining chair which Jimmy, in a fit of domesticity, had once begun to paint.

Her guitar was leaning against the opposite wall, exposed to the light by the removal of Jimmy's leavings. She hadn't seen it for at least ten years but, recognising an old friend she crossed the room and picked it up. It took a while to get it in anything that resembled tune.

'Good enough for folk,' she murmured and began to sing:
I set my back against an oak
Thinking it was a mighty tree.
But first it bent and then it broke
As did my love prove false to me.

She missed him. His cheerful eccentric presence filled a lot of space. *No point being sentimental* she admonished herself, *he's gone. Tears will achieve nothing.* Still embracing the guitar, she wiped her nose with the back of her hand.

'Mum?'

She looked up and saw Catrin, or some apparition that looked a lot like her, standing in the doorway. Jumping to her feet, dropping the guitar, which landed on the floor with a boom and a clatter, she confronted the figure in the doorway with a mixture of hope and wonderment.

'How did you get here?'

'Borrowed Di's Land Rover.'

Gaynor wrapped her arms around Catrin, stroking her hair, her shoulders and her back, making sure she was real. Then she held her at arm's length for a more detached appraisal. There was a wide gap between the tops of long leather boots and the bottom of a pair of very short satin shorts. Underneath a grubby anorak which she might have borrowed from a passing tramp, Gaynor could just see a frilly shirt, unbuttoned almost to the waist and just about contained by a very tight-laced bodice.

'What, exactly, have you come as?'

'I was in a hurry,' Catrin explained. 'Didn't have time to change. This is my working gear.'

'What?' Gaynor stared at her daughter. This was the worst, the most horrible...there had to be an explanation...someone to blame. 'Wh...where is he?' she managed at last. She seemed to have developed a stutter.

'Who?'

'Miles Hollowtree.' Gaynor said it slowly, deliberately, the word trailing off into a shudder.

'In jail, as far as I know. Last time I saw him he was being dragged out of the quarry by two big fat cops.'

'They got him?'

'Yeah. For all I know he's still in the nick. You could keep him there if you told them he fucks young girls.'

'Catrin!'

'I'm in the business now. I've heard all the rumours. He used to be on 'Top Of The Pops'.'

'Yes...but...?'

'You didn't seriously think I'd want to shag that ancient stick insect?'

'But...' Gaynor's eyes ran over the fiendish costume.

'I'm a singer, Mum.'

'What kind of singer? You look like Sally Bowles.'

'I'm a pirate wench. You know? William Taylor's jilted sweetheart? You used to sing me "William Taylor" when I was a kid.'

'So, it's my fault then?'

'It's an act. We're a fusion band – folk inspired with a prog rock beat – kind of Fairport Convention on heat.'

'Right.' Gaynor tried to digest this piece of critical analysis, but couldn't.

Catrin chuckled. 'I'm a bit too old for him, anyway. His girlfriends are all innocent kids, just sixteen – or are they?'

'We think so. We don't know the exact course of events.'

'So he buggered off to L.A. just in case?'

'Bron was going to kill him.'

'That's a bit extreme.' Catrin paused, reading her mother's stern expression. 'He didn't? Not Eirlys?'

Gaynor hung her head. 'I didn't know.'

'Did Dad?'

'Your father wouldn't,' Gaynor blurted out before she could stop herself. 'He wouldn't condone...'

''Course he wouldn't. He's just a prat, really, isn't he?'

'He's still your father, Catrin.'

Catrin thought about it for a moment. She shrugged. 'Got any tissues?'

'Are you all right?'

'I want to take my face off,' Catrin explained patiently. As if talking to a child with learning disability. 'Like I said, these are my work clothes. I've got mascara in my eye and I'm eating my lipstick.'

'Are you hungry?' In spite of her daughter's rudeness, Gaynor was anxious to please. 'There's a pizza in the freezer.'

Catrin beamed at her. 'Pizza would be good.'

II

'Go on, mate!' said Terry to an anxious-looking Romanian waiter. ''Tis good English beer. You'll like it, I promise you.' He waved an open can of Chedgy's under the man's suspicious nose.

The waiter politely declined.

Crestfallen, Terry walked across the room to where Jimmy had taken a seat next to Mary and held the can out to him.

Jimmy shook his head.

Terry stepped backwards as if Jimmy had bitten him. 'Whassup, mate?'

'Oh, nothing.'

'Are you feeling ill?'

Jimmy could think of nothing useful to say.

Terry wandered away drinking the beer himself, stopping now and again at a table to sample one of the stupidly small food offerings. 'They'm really tasty,' he said through a shower of puff pastry.

Jimmy slumped forward in his seat, head bowed, wondering what horror was coming next. So far there had been no sounds from the inner meeting room to suggest rampage or battle. All he could do was wait.

After an eternity of apprehension Rosie, Estelle and Frankie emerged from the inner room talking quietly among themselves.

Frankie bounded over to Mary's side and took her hand. They smiled at one another.

Estelle and a subdued-looking Rosie approached Jimmy.

'I'm sorry, Jimmy,' Rosie said.

'Is Gaynor at home?' Estelle asked him. She sounded concerned.

'As far as I know,' Jimmy said.

'I think we should go see her. I texted her but there was no reply. Rosetta has something to say to her.'

'There's no buses.' This sounded lame, even to Jimmy, but he couldn't think of anything else to say.

Terry, buzzing around the edge of the conversation like a busy bee, sprang to the rescue. 'There's room for us all in my van.'

'Thank you, Terry,' said Estelle. 'My PA will get us a cab.'

III

Catrin ate heartily. She and Gaynor were sitting opposite one another sharing a giant pizza and washing it down with large mugs of coffee. The atmosphere in the kitchen was warm and happy.

Gaynor had realised that she was hungry.

'Mum,' Catrin hesitated and then plunged in. 'I'm not going to uni...'

Hot coffee gushed into Gaynor's windpipe. She choked and gasped. 'What?'

'Not now anyway,' she added, noting her mother's stricken face.

Gaynor recovered her powers of speech. 'It's a dream, Catrin.'

'We've got a recording contract. Mickey Xavier was at the gig. He's signed us up.'

'But...but...even if he's honest, which I doubt, there's no money in it, not now, never was really, except for a few. It's all downloads from the internet now. You'll starve. Oh Catrin, I never thought you'd be the sort of silly girl who wants to be a pop singer on the *X factor* or,' Gaynor shuddered, '*Britain's Got Talent*.'

'I am a singer and a musician with a folk/rock fusion band. Mind you,' Catrin paused to view the lowlands of TV talent shows from the lofty peaks of the artistic high ground, 'if that's what it takes...'

Gaynor stared at her daughter's recently scrubbed face, her practised eye looking for the mutinous child beneath the mask. She couldn't find it. Admonition would get her nowhere, so she tried reason. 'A degree is real, a qualification.'

'For what, exactly?'

'A Cambridge degree, Catrin. It opens doors.'

'Depends on whether or not you want to go through them, doesn't it?'

'You think that now,' Gaynor said desperately, 'but you're young. You think...' She was casting around for some meaningful psychological analysis. 'There's no need to reject Cambridge just because you're afraid you won't get in. You've got the ability, you just need the confidence.'

Catrin helped herself to another slice of pizza, bit into it, and chewed, thinking all the while.

'I expect I could get into Cambridge actually, if I wanted to, but I don't.'

Gaynor slumped over the edge of the table clutching her cooling mug of coffee in a claw-like fist.

'If you think so much of Cambridge,' Catrin advised her, 'why don't you go there yourself?'

'Don't be silly!'

'Why not?' Do a masters or something.'

'The trouble with dreams, love, is they don't come true.'

'What about Plogoff?' You've showed us everything there is at Plogoff, except the power station.'

'They didn't build it.'

''Cos you won, right? And Cruise – all that stupid sitting down in the road singing, getting arrested. Where's Cruise now?'

'Armed with conventional warheads and pounding the Middle East last time I looked.'

'You won, though, didn't you?'

'It's not that simple.'

'It could be.' Catrin looked at the piles of paperwork her mother had shoved to the far end of the table. 'Tell school to go and fuck itself. Get Dad to support you.'

Gaynor could feel what was left of her world crumbling around her, laid into with a wrecking bar by her once biddable and intelligent daughter. 'Just like that?'

'Yeah. Dad gets paid plenty. Ask him. He's really guilty that he fucked up.'

Gaynor frowned. She was finding all this hard to follow.

'He pitched up at the gig, which was mega embarrassing. He begged me to come home and talk to you.'

'That was good of him,' Gaynor said without much conviction, She considered telling this unexpectedly mature version of her daughter how the land lay between herself and Jimmy, but decided against it. Her immediate priority was Catrin, who, though apparently grown-up, confident and decisive, remained foolhardy.

'I can't make you go to university,' she said, after a tense silence during which both women looked from each other's faces to random objects around the room.

Catrin fiddled with the zips on her thigh-high boots, then looked up and nodded.

'Promise me one thing,' Gaynor continued. 'Come back to school, just for a few weeks, do your A levels. You never know when you might need them.'

Catrin smiled. 'OK,' she said in a tone reminiscent of her father. 'Deal!' Then, as if nothing of much importance had happened, she cleared the dirty plates and mugs from the table, dumped them in the sink and turned on the hot tap.

Gaynor retrieved the box of dirty dishes from the oubliette. 'Sorry,' she said passing them to Catrin, who piled them up in the soapy water and scrubbed.

Energetically stacking dishes on the draining board, Catrin returned to the subject of school. 'You don't like Al Messenger, do you?'

Gaynor was taken aback. 'How can you tell?'

'Obvious, isn't it? He's a twat. Kids call him Ally Pally.'

'Why?' Gaynor could not stop herself from laughing.

'Gets in your personal space. He thinks it's cool, but it's a well-known fact that he is, in fact, a twat.'

This was undeniably true. Gaynor took a tea towel off the rail in front of the Rayburn, dried the dishes and bustled round the kitchen putting them away.

When they'd finished the washing-up they sat down again at the table and gossiped about school, about Catrin's band and their ridiculous hangers-on and about Rosie.

'She's dumped Chaz. Gone to find her mum.'

Gaynor relaxed. She felt happier than she had done for days, months, really, if she thought about it.

'She'll go to Cambridge. She's my good twin, see?'

It occurred to Gaynor, watching and listening to this cheerful young woman, that, though she had lost a daughter, she had found a friend.

They were interrupted by a knock on the back door

Gaynor jumped to her feet. 'Estelle!' She ran to the door and opened it.

Estelle entered the room. 'Gaynor! Hi!'

The elegance of her visitor was not lost on Gaynor. Her eyes darted frantically round the kitchen. From the cobwebs and the accumulations of dust on the dresser her failings as a home-maker jumped out at her. 'The place is a tip, I'm so sorry,' she blurted.

'When did either of us ever do housework, Gaynor?' Estelle smiled at her and time jumped backwards by seventeen years or more to when they were an island of civilised discourse on literature, politics and the arts surrounded by a sea of domestic mayhem, wailing children breaking on the shore from time to time seeking comfort for complaints or injury.

The two women hugged each other.

Rosie, who had entered behind her mother and hovered discreetly in her wake, went over to Catrin's side. Both girls watched their mothers, awkward but intrigued.

Gaynor and Estelle separated and looked at each other.

'I brought Jimmy back with me,' Estelle said tentatively.

Gaynor looked at the back door behind which people could be heard whispering. 'Don't ask,' she said, her tone both dismissive and indicating that she had much to tell.

Jimmy crept into the room followed by Frankie, Mary and Terry, who was carrying a cardboard case of beer cans.

'Tea?' said Gaynor. She turned to ask Catrin to put the kettle on but found only empty space and a draught coming in from the hall. The girls had run for cover.

'Anybody like a beer?' enquired a jovial Terry.

'Shut up, Terry!' Jimmy said.

'Come on! We ought to be celebrating.' He deposited the box on the dresser, took out two cans and offered one to Jimmy.

Once more Jimmy declined. 'No thanks, mate. Not now.'

In spite of everything, Gaynor could not help looking anxiously at her husband. 'Are you all right, Jimmy?'

'Not really.' Jimmy cleared his throat. 'I owe you an apology, an explanation and…er…'

Gaynor took his hand and led him to a chair. 'Sit down, Jimmy. You look awful.' The dejected penitent dog had come home once more. This time he looked as if he had been in a fight.

'Thanks,' he said, and gave her an apologetic smile.

At least, she supposed, they would now be able to deal with the situation in a civilised manner, but she still felt hurt.

IV

Lady Alexandra sat alone in the bar of the Jolly Collier. Before her on the scrubbed pine tabletop sat a row of cups and glasses containing the dregs of assorted non- alcoholic drinks, the obligatory driver's portion. Long lengths of rolled-up paper were propped against a neighbouring chair.

Brightly coloured images succeeded one another in a meaningless procession across the big screen. There was no football on Thursdays. A handful of regulars sat round tables playing cards or dominoes or just chatting and the occasional disappointed folkie wandered in from the back bar to order.

Ivan the landlord arrived to clear away the empties. 'You been stood up, my love?' he asked kindly.

'You could say that.'

A displaced folkie, waiting by the bar, turned to look and listen.

Alex gathered up her possessions, thanked the landlord and walked out of the pub.

V

In the Manor farmhouse kitchen Jimmy and Gaynor sat on opposite sides of the table.

'I'm sorry,' Jimmy began.

Estelle loitered, waiting for a suitable moment to make a polite exit. Mary and Frankie, on their way to the back door, were trying to persuade Terry to accompany them.

'Yes…?' said Gaynor.

'Miles… We had a fight.' He extended his injured hand across the table for her inspection. 'Turns out he's a twenty-four-carat bastard.'

Estelle caught Gaynor's eye and nodded in vehement agreement, before taking the opportunity to say, 'I should go.' She took a phone out of her handbag.

'You can stay here,' Gaynor said eagerly, adding more cautiously, 'if you'd like to.'

'That would be lovely. I'll go find myself a room.'

'Front right is the best of them, next to the bathroom,' Gaynor suggested. 'You might recognise some of the cobwebs.'

Estelle grinned at her old friend and moved towards the door.

Terry, however, stood his ground. 'We ought to have a celebration first, now we'm all together again.'

Mary took his arm gently.

Frankie stood over him.

'It's been a long time...' Terry's voice tailed off.

Someone was hammering on the front door. It echoed down the passage like a detonation from one of the quarries.

'It's the coppers!' Terry yelped, looking round for somewhere to hide.

This was met with an aggrieved Greek chorus of 'Shut up, Terry!'

Terry backed into the Rayburn and stayed there, sulking, until smoke started rising from the seat of his pants and he sprang away cursing and patting his denim-clad buttocks. Nobody laughed. Footsteps could be heard crossing the yard, then a woman's voice crying 'Jimmy!' with the full force of her lungs.

Alex let herself into the kitchen and walked through an affronted silence to the table, where, sweeping everything else aside, she dumped a pile of rolled-up plans and papers. Exercise books and folders flopped over the edge on to the floor.

'Do come in,' Gaynor said icily.

Alex was annoyed. 'Jimmy! Where were you?'

'Here,' said Jimmy.

'You were supposed to meet me. I've been sitting in that pub, all on my own since eight o'clock! It's now...' Alex looked at her watch.

Gaynor remained calm. 'Ah yes! The strumpet from the folk club.'

'Excuse me! I am not a strumpet. For your information, I am Lady Alexandra Archbold!'

'Well, your ladyship,' Gaynor said evenly, 'perhaps you'd like to tell us why you were supposed to be meeting my husband in a pub.'

Jimmy felt that he should intervene at this point. He also knew that it would be hopeless. 'I can explain.'

'Yes, you can always explain, can't you, Jimmy?' said Gaynor. 'Now, perhaps, you'd like to explain to me what you've been getting up to with this person.'" She realised she was losing control.

'For God's sake, Alex. Tell her what's going on,' Jimmy said.

It had been a long time since anybody had issued Lady Alexandra with instructions in this peremptory manner. She was annoyed.

'I will if you will, Jimmy,' she said coquettishly. 'You said you were going to tell me what goes on at The Boquerie.'

'The Boquerie!' Gaynor shouted, unable to cling to her dignity any longer. 'You mean that sleazy so-called nightclub in Bath?'

'Yep,' said Alex. 'My husband owns it.'

'Bully for him!' Gaynor yelled.

'I only went there once,' Jimmy muttered. He could see no way of convincing his wife that he was telling the unspun truth.

VI

Catrin and Rosie were sitting on the stairs, side by side on the fifteenth step, out of sight, but within earshot of any major developments in the kitchen. They had crept out of Catrin's bedroom to see who was knocking on the front door and were now straining their ears listening for sounds of fighting. Little percolated through the thick oak door of the kitchen.

'Your mum's in there with your dad?' Catrin said, trying not to sound too nosey.

'They've sued for peace. It's about money mostly, like Bretton Woods.'

'Money?'

'For me. I'm going to uni and my mother's going to give me an allowance.'

'Wow! She should do after dumping you like that.'

'It's complicated,' Rosie frowned. 'Nan and Dad, they wouldn't let me go with her.'

'But she's your mum.'

'There was this thing, back in the nineties, about people taking babies out of the country.'

'Moral panic?'

They both nodded wisely.

'And what with my mother being...'

'Black?'

'Didn't stand a chance, did she?' Rosie shrugged and shook her head, 'Loves me, doesn't he? Silly old sod.'

Catrin concurred. 'He loved *her* too. Mum always said he was bitter.'

'It wasn't him, not all of it, anyway. She just had to leave Crubscombe. She said it was strangling her, slowly, like all those wild plants in the quarries.'

'Was it about, you know...racism?'

'I guess it didn't help.'

'But, she had friends. We're not all like that.'

Rosie shrugged. 'Speak for yourself, Catrin.'

A fusillade of shouting that even ancient oak could not contain erupted from the kitchen.

'Do you think they might be about to kill each other?' Catrin speculated.

They put their arms around one another and sat together on the dusty staircase, like the babes in the wood, contemplating the unimaginable width and depth of adult folly.

VII

Resisting his friends' attempts to march him out of the back door, Terry had been taking in the dispute at the table with goggle-eyed fascination. Once he'd grasped its essential meaning he yielded to a reckless compulsion to intervene and addressed Gaynor.

'You don't think she,' he ran an appreciative eye over Alex, 'is carrying on with your Jimmy, do you, missus?' He was seized by a raucous guffaw. 'I seen her down the club. She've got a handsome young man what can play the guitar like Richard Thompson.'

'Thank you, Terry,' Jimmy murmured, with a hint of bitterness.

For a moment there was silence.

Frankie spoke first. 'It's true,' he said to Gaynor. 'I see everything that goes on in the club.'

Gaynor thought it over. For all her reservations about Frankie, she had never known him to lie. She looked at Estelle, seeking confirmation, and found it.

'It's true,' Mary said.

'Of course it's bloody true!' said Alex. 'No disrespect, Jimmy, but...'

Jimmy and Gaynor looked across the table at one another. Gaynor bit her lip.

Jimmy fiddled with an ear lobe and ran his free hand through his curls, as if he were attempting to detach them from his scalp.

Estelle walked quietly out into the hall.

Mary and Frankie finally succeeded in hustling Terry out of the back door. As they dragged him through the utility room his voice, loud and cheerful, could be heard suggesting: 'Shall we go to the pub, then?' The back door slammed shut, cutting off their response.

Alex hung around.

'I'm sorry I called you a strumpet,' Gaynor said at last.

'No worries,' Alex chirruped. 'Just a bit of a misunderstanding.' She turned to Jimmy. 'Now, if we could get down to business?'

'Why don't you come back tomorrow?' Jimmy suggested. 'Bring young Sam with you so that we can go through all this stuff together, and I'll tell you what Miles said about the Boquerie.'

Alex gathered up the paperwork and headed for the back door. 'Promise?'

'Believe me,' said Jimmy, 'I would be more than delighted to dump both Miles and your husband in the shit.'

Once Jimmy and Gaynor were alone, there was another guilty silence.

'Sorry,' they said simultaneously.

'I fucked up.'

'So did I.'

'I've made an even bigger mess than you have,' Gaynor insisted. 'I didn't even understand my own daughter.'

'Not sure I know her these days,' Jimmy admitted.

'I suspected you of being unfaithful.'

'It could be worse than that.' Jimmy was only half joking.

'You're not ill, are you?'

Touched by her concern, Jimmy explained what had really been going on between him and Alex.

VIII

The following morning Gaynor broke with the habit of her entire working life and threw a sickie. The second in-service training day at Hales Mead promised 'team building' and 'role play', so her conscience was not much troubled. Jimmy, as was his custom on a Friday morning, was 'working from home'. They decided to provide a working breakfast for their guests.

Shortly after everyone had got up, three guilt-ridden parents had taken Catrin and Rosie aside, pressed cash into their hands and sent them to the Co-op for provisions.

'Go and get your mother something decent for breakfast,' Jimmy had shamefacedly instructed them.

'Get something nice for your father,' said Gaynor. 'He looks as if he hasn't eaten for a week.'

Estelle intercepted them in the utility room. 'Get something good to eat and,' she lowered her voice, not wishing to cause embarrassment to her hosts, 'real coffee.'

The girls took their mission seriously, purchasing the most expensive coffee and free-range organic eggs, stripping the shelves of smoked salmon and raiding the freezers for baguettes and croissants.

'Is this what they like?' Rosie asked as they bore their expensive cargo down Crubscombe Hill.

'We usually only have it at Christmas.'

'Why are they being so nice?'

Catrin shrugged and hefted her bulging rucksack into a more comfortable position on her shoulders. 'Up to something, I expect, as usual...'

Alex and Sam arrived at eleven o'clock. They sat at the table with Jimmy and Gaynor devouring brunch, while Catrin and Rosie topped up plates of scrambled eggs, smoked salmon, newly baked bread and croissants. Even the Rayburn was behaving itself. Warm air and baking smells wafted round the kitchen. The sun sent tentative fingers of light in through the window.

Jimmy, as promised, opened the proceedings by telling the sorry tale of Miles' revelations and their subsequent fight.

Estelle, who had taken it upon herself to supervise the coffee, dumped a fresh pot in the centre of the table. 'That man!' she exclaimed. 'Don't bother reproaching yourself, Jimmy. I was once obliged to kick him down your back stairs.'

Gaynor looked up at her friend with shocked approval. 'That was you?'

'I never told anybody, like you don't. He was your friend. Hezekiah had his suspicions, but I didn't enlighten him; didn't want him doing jail time for that –' she stopped for a moment, as if weighing up the sensibilities of her audience – 'piece of shit.'

All round the room heads nodded.

Jimmy turned to Alex, apologetic, nonetheless. 'I'm afraid that's all I have. You'll need witnesses. It's a start. I don't see Miles giving evidence in court, but I can try to find someone who will.'

Gaynor, sitting next to him, put her hand on his arm. 'Someone might talk to a woman. I've taught a lot of teenage girls.'

Catrin strolled over to the table, ostensibly to collect dirty dishes. 'I can help,' she announced to the gathering. 'I'm in the business.'

Gaynor smiled at her daughter, but she looked anxious.

'Don't laugh! A lot of bands play the Boquerie. Not our scene, but I know some of the people. Bet they know what's going on. I can find out where all the old pervs' knocking shops are.'

'Catrin!' Jimmy was shocked by his daughter's uninhibited sharing.

'Would you help us?' Alex took her boyfriend's hand and squeezed it. He put his arm round her.

'Sure,' Catrin said cheerfully. 'Do us all a favour to kick those old bastards up the arse. People like them run the business. You were trying to warn me about it, weren't you, Mum?'

'It would appear that I didn't need to,' said Gaynor, torn between censure and admiration.

'We'll all do what we can,' Jimmy promised. He was beginning to understand the new reality, or, rather, the old reality for what it was. For all he knew about the misdeeds of his colleagues and associates, all the nods, winks and deals that bound the superficial freemasonry in which he'd operated, he was not omniscient. He had never penetrated the drifts of exploitation and misery that still lay hidden in the deeps and the shadows.

'Thank you,' murmured Alex. She stood up and, with Sam's help, unrolled a dieline copy of a large and detailed map. They spread it out on the table, anchoring it with coffee pots, mugs and school folders.

Sam pointed out local features that were still visible, measurements and old boundaries to Jimmy and Gaynor. 'I'm pretty sure,' he concluded, 'that the quarrymen's social club is on your land.'

Jimmy looked nervously at Gaynor.

'This is your terrible secret, is it, Jimmy?' she asked him earnestly before laughter consumed her.

He'd got it wrong again.

IX

After the guests had dispersed, Alex and Sam to the upstairs flat at 1A, Archbold Terrace, and Estelle to be reunited with her PA in

Bristol, and onwards to Heathrow, Jimmy and Gaynor sat in front of the Rayburn. Jimmy had dragged a second old armchair out of the dining room. It smelled a bit musty but it was comfortable. They warmed their feet and chatted amicably. Decisions had been made.

Gaynor conceded the club to her husband. It was part of him. Furthermore, since the malign influence of Miles Hollowtree had dissipated, scattered, as it were, to the four winds, like the shade of Sauron, she was regaining her long-lost affection for it.

Jimmy, in return, had agreed to carry on working, allowing his wife to resign from her job.

'I used to love it,' she said wistfully.

'Go part-time. Just teach the sixth form.'

'That might depend on how I frame my resignation to Al Messenger.'

'Ah well. You know what we used to say at university?'

'The universal student philosophy?' Gaynor chuckled.

'Fuck 'em all!' they chanted together.

'What are you going to do with your time?' Jimmy asked.

'Not a lot. Get the old quarries sorted, help you dig up more dirt on Archbold, help Alex and Sam.'

Jimmy looked thoughtful. 'The two could go together, of course.'

'You mean blackmail Archbold?'

Jimmy tutted and shook his head. 'Oh no. That would be unlawful. But don't despair. We can support Alex in the matter of her divorce settlement and ask her charity to give us some funds to make a start on the quarries.'

Gaynor sighed. 'It goes deeper than that, though, doesn't it? All those campaigns we've been involved with, all those...'

'Little victories?'

'Haven't changed anything really.'

'It could be more than a life's work,' Jimmy conceded, 'to bring down the patriarchy.'

'Would you…?'

'We could have fun trying.'

'Can we work together again?'

'Absolutely,' said Jimmy, and this time he meant it.

AUGUST 2013

Summer came at last, quite a sunny and agreeable one in the end. The old quarrymen's club, Gents' urinal restored, more or less, to working order, was hot and heaving. Even some of the old villagers, allies of the Chawners, were there, partaking of good, cheap beer and letting bygones be bygones.

There'd been a gathering earlier that evening at the Boundary Stone, a service, led by the vicar, to commemorate the tragic demise of Jason Chawner, and to celebrate the new Crubscombe Plan.

Everyone had left flowers on the rock, even Catrin and Rosie, moved to generosity by success in their A levels. Frankie had joined the gathering too, accompanying Mary. During the vicar's address on the subject of love and solidarity she'd slipped her hand into his. He'd looked down at her and smiled.

It being a Thursday Jimmy had declared that the celebrations would continue at the folk club.

Another cracking night. A couple of well-respected, almost famous, folk acts had blown in and given of their best, some of the older villagers got up and sang top ten favourites from the 1960s and 70s, while Frankie, not entirely de-fanged by love, kept an eye on the folk purists, still a possible source of insurrection.

'Folk is the people's music,' Jimmy had reminded them, 'and these are the people.'

He instructed Terry to fill the potential insurgents' pewter tankards with free beer.

But more, much more than these minor triumphs, Gaynor was there. She'd even sung a couple of songs, one of them with his guitar accompaniment. And Catrin had dropped in, with some members of her band, and sung 'William Taylor', a traditional version, fortunately. He blanched at the thought of how much free beer he'd have had to distribute to atone for 'Seafaring Girl'.

Rosie, recently returned from a holiday in the United States with her mother, was there too, chatting happily to her father and Mary, and to some of the Dandos' neighbours from Apple Close.

The first interval came.

The second half began with Mary singing 'Seeds Of Love', sweet music wrapping everybody in their dreams: for Catrin and Rosie and all the young ones, the highway to success; for the villagers old residents and new, the promise of a beautiful country park. Led by Jimmy and Gaynor, the campaign was already under way.

Alex's charity had already provided funds for some basic improvements. The orchard wall was to be moved a couple of hundred yards west of its previous location, in accordance with the old maps and deeds young Sam had found in the Aggrementos estate office. The Boundary Stone Rock was to be become a public viewing point with neat footpaths and a line of limestone boulders between the stone itself and the edge of the abyss. There would be a wooden bench dedicated to the memory of Jason Chawner.

Jimmy allowed Terry to refill his glass and carried it carefully out of the door across what had been the car park to smokers' corner where a discussion about the sewers of ancient Rome was in progress.

'Ancient turds!' declaimed Cyril. 'If you dig them out and analyse them you can tell what the Romans used to eat.'

Jimmy wondered where, in future, he was going to accommodate the 'brains trust'. Perhaps he would offer them more comfortable chairs.

He went back into the hut, stepped into the circle of light in front of the bar and closed the formal proceedings of the evening. 'Thank you all for coming, ladies and gentlemen, and now, for the survivors, let the music begin! The third half, no MC, no running order, just jump in when you feel like it.'

Then he made his way through the drinking, chatting crowd till he found Gaynor gossiping to old acquaintances. He put his arm round her and kissed her silver-threaded hair as the band launched into a French café waltz.

Down by the pig farm a late-night motorist, arriving at the T-junction, noticed that the grass verges and hawthorn hedges had been cut back. His headlights picked out a brand-new road sign, pointing in two directions: Frome 3 – Shepton Mallet 14.

Civilisation was coming for Bohemia.

ACKNOWLEDGEMENTS

Many thanks to Gill Harry and Brenda Bannister and the readers at Silver Crow Books who have given me so much guidance and support through the publishing process; to Alison Clink and Frances Liardet for hospitality, encouragement and friendly criticism at their summer boot camps; to Frome Writers' Collective, many of whose writing groups listened patiently to early drafts of 'Bohemia'; to Chris Molan for the lovely artwork on the cover; to Frances and Douglas at SPP and to all the folk clubs and sessions that have inspired me – and put up with my singing.

I'm also grateful to the family of the late Harry Robertson, who allowed me to quote from his song 'Wee Pot Stove'. For those who'd like to know more, go to www.harryrobertson.net.

'The Ballad of Drum Snot', mentioned in Chapter 8 was written by Brian O'Rourke. All the other songs are traditional.